LIFE REMAINS

Alex Walters

ALSO BY ALEX WALTERS:

The Shadow Walker
The Adversary
The Outcast
Trust No One
Nowhere to Hide
Late Checkout
Murrain's Truth (short stories)
Dark Corners
Snow Fallen
Stilled Voices
Candles and Roses
Death Parts Us
Their Final Act
Expiry Date
For Their Sins
Winterman
Small Mercies
Lost Hours

STILLED VOICES

Copyright © Michael Walters 2021
Michael Walters has asserted his right to be identified as the author of this Work in accordance with the Copyright, Designs and Patents Act 1988.

This is a work of fiction. Names, characters, places and incidents are a product of the author's imagination. Locales and public names are sometimes used for atmospheric purposes.
Any resemblance to actual people, living or dead, or to businesses, companies, events, institutions or locales is completely coincidental.

CHAPTER ONE

He was coming to his own domain. Where he felt most comfortable, especially at night. For a short time, he could be alone in a place that felt uniquely his.

The lift door opened, and he pushed the trolley out into the corridor. The trolley was heavy and should have been handled by two members of staff. Staffing shortages meant he generally ended up manoeuvring it by himself. He was happy with that. He was strong enough to cope, and it gave him more time by himself. When he came down here, especially at night, he preferred to be alone.

No one would miss him for another half hour or so. His colleagues all did the rounds as slowly as possible, especially at night. It was a way of filling the time, alleviating the boredom. Of scoring a few more small points against those in charge.

He had no idea what the rest of them did with the time. Sneaked out of the building somewhere for a clandestine smoke or even something more. He didn't care. His own preference was innocuous enough. Just to spend time down here by himself, enjoying the solitude. The sense of power.

More than anyone realised, he was in control here. The one who decided whether they lived or died. Others might claim that power, and some saw themselves as more qualified for the role. But they rarely exercised their power, constrained as they were by some notion of ethics, of decency, he would never begin to understand. Power became power only when used.

He pushed the trolley along the bleak white-painted corridor. Away from the patient-facing parts of the hospital, the decor was less well maintained. The walls were stained, the paint peeling in places. The lights were motion-activated, illuminating only as he walked towards the darkness. As a result, it was dimmer down here, shadows clustered more thickly in the corners. Exactly as he liked it.

He turned at the end of the corridor and pushed the trolley along the next corridor to the loading bay. The hospital laundry was handled off site by a commercial provider, and his job was to unload the laundry bags ready for collection early in the morning. There'd be a reciprocal run to collect the fresh laundry for delivery to the wards. The process had been explained to him at length during his induction training, but he'd taken in only as much as he'd thought would be useful.

He unloaded the large bags from the trolley and left them stacked in the allocated place, then pushed the trolley back along the corridor towards the central service lifts. As always, his objective was to complete his duties as quickly as possible, to allow him maximum time by himself. Before he reached the lifts, he turned into a side corridor and left the trolley out of sight. The chances of anyone else coming down here in the small hours were remote, but he preferred to be cautious.

Having deposited the trolley in its hiding place, he continued along the corridor past the lifts. He'd familiarised himself with every inch of the basement area. It was used mainly for storage – everything from cleaning products to clinical equipment to pharmaceuticals. From time to time, he and a colleague came down here to collect supplies for distribution to the wards and departments. Predictably, he'd never been allowed to carry out those duties by himself. Pilferage and petty theft were recurrent problems, and management were understandably concerned to ensure employees were not led into temptation.

He didn't much care. When he wanted to help himself, he did. The half-hearted security was a minor inconvenience, a small hurdle to overcome. And that, repeatedly, was what he had done.

At the far end of the basement area, below the main hospital entrance, he passed through a set of double doors. The decor and surroundings immediately improved. There were outpatient departments here accessed from the main public lifts, and, tucked discreetly away at the end of the corridor, the hospital mortuary. By day, these areas would be busy with patients, but now the corridors were silent and empty.

He always made a point of coming along here, even though his time was limited. This was the heart of his kingdom. He never went inside, even though one of his several duplicate keys would have allowed him access. There were times when he'd been tempted. Just to go in and stand looking at the rows of storage units, hearing the silent voices calling to him. But the risk was too great. If he were found wandering about in the corridors at this time he'd have no difficulty coming up with an excuse. But his presence in the mortuary would be much harder to explain.

He was happy to do no more than pause briefly outside its doors, sensing the power within, knowing how easily he could commune with its inhabitants if he chose. He drew something from that, an energy he knew would help sustain him.

Having paid his usual obeisance, he headed back through the double-doors into the restricted areas. He'd organised himself a private room, tucked away at the rear of the basement, an unused storage area where he could remain concealed from any unexpected visitors. He'd furnished the room with an abandoned office chair he'd discovered elsewhere in the basement and various other pieces of furniture. He generally whiled away ten or fifteen minutes there. This was when he thought and planned.

The intensity of his thought down here was different. He was at the centre of his kingdom, everything in reach. He could see how it fitted together. He could discern the patterns. He could work out exactly what he needed to do, and the order he ought to do it. Everything came together.

He had to limit his time here – he had no desire for his absence to be noted – but that intensified the experience. He could almost see them all up there, the staff and the patients. He could see what they were doing, those who were working and those who were not, those who were waking and those who were asleep. Those worthy of his attention, and those who were not.

Those who deserved to live. And those who did not.

He sat for ten minutes or so, his mind probing the spaces above. Finally, as if awaking from sleep, his eyes snapped into focus. He had one more task to complete before he returned upstairs.

He walked back along the corridor and stopped in front of one of the many closed doors. He'd had less difficulty obtaining the duplicate key than he had expected. But they were as careless here as everywhere else. He shouldn't have been surprised, but he still had a tendency to overestimate them. Perhaps that was just as well. It prevented him becoming complacent.

He opened the door and stepped into the storeroom. Closing the door quietly behind him, he relocked it from the inside, and only then turned on the lights.

He was gradually learning more about the products down here and their various uses. None of the really serious items were stored here, of course. Even those fools were smart enough to realise that the Class A drugs and similar items needed to be stored more securely. But there was plenty down here for his purposes.

As always, he selected a small number of items and slipped them into his pockets. He made a point of not taking too much of any one item. He presumed that some kind of periodic inventory was carried out, but he imagined the checks were not precise. As long as he avoided raising any immediate suspicion, he should be able to continue for as long as he needed.

Satisfied, he turned out the lights, unlocked the door and stood for a moment listening. Then he stepped outside into the corridor. Finally, he relocked the door and slipped the key back into his pocket.

He returned to where he had left the trolley and pushed it back towards the service lift. Another satisfactory night.

Another step towards his objective. Slowly, the plan was coming together, the pattern forming in the way he wanted. It wasn't yet fully in focus, but it was within his reach.

And only he could see it. Only he could read the connections, see the links, identify how the parts fitted together.

Only he could see which deaths were needed before the pattern was complete.

CHAPTER TWO

Kenny Murrain stepped into the main hospital foyer and paused. He didn't know how many times he'd been here over the last few weeks. Each time he'd hoped things would be different. That there'd have been some change, some positive development. But the news was always the same. He assumed, though no one seemed prepared to confirm this, that in practice that meant the news was becoming worse.

It was cold outside, though spring was finally on its way. There was blossom on some of the trees, burgeoning buds on others. The days were growing longer. It was normally a time when Murrain felt optimistic, as if the coming year might have something new and better to offer. This year he felt nothing but gloom.

The foyer was thronged with people – visitors on their way to see patients, former patients waiting to be collected, hospital staff passing through in the course of their duties. At the far side there was a small cafe serving coffee and snacks to visitors, one of several in the building. Murrain ran his eye idly across those sitting at the tables.

She was sitting by herself, staring through the window at nothing in particular.

He was tempted just to walk by. It wasn't exactly that they'd been avoiding one another. That had been impossible in the circumstances. But their paths had crossed only up on the ward, and it had never seemed appropriate or tactful to exchange more than the usual platitudes.

He'd been spared the need to interact with her at work, partly because she'd been on compassionate leave since it had all happened, and partly because Marty Winston, the superintendent in charge of the team, had taken responsibility for handling the welfare issues. Murrain had resented that at first, feeling edged out of the picture. But

Marty had been right. Murrain had barely been in a state to take care of his own welfare, let alone anyone else's.

If he pretended he hadn't seen her, it would be yet another example of his weakness, his inability to step up when it mattered. A trivial example compared with everything that had happened, but still indicative of his failings.

He made his way over to the cafe, positioning himself close to her table. 'Marie.'

She looked up. 'Kenny.'

'Can I get you another coffee?'

She glanced down at her empty cup, and for a moment he thought she was going to refuse. 'Yes, why not? Thanks. A cappuccino, if that's okay.'

'Won't be a moment.'

While the coffees were being prepared, he looked back at her. She was sitting motionless, her gaze fixed on the empty cup in front of her. It was impossible to tell what she was thinking.

When he returned, she stared at him as if only now registering his presence. 'Sorry, Kenny. My mind's – well, you know…'

'Of course. I take it there's no news.'

She gave a barely imperceptible shake of the head. 'Same as ever.'

'At least it's not bad news.'

'Isn't it? The longer this goes on, the worse the outcome's likely to be. They're not optimistic.'

Murrain wanted to argue with her, tell her the doctors had offered him a more positive prognosis. But they'd both been given the same information, even if they'd chosen to interpret it differently. That was understandable. She didn't want to allow herself the luxury of hope.

'Christ, I'm sorry, Marie. I wish…'

'It wasn't your fault, Kenny.'

'None of that matters now, anyway. It happened.'

'I thought he was all right, you know? That night, I mean. I was praying and praying after he'd been swept away. Then when we found him, swept up on the bank, I thought…'

Murrain knew exactly what she meant. He'd been though the same sequence of emotions himself. The initial horror at that dramatic surge of water along the bank. The realisation that Joe Milton had been swept away by the sheer force of the water. Then the euphoria, only a little later, when they'd found his body washed up by the river. Murrain had barely been thinking coherently, but he and Marie had administered CPR until the ambulance had turned up. At that point, he'd thought the worse of it was over. Joe would spend a night or two in hospital getting checked over, and everything would return to normal.

But the following day Marie had phoned from the hospital to break the bad news. Joe had remained in a coma and the prognosis was at best uncertain. The consultant had later given Murrain a detailed explanation he hadn't really followed, but it amounted to the fact that, for precious minutes, Joe's brain had been starved of oxygen. The precise cause of the coma remained uncertain, but – though no one had ever said the words out loud to Murrain – there were fears the outcome might be lasting brain damage.

Even then, he'd expected the future would soon become clearer. But they were nearly three weeks on, and nothing had changed. Marie spent the days sitting by Joe's bed desperately hoping for an improvement. Murrain came here after work most days, and phoned regularly to check for developments. They remained trapped in this hellish limbo.

'Why now?' She was talking more to herself than to Murrain. 'Why the hell did this have to happen now? When we'd just finally got together.'

He could offer no answer. It was just how life was. When you finally thought things were running smoothly, the fates screwed you over. 'All we can do is hope.' He was conscious how feeble his words sounded.

'What about Edward Crichton? Any news on him?'

Murrain hadn't expected the question. He assumed that Marie would be too focused on Joe's condition to worry about the wider case they'd been involved in. It was Crichton they'd been trying to stop when it had happened. Murrain supposed they'd succeeded. They'd prevented two innocent people from being killed. In the end, the only casualty had been Joe. And, most likely, Crichton himself.

They still didn't know for sure. Crichton had been swept away in the same surge of water that had dragged Joe from the shore. But his body hadn't yet been found. The river itself wasn't particularly wide or deep in normal times, and Murrain had expected to find the body shortly after they'd found Joe's. But nothing had turned up. 'Nothing at all,' he said now in response to Marie's question.

'I don't like it.'

Murrain shared her unease. Something about Crichton had disturbed him from the start. There'd been moments, out there in the pouring rain that night, when Murrain had felt Crichton had entered his head. As if Crichton had been the one in control.

He'd found himself thinking of Crichton almost as something other than human. It was nonsense, of course. Crichton was flesh and blood. It might be that he had unusual gifts. It might even be that his talents were greater than anything Murrain had experienced. But none of that made him superhuman. He was no more capable of surviving those waters unharmed than Joe had been. The only question was whether he'd been luckier.

It was possible. If he'd been washed up on the far bank or further downriver still conscious, it wouldn't have been difficult for him to have made a successful escape. He'd have been soaked and freezing, but Murrain had little doubt about Crichton's resilience.

All they could do was continue the hunt. It didn't help that the intelligence services had, as so often, been less than co-operative. They regarded Crichton as their business and were unlikely to change their views at the behest of some tin-pot local force. It was possible they'd already tracked down Crichton and taken him back into their clutches. Although, from everything he'd seen of their work, Murrain doubted it.

'He scared me,' Marie said. 'He scared the bloody life out of me. There was something about him.'

'We'll get him, Marie. If he's out there, we'll get him. And if he's not, we'll find the body sooner or later.'

'In the meantime poor Joe just lies there. What do you think's going on in his head, Kenny? He might be conscious. He might be aware of what's happening.'

Murrain avoided her eye. He knew what she wanted to ask of him. Could he somehow use his gifts – whatever they were, however they might work – to communicate with Joe? The same thought had occurred to Murrain himself. But it just didn't work like that. It wasn't something he could control. Sometimes it was there. More often, it wasn't. Sometimes it helped. More often it didn't. Even when it did, the results were frequently unexpected. When he'd first visited Joe here, he'd tried. But there was nothing. Not even the static or white noise he sometimes encountered. Just the absence of a connection.

'What do the doctors say?'

'They don't seem to know any more than I do,' she said. 'Or if they do, they're not saying. There are signs of brain activity, but they won't commit themselves to their significance.'

'There are plenty of instances of patients making full recoveries from this kind of state.'

'And more cases where they haven't, and the chances of recovery grow slimmer with every passing day.' She pushed her cup away and bent over to collect her bag. 'I'd better be getting back up. Are you coming?'

'I'll follow you up.'

'I do mean it, you know, Kenny. None of this was your fault. You helped save his life.'

Murrain nodded, not trusting himself to respond. Whatever anyone might say, he was always going to blame himself. He should have acted more quickly. He still didn't know why he hadn't. Something had prevented him. He hadn't been able to explain it then, and he couldn't explain it now.

He watched her walk towards the lifts. She was right, he thought. There was something scary about the mysterious Edward Crichton. Whatever had happened that night, whatever had prevented Murrain from acting the way he'd wanted, it was all connected to Crichton. Crichton shared Murrain's distinctive gifts perhaps at a level Murrain himself couldn't even imagine. But he'd begun to suspect there was more than that.

Whatever the truth might be, he wouldn't feel comfortable until they'd finally tracked Crichton down. Alive or dead.

CHAPTER THREE

How the hell had he ended up here?

Kyle Amberson still didn't know, two years on. He could trace the sequence of events that had resulted in him living and working in this place. But he couldn't replicate the state of mind that had made each of those steps seem, at the time, quite natural, if not inevitable.

There had been Anna, obviously. That had been a big part of it. She was what had brought him up to the north west in the first place. There'd been a period, probably several months, when he'd assumed they'd end up living together, get married, make a joint life for themselves up here. Whether she'd shared that expectation, he now had no real idea. He couldn't recall they'd ever seriously discussed it. It was only when she almost casually took up with someone else that it occurred to him that, in her eyes, they'd never been much more than friends. They still were, he supposed, though he hadn't seen her in the best part of a year. From what he'd heard, she was now happily living with the man she'd left him for.

Then there'd been the work. When he'd decided to move up here, he'd needed to find something. He'd worked as a locum for a while, and then the practice here had invited him to join them on permanent basis. The relative stability had appealed, and he'd willingly taken up the offer. He largely enjoyed the work, and the practice was efficient and well regarded. His income was less than most of his patients probably assumed, but he'd never wanted an extravagant lifestyle and he earned enough to meet his needs.

It was just that he'd never envisaged ending up somewhere like this. Not that there was much wrong with the place itself, and the location had its compensations. But it was essentially a functional, slightly bleak northern market town which had undoubtedly seen better days. There were pockets of deprivation and of relative wealth, and he encountered instances of both every day in his work. There was nothing wrong with the place but nothing particularly attractive or inspiring either.

The main compensations were that a thirty minute drive in one direction would take him out into the Peak District, while a thirty minute drive in the other took him into central Manchester. When he'd first moved here, particularly when he was with Anna, they'd taken frequent advantage of that. Now, he spent most of his time here. He'd occasionally head into the city for a drink with mates, and every now and then they'd have an excursion into the countryside. But his old friends were drifting into serious relationships and he found himself left more and more to his own devices. Most weekends, he felt too tired to do much more than head to the supermarket for his weekly shop before settling down to watch the football on the TV.

He wasn't due back at the practice for another twenty minutes. He made a point of getting out at lunchtime, if only just to buy a sandwich and a cup of soup. Today was a half-decent spring day – still chilly, but with a clear sky and the scent of renewal in the air.

Instead of heading back to the practice, he found an empty bench in the market square and sat sipping at his soup. Behind him there was the attractive brick-built edifice of the town hall, but the market square itself had little to commend it. It was the usual wasted opportunity, a pigeon-filled space surrounded by anonymous concrete shops and offices from the 1960s. It could easily have been transformed into an inviting location if the buildings had been designed as a tribute to the Victorian grandeur behind him. But nobody had cared enough or had had enough funding to produce anything of that quality.

Various shoppers, mostly elderly, shuffled past him. That was another thing about the place. It seemed increasingly to be dominated by old people, or at least by people who seemed old to Kyle. He saw that in the surgery too. Sometimes it felt as if the majority of his patients were geriatrics. It probably wasn't true, any more than it was true of the population of the town in general. But most younger people would be working at this time of day. The only sign of a newer generation were the hordes of teenage schoolchildren who descended on the square every lunchtime. Kyle always timed his break to avoid their mass invasion.

So, if not here, where had he envisaged himself? He'd originally had ambitions for a more specialist medical role but – partly again because of his ultimately unrequited pursuit of Anna – he'd drifted into general practice as offering more flexibility in location and lifestyle. He'd never really regretted the decision. He enjoyed the interaction with the public. He didn't resent the fact that his role was often more that of counsellor than medical advisor. He liked being able to establish a more personal relationship with some patients.

That was important. And it was particularly important in this particular town. A shadow hung over the place that he and his colleagues could never entirely dispel. It was a long time ago now, of course, or it seemed so to a young man like Kyle. Nearly twenty years. But people here had long memories. Too many of them had been directly affected and they weren't likely to forget. Against that background, trust was hard to regain and all the more precious.

Kyle finished his soup and sandwich, throwing the packaging into one of the market square bins before heading back.

It was just up the road, he thought. Only a few hundred metres away. The place where the man had been based, where he'd carried out much of his consultation work. There, and in the dozens of homes that he'd visited. He'd been liked, well-respected and, yes, trusted. They'd all believed in him, confident he had their best interests at heart. Perhaps, in his own twisted way, he'd come to believe that too.

It was a risk of the profession, Kyle thought. You were taught to trust your own judgement, to deal confidently with uncertainty or ambiguity, to convince your patients you knew what you were doing. That didn't mean you acted blindly or ignorantly, but it did mean you had to exude an air of authority. Most learned to strike the balance appropriately, but Kyle could see how easily you might begin to believe your own publicity.

He hurried across the street, suddenly feeling cold in the early spring afternoon. His own fault. He'd brought in only his light overcoat today, fooled by the brightness of the day, but winter still lingered in the air. As he reached the entrance to the surgery, he glanced behind him and hurried through the doors with the air of a man pursued.

CHAPTER FOUR

'Any suspicious circumstances?'

DS Paul Wanstead squinted and made a play of studying the report on the screen in front of him. There was the usual element of theatre in his behaviour, Bert Wallace thought. Wanstead liked to be seen as a copper of the old school, mildly bemused by the technology that was now an unavoidable part of their lives. He was actually far more adept in using that technology than the rest of them.

'Not entirely clear,' Wanstead said, 'other than that the death was unexpected. The coroner's officer had some concerns and wants our view. You want me to print this off?' As always with Wanstead, it sounded like a question expecting the answer 'no'.

'Might be useful.' Wallace had learnt long ago not to take Wanstead's temperament at face value.

'I think it's partly the location.' Wanstead set the printer running. 'They've long memories over there, and who can blame them?'

Wallace recalled the address. 'Oh, yes, right. I can see that.'

'Probably why there was a reluctance to sign off the death certificate.'

Wallace had picked up the printout and was studying the detail. 'Not too old, then?'

'Sixty-five. No age. But people die for all kinds of reasons. Not all of them suspicious.'

'Looks like one for the medics, really. See what the post-mortem comes up with.'

'That'll be the clincher. They just want us to have a look at the scene. See if we should get it examined properly while it's still fresh. Coroner's officer said he'd meet you there. Chap called Fraser.'

'Okay, I'll get over there.' Wallace was only too happy to get out of the office. There was an atmosphere hanging over the place that made her feel uncomfortable. She'd never thought of herself as the sensitive type, but the past few weeks had been increasingly difficult.

It was partly just the empty desks. An all too visible reminder of those who were absent. The usual humour, the jokes and badinage that normally kept them going even through the worst moments, had dried up. Cops were known for their gallows humour, and not much was considered off-limits.

The exception was the death of a fellow officer, particularly a death in the line of duty. They weren't at that point yet, but everyone knew how serious the situation was. You could feel it all over the building, and it was most intense among Joe Milton's own team.

What had happened wasn't something abstract. It was the loss of someone who wasn't just a fellow officer, but someone they all thought of as a friend. Straightforward, pragmatic, down to earth Joe Milton. Someone who'd always just been there, getting the job done in his usual no fuss way. Now, suddenly, he wasn't.

She could tell it had hit Kenny Murrain hard, though he'd never been one to let his feelings show. Kenny had seen Joe almost as a protégé, and there'd been something almost paternal in his relationship with the younger man. Murrain blamed himself for what had happened. Survivors' guilt, they called it, didn't they?

Then there was Marie Donovan. Heaven knew what it must be like for her. The word around the office, immediately before the incident, had been that Marie and Joe were an item. There'd been gossip for months beforehand, mostly disseminated by Paul Wanstead, which Wallace had taken with a dollop of salt. But it had begun to look as if there was something more substantial in it, just at the point when this had happened.

Marie was absent on compassionate leave. Kenny Murrain had spent a few days on leave before returning and throwing himself back into his work. Whether or not that was wise, Wallace had no idea, but that was for others to worry about.

She was musing on these issues as she drove around the M60 towards her destination. It wasn't a side of the city she knew well, so she was following the Satnav blindly. She hadn't been sure what to expect – the initial briefing note had provided little information – but her destination turned out to be an unassuming bungalow in a secluded avenue on the edge of the town. She pulled into the kerb and looked around, taking in her surroundings.

It was a not unattractive little estate, probably dating from the 1950s or 1960s. The houses were all different, built to a personal specification rather than off a standard blueprint. None of them was particularly grand – two or three bedroom homes for couples or families – but they looked well maintained and tidy. There was the usual array of carefully cultivated front gardens – neat lawns, trimmed shrubbery, flowerbeds with the first snowdrops beginning to show.

She climbed out of the car and walked up to the gate. As she did so, the front door opened and a young man stepped out, waving to her. 'Hi. DC Wallace, I presume. I'm Danny Fraser.'

'Pleased to meet you. Yes, I'm Bert Wallace.'

He raised an eyebrow but was clearly too polite to ask the obvious question.

'Roberta. But everyone calls me Bert.' She smiled. 'More than Roberta, anyway.'

'I can see that. That's why I call myself Danny. I never forgave my parents for christening me Danbert.'

It took her a beat to realise he was joking. She decided that she probably rather liked him. 'You'd better show me what's what. I've not been given much in the way of background.'

The inside of the house appeared to be as well maintained as the exterior. She'd half-expected the decor to be that of an elderly person. Like her own nan's, slightly old-fashioned and filled with fussy knick-knacks and ornaments. But this wasn't like that. It was a house decorated by someone with at least half an eye for interior design. The style was relatively minimalist, with plain white walls and a few well-selected pictures and ornaments, but the place still managed to feel welcoming and cosy.

'The deceased was a woman called Margaret Perry,' Fraser said. 'Sixty-five years old. Supposedly in good heath according to her GP.'

'Who found her?'

'Her son. Gregory Perry. Lives in Wilmslow. He'd tried to call her and got no answer, so he'd popped over to check she was okay. He found her sitting in that armchair.' Fraser pointed to a chair positioned opposite the large television screen. 'This was Sunday evening. Doc reckons she'd probably been dead since early that morning, though they've not yet been able to give us a precise time. Son had phoned around lunchtime, as he usually did if he wasn't popping over in person, apparently. No answer, but he wasn't too concerned. Then he tried again a couple of times over the afternoon and started to get worried.'

'Must have been a shock for him.'

'A complete shock, he reckons.'

'So why did he come over?' Wallace had never been a sentimental person, and certainly not a superstitious one, but there was something about the empty chair she found disturbing. If she were asked to sit in it, she knew she wouldn't be able to.

'He was concerned, I guess.'

'She didn't have a mobile?'

Fraser gestured to the coffee table in the centre of the room. 'It's there. Switched off. The son had tried that but just got the voicemail. He wasn't surprised by that. Reckoned she wasn't keen on using it.'

'So what did the son do when he found her?'

'Called an ambulance. She was pronounced dead by the paramedics and shipped off to hospital. The paramedics couldn't ascertain an obvious cause of death and apparently neither could the hospital medical staff. The GP's confirmed there were no reported underlying health conditions. So the death was categorised as undiagnosed and unexplained, which is why we're involved.'

'Something like a cardiac arrest wouldn't be easy to diagnose without a postmortem, presumably?'

'We're all waiting on the postmortem. Everything seems to take so long these days.'

'Tell me about it.'

'But everyone's a bit wary. Which is why my boss thought there were grounds to involve you at this stage.'

'You mean because it's here. In this town, I mean.'

'It sounds daft, doesn't it? After all these years.'

'Who knows? I mean, it does to me. Lightning doesn't strike in the same place twice. There's no more reason to worry about an unexplained death here than anywhere else in the country. Unless you're suggesting some kind of sick copycat killing?'

'Nothing that definite,' Fraser said. 'It's more that a lot of people got their fingers burned back then. They know they should have spotted something wrong before they did. They don't want to be caught out twice.'

'But we're talking – what? Fifteen, twenty years ago.'

'Still some of the same people involved, though. People who were in junior roles then, but who've got the real responsibility now. I've seen it a few times. It's the ones like this that make them jittery, at least till they get a clear diagnosis.'

'The burdens of power, eh?' Wallace said. 'So do you think there are any suspicious circumstances here?'

'As far as we know, Margaret Perry died alone. She seems to have died peacefully, from the appearance of the body. She was just slumped in the chair.'

'Was she watching TV?'

'We assume so, but we're not sure. The TV was off by the time the son got here, but it's got some power-saving timer that turns it off if there's been no activity for a while.'

'Nothing sounds suspicious.'

'There were just a couple of things that raised questions.'

'Go on.'

'The first is that there were two mugs in the sink. Both used and left there ready to be washed.'

'Maybe she'd had two coffees. I need more than that just to get started in the morning.'

'Her son reckons she normally just rinsed out her coffee mug and reused it.'

'Doesn't prove much. Maybe one of the mugs was from the previous evening and she hadn't got round to washing it. Maybe she'd left one in another room and forgotten about it. There could be countless explanations.' Wallace was acutely conscious of how many dirty mugs were sitting in her own sink. In her eyes, the presence of only two unwashed cups was evidence of impressive domestic efficiency.

'Then there was the front door.'

'Front door?'

'The son reckoned she always kept the front door double-locked and bolted when she was in the house. She had a bit of a thing about security, apparently, after she was burgled a year or so back. It wasn't long after her husband died, so it left her nervous.'

'Understandable.'

'When the son arrived here, he wasn't worried at first. There were lights showing in the house so he assumed Margaret must have turned them on. But they'd probably been left on since the morning. There was no answer when he rang the doorbell. He had his own set of keys but he expected the front door to be bolted from the inside.' Fraser gestured towards the patio doors at the far end of the sitting room. 'She had those fitted after the burglaries. Toughened glass, state of the art locks, all that stuff, but the son had a set of keys.'

'And the front door?'

'He reckons when he went to let in the paramedics the front door was unbolted.'

'He's sure about that?'

'Well, no. Not absolutely. He was in a state, and he

admits he might have unbolted and unlocked the door without thinking about it. You know how it is when you do something on automatic pilot. It was only afterwards, when he'd finished dealing with the paramedics, that it occurred to him he couldn't remember doing it.'

'So we don't have a lot,' Wallace said. 'Two mugs in the sink and the possibility that the front door wasn't locked in the usual way.'

'That's about it, yes.'

'So what's the suggestion? Even if we accept these things mean something, it doesn't sound like an intruder.'

'More like a visitor. Someone she knew.'

'Any obvious contenders?'

'The son reckons she had several friends locally, mainly women of a similar age. Widows like herself. But we don't really have the resources to start carrying out that kind of investigation.'

Wallace was beginning to see where this was heading. 'If this mysterious visitor had been responsible for her death, why would they leave two coffee cups in the sink? Surely you'd want to dispel any suspicion there'd been a second person there?'

'That's why you're the detective and I'm just the humble coroner's officer.' Fraser smiled. 'But, yes, that thought had occurred to me. I'm just doing what I'm told.'

Wallace looked around the room, conscious if it was to be examined as a potential crime scene, they should take care not to compromise any evidence. As far as she could see, there was little of interest. A shelf of anonymous paperbacks. The television with a cable set-top box on the table beneath it. The fateful armchair and its equivalent on the far side of a matching sofa. 'When do you think we'll get the postmortem results?'

'It's likely to take a few days. We need to get the medical history summary from the GP for the pathologist. We've been told informally by the GP that there's nothing of interest in there. But nothing will get signed off till they've been through all the relevant hoops.'

'I get the picture. It sounds thin to me, but if there are concerns we might as well roll with it. I'll recommend we'll treat it as potentially suspicious until we have good reason to think otherwise. We can get the house examined by our CSIs before there's any risk of the scene being contaminated.' She looked down pointedly at their feet on the carpet. 'Speaking of which…'

'Perhaps we'd better get out of here.'

'I don't know what they're likely to find, to be honest. We can check the two mugs, obviously, and for any unexplained prints, so we'll have to eliminate all those who we know have been in the room since the death. Perry herself, the son, the paramedics. You. Anyone else?'

'I don't think so,' Fraser said. 'This is the first time I've been in here. Just seemed like a sensible place to meet, so you could get a feel for what had happened. Gregory Perry was happy to lend me his keys to look round for myself.'

'What's his attitude to all this?'

'I'm not sure he's thinking straight yet. I don't think he believes there's anything suspicious about his mother's death. But now the question's been raised, he's looking for reassurance.'

'Understandable enough.' Wallace took one last look around the room, before turning back to Fraser. 'Okay. let's get out of here before we do any more damage.'

CHAPTER FIVE

Murrain sat for another fifteen or so minutes in the hospital cafe, slowly sipping his coffee. He needed time to think about what he'd been discussing with Marie. It didn't matter what anyone said. He'd failed. He'd known even on that night, though he'd never envisaged that the ultimate victim might be Joe. At the moment he needed to act, he'd been unable to do so. He'd never be content now until he knew how or why.

Which might mean, as his wife Eloise had characteristically pointed out, that he'd simply never be content. No change there then, she might well have added. But the issue nagged at him. At the time, it had felt as if he was being physically constrained, as if someone or something had been gripping his limbs. What he couldn't work out was whether this had been connected with Edward Crichton and whatever gifts he might have possessed or if it simply reflected some psychological weakness in his own make-up.

It would be easy for him to assume Crichton had somehow been in control of the situation. Murrain's own gifts could offer insights that sometimes surpassed anything that was rationally explicable. He knew also that Crichton's abilities exceeded his own. Was it possible Crichton might be able to influence or affect others' behaviour?

Murrain had to assume so. They'd never fully explained how Crichton's previous victims had been lured from their homes in the small hours of the morning. Perhaps that had been another example of Crichton's ability to bend others to his will.

He had been sitting, lost in these thoughts, the last dregs of coffee going cold in front of him. Now, as if waking from a daze, he became conscious of someone addressing him. A young woman was standing beside the table holding a tray. He had no idea what she'd just said to him. 'Sorry, I was miles away.'

'I was just asking if this seat was free.' She gestured with her tray towards the rest of the cafe. 'All the tables are taken, so I was hoping you wouldn't mind?'

'No, no, of course. I'll be going in a minute anyway.' As if to demonstrate he was speaking in good faith, he swallowed the last few mouthfuls of his drink. The young woman was unloading a coffee and a pastry from her tray. It was only when she'd finally settled herself that she finally looked up at him.

He'd been correct, he realised. He'd thought she seemed familiar when she'd first spoken to him, but it had taken his fogged brain a minute or two to place her. 'I'm sorry. It's Gill, isn't it?'

She gazed back at him with baffled curiosity. Then her expression cleared. 'Oh God. I didn't recognise you. I just hadn't expected...'

'There's no reason why you should have. Must be three years at least. And we'd all had one or two too many by the end of the night, from what I remember.'

'I can still remember the hangover, to be honest.'

It had been a Christmas do, Murrain recalled. He always steered clear of the big parties that various departments organised, but he'd felt obliged to organise something more intimate with the immediate team, just a sociable evening out with them and their partners. That year, they'd held it at a local Italian place, and it had been more than usually lively, ending up with most of them repairing to a nearby pub for a few more glasses. Murrain wasn't much of a drinker, but had been happy to go with the flow, he and Eloise sitting contentedly nursing their respective beer and red wine while the younger team members took things a little further.

That had been the last time he'd seen the woman sitting opposite him. At that point, Murrain had assumed Gill and Joe Milton were set up together for life. He'd been surprised when, just a few months later, Joe had told him Gill was taking up a job with the OECD in Paris. Even then, Murrain had assumed the split would be temporary, and he knew Joe thought the same. Or at least had pretended to think so.

But Gill's work contract had been extended and it had become clear to Joe that, in the end, she'd chosen her career over their relationship. Whatever the rights and wrongs of it, he'd finally acknowledged the relationship was over, and that Gill would never be returning.

Except, Murrain added to himself, here she was.

'You're here to see Joe?'

'I'm still not sure if it's a good idea. That's one reason I'm lurking down here, trying to screw up the courage...' She hesitated, as if she'd been about to say something different. 'How is he, exactly?'

There was no point in trying to sugar the pill. 'Still unconscious. Unresponsive. I'm sorry.'

'That's what I'd understood. I was hoping there might have been some change.'

'Not yet.' He hesitated. 'The prognosis isn't particularly positive, I'm afraid. We can only hope.'

There was a long silence as she took a mouthful of coffee. 'I'm beginning to think I shouldn't have come.'

'The consultant thinks it's a good idea for him to hear familiar voices,' Murrain offered. 'They don't seem to know what might be going on in his head. How responsive he might be to external stimuli.'

'I don't know how welcome my voice would be.' She picked up her pastry and gazed at it as if wondering about its edibility before dropping it back on to the plate. 'I wasn't entirely telling the truth just now. I said I was lurking down here to pluck up courage. That wasn't quite true. I've already been up there. But I saw someone was already sitting with him.'

Murrain nodded, but could think of no immediate response.

'I think she was a colleague,' Gill went on. 'She looked familiar.'

'Marie Donovan,' Murrain said. 'Yes, she's a colleague.

But also, well, more than a colleague.'

'Ah.' Gill picked up the pastry again and this time took a large mouthful, making a play of dealing with the cascading crumbs. 'I wondered about that.'

'Probably better you know.' Murrain was conscious he was articulating all this very clumsily. 'But, yes, they're together. Quite a recent development.' His tone suggested he was defending Joe against some accusation that hadn't been made.

'Right.' Gill took another bite of the pastry. 'Christ, the poor woman.'

'It's hit her hard. She's been through some tough times before. I don't know if that makes it easier or harder.'

'I imagine nothing makes it easier. What do you think I should do?'

'Do?'

'I mean, should I go up there? I don't want things to be awkward. She must be going through a hell of a time. I don't want to add to it.'

'I can see that.' Murrain had no idea what advice to offer. 'Did you come over specifically because of Joe?'

'Not entirely. I was planning to come back at some point. See various people.'

'Including Joe?'

There was a hesitation which Murrain thought probably answered his question. 'I don't think I treated Joe very well.'

'It's none of my business, Gill.'

'Maybe not, but I know – well, Joe saw you as a bit of a father figure. He must have talked to you about what happened.'

'Like I say, Gill—'

'I was cowardly. I knew our relationship was grinding to a halt. It wasn't Joe's fault. It was mine. I needed something more than just being a copper's wife living on an anonymous estate in Sale.'

'I'm sure Joe never thought…'

'I knew when I took up the job in Paris I was effectively

ending the relationship. But I never admitted it, not even to myself and certainly not to Joe. He genuinely thought it was a temporary break and I'd be back in six months. I should have been straighter with him.'

'I think he probably knew too, really.'

'Maybe. But I wanted to apologise to him. He's a decent guy. He deserved better.'

'These things happen, Gill. It wasn't your fault either.'

'I just felt he was owed an explanation at least. I'd been trying to contact him, but he didn't respond to any of my messages. Then someone told me about – well, what had happened. They'd seen it reported in the Evening News.'

'It was a shock to us all.' Murrain was keen to move the conversation on, conscious he had no answers to anything Gill was saying. 'Look, I'm heading up to the ward myself. Why don't you come up with me? I can introduce you to Marie. That might make it easier. I'm sure she won't mind you being here.' He wasn't remotely confident of that, but he had no right or ability to prevent Gill from visiting Joe. All he could do was try to prevent it escalating into a major incident.

'It might help. If you don't mind.'

Murrain was already regretting his offer, but could see no way back now. At least he could get it over quickly. 'Shall we head up?' He pushed himself to his feet, keen to signal the discussion was finished. Gill swallowed the final dregs of her coffee and rose to follow him across the lobby towards the lifts.

CHAPTER SIX

'Christ,' Bert Wallace said. 'So they were right to be jittery?'

'Looks that way, doesn't it?'

Wallace had commandeered one of the small interview rooms to meet Danny Fraser. She'd thought it better to speak to him in private and find out exactly what he had to say, rather than setting the inevitable rumour mill running.

'And they're sure?'

'It's only a preliminary view from the pathologist. Obviously, they've still got to carry out the postmortem and the full toxicology reports could take days if not weeks. But the pathologist asked them to do some initial work on the blood and urine samples.'

Wallace looked at the note he'd given her. 'Diamorphine? That's basically heroin, isn't it?'

'More or less. And Margaret Perry doesn't sound like anyone's idea of a junkie.'

'So we're talking unlawful killing.'

'Let's just say the coroner's keen to kick the case in your direction.'

'I guess that's what we're here for.'

'At least it's been handled the right way.' Fraser said. 'Nobody can accuse us of not doing this by the book. How are your CSI people doing?'

'They're over there at the moment. I called the senior CSI for an update while I was waiting for you. He reckoned there was no sign of a break-in. As you said, Margaret Perry was keen on security, so he's sure no-one could have got in there without leaving some obvious signs. If there was someone with Margaret Perry, they'd been allowed into the house.'

'So what does that mean?'

'Could mean anything. Could mean it was someone she knew. Could mean someone sweet-talked their way in. Perry doesn't sound like the vulnerable type, but even the smartest people can be fooled.' She paused. 'Then there's the son.'

'The son? Really?'

'We have to look carefully at those closest to the bereaved. He could easily have had the opportunity. The question is whether he had the motive and the means.'

Fraser was silent for a moment. 'He might have had. The means, that is. He's a hospital pharmacist. That might be another reason why there was some jitteriness about the case.'

'It might have been useful to have known that from the start.'

'I only found out myself just before I came over here. Nobody had thought to include it in the briefing notes. It was only when I broke the news about the diamorphine that my boss mentioned it. In a tone that suggested I should have already known, obviously.'

Wallace smiled. 'That's a management style I've come across once or twice.'

'I'm getting used to it.'

'So the next question is does he have the motive? Don't suppose you've been given any unexpected insights on that front?'

'Nothing. As far as I'm aware, he's the only child, so I guess he'll inherit her estate for what that's worth. But there's no sign that Margaret Perry was wealthy. I can't imagine she'd have had enough to make her worth killing.'

'You'd be surprised how little it takes sometimes. But it doesn't sound like a strong motive in itself. And it takes us back to the question we discussed at the house. He could have washed the second mug and relocked the front door the way his mother usually did, letting himself back out through the patio doors. We wouldn't even have suspected a second person had been there. He was the one who drew our attention to the front door.'

'Some kind of double bluff? If he knew we'd identify the cause of death eventually, maybe he thought his only option was to persuade us there'd been an intruder.'

'Whatever the truth, it sounds like we're likely to have a major investigation on our hands. And a potentially sensitive one. The media will be all over this one.'

'Not a nice thought.'

'It depends what we actually have here. If the killer was her son, it's potentially just a one-off. Awful and tragic, but not a multiple killer. But if it wasn't…'

'I'm not sorry it's all above my pay grade.'

'Is that right?'

'I just do the legwork. It's now being escalated through the formal channels. Just thought you'd like a heads-up.'

'Thanks for that. It's good to be warned before it all hits the fan.'

'Keep it confidential for the moment. I'm not sure I'm supposed to have told you.'

'I'll act suitably surprised. But it's good to be forewarned. There's never a good time for an investigation like this, but it's going to be a real challenge right now. We're a couple of key people down in the team.'

'I'll keep you posted if I hear anything else in the meantime.' He hesitated. 'I'd be grateful if you could keep me up to speed too. I don't mean anything confidential. Just the odd update. It's one of the frustrations of my job. You get involved at the beginning, then don't hear another word. Would be interesting to know where this one's going.'

'I'll do what I can. Though I probably won't be able to tell you much beyond what we release to the media.'

'Yes, of course. It's just curiosity, really.'

'Thanks again for the heads-up. I'm very grateful.'

'Pleased to help.' He looked as if he was about to say something more, but in the end he rose from the table. 'I'll leave you to get on. You must be busy.'

'From what you've told me, I've a feeling I'm about to become a whole lot busier.'

CHAPTER SEVEN

Kyle Amberson's early afternoon appointments had mostly been routine, the mixed bag of ailments and anxieties that form the daily life of any General Practitioner. None of the issues had been serious, at least not from a medical perspective, and in most cases he could offer little more than a sympathetic ear, some lifestyle advice, and the odd low level prescription.

The rest of the afternoon would be spent making house calls, listening to a similar litany of questions and concerns. The practice made fewer and fewer house calls these days, but they maintained the service for those who were housebound or unable to attend the surgery unattended. They rotated the task among the team across the week, part of a working pattern that also covered the evening and weekend surgeries.

Amberson enjoyed the opportunity to see patients in their own homes. It was his only chance to gain a sense of the person beyond the immediate consultation. It was difficult for a GP to build up any kind of relationship with patients these days. The days of the old-fashioned family doctor were largely gone. Except for those with more chronic or recurrent conditions and a few of the older patients who insisted on seeing a familiar face, most patients rarely saw the same doctor twice.

That was perhaps no bad thing. In these parts they'd received a powerful lesson in the potential perils of that kind of doctor-patient relationship. At a personal level, Amberson felt more secure knowing his work was scrutinised by a team of colleagues, reducing the risk of errors and unfounded accusations, and he knew his colleagues felt the same.

But it was nice, on these home visits, to establish a slightly more personal connection than was possible in the surgery. Many of these people were lonely and only too grateful for a few minutes conversation with a friendly face. He had no illusions that some of the supposed medical concerns were concocted, consciously or otherwise, for that reason. Again, that was fine. It was probably one of the most useful contributions a GP could make.

His first couple of appointments were straightforward – an elderly couple with the husband suffering from mild dementia, and a widower of a similar age who needed some changes to his diabetes prescription. His third appointment was further out of town, with a younger woman who had sustained serious physical damage in a motorcycle accident. After several months in hospital, she'd returned home with a care plan that involved regular visits from her GP as well as periodic outpatient attendance as she made her slow progress towards recovery.

Amberson was keen to meet her. The visits to date had been conducted by various of his colleagues, who'd returned with a wealth of anecdotes about an apparently remarkable woman. Or, more accurately, two remarkable women. The patient was a character called Vivian Turnbull. If Amberson was unsure about his own reasons for ending up in this rainy northern market town, he was even more baffled as to how someone like Turnbull had finally settled here.

She was a Mancunian by birth, which was perhaps part of the answer, but she'd spent most of her adult life travelling the world. Despite his relative youth, Amberson had recognised the name instantly. In the 1980s and 1990s, she'd gained a reputation as a television correspondent reporting from the world's most troubled and battle-scarred regions. She was the figure who travelled into the places where her colleagues, male or female, were reluctant to go.

Amberson had only vague recollections of Turnbull's appearances on TV, though he knew she'd been something of a celebrity. She'd resolutely stuck to the nitty-gritty of everyday reporting rather than accepting any of the 'front woman' roles that had no doubt been offered her. When she'd eventually retired from her reporting role, she'd stepped quietly out of the limelight and returned to her roots, accepting a visiting lectureship in journalism from one of the city's universities.

Her partner was Romy Purslake, now in her early sixties and with an equally extraordinary life behind her. Although Amberson was hazy about the precise details, Purslake's life had apparently encompassed a period on the hippy trail in India in the 1970s, an academic career initially in Cambridge and then the US, the production of several volumes on topics ranging from literary criticism to feminism, and a period as a niche 'talking head' on television and radio. Turnbull and Purslake had met at some point on their respective travels, and, after an itinerant few years, had set up home together, initially in London before moving north with Turnbull's retirement. These days both lived relatively quiet lives, focused on their respective teaching and writing.

The quiet was only relative, though, which had been one reason for Turnbull's accident. Both women remained adrenaline junkies, engaging in potentially hazardous activities from microlighting to mountain climbing. Both rode motorbikes as their primary mode of transport into the city and to tour the Peak District and further afield. During one of those trips, Turnbull, had left the road and ended up crashing into a thicket of trees. Somehow, as a result of her protective clothing and survival instincts, she'd emerged alive if badly injured. She was only now approaching a return to something like full fitness.

Amberson's colleagues had informed him that, though Vivian Turnbull had a fearsome reputation for not suffering fools gladly, in person she was a personable and likeable individual who clearly enjoyed having even a temporary audience. All in all, it was an experience he was looking forward to.

The satnav led him up towards the edges of the Pennines. After another half mile or so, he was instructed to take a left turn into a single track road. He was now within a few hundred metres of the house, although for the moment it was concealed by woodland.

As the road curved to the right, he saw the house and gave a low whistle. It was an impressive place, a large old farmhouse extensively renovated in the recent past. He'd been given various descriptions of the place by his colleagues, but the house was more attractive and welcoming than he'd expected. The renovations had been sensitively handled and the house looked at if it had been standing in that spot, largely unchanged, for two hundred years or more.

He turned in at the gate and followed the drive towards the house. This side of the garden was given over largely to lawn, but he glimpsed a more cultivated garden at the rear with an impressive view out over the valley beyond. Manchester was only a few miles behind, but this felt like a different world. The house was surrounded by trees swaying gently in the spring breeze. The landscape was gently rolling farmland overlooked by dark hills. It was a fine day, fresh and breezy with a few white clouds scudding across the sky. A very different proposition from the cramped backstreets where he'd spent the early part of the afternoon.

A white van was parked by the front door, its side panels depicting an image of a rather excessive floral arrangement with the words 'J Gibbons - Florist' beneath. A young woman was standing by the front door, her arms filled with a bouquet of flowers, as she waited for the door to be answered.

Amberson grabbed his bag from the boot of the car and strolled over to the house. The young woman turned to him with an expression of hope. 'Are you the householder?'

'Sorry. Just visiting myself.'

'It's just that I don't seem to be getting any answer. I'll just have to leave these somewhere, but I'm always a bit reluctant just to stick them by the front door.'

Amberson frowned. 'She should be in. I'm her GP. She

knew I was coming.' He knew Vivian Turnbull had been using a wheelchair in the first weeks after her return home, but had now progressed to a pair of crutches. 'She's been in an accident, so it might take her a few minutes to get to the door.'

'I've been trying for a while now.' She stepped back. 'You have a go.'

Amberson wasn't sure why his efforts were any more likely to be fruitful than the woman's, but he reached past and pressed the bell again, listening for any sounds of movement from within. He could hear the sound of the bell but nothing else.

Amberson wasn't sure whether he should be concerned. From the descriptions provided by his colleagues, he couldn't imagine Turnbull was the vulnerable type, but it was possible she'd had a fall. After a moment's thought, he delved into his bag and brought out the set of notes he'd printed, which included Turnbull's address and her landline and mobile phone numbers. 'I've got her phone numbers. I'll try those.'

The landline rang for a few moments and then cut to voicemail. He waited a few more minutes and tried again. Again, the call rang and then he heard a female voice telling him to leave a message after the tone. He ended the call again without leaving a message and then tried the mobile number, with the same outcome.

He was feeling more anxious now. There were countless reasons why Turnbull might have failed to answer the door. Perhaps she'd fallen asleep. Perhaps she was using headphones and had lost track of the time. But none of the possible explanations entirely satisfied him. His impression from his colleagues had been that Turnbull was razor-sharp in everything she did, that she wasn't the type to lose track of the time or forget an appointment. 'Look, I'm going to take a look around the back, just to check everything's all right. You can just leave the flowers if you like.'

She hesitated. 'No, I'll come with you. There might be

somewhere I can leave the flowers at the back.'

Amberson wasn't entirely sorry she'd rejected his suggestion. Even as Vivian Turnbull's GP, he felt slightly awkward at the prospect of peering into her house uninvited. At least the woman could confirm he wasn't just a peeping tom.

He led slowly along the side of the house, peering in at the windows he passed. In the brightness of the afternoon, he could make out only the dim outlines of the interiors. The two front windows belonged to some kind of formal living or drawing room and to a second room lined with books. Both looked smartly furnished but showed no signs of life.

They continued their progress around the house, taking a paved path to the rear garden. The view from the rear of the house was spectacular, the fields falling away towards a valley crossed by the silver line of a river, before rising again towards the hills beyond. The rear garden was more cultivated than the front, a large polytunnel partly concealed behind a row of trees at the far end. In between was an attractive array of flowerbeds, the first daffodils and crocuses beginning to show, interspersed with lawns and shrubbery.

The area immediately in front of the house had been laid out as a stone patio with a mix of garden furniture. A pair of patio doors led into the house, one of the doors standing open.

Amberson walked cautiously to the open door, not wanting to startle Turnbull if she was sitting inside. 'Hello. Ms Turnbull? It's Dr Amberson. I'm due to see you at 3.30.'

Music was playing quietly somewhere. A classical orchestral piece Amberson didn't recognise. Otherwise, the house was silent. He stood in the doorway, feeling awkward about progressing further. 'Ms Turnbull?'

Finally, he took a further step forward and stopped. A woman was lying on the sofa at the far end of the room, apparently asleep. 'Ms Turnbull?' He raised his voice slightly in an attempt to wake her.

That was where the music was coming from. A pair of headphones lay on the carpet by the sofa, the melody leaking softly from the speakers. 'Ms Turnbull?'

His initial suspicion was hardening into certainty. He gestured for the young woman to remain outside and cautiously approached the sofa. The woman was lying face down, her face buried in the cushions, her legs encased in plasters. Vivian Turnbull.

Amberson gently touched her shoulder, still concerned about startling her. But he already knew the truth. He placed his fingers on her neck and sought a pulse, but could find nothing. The flesh was warm to his touch.

Knowing he needed to be absolutely certain, he carefully eased her body round until she was lying face up. By now, he had no doubt.

She hadn't been dead for long, he thought. Less than an hour, probably, although the warmth of the room made it difficult to be sure. She looked peaceful, as if she'd died quietly in her sleep. Perhaps an undiagnosed heart condition.

Amberson was on the point of moving away from the body, intending to call for an ambulance, when he heard a movement at the end of the room. He looked up, startled, having assumed he was alone in the house. The living room door had been opened, and a middle-aged woman was standing in the doorway, her expression a mix of horror and fury.

Before he could speak, she was striding towards him, looking as if she was preparing to drag him away physically. 'Who the bloody hell are you? And what the bloody hell do you think you're doing?'

CHAPTER EIGHT

Kenny Murrain paused outside the door of the private room and gestured for Gill to wait. 'I'll let Marie know you're here, if that's okay.'

'I think that's sensible,' Gill said. 'Thanks for doing this. I appreciate it's going to be a little awkward.'

You can say that again, Murrain thought to himself. 'We're all in rather a state about this. I don't want to cause Marie any unnecessary distress.'

'I don't need to go in,' Gill said. 'I don't want to make this any worse than it already is.'

'You've every right to see him. You're still friends. I'm sure Marie will appreciate that. And anything that might speed his recovery...'

'If you think it's the right thing to do.'

Murrain had no idea what might be the right thing to do, and he wasn't remotely comfortable with the responsibility that seemed to have been shunted in his direction. But there was little point in arguing now. 'Give me a second.'

He quietly opened the door, and stepped inside. 'How is he?' he said to Marie Donovan.

Donovan was a striking looking woman in her mid-thirties who normally gave the impression she could cope with anything life might throw at her. Now she looked exhausted and careworn. Murrain wondered when she'd last slept. 'Kenny. You were longer than I expected...' She had clearly read his expression. 'What is it?'

'Another visitor for Joe. She's waiting outside.'

'She?'

'Gill.'

'Ah.' Donovan was silent for a moment. 'I suppose it's understandable she'd want to come. In the circumstances.'

'Anyone who knows Joe will want to help him.'

'Yes, of course.'

Murrain could almost read the thoughts running

through Marie's head. Joe's mother and father were both dead, and he had no other close family. Other than his colleagues and a few friends, few people were likely to turn up here. It would be churlish of her to turn away someone who, in her own way, no doubt cared about Joe's fate. 'I'll bring her in.'

Murrain opened the door and gestured for Gill to join him. 'Marie, this is Gill. Gill, Marie Donovan.'

Gill awkwardly shook Marie's hand. 'I'm sorry. I just thought I ought to come. I won't intrude.'

Marie gestured for Gill to take one of the available chairs, sitting herself back down beside Joe. 'I'm pleased you could make it over. The doctors say it might helpful for Joe to hear familiar voices, though I don't know if they're just saying that to make us all feel less useless.'

'He looks better than I'd expected,' Gill said.

'There were no serious physical injuries,' Marie said. 'Just some bruising and a minor breakage to one of his wrist bones. He was lucky—' Marie stopped. 'Well, he nearly was. They don't really even know what the cause of this is. Whether it's some psychological effect of the unexpected trauma or if he really has suffered some form of brain damage. They've found nothing in the scans, but who knows?' She paused again, as if conscious she was talking too much.

Gill shook her head. 'It's an awful business. He always said it was part of the job, but I didn't really believe it.'

'Trust me. It's very much part of the job.' It was impossible to read Marie's tone.

Murrain lifted a chair from a stack in the corner, and joined the two women sitting by Joe's bed. 'Still no change then?' he said, hoping to move the conversation on.

'Nothing at all.' Marie reached out and touched Joe's hand, as if staking a proprietorial claim to him. Gill shifted awkwardly on her seat. 'There's no clear prognosis from the doctors. I get more worried with every day that goes by.'

'I'm so sorry,' Gill said. 'If there's anything I can do…'

'I don't think there is. But thank you.' At first, Marie had seemed over-garrulous. Now she seemed almost to have shut down, as if she'd run out of words.

Gill looked at her for a moment, as if about to offer some response she'd then thought better of. Murrain could feel the tension growing between the two women. He wondered what impulse had brought Gill back at this moment, beyond a natural concern for Joe's welfare.

Murrain turned his attention back to Joe. Amidst the tangle of cables and tubes attached to his body, he scarcely even looked ill. He seemed only to be sleeping, as if he might wake at any moment. Perhaps, Murrain added silently to himself, that's exactly what he would do.

Murrain gazed fixedly at Joe, trying to see if he could forge any kind of communication with him, any kind of link. There had been a few occasions when he'd felt as if he could tune into others' thoughts. Not in a coherent, telepathic way, but in the sense he felt somehow on the same mental wavelength as the other person. As if he had an insight into their emotions or their feelings. It had usually happened in moments of extreme duress, and once or two had helped him through tricky confrontations.

But it was an all too rare experience. Much more commonly, as now with Joe, there was simply nothing. He stared at Joe for a moment longer, willing himself to sense or feel something, but he knew no response would be forthcoming.

The two women were both still sitting in silence. After a moment, as if aware Murrain's attention had switched back from Joe, Gill said to him, 'I'd probably better go. I just wanted to see how he was.'

'I'll walk down with you.' Murrain was conscious he almost sounded as if he were escorting her off the premises, but Marie probably needed a few more minutes alone with Joe to regain her equilibrium. He turned back to Marie. 'I can come back if you'd like me to sit with Joe while you grab yourself a bit more of a break.'

'I'm fine. You need to be getting back to work.'

'You've got my mobile. If you need anything or if anything happens, call me whenever you need to.'

'I'll do that, Kenny. Thanks.'

It sounded like a dismissal, and he followed Gill back out of the room, closing the door behind him. Gill was waiting at the end of the ward by the nurses' station.

'I'm sorry,' she said. 'That was a mistake, wasn't it? I shouldn't have gone in there.'

'It was always going to be difficult. Marie's been through a hell of a lot. And there's no end in sight with this.'

'Was it serious between them?'

Murrain noted the past tense. 'It's serious. Relatively recent, but all the more serious for that.'

'Recent?'

'I don't know the details. It's none of my business. They've been together for a while, but it had recently moved to – well, to another level, let's say. So, yes, serious.'

'Yes, of course. I just wanted to know where things stand. So I don't put my foot in it.'

It was at moments like this that Murrain wished his gifts would allow him more mundane insights into others' thoughts or feelings. There was something in Gill's expression he couldn't interpret, but it made him feel uneasy. 'How long are you over here for?'

She appeared to hesitate before responding. 'I'm not sure. I'm just weighing up a few career options. There are a couple of opportunities over here I'm interested in. It's all rather in the air at the moment.'

Murrain already felt as if he'd been drawn into a conversation he'd rather have avoided. 'Well, good luck with it all.' He looked pointedly at his watch. 'I'd better be getting back.'

'Yes, of course. Thanks for helping me out in there, and thanks for all you've done to help Joe.'

'I just want Joe to make a full recovery. That's all.'

'Yes, of course.' Gill's gaze shifted back down the ward

towards the door of the room where Joe lay. 'That's what we all want, isn't it?'

CHAPTER NINE

'Just get away from her. Whoever the hell you are, just get away from her!'

Amberson had been crouched on the floor beside the sofa as he checked Vivian Turnbull's pulse. Now, unnerved, he scuttled backwards as the woman strode towards him. 'I'm Dr Amberson. From the practice. I had an appointment—'

'Just what the hell's going on here. How did you get in—?' The woman's gaze had drifted towards the sofa, and Amberson saw her expression change. 'What have you done?'

'I haven't done anything.' Amberson was still on the floor, his body curled defensively as if he was about to be struck a physical blow. 'I just came in and found her lying like that.'

The woman had taken Vivien Turnbull's wrist and was clearly trying to check her pulse as Amberson had done. He could tell she'd already reached the same conclusion.

'We need to call an ambulance,' Amberson said. 'I was just going to do that.'

The woman turned back to look at him with a face that revealed nothing of her emotions. 'It's a little too late for an ambulance. I'm calling the police.' She stopped, and her gaze shifted past Amberson towards the patio doors.

The young woman was standing there, the bouquet of flowers still clutched in her arms. Her mouth was open.

'And who the hell are you?'

The young woman looked on the point of tears. 'I'm a florist. I've a delivery for a Ms Turnbull?'

Amberson scrambled to his feet and took a step forward. 'Look, we need the police and an ambulance—'

The woman gave him a look that froze him in his steps. 'Don't move. Either of you. You're staying right there until the police arrive.'

'I've no intention of doing anything else. I just want to

help.' He looked across at the young florist. 'I'm sorry. I think we'd better do as she says.'

The woman glared at him and pulled out a mobile phone. He watched as she dialled 999 and explained the situation to the call handler. 'I don't know,' she said finally, 'but, yes, I'll stay on the line.' She looked up at Amberson. 'She wants to know if I think you're dangerous.'

'I'm just a GP.' Amberson had taken a few steps back in an effort to look as unthreatening as possible. 'I was due to visit Ms Turnbull this afternoon. That's all.'

'I'm just a florist.' The young woman held up the flowers as if in evidence.

'Yet you just walked into the house?'

He gestured towards the patio doors. 'I came in to check whether she was all right, and…'

'She wasn't?'

'No, she wasn't. There was no sign of any pulse.'

The woman's face gave no clue as to whether or not she believed the account. She spoke again into the phone. 'No, it's fine at the moment. Just tell them to be as quick as possible. Okay, I'm sure I can hang on for that long.' Her gaze switched back to Amberson. 'Police should be here in less than five minutes. I take it you're going nowhere.'

'Of course not. I've nothing to hide.'

He assumed that this was the formidable Romy Purslake. If so, he was slightly taken aback at her seemingly dispassionate response to her partner's death.

The three of them stood, motionless and silent, until they heard the sound of the front door bell. She backed away, still watching him, opened the living room door and stepped back into the hall.

She returned a moment later accompanied by two paramedics, followed by a pair of uniformed police officers.

Following the woman's directions, the two paramedics immediately began to tend to Turnbull's body. The two police officers, on the other hand, headed directly towards him. 'Can you and your friend here step back out into the hall, please, sir?'

'She's not my friend. I ran into her outside the house just now. Look, I'm Dr Kyle Amberson, Vivian Turnbull's GP. I—'

'Do you have any ID, sir?'

The police officer had led Amberson and the florist out into the hall, and now discreetly closed the living room door behind them. Purslake, presumably at the police officers' instructions, had retreated to the kitchen at the far end of the hall, though Amberson could see she was watching them. He reached into his pocket and found the official ID he used for home visits.

The police officer scrutinised it for a moment. 'Well, if that's real, it proves you're a GP at least.' His tone made every word in the sentence sound ambiguous.

'Of course I'm a GP.'

'And you say you're Ms Turnbull's GP?'

'That's why I'm here.'

'Ms Purslake doesn't recognise you.'

'There's no reason why she should. This is the first time I've visited. We're a group practice. Previous visits have been carried out by my colleagues. I just happened to be the doctor on duty today.'

'Can you tell me exactly how you discovered Ms Turnbull just now, sir?'

Amberson took a breath, wanting to give as clear and convincing account as he could. Both officers were stony-faced, watching him intently, as he briefly described his earlier actions. 'I thought she might have had a fall or injured herself. I'd run into this young woman outside, so we came round to the rear of the house to check. The patio doors were open. I looked into the room and saw Ms Turnbull lying on the sofa.'

'Then you entered?' The officer made it sound as if he were accusing Amberson of house-breaking.

'I just had the sense that something wasn't right—'

'You had the sense?'

'I don't know. Just an instinct. She seemed too still. I'm

a doctor. It's not the first time I've…' He trailed off.

'Not the first time you've what, sir?'

'Encountered a dead body, I suppose.' Amberson lowered his voice, conscious of the young woman beside him and of Purslake in the kitchen, just yards from them.

'Is that right, sir?'

'I don't know exactly what it was. But something made me go in and check she wasn't just asleep.'

'And she wasn't?'

'Of course. You've seen how—' He stopped short. 'Are you accusing me of something?'

'Just trying to ascertain the facts, sir. So you entered the room?'

'I entered the room and called Ms Turnbull's name again. Then I tried to wake her, but I was already becoming sure she was beyond that. I checked for a pulse but couldn't find any. I was on the point of calling an ambulance. Ms Purslake came in at that point and took control of everything.'

'How long do you estimate you were with Ms Turnbull in all, sir. I mean, before Ms Purslake came in.'

'No more than a minute or so.'

The police officer turned to the young woman. 'And can you vouch for all this?'

'It's exactly as he said. I was watching from the door. All he did was check her pulse.'

'So what do you believe was the cause of Ms Turnbull's death, sir? Using your professional experience.'

'I'm really not in a position to say. There are a number of possible causes of an unexpected death.'

'You don't believe there's anything you could have done for Ms Turnbull?'

Amberson made an effort to control his frustration with what felt increasingly like an interrogation. 'I don't know for sure. But I think she was already dead when I entered the room.'

'I understand, sir.'

'So what happens now?'

The police officer glanced at his colleague, for the first time looking slightly at a loss. 'We'll take contact details from you both, sir. Both your work and your home contact details, please. You're based in a practice in town?'

Amberson provided the address and phone number, and the young woman handed over a business card. The second officer, having taken the details, retreated to the end of the hallway and pulled out his phone. Clearly calling their workplaces to check their credentials.

The officer returned and nodded to his colleague. 'Checks out.'

'In that case, you're both free to go. We'll be in touch to arrange for you to provide a formal statement.'

'A statement?'

'Just routine, as you were the people who discovered the body.'

'I feel as if I ought to say something to Ms Purslake before I leave.'

'I don't think that would be a good idea, sir. She's a little shaken, as you can imagine.'

Shaken wouldn't have been the word that Amberson would have used to describe the woman who'd accosted him earlier. But that was perhaps just surface bravado. 'No, of course.'

Amberson was relieved to get back out into the fresh air. Outside the front door, he and the young woman stood for a moment, both clearly trying to absorb what had happened. The young woman was still holding the flowers. 'What do I do with these?'

Amberson offered her a half-hearted smile. 'Is there a message?'

She looked at the label on the flowers. 'From all at work. Get well soon.'

He shook his head. 'I think you'd better take them back. It's a bit too late for that now.'

CHAPTER TEN

'Okay,' Murrain said. 'Let's get started.'

This was the kick-off meeting for the investigation into Margaret Perry's death. Murrain and Bert Wallace had had some discussions with Paul Wanstead, but this was the first time they had brought together what was likely to be the core team.

'First of all,' Murrain continued, 'let me do a few introductions. Do we all know Colin Willock?'

DS Colin Willock looked around the table with the air of a zoologist examining an interesting new species of mammal. 'I've come across most of the team, one way or another, but there are one or two unfamiliar faces.' He gazed pointedly at Bert Wallace.

'Good afternoon, Colin,' she said. 'Bert Wallace.'

'Bert?'

'It's a long story.'

'You'll have to tell me sometime.' He smiled in a way Murrain assumed was intended to be charming.

'Sometime.' Wallace's tone suggested she remained uncharmed.

'Anyone else you don't know, Colin?' Murrain asked.

'No, I think that's everyone.'

Murrain suspected there were other members of the team unfamiliar to Willock but they were beneath his interest. Murrain had already begun to form an opinion of Willock. He knew of Willock by reputation – and most of what he'd heard had been negative – but he tried not be prejudiced by hearsay. It wasn't as if he'd had much choice about accepting Willock into the team. In the absence of Joe and Marie, he'd been scraping around for whatever resources were available. For whatever reason, Willock had been top of the availability list.

Murrain had sought Paul Wanstead's view, on the basis that Paul knew most what there was to know about individuals across the force. On this occasion, Wanstead had remained unusually non-committal, saying he too knew of Willock only by reputation. That should probably have told Murrain all he needed to know.

But Willock was here and there wasn't much Murrain could do about it. He'd already succeeded in rubbing up one or two of his colleagues the wrong way, and Murrain knew he was going to have to keep an eye on things. But that wasn't so unusual. It was just that Murrain had grown accustomed to working with a team who were generally cohesive and mutually supportive. Which might be testament to his own management skills or – more likely – just down to pure dumb luck.

'Okay,' he said. 'Talk me through it. Bert?'

He'd already read the briefing file pulled together by Bert Wallace but he always liked to hear a verbal summary of the key points. He knew from experience that hearing a description of the facts was more likely to trigger a response from his own distinctive gifts.

Bert Wallace took them through a characteristically concise summary of the case, beginning with Gregory Perry's discovery of his mother's body and ending with the pathologist's preliminary conclusions about the cause of death.

'How soon till we get the full postmortem findings?' Murrain asked.

'At least a couple of days,' Wallace said.

'And how definite do we think the pathologist's conclusions are? I mean, is he likely to change his mind?'

'I spoke to him about that,' Wallace said. 'He seems pretty sure. It's like it is with all those experts. He was reluctant to commit himself completely without having all the evidence. He said it was conceivable the postmortem might reveal something unexpected, but he couldn't envisage how it might change his mind.'

'So it looks as if we can safely proceed on the basis that Margaret Perry was poisoned. Who are the potential suspects?'

Wallace shrugged. 'There aren't any.'

Willock gave a snort. 'There are always suspects.'

Wallace closed her eyes for a moment. 'Yes, of course. What I mean is that there's no one who stands out as an obvious suspect at this point. The closest is the son, if only because he supposedly discovered the body.'

'Tell us about the son,' Murrain said.

'The main thing about him is that he's a hospital pharmacist.'

Willock repeated his snort. 'You said there are no suspects?'

Wallace ignored him. 'So, yes, he might have had the means to procure the diamorphine. It's possible he had the opportunity. But his mother had been dead for some hours before the son found her. If he'd killed her, that must have involved a previous visit, either on the morning of her death or late the evening before. He and his wife deny he left the house except for a short visit to the local supermarket.'

'Wife's alibi's not worth the paper it's written on,' Willock said.

'Maybe not,' Murrain said, 'but we need something substantive to challenge it.' He'd had the first glimmerings of his familiar feelings while Wallace had been talking about Gregory Perry. As always, nothing he could easily pin down. Just a break in the usual white noise, the distant echoes of some kind of signal.

'The second mug suggests the killer was likely to have been someone she knew,' Will Sparrow said.

Sparrow was a relatively young DC. In Murrain's view, he lacked Wallace's intuitive intelligence, but made up for it with a solid doggedness that would probably take him a long way in the force. He was already beginning to develop an air of gravitas appropriate to seniority.

'Which could be another pointer towards the son. Any other contenders?' Murrain asked Wallace.

'Not many,' Wallace said. 'She had a number of friends, mainly women of roughly her own age. It's hard to see what motive any of them might have had to kill her.'

'Other than that, there are no obvious contenders,' Wallace went on. 'She doesn't seem to have had many visitors. Not that she was a recluse. But when she was meeting friends, she generally went out to some local cafe.'

'Okay,' Murrain said. 'I assume we're following up with all her close friends. They might at least have some ideas about other people who visited Perry's house. Perry might have been more open with them than she was with her son.'

'If she was having a wild and passionate affair, you mean?' Wallace smiled.

'Anything's possible. But even if she was just, well, seeing someone, she might not yet have shared that with her son. Or she might have had other reasons for not telling him the whole truth. Maybe something about her finances or health. Parents don't always confide in their children, especially if they're embarrassed or worried about something.'

'We can check out her finances,' Wallace said. 'And see if her GP has anything to tell us. My understanding is that she was in good health. That was one reason there were suspicions about the death.'

'Any news from the CSIs or forensics?'

'We're still waiting on the forensic reports,' Wallace said. 'In terms of the crime scene, we've eliminated the obvious fingerprints – Perry herself, the son, the paramedics. There are a number of others which we're working through but nothing significant so far.'

They spent the remainder of the meeting allocating duties and responsibilities to the various enquiry teams, and the meeting eventually broke up. Colin Willock lingered after the others had left, waiting while Murrain finished talking to Bert Wallace.

'She seems a smart lass,' Willock said, when Wallace had left.

'She is,' Murrain agreed. 'One of our up and coming officers.'

'Maybe a bit pushy?'

'Pushy?'

'Perhaps that's not the right word. A little dominant, maybe.'

'For a woman, you mean?'

'No, not at all. Of course not. I just meant for her experience. She's quite young.'

'And very good. What can I do for you, Colin?'

'I just wanted to be clear about my role here.'

'Weren't you clear what we agreed just now? I mean, the allocation of tasks.'

'I meant more generally. I felt a little excluded in that meeting.'

Murrain was gathering together his papers. 'Excluded? In what way?'

'I was expecting you to seek my input more actively. The meeting seemed to be very focussed on DC Wallace.'

Murrain noted the use of the rank. 'She's done a lot of the early legwork on this case, Colin. It seemed sensible for her to lead the briefing.'

'At this stage, yes. I can see that. But as we proceed…'

'What are you trying to say, Colin?'

'Just that I'm assuming that, once I've got my feet under the table, you'll be looking at me as your number two.'

Murrain straightened up and gazed at the other man for a moment. 'That's not really how I work, Colin.'

'I just—'

'We're a team, Colin. We have our distinctive parts to play. We have different talents and experiences, and we all bring something to the party. I expect everyone to make a contribution.'

'I just thought that in the absence of Joe Milton—'

'Colin, as you know, I've worked with Joe for a number of years and I've come to respect his contributions. I'll no doubt come to respect yours in the same way in due course.' The words had emerged more bluntly than he'd intended, but that was probably no bad thing.

'I just thought—'

'We don't operate in terms of a pecking order here. If you do a good job, people will treat you accordingly.'

'Are you suggesting I don't do a good job?'

'I've never worked with you, Colin, but I'm looking forward to doing so. I'm sure you're an excellent officer. That's all I'm interested in.'

'I get the message. I'd always heard that you did things differently.'

Murrain had been about to leave, but now turned back to face Willock. 'What do you mean by that?'

'Just that I'd heard you work in your own way. From what people say—'

'What do people say?'

Willock clearly had no answer he was prepared to offer. 'I didn't mean…'

'I do things by the book, Colin. I've got a good team and I trust them. I hope you're going to become part of that team. You'll be very welcome.'

Willock looked as if he was on the point of making some response when Paul Wanstead stuck his head round the door of the meeting room. Murrain had long suspected Wanstead had some sixth-sense for knowing when to intervene. 'Sorry to interrupt, guv. Can I have a word?'

CHAPTER ELEVEN

'We were just finishing anyway,' Murrain said. 'Thanks a lot, Colin. Keep me posted on how you're settling in.'

Willock was clearly smart enough to know when to beat a dignified retreat. He nodded to Wanstead and left, closing the door perhaps a little too firmly behind him.

'I won't ask what all that was about,' Wanstead said.

'Best not. What can I do for you, Paul?'

'Thought you'd like to know we might have another one.'

'Another one?'

'Unexplained death. Not unlike the Perry one. An intriguing one. Woman called Vivian Turnbull.'

'Go on.'

'May be something and nothing, of course. Would probably have sailed under the radar if we hadn't already been dealing with the Perry case. As it is, I've just had a call from the coroner's office.'

'What's the story?'

'An interesting one. Her GP was with her when she was found dead.'

'If the GP was there, what's the issue?'

'GP reckons he arrived to find her already dead. She hadn't answered the door, so he'd gone round the back of the house and found the patio doors open. She didn't respond when he called her name so he went in to check she was okay.'

'And she wasn't?'

'He reckons not. He was in the process of checking her pulse when Turnbull's partner turns up, finds this strange man standing in the living room and understandably assumes the worst.'

'That's quite a scenario. Must have been a hell of a shock for the partner.'

'You'd think,' Wanstead said. 'That's the other interesting thing.'

'You know how to tell a story, Paul.'

'The PCs who arrived to deal with it reckon she seemed remarkably sanguine about Turnbull's death. Not unconcerned, but unemotional. More concerned about the presence of the GP.'

'Grief hits people in strange ways,' Murrain said.

'I'm just telling you what the PCs reported. Then there's the question of who Vivian Turnbull is.'

Murrain had the impression that Wanstead had been saving the best part of his story up for last. 'Put me out of my misery.'

'Doesn't the name ring a bell?'

It hadn't initially, and it still took Murrain another moment to place the name. 'The war reporter?'

'That's the one. Went where the men didn't dare to, or whatever it was they used to say about her.'

'I remember.'

'And her partner's Romy Purslake,' Wanstead said. 'Academic. Used to be on TV a lot as well. She's the one who's really pushing this. She's adamant the death is suspicious. I imagine the coroner would have been minded to push it in our direction anyway in the light of the Perry case, but Purslake banging on the door made the decision easier, I'm sure.'

'Does it sound suspicious?' Murrain asked. 'People do die unexpectedly.'

'Who knows? Turnbull had been badly injured in serious motorbike accident a few months back. That was why she was receiving visits from the GP. I guess it's possible her death might have resulted from some delayed effect of the accident, or that she died naturally from some other cause. We won't know till we get the postmortem report.'

'Doesn't sound a lot to go on. Maybe Purslake is just channelling her repressed grief into pursuing this.'

'That was my thought,' Wanstead agreed. 'Sounds like she's the practical sort. I can imagine she wouldn't waste her time on wailing and gnashing of teeth, if there's a good campaign to be fought.'

'What about the GP? Anything of interest there?'

'Not on the face of it. He didn't know Turnbull personally. It's a group practice so they make visits on a rota basis. There happened to be an independent witness present who supports his account, so looks like he's in the clear.'

Something had been stirring in Murrain's mind while Wanstead had been talking. One of his familiar sensations. Nothing strong, and certainly nothing clear. A minor mental tremor somewhere in the depths of his brain. Triggered by – well, what exactly? Something that Wanstead had said, he thought. He tracked back through Wanstead's words, trying to pinpoint the moment when he'd felt that sensation.

Wailing and gnashing of teeth, perhaps. A fairly characteristic Wanstead phrase.

'You okay, guv? Another of your brain farts?'

If it had been almost anyone else, Murrain might have been annoyed. But he'd worked with Wanstead long enough to know the other man wasn't mocking him. 'It was when you talked about Purslake not wasting her time on wailing and gnashing of teeth—'

He could feel it again, a little stronger this time. Bubbling away, trying to tell him something. And an image of some kind. An image he couldn't fully discern or interpret. A figure. A woman. Someone formally dressed…

Then it was gone.

'Anything useful?' Wanstead asked.

'Not really,' Murrain said. 'Or at least nothing I can make sense of at the moment.'

'I don't envy you that, guv. I think I'll stick to the old copper's gut. Which is sizeable enough, in my case.'

'You're fitter than all of us, Paul.'

'Fitter than poor Joe, anyway. I take it there's nothing new?'

'Not as of this morning.'

'I hear young Gill's turned up like a bad penny.'

Murrain sometimes felt that Wanstead's ability to tap into the grapevine was more remarkable than any gifts Murrain himself might possess. 'You keep your ear to the ground, don't you, Paul?'

'I've found it pays. It's true then?'

'She was at the hospital this morning, yes.'

'I take it Marie was there too?'

'You must know full well she was there. I don't know what your sources are, Paul, but they never let you down. Since you're so knowledgeable, what exactly is the deal with Gill?'

'In what way?' Wanstead's expression was one of wide-eyed innocence.

'I'd understood she and Joe had well and truly split up.'

'They have,' Wanstead said. 'At least as far as Joe's concerned.'

'Gill doesn't see it that way?'

'What was your impression when you met her today?' Wanstead asked. 'I mean, I take it there's a reason you're asking me these questions.'

'Fair play. I was left feeling a little uneasy, shall we say? I think she expected to get an opportunity to see Joe by herself. She dropped hints about pursuing her career over here…'

'Did she now?'

'Something you hadn't picked up on your famous grapevine, Paul? I don't know how serious she was. But I had the impression she wasn't hurrying back to Paris.'

'Now you're making *me* uneasy,' Wanstead said.

'You think Gill might be harbouring hopes of getting back together with Joe?'

'I've no idea. The split-up was an odd business. For a long while, Joe didn't even want to believe it had really happened. He thought she'd just gone to Paris for a while for her work, and then she'd be back and things would continue as before.' Wanstead shook his head, with the air of one who'd witnessed all the follies of mankind. 'I told him it didn't usually work like that, but he didn't want to hear it. To be honest, I thought Gill was only too happy to string him along. Keep her options open as long as she could.'

'When did that change?'

'Gradually. Joe realised Gill was showing no sign of returning. Things dragged on. Marie came along and things grew more serious in that direction. There were rumours that Gill was seeing someone else.'

'Was she?'

'I think there was something in it, but how much I've no idea. Anyway, at some point, Joe went from hoping they might somehow get back together to being certain they wouldn't.'

'And Gill?'

'That's the question, isn't it? She's made all the running in this, but she's never quite cut the ties. Didn't put any pressure on Joe to sell up the house they'd bought together.'

'Joe thought that was because she was being helpful. Letting him sort things out in his own time.'

'Maybe she was. Not for me to judge.' Wanstead's tone suggested he was only too happy to do so. 'But it kept her options open for that much longer.'

'You're an old cynic, Paul.'

'You brought the subject up. I'm just telling you what I felt. I know I'm probably biased. We both are. Interesting she should turn up again now, though.'

'Maybe she's just concerned about Joe. That would be natural enough.'

'If we're both brutally honest with ourselves, it may not matter much anyway,' Wanstead said. 'We don't even know what sort of future Joe may have. If any.'

'Maybe that's why I'm feeling so protective of his wider interests. The whole thing's such a bloody mess.' He was keen to move the conversation on. 'Okay, what about this Vivian Turnbull case?'

Wanstead took the hint. 'No sense in doing too much

until we've got the postmortem results, or at least something to indicate it's worth pursuing. We could well be wasting our time. We've got the CSIs going over Turnbull's living room in case there's any evidence there that might otherwise be compromised. We'll be taking statements from Romy Purslake, the GP who found the body and the other witness. I'm not sure it's worth doing too much more till we've some justification.'

'What about Purslake? Is she likely to kick up a stink in the meantime?'

'It's possible. She's pressing us to do something.'

'Maybe I should have a chat with her. Let her see we're taking it seriously. We don't want her as a loose cannon. I'm sure she's got the media contacts to cause us some grief.'

'My thoughts exactly.' As so often with Wanstead, Murrain was left with a sense that he'd been manoeuvred into doing what Wanstead had intended all along. 'Oh, and guv…?'

'Yes?'

'Not my place to say it, but if I were you, I'd keep an eye on Colin Willock.'

'Any particular reason?'

'Like I say, not my place. But he comes with a bit of a reputation.'

Murrain was tempted to ask more, but was conscious he was being led into territory that left him professionally uncomfortable. They were a close-knit team, but it was important not to abuse that. He smiled. 'Comment noted, Paul. And, like you say, not your place.'

CHAPTER TWELVE

'A Detective Chief Inspector?' Romy Purslake said. 'I'm honoured. I'm assuming this is one of the privileges of celebrity.'

'We try to give the same attention to everyone, ma'am,' Murrain said blandly.

'Of course you do. Please do come in.' She stepped back and ushered him into the hallway. 'Your people have finished in the living room now, I'm relieved to say.'

'My condolences to you,' Murrain said. 'It must have been a dreadful shock.' He could see now what Wanstead had meant about her emotional state. He was already mildly taken aback by her apparent energy and focus.

This was one of the reasons he'd been prepared to make this visit. It was an opportunity to meet her face to face, to gain any insights offered by her physical presence.

Murrain was conscious that, if there should be anything suspicious about Vivian Turnbull's death, her partner would be at the top of the list of suspects. It was possible she was creating a stir now to deflect the police away from that conclusion.

He'd felt something when she'd first answered the front door, though he'd have been hard pressed to ascribe any meaning to the sensation. Now, as they walked down the hallway to the living room, the feelings had reduced, though there was still something there, a low level murmur like the distant sound of traffic.

'They were very thorough, your colleagues.'

Murrain assumed she was referring to the CSIs, who had been examining the site of Vivian Turnbull's death. 'They have to be. Their work's critical to our investigations these days.'

'Although I'm not sure what they hoped to find in here,' Purslake said as she led them into the room.

'They generally find anything that's there to be found. We don't prejudge its significance.'

She was clearly only half-engaged with the conversation. At her invitation, Murrain sat in one of the armchairs, recalling that Turnbull's body had been found lying on the sofa.

'Can I get you some coffee or tea?'

'If it's no trouble. Coffee, please. Just milk.'

He was keen to have a few minutes to examine the room in which Turnbull had died, to see whether the room itself might provoke any mental response.

It was a handsome-looking room, decorated in a relatively modern style that felt slightly at odds with the age and character of the house. There were exotic-looking pictures on the walls and various ornaments which Murrain assumed were testament to the two women's travels. The room was large enough to accommodate several armchairs as well as the substantial sofa. Bookshelves, closely packed, lined the far wall. The place had a welcoming feel and Murrain guessed it would be a cosy place to spend an evening.

He looked across at the sofa on which Vivian Turnbull had died. It was a large, solid piece of furniture, plenty large enough to hold an adult body. As he gazed at it, he experienced a return of the sensation he'd felt on the doorstep.

He sat for a moment, trying to interpret what he was feeling. A sensation of loss, perhaps of departure, he thought. The emotion you might experience as you depart for a lengthy journey, perhaps. There were other sensations he felt less able to define. As far as he could tell, there was no sense of fear or anxiety. If anything, he felt almost the opposite. Reassurance, resolution, perhaps.

As so often, he cursed the imprecision of what he was feeling. It was like trying to disentangle the layers of flavour and ingredients in a particularly complex dish – a hint of this, a trace of that, much of it remaining tantalisingly out of reach.

Before he could think further, Purslake reappeared bearing two mugs of coffee. She placed one down on the occasional table beside Murrain and then, almost defiantly, sat herself on the sofa opposite. 'Now what I can do for you? I've already given a statement to that nice young man.'

The nice young man in question had been Will Sparrow who had visited the house, along with the CSIs, to take a formal statement from Purslake. Murrain had read the statement before setting out but it had told him little unexpected. Purslake had related that she'd returned earlier than usual from her work at the university, had walked into the living room and been startled to find Dr Amberson crouching over her partner. It had taken her only a few seconds to realise all wasn't well and, in her shock, she'd jumped to the obvious conclusion.

'First,' Murrain said, choosing his words with care, 'I wanted to reassure you that we are taking this extremely seriously—'

'I'd hope so.'

'Although you need to understand there are only certain steps we can take at this stage.'

'Is that police-speak for "bugger all"?'

'I don't want to mislead you about the level and nature of our current activity. At this point, we don't even know if a crime has been committed—'

'Vivian is indisputably dead.'

'But we don't yet know the cause of death. Tragic as it may be, people pass away for many different reasons.'

'I hate that euphemism,' Purslake said. 'Pass away. Pass on. Or these days just "pass". "I'm sorry to hear that such and such has passed". No, she hasn't. She's dead.'

Murrain was unsure how to respond to this diatribe. 'My point is she may well have died from natural causes. Until we ascertain otherwise, we can't authorise a full-scale investigation.'

'So how long will it take to ascertain the cause?' There was a trace of mockery in her echoing of Murrain's language.

'It's likely to take a few days for the postmortem to be

completed.'

Purslake snorted expressively. 'And of course it can't be done more quickly than that.'

'I'm afraid it's not within my control. They'll no doubt expedite it as much as possible.'

'No doubt.' Her voice dripped with irony. 'And in the meantime whoever did this is getting away with it.'

'We're taking as much action as we can, Ms Purslake. That was the reason for calling in the CSIs. If there is a crime to be investigated, any evidence here won't have been compromised.' He wondered how to formulate his next question. 'If I may say so, you seem very certain we should be investigating Ms Turnbull's death. Do you have any particular reason to believe that?'

For the first time Murrain had the impression Purslake was unsure how to respond. 'First, Viv was as fit and healthy as any woman of her age could be.'

'Even so,' Murrain said, 'it's possible she might have been suffering from some undiagnosed medical condition. I understand she'd been involved in a serious motorbike accident fairly recently?'

'She had. And that itself was unexpected. Viv was an extremely skilled motorcyclist.'

The sensation Murrain had felt a few minutes earlier had returned, stronger than ever. 'What are you implying, Ms Purslake?'

'I'm simply stating facts. I was shocked when Viv was involved in that kind of accident.'

'Accidents happen. Even to the most skilled and cautious drivers. Sometimes it's outside their control.'

'I understand that. Just as I understand that apparently very healthy people can die unexpectedly. But when two such incidents occur within a few months to the same individual…'

'It may still be coincidence.'

'I can understand it would be more convenient for the police if there were no crime to investigate.'

Murrain resisted rising to the bait. 'If there's evidence of a crime, we'll investigate. But we need evidence. Forgive me, but you seem to be implying someone might have wished Ms Turnbull harm. Do you have any reason to believe that?'

'You'll be aware of Viv's background. I think it's possible that in the course of her career she might have made some – well, I'm not sure enemies is the right word. Antagonists is perhaps a better description. If, as she did, you've devoted a substantial portion of your life to probing into the actions of questionable regimes, you're bound to incur some resentment.'

'But she'd retired from her journalist career some years ago, I understand? With respect, Ms Purslake, this does seem to be nothing more than speculation. There don't, as yet, seem to be any substantive reasons to believe there was anything suspicious about Ms Turnbull's death.'

'I appreciate that, and there's probably little I can do to persuade you otherwise at this stage. I just want to ensure that, if the postmortem does provide the evidence I'm fearing, you're in a position to take whatever action is needed.'

'I can assure you that, if we do have evidence of criminality, we'll take the appropriate action.' The sensation at the back of Murrain's mind had grown even stronger as they'd been talking. He sat back in the armchair, trying to grasp what the sensation was trying to tell him.

'Are you all right, Chief Inspector?'

'I'm sorry, Ms Purslake. I was just thinking about what you've been telling me.' The meaning, whatever it might have been, had frustratingly slipped away. He was left with a feeling, probably not much more than the usual copper's instincts, that Purslake was holding something back. 'Can I ask you again, Ms Purslake? Do you have any reasons to believe someone wished to harm Ms Turnbull?'

'There are aspects of Viv's past that I know little about, for all our closeness. Not necessarily for any sinister reasons, but simply because each of us was our own person. There are parts of my life I never shared with Viv, and I imagine there were parts of her life she didn't share with me. It didn't matter.'

'I've noted what you've said.'

'What about the doctor?'

'Doctor?'

'The GP who was here. Are you talking to him?'

'We've taken a statement from him.'

'But are you looking into him? Who he is, what his background is?'

'If there's a need for an investigation, we'll pursue every avenue, of course.'

'He was here, in the house. He'd let himself in. He could easily have been responsible for Viv's death.'

'As I say, if it proves necessary we will investigate every possibility.' Before she could interrupt again, he rose to his feet. 'I won't detain you any longer, Ms Purslake. I just wanted to let you know how matters stood.'

'Which is more or less where they stood at the time of Viv's death.'

She led him back to the front door. 'I look forward to hearing from you, then. And I hope you come bearing reassuring news.'

It was only after she'd closed the front door after him that it occurred to Murrain to wonder exactly what kind of news Purslake had in mind.

CHAPTER THIRTEEN

'I'm not sure what else I can tell you,' Kyle Amberson said.

Dr Andrew Carnforth leaned back in his large office chair and gazed at Amberson over his half-moon reading glasses. Like most of Carnforth's behaviour, the act was calculated to produce an effect on the person he was talking to. Amberson assumed Carnforth had perfected these stylistic quirks through decades of interacting with patients, his distinctive approach to a 'bedside manner'.

There was no question that it worked. Carnforth's current demeanour was intended to convey a mix of authority, quasi-parental concern and mild disapproval, as if Amberson was a mildly recalcitrant teenager.

They were all partners here, and in theory all had equal standing. But no one doubted that, for all practical purposes, Carnforth was the senior partner, simply because he had been one of the original co-founders. As the most recent joiner, Amberson was at the bottom of the pecking order.

He didn't particularly mind that, and it made little difference to his daily working life. He'd found he was listened to if he had something useful to contribute, and he was easy-going enough to accept his colleagues' long-established ways of doing things. But it was galling to find himself being treated like an errant schoolboy.

'I just want to reassure myself that there are no aspects of this unfortunate incident that reflect badly on us.'

Amberson made an effort not to rise to Carnforth's words. 'I don't see why there should be.'

'I just want to be confident everything was done by the book.'

'There's nothing to tell. I arrived at the house and rang the doorbell but there was no answer. I was concerned, so I made an effort to check everything was all right.'

'Did you have any reason to think it might not be?'

'Ms Turnbull had recently been involved in a serious

accident. I thought it possible she might have had a fall or be in difficulties in some way. If I'd decided to leave, that might have reflected more badly on the practice. It might have made us look negligent. Particularly given the way things turned out.'

Carnforth gazed at Amberson for a few moments, as if suspecting him of irony. 'Although you were too late to offer Ms Turnbull any assistance.'

'Unfortunately, yes. If anything, I only regret that I delayed as long as I did. If I'd gone straight round to the back of the house...'

Carnforth shook his head vehemently, clearly wrong-footed by Amberson's response. 'I'm sure you behaved entirely appropriately. We can't just go barging into our patients' homes without good reason. You weren't to know what had happened.'

'I'm just sorry I didn't arrive in time.'

'Of course, Kyle. I'm sure we all appreciate exactly how you feel. What's your view about the cause of death?'

'I think that'll have to wait on the postmortem. To be honest, I barely had time to examine her—'

'Ah, yes. You were interrupted by Ms Turnbull's – partner, I understand?' He placed a mild emphasis on the word 'partner' as if questioning its appropriateness.

'It was unfortunate, but understandable in the circumstances. I tried to explain why I was there, but she wasn't in a state to listen. Fortunately, it wasn't long before the police and paramedics arrived.'

'You are sure Ms Turnbull was already dead when you arrived?'

'As sure as I can be, yes.'

'As sure as you can be,' Carnforth echoed.

'There was no sign of life. I'd been unable to find a pulse. If I hadn't been interrupted, I'd have carried out a more thorough check, but I've no reason to doubt my initial judgement. And that was confirmed by the paramedics.'

'Who arrived some minutes after you did.'

'Nothing changed in those few minutes.'

'I just want to ensure I have a full understanding of the circumstances. In case there should be a challenge subsequently.'

'A challenge? From who?'

'Possibly from Ms Turnbull's partner.'

'Has she registered a complaint?'

'She did give me a call.'

Carnforth had presumably been holding back this piece of information to ambush Amberson. 'What did she say?'

'She was mostly concerned about the cause of Ms Turnbull's death. I told her that now had to be a matter for the pathologist.'

'Did she say anything about me?'

'She was concerned by your presence in the house. She implied that, if she hadn't been startled by that, she might have been able to do more to assist Ms Turnbull—'

'That's nonsense,' Amberson said. 'If anything, I might have been able to do more if she hadn't interrupted me. With respect, I believe Ms Turnbull's partner is an academic, not a medical doctor.'

'I'm merely relaying what she said. I had the impression she wasn't the sort to give free rein to her emotions. She struck me as the practical type, who prefers to express her grief through substantive actions.'

'Such as registering formal complaints?'

'I just want to ensure we're prepared for any eventuality, Kyle. It's important that we protect our reputation. You must appreciate that. Especially in a place like this.'

'I'm not sure I understand.'

'You're a young man, Kyle. But you know the history in this town. Many people placed their trust in a man who betrayed it in the most egregious way.' He picked up the expensive-looking fountain pen which always sat in a holder at the rear of his desk. Amberson had never seen Carnforth use the pen for writing. Like the other members of the practice he carried out most of his work on-line. The pen was utilised more as a visual aid. He tapped it gently on the surface of the desk with the air of a magician performing a particularly subtle trick. 'Some of our patients were his patients. Others had relatives or friends who were. Almost everyone in the area knows of someone – if only the relative of a friend of a friend – who was. People haven't forgotten.'

'That doesn't surprise me.'

'We have to be doubly careful. If there's any suggestion of scandal, people are likely to think the worst. They may start imagining problems that don't exist.'

'It's a very different situation, surely? We're a group practice with all kinds of checks and balances in place.'

'That's exactly why we have to ensure we apply the checks and balances. I just want you to reflect on everything you did with Ms Turnbull. Just to ensure that, in retrospect, there's nothing you could have done better or differently. Even if you think there's nothing – and in my experience with the benefit of hindsight there's usually something – please also think about what criticisms others might level at you, particularly if there should be a formal complaint. I want to ensure we're fully prepared.'

'But I don't—'

'One more thing, Kyle. Until this matter's resolved to everyone's satisfaction, I think it's probably better if you don't carry out any home visits.'

'Are you saying you don't trust me?'

'That's not the point. I just want to ensure that we're beyond reproach here.'

'You think I'm a risk?'

Carnforth sighed. 'Please don't be wilfully obtuse, Kyle. No-one is suggesting you're a risk or that you're at fault in any way. I just wish to ensure there are no possible grounds for us to be criticised.'

'What do the others think about this?'

'Everyone understands the importance of protecting our reputation.'

'Would you prefer me to resign from the practice? Is

that what this is about?'

'The thought hadn't crossed my or anyone else's mind. You're an excellent GP and a credit to the practice. No one's suggesting you shouldn't continue here or that you shouldn't see patients. You're a very valued member of the team.'

Amberson had already decided there was little point in continuing the discussion. There was no possibility of persuading Carnforth to change his mind. The real question was what this meant for Amberson's future in the practice. On the one hand, he had no desire to work in an environment where he wasn't trusted. On the other, he was damned if he'd allow Carnforth to drive him out for no good reason. 'If I'm such a valued member of the team, I'd better get back to work. I'm already late for my next appointment.'

He left the room before Carnforth could respond, taking care not to slam the door behind him. Still silently seething, he returned to his own consulting room, and summoned his next patient.

CHAPTER FOURTEEN

'Do you mind if I join you on this one, Bert?'

Colin Willock was stooped over Wallace's desk in a manner some might have found intimidating. She'd been aware of his presence for some seconds but had been determined to make him speak before she looked up. 'Sorry?'

'I understand you're interviewing Gregory Perry. I wondered if you'd mind if I joined you?'

'I'm just taking a statement from him at this stage.'

'But he must be our prime suspect, surely?'

'There's no one else in the frame. But the only evidence against Perry is purely circumstantial.'

'He discovered the body and he works as a hospital pharmacist,' Willock said. 'It's a start.'

'But no more than that.'

'That's why I'm keen to see the whites of his eyes. I flatter myself I know when someone's lying to me.'

Wallace guessed this wasn't the only way Willock flattered himself. 'You're welcome to join me. I just don't want to make the interview too heavy at this stage. I'd rather he trusts us enough to speak openly.'

'If he's guilty, he won't trust us anyway. But I take your point, Softly, softly and all that.'

Wallace had actually wondered about asking Kenny Murrain to join her at the interview, because she knew Murrain really did have an instinct for when people were lying, or at least for when what they were saying might be significant. Given Murrain was still out visiting Romy Purslake, she couldn't see any good reason to refuse Willock's request.

As if reading her mind, Willock said, 'Where's that boss of yours, by the way? Does he ever come into the office?'

'I don't keep track of his activities. He's been through a lot recently. We all have.'

'An officer down. I can see he'd feel bad about that.

You'd have to worry about whether you'd been negligent, wouldn't you?'

She gazed at Willock for a moment, but offered no response. 'Perry's down in reception. We're in Room 4 if you want to wait for us there.'

Willock smiled. 'Message received. The wagons have been circled. I'll see you in Room 4 then.'

Wallace walked past him out into the corridor. She stood for a moment, forcing herself to calm down, and then headed towards the lifts.

Perry was sitting in the small waiting area beside reception. He was a tall slim man in his early thirties, his pale hair already thinning. He looked nervous, drumming his fingers on the arm of his chair and staring fixedly at the ground as if to avoid catching anyone's eye. There were no conclusions to be drawn from that, Wallace thought. Most people felt nervous when they first came into this place.

'Mr Perry?'

'Yes, that's me.'

'Good to meet you, Mr Perry. I'm DC Wallace. Good of you to come in.'

'Anything I can do to help. It's all been a dreadful shock, especially now we know…'

'My sincere condolences to you. We'll do everything we can to bring to justice whoever's responsible for what happened to your mother.'

'Thank you.'

Wallace led him over to the security barriers, waiting till the receptionist had allowed him through, and then took him to the lifts. 'We're just on the third floor. It'll be myself and DS Willock talking to you.'

'I didn't realise—'

'It's nothing formal. It's just useful for there to be two of us so we can ensure we don't overlook anything. We appreciate you've already provided a statement to the uniformed officer, but we'd like a further discussion now we know the cause of death.'

'I'm not sure there's much else I can tell you. I just want

to know what's behind this. I can't understand why anyone would want to do this to mum.'

'This is us,' she said, as she ushered him out of the lift and along the corridor. She pushed open the door of Room 4. Willock was sitting on the far side of the table, and made no effort to rise. She gestured for Perry to take a seat opposite him and sat herself at the end of the table between the two men. She suspected Willock had been trying to engineer an adversarial set-up but she was keen to establish a less formal arrangement. She wanted Perry to relax and talk.

'This is DS Willock,' she explained to Perry. 'First of all, we'd both like to offer you our sincere condolences and sympathy. We realise that this must have been an awful shock to you, particularly now we know the circumstances.'

Willock had been drumming his fingers impatiently on the table top. Now he leaned forward and stared at Perry, as if trying to read the contents of Perry's brain. 'Tell us about how you found your mother.'

Perry blinked. 'I don't know if there's anything I can add to my statement. I was worried because mum hadn't been answering the phone—'

'Do you have any reason to believe she might have come to harm?' Willock asked.

'Not at all. She's in good health for her age. I just wanted to be sure she was okay.'

'So what did you do?'

'I knew I wouldn't be able to get in the through the front door because mum generally keeps it bolted. I've a set of keys for the rear patio doors, so I thought I could let myself in that way if I couldn't see any sign of her.'

'You didn't have any qualms about entering your mother's house without permission?'

'She's my mother. She wouldn't have minded me being in there.'

'Just tell us how it happened, Mr Perry.' Wallace was annoyed at finding herself involuntarily cast in the role of 'good cop'. 'In as much detail as you can. There may be something you saw that could be helpful to us.' Perry lowered his head for a moment, and she took the opportunity to glare at Willock. Willock smiled back.

'There's not much to tell,' Perry said. 'I made my way round to the rear of the house – there's a passageway between mum's and the house next door. She's got – she had a bit of a garden at the back. Nothing much, but enough to keep her busy in the summer…'

Willock had resumed his drumming, clearly willing Perry to get on with his narrative.

'Anyway,' Perry continued, 'I approached the patio doors and peered inside.'

'Could you see your mother at this point?' Willock asked.

'No. I could see the TV was off, but mum's armchair was facing away from where I was standing. I tapped gently on the window at first. I didn't want to startle her if she was asleep. I waited a bit and then tapped a bit louder. By this stage, I was getting concerned. Mum's usually bustling about the place. So I went in. I called but there was no reply. That's when I saw her—'

'If you're finding this distressing, Mr Perry, we can take a short break. Get you some water, perhaps?'

'No, no, I'm fine. It was just a shock, seeing her like that. Somehow I knew straightaway she wasn't just asleep.'

'How could you possibly have known that, Mr Perry?' Willock asked.

'Just something about the way she was sitting. It didn't look natural. Not the way you'd sit if you'd just dropped off. I called her name again, just in case. Then I walked forward and – well, took her hand… It was cold, even though the heating was on. I don't think I had much doubt by this point, but I tried to see if I could find a pulse. I'm no expert, but I've done a first-aid course at work and – well, there was nothing…'

'So you're confident she was dead when you entered the house?' Willock said.

If Willock's intention had been to play nasty cop to her nice cop, Wallace reflected, he was certainly succeeding.

'Like I say, I'm no expert. But I was fairly sure she'd been dead for some time before I arrived. The paramedics confirmed that, and I'm assuming the pathologist would have provided you with an estimated time of death.'

'Assuming you're telling us the truth about the time you arrived at your mother's house,' Willock said. 'And about this being your only visit over the weekend.'

'Oh, for goodness sake. My wife can vouch for my movements.'

'She was with you the whole time?'

'Pretty much. I went to the local supermarket on Saturday evening on my own, but I wouldn't have had time to get over to mum's and back, as well as getting the shopping. Other than that, we were together the whole time.'

Willock nodded. 'You're a pharmacist, aren't you, Mr Perry?'

'Yes. At the hospital.'

Willock wrote something in his notebook as though Perry had confirmed some critical point. Wallace expected him to continue his questioning, but instead he fell silent. More mind games.

'Tell us what happened after you found your mother's body, Mr Perry,' she said. 'If it's not too distressing for you.'

'I wasn't sure exactly what to do, so I called 999 and asked for an ambulance. The operator asked me some questions about mum's condition, but I think they accepted my view that she was likely to have – well, passed on. The ambulance got there quite quickly, though it seemed an age while I was waiting. After that, I just left them to it. But they confirmed what I'd thought.'

'You let the paramedics in through the front door?'

'Yes. That was one of the odd things. I mentioned it in my statement. Mum always kept the front door bolted and deadlocked after she was burgled. But I've no recollection of unlocking it to let the paramedics in.'

'You think it was already unlocked?'

'I wasn't really thinking very clearly. You sometimes do these things on automatic pilot, don't you? But I've no recollection of having done it.'

'And you don't think your mother would have left it that way?'

'If she had, it would have been the first time. Even when I was there, she always insisted on relocking and bolting the door once I was inside.'

'You said there were two mugs in the sink?'

'I went into the kitchen to get out of the way while the two paramedics were checking over mum. I noticed it again because it wasn't typical of her. She was the kind of person who normally washed up after herself as she went. If she'd just had coffees by herself, she wouldn't have left one dirty mug in the sink, let alone two. Even if she'd had a visitor, she'd normally have washed up after as soon as they'd left.'

'So what are you suggesting, Mr Perry?' Willock said.

'I'm just telling you what I noticed.'

Willock peered at Perry across the table. 'What have you been told about your mother's death, Mr Perry?'

'Only that it appears to have resulted from an overdose of diamorphine.'

'As a pharmacist, you'll be aware of the drug?'

'Yes, obviously. It's an opioid. A form of heroin. We used it as a painkiller in the hospital, though only in serious cases.'

'Are you aware of any reason why the drug should have been present in your mother's body?'

'Of course not. Like I say, it's used in cases where the pain is substantial. With cancer patients or post-operative patients suffering severe pain. There's no reason why anyone should have used it on mum. She wasn't ill, let alone in pain.'

'And yet there it was,' Willock said. 'Do you have access to diamorphine at work, Mr Perry?'

'Is this an accusation? Are you accusing me of killing my own mother?'

'We're simply trying to ascertain the facts, Mr Perry. I assume that, as a pharmacist, you do have direct access to diamorphine.'

'It's a controlled drug so there are very strict safeguards on its use.'

'I'm sure there are, Mr Perry. Though I imagine someone with your experience might be aware of ways to circumvent them?'

'That's an outrageous suggestion. I carry out my work with absolute rigour—'

Wallace held up her hands. 'I'm sure you do, Mr Perry. And I'm sure DS Willock didn't intend to suggest otherwise.'

Willock was smiling, clearly pleased he'd succeeded in getting under Perry's skin. 'I was merely asking a question, Mr Perry. I'm sure your own behaviour is above reproach. My question was whether the procedures might be open to abuse by a – less scrupulous individual.'

'There are very tight procedures,' Perry said, coldly. 'I think it would be very difficult for anyone to access these kinds of drugs inappropriately. But I'm not an expert in law breaking. That's more your field.'

'I certainly wouldn't want you to speculate outside your area of expertise, Mr Perry.' Willock was still smiling.

'Perhaps we should move on,' Wallace said. 'You indicated in your statement that your mother had a number of close friends who might have paid her a visit.'

'I gave your colleague the names of the ones I knew.'

They'd already begun to contact some of the individuals Perry had mentioned in his original statement. They had all been women of roughly the same age as Margaret Perry, some living alone as she was, some married. So far they'd identified no one who might have visited Margaret Perry on the weekend of her death. 'Do you think your mother had other friends beyond the names you've given us?'

'It's possible,' Perry said. 'I was close to mum, but she was still very independent and very much lived her own life. She told me about her friends when there was a reason to tell me, and obviously some were people she'd known for years. But there might have been others. She was quite an active woman. Involved in various local groups and societies. She knew a lot of people.'

'Any information you can provide us on those groups would be useful.'

'I'll see what I can remember. Some of it will be a bit vague, I'm afraid. For example, I know she was a member of a book group but I've no idea who the other members were. I assume you've been going through her possessions and documents?'

'We're still doing that,' Wallace said. 'It's given us one or two leads so far, but your mother doesn't seem to have kept much personal material. Most of it's just formal documents – copies of bills, bank statements, that kind of thing.'

'Mum was always more the practical type. She had a few photographs of me and my dad from over the years, but she wasn't a big one for that sort of stuff.' He finally allowed himself to smile. 'But if you wanted an electricity bill from five years ago she could put her finger on it straightaway.'

'Anything you can come up with could potentially be helpful to us,' Wallace said. 'Is there anything else you can tell us about your mother that might be helpful?'

'She was just an ordinary middle-aged woman. I don't mean that disparagingly, but there was nothing out of the ordinary about her at all.'

'What about your father? What kind of man was he?'

'Again, not much to tell. He was a few years older than she was. He retired a couple of years ago from the Civil Service. He died within a year of retiring. Heart attack.' Perry shrugged. 'It's not uncommon, apparently. But again he was just an ordinary bloke. Comfortably off with a decent pension, but not what you'd call wealthy. Played a bit of golf, but didn't do much else once he stopped work.'

'You can't think of any reason why anyone might have wanted to harm your mother?'

'Not at all. As I said in my statement, there doesn't seem to be any sign of anything missing from mum's house, so it can't have been a burglary. I can't imagine why anyone would have any reason to harm her.'

Willock was sitting back in his chair, playing with his pen in a manner that suggested he'd lost interest in the discussion. 'Are you your mother's sole heir, Mr Perry?'

'I'm her only child. So as far as I'm aware I'm likely to be the major beneficiary in her will. But I've not looked at the detail yet or spoken to her solicitor.'

'She never told you what was in her will?'

'She told me she'd made one and I know she updated it after dad died. As far as I'm aware I was the sole or at least main beneficiary, but we never really discussed it. As I say, she wasn't a wealthy woman. The mortgage is paid off on the house, so there'll be that, but otherwise I don't expect the estate to be worth much.'

'Still, any additional windfall is always worth having, I guess,' Willock said.

'Not at the expense of my mother's life.'

Wallace decided it was time to interrupt. 'I think that's probably all we need from you for the moment, Mr Perry. Obviously, any additional information you can give us about your mother's contacts or friends will be useful to us. But we don't need to take up any more of your time now.'

'I'll see what more I can come up with.' Perry was still watching Willock, with the air of a mouse observing a cat about to pounce.

'I'll take you back downstairs.' Wallace deliberately placed herself between the two men. 'Thanks again for your time.'

'Yes, thank you, Mr Perry,' Willock said from behind her. 'That's really been very helpful.'

CHAPTER FIFTEEN

That was the best thing about the job. No one noticed you. You were just part of the fabric of the hospital. Almost literally so, of no more interest or worth than the grey walls, the blank tiled floors or the rows of identical doors. It wasn't even that they disliked or despised you. They barely even registered your existence.

There were exceptions. Some of the junior nurses, the cleaners, the maintenance people, some of those were friendly enough. They might stop and chat, crack a joke, exchange the banter people do in a workplace.

He'd quickly identified the more sociable characters, and mostly tried to avoid them. The last thing he wanted was to make small talk, blether on about something that held no interest for him. If he saw those types heading towards him, he turned and walked the other way.

Not that he was unfriendly. If he couldn't avoid contact with someone who wanted to chat, he responded willingly. In the rest room, he talked amiably to his colleagues, even if he made a point of quickly hiding himself behind a copy of the Mirror or the Sun. He didn't want anyone to think he was aloof or considered himself superior. He just wanted not to be noticed.

If anyone had asked his colleagues about him, they would hardly have an opinion to express. Pleasant enough. Bit of a quiet one. Keeps himself to himself. As people always said when interviewed about their neighbour who'd turned out to be a serial killer.

He'd laughed to himself when that thought had occurred. Most people were unobservant. They had family, friends, but anyone outside that circle passed almost unnoticed.

He could walk the corridors here, dressed in his standard green uniform. No one would even consider why he was there. If he was pushing a trolley, regardless of its contents, no one would question what he was doing or where he was going. If he looked suitably purposeful, nobody would think to challenge him.

He didn't abuse this. He just got on with his job, carrying out the tasks he was given, performing the routine duties at the specified time. He didn't want anyone questioning his work or his performance. But there were busy periods and less busy periods, and he took advantage of the latter to do what he really wanted.

In the early weeks, that had been to get to know the hospital, to familiarise himself with the layout. It was a rambling place – a series of newer units added piecemeal to an original Victorian core – and there was no obvious logic to its design. Patients were directed to the various wards and departments by a complicated arrangement of signage, but he quickly discovered that, if you knew which way to go, there were short cuts unknown to most of the general public. Some of these were explained to him by colleagues – often in the manner of someone sharing a piece of arcane lore with a neophyte – but many he'd discovered for himself. The trick was to hold the overall shape of the place in your head, rather than trusting the signs, so you could identify the sometimes unexpected proximity of one part of the building to another.

Within a few weeks, he could make his way around the place with remarkable efficiency, buying himself precious free minutes after completing a task. After that, he'd set about identifying other aspects of the building that might be useful to him – places where he could conceal himself, or could leave a trolley to free himself for some diversion. Places where he could temporarily hide anything he appropriated, prior to taking it off site at the end of his shift.

The most useful area was, of course, the basement, which he explored at greater leisure whenever he was working the night shift. That was his real kingdom, where he could operate with much greater freedom, particularly outside daylight hours. That, for him, was the heart of the place.

Once he knew that the building was his, he focussed on the people – the staff and the patients. The staff were easier, of course, if ultimately less important. With some exceptions, they were mostly based here permanently and he could develop his knowledge of them over time. He couldn't know them all, but he gradually identified and selected those likely to be of most interest to him.

His interests lay at all levels in the hospital hierarchy. Anyone, essentially, who he thought might be of use. For the moment, he was mostly simply observing these individuals, while remaining inconspicuous himself. When the moment came, he'd inveigle himself into proximity with those who mattered. That was one of his talents, and the hospital's usual barriers of status and social standing wouldn't stand in his way.

He'd already started making approaches to some individuals. They hadn't realised he was doing it, of course. They just thought he was exchanging the odd pleasantry as they passed in the corridor or he carried out some activity in their vicinity. The fact that he was seen as a quiet, reserved individual made these people more responsive if he made a point of talking to them, as if he'd decided they alone were worthy of his attention.

These initial contacts had already paid some dividends. He'd extracted information from them without them even realising that he was doing any more than making idle conversation. He knew about the layouts of some specific wards, he knew where sets of keys were stored, and he was learning more about some of the patients.

It was the patients he was really interested in. Especially, the patients likely to be in here for some time. Most of the people were in here for a day or two, and then shipped out as quickly as possible. He was more interested in those here for longer, those with some kind of chronic illness or a condition which required some particular care. Those not necessarily at death's door, but at least waiting in some adjacent anteroom.

For the moment, he was still working out the pattern,

determining how many and what sort would be needed to achieve his objectives. The overall architecture was still unclear. He had an idea of the shape and the scale, but the precise profile of targets remained elusive.

Inspiration would come. He needed to create something substantial. Its heart lay here, in this building, but he was also casting tendrils outside into the wider community. That was needed for balance.

He had already identified some possible targets. Not all of them would be chosen, but he needed to make allowances. Some would be discharged before he was ready. Some would die naturally before their time. Some would simply not be right. But he'd already found some initial favourites – a couple of elderly patients in the geriatric wards unlikely to be released soon, a boy and a girl in the children's wards suffering from cancer. And the police officer. The police officer who was showing no sign of recovering from his coma, and who might never do so. He was perfect. Previously fit and healthy. An officer of the law. A normally strong and sensible individual, at the centre of emotional attentions he knew nothing about. Above all, the man who had already unwittingly sacrificed himself to help deliver this outcome.

He thought through all his as he sat in the porters' rest room, enjoying his brief break. He closed his eyes and concentrated, letting his mind wander through the corridors and rooms around him. It was almost an out of body experience – drifting into rooms and spaces normally inaccessible to him, the sense of complete freedom…

'Sleeping on the job?'

He opened his eyes. As he'd expected, his solitude had been short lived, and a couple of his colleagues had burst into the room and were busying themselves with the kettle.

'Just thinking,' he said, with a faint smile.

'You don't want to start doing any of that stuff, mate.' His colleague laughed. 'Dangerous bloody habit.'

He nodded, going along with the joke. 'Aye, you're probably right. I'll bear that in mind.'

CHAPTER SIXTEEN

Marie Donovan stopped at the entrance to the café and looked around. For a moment, she thought her suspicions had been wrong. The place was busy, as it always was around lunchtime as visitors, staff and the occasional patient came in to grab themselves a sandwich or a light lunch. Most of the tables were full, and there was the usual throng around the serving counters.

She was growing all too familiar with this place now, as with most of the hospital's public areas. She spent most of the day sitting beside Joe's bed – or at least as long as they'd allow her to – but found she needed a break every now and then.

She varied her routine, if only in an attempt to preserve her own sanity. Sometimes she went for a walk in what passed for the grounds outside. There wasn't much out there – car-parks and a motley assortment of buildings detached from the main hospital – but a short walk would bring her to a small park at the rear of the site, where if the weather was good she might sit and eat her lunchtime sandwich.

If it was raining, she just came down here, bought herself a snack and maybe a newspaper, and sat for half an hour thinking about nothing in particular. It gave her a brief opportunity to do something other than stare at Joe's face, wondering if those eyes would ever open again, and how things would be if they did. On one occasion, instead of coming in here she'd tracked down the hospital's chapel. She'd gone in mainly from curiosity. It was empty and she'd sat for a while, wondering if she should pray for Joe. She'd never been a religious person and she had no faith she could draw on. In the end, she'd simply thought about Joe, and about the future they'd been expecting to create together. Afterwards, she couldn't say whether the experience had left her comforted or more despairing.

Today, though, she'd come down here with a purpose. Since her brief encounter with Gill a couple of days before, she'd been feeling uneasy. It was partly that she felt some guilt at the way she'd behaved towards Gill. Marie had been fully aware of Joe's previous relationship, but after all that had happened she hadn't thought about Gill at all. That had perhaps been remiss in itself. Even if Joe's relationship with Gill was long over, they'd remained on good terms and Gill arguably had a right to know what had happened.

Marie knew she'd hardly been welcoming. She'd said nothing, but she'd made it very clear she didn't want Gill there. It was to Gill's credit, Marie supposed, that she'd taken the hint so quickly and departed.

Marie wasn't sure she'd have behaved any differently if she'd been able to relive the encounter. She hadn't intended to be unfriendly or unwelcoming. But, almost without realising it, Marie had perceived Gill as – well, perhaps not a threat exactly, but as someone who had access to a part of Joe different from anything Marie knew. Someone who had lived with Joe in a way that Marie as yet hadn't – and, she forced herself to add, might never do. Someone who'd known Joe for longer than she had, and at a different time in their lives.

Gill had been the last person Marie had wanted to encounter by Joe's bedside, and she hadn't been sorry that the visit had been so fleeting. But every moment since she'd been expecting that Gill would reappear, and she'd been preparing herself for that moment.

Marie's anxiety had been increasing to the point where she'd begun to fear she was growing paranoid. On a couple of occasions she thought she'd glimpsed Gill, first leaving the hospital entrance lobby through the main doors just as Marie had emerged from the lifts, and then later waiting at the counter while Marie had been sitting in the café reading her newspaper. Marie had looked up in time to see the woman she thought might have been Gill accept a takeaway coffee and leave.

So what did that mean? That Gill had continued to visit the hospital, even though – at least as far as Marie was aware – she'd not returned to see Joe? Was she waiting for a moment when Marie was away from Joe's bedside, or had she already taken advantage of one of Marie's brief absences? Marie thought that unlikely. The nurses tended to mention to her the few other visitors who had been in to see Joe, mostly his other colleagues from work.

That was one of the reasons she had come down to the café. Since her last supposed sighting of Gill in here, Marie had been alert for any further evidence of Gill's presence in the building. If Gill really had been hanging around the hospital there were few places she could go. Most of the available waiting areas were attached to specific departments, usually with receptionists, so it would be difficult for anyone to sit there inconspicuously. There was the small café and larger waiting area in the entrance lobby. And there was the main café where Marie was currently standing.

Marie gazed around the room. There was a woman sitting at one of the window tables who from the rear bore a strong resemblance to Gill. At first, Marie had taken the woman to be part of a couple, as she had been talking to the man opposite. But now the man was leaving the table, Marie saw they were strangers after all, just two people who had shared a table and struck up a brief conversation in a crowded café.

Marie walked slowly down the line of tables until she drew level with the woman, and looked at her in profile. The tables were packed closely together and it took her a few moments to ease her way through to the window table. 'Gill.'

It was difficult to tell whether or not Gill was surprised by Marie's presence. Her face remained blank, expressionless.

Marie gestured to the empty chair opposite Gill. 'Do you mind if I join you?'

'The seat's free.'

It was clear that Gill wasn't going to make this easy. But then, Marie thought, why should she? 'I just noticed you across the room. I wanted to apologise for the other day.'

Gill's face remained as unrevealing as ever, but for the first time her eyes registered some interest. 'You've nothing to apologise for.'

'I made you feel uncomfortable. I more or less drove you away.'

'You didn't make me feel uncomfortable. And it takes more than that to drive me away.'

The response wasn't exactly what Marie had been expecting, and the final words sounded almost threatening. 'Well, anyway, I'm sorry.' She'd been about to add that Gill should feel free to visit Joe whenever she wanted, but in the face of Gill's response the offer felt almost unreasonably proprietorial.

'Don't be. You're upset about what's happened to Joe.' For the first time, Gill smiled although the smile didn't entirely reach her eyes. 'When you've known him for such a short time, too.'

'Long enough for me to know what he's like.'

'He's not an easy person to get to know,' Gill said. 'He doesn't reveal much of himself.'

Marie decided to move the conversation on. 'I understanding you're living in Paris? That must be exciting.'

'I guess so. I don't know if I'll stay.'

'It must be a tremendous opportunity, though? To get to know a new place like that.' Marie was conscious her capacity for small talk had severe limits, particularly when speaking to someone who offered little in return.

'It has its moments.'

'So where are you thinking of moving on to?'

'Back home, of course.'

'Back to Manchester, you mean?'

'Back home.'

'What about your job in Paris?'

'I don't know whether I want a new contract. I can look for something here. Once I'm settled.'

There was an odd flatness in Gill's tone, as if the emotion had been drained from her words. 'Well, good luck in whatever you decide to do.'

'You too. Whatever you decide to do next. I'm sorry about Joe.'

'It's too early to be pessimistic. I'm sure he'll pull through. It's just a matter of time.'

'I'm sure it is. That's why I'm here.'

'I—' Marie could think of nothing to say in response. 'Look, I'd better get myself a coffee and a sandwich. I've not eaten all day. Can I get you anything?'

'I'm fine.'

'Well, if you're sure.' Marie rose and made her way through the tables towards the counter, glad to have ended the conversation. She'd been taken aback by the unexpected coldness of Gill's response. She anticipated a degree of awkwardness, but had assumed Gill would be open to a conciliatory move. But nothing had been forthcoming, just a series of statements that increased Marie's discomfort.

She owed Gill nothing, and she'd be happy never to encounter her again. She could live with that. None of it would matter once Joe recovered.

She reached the counter and turned to look back. Gill had already left, and the table she'd been sitting at was empty.

CHAPTER SEVENTEEN

Murrain felt the pulsing in the back of his brain, stronger and more intense that anything he'd experienced in a while. 'You're sure about this?'

'We've not conducted the postmortem yet so that will most likely tell us more, but I've got the results of some of the toxicity tests.' Dr Gerry Hayward was silent for a moment at the other end of the line. 'I had the tests expedited. It somehow didn't feel right to me.'

'I thought you were supposed to be a man of science.' Murrain had known Hayward for a long time, and they'd developed a friendly and mutually respectful relationship.

'And I thought you were supposed to be a detective,' Hayward said. 'But I know how you work.'

'More than I do,' Murrain conceded. 'But what do you mean when you say it didn't feel right?'

'Just experience, I guess. Or maybe I was just a bit spooked by the Perry case. That was unexpected. Of course, apparently healthy people die unexpectedly all the time, but Vivien Turnbull always seemed more healthy than most. Maybe that was it, if I'm honest. I still saw her as that apparently indestructible figure who used to report from the world's war-zones. It just seemed incongruous that someone who'd survived all that should just pop her clogs without warning and for no apparent reason.'

'You realise this is sounding less scientific by the second?'

'Well, it made me rush through the tests and it turns out I was right to do so.'

'Diamorphine again?'

'Just like the Perry case.'

'And we're talking unlawful killing?'

'I'd have said so. There's no medical reason she should have been taking it, and there's no indication of any prescription on her records.'

'It wouldn't have been used as a painkiller during her

period in hospital?'

'It's conceivable it might have been used as a painkiller after she was operated on, but there's no record of that. Something for you to check out with the consultant in case it's been misrecorded, but I think that's unlikely.'

'And that would have been months ago.'

'Quite. There's no reason why she should have been in significant pain now, and no reason she should have been using anything other than low-grade painkillers at most.'

'Is it possible she'd become addicted to it and was somehow accessing a supply?'

'I've seen no evidence of recurrent use, though that's an area where we might discover more from the postmortem.'

'So we're left with an unlawful killing.'

'Either straightforward murder or assisted suicide.'

'Assisted suicide? Is that possible?'

'It's conceivable. If she'd wanted to take her own life and persuaded someone to help her. But I've only ever encountered it in the context of euthanasia – individuals who are terminally ill or have some kind of severe degenerative disease, for example. There's no record of Vivian Turnbull suffering anything like that.'

'Okay, Gerry, thanks for the heads-up. I'd better get on with doing something about it.'

'I'll let you have the postmortem report and everything else as quickly as I can. Good luck with it. Suspect you're going to need it.'

Murrain finished the call, reflecting on what Hayward had told him. Two deaths, mostly likely murders, with the same MO and in broadly the same geographical area. But it was difficult to see any link between the resolutely ordinary Margaret Perry, a woman of moderate means, mundane lifestyle and limited horizons, and Vivian Turnbull, a former globetrotting celebrity correspondent who had routinely dealt with situations and experiences most people could scarcely contemplate. If there were links between the two, they were likely to be – what? Historical? Family?

The pulsing was still there in the rear of his brain, trying to communicate some message to him. There's been a moment, when he'd mentioned Margaret Perry's name to Hayward, when he'd felt something more, one of those jarring moments he sometimes experienced when there was a knocking on his mental doors. But the door had remained firmly shut, and he had no idea what was waiting on the other side.

He made his way through to the open plan office next door to break the news to the team. He paused before entering, and saw through the glass partition that Colin Willock and Bert Wallace were engaged in what looked to be a heated discussion.

Murrain opened the door silently and stood for a moment in the doorway. Willock and Wallace appeared not to have registered his presence, although Will Sparrow, sitting at a desk opposite, was watching him with semi-concealed amusement.

'If it had been left to you,' Willock said, 'we'd have all been having a nice cosy little chat. Not trying to pin down a bloody murderer.'

'I wanted to encourage him to talk, Colin. None of your nice cop, nasty cop game-playing. He clammed up like I knew he would.'

'Suggesting he's something to hide. You need to learn some proper investigation technique, Roberta. You're not chatting with your girlfriends over prosecco now.'

The use of her full forename and the sexist comment were clearly intended to provoke Wallace, but Murrain knew she had more sense than to rise to the bait. He closed the door noisily behind him. 'What's going on?'

Willock was obviously surprised by Murrain's arrival. 'Just sharing my experience of interview technique, guv. A bit of coaching.'

'Is that right?' Murrain turned to Wallace. 'Who've you been interviewing?'

'That was the point,' Wallace said. 'It wasn't a formal interview. We were just talking again to Gregory Perry. It became more aggressive than I'd personally have preferred at this stage.'

'He's our prime suspect,' Willock said. 'We wanted him under pressure.'

'You think he killed his mother?' Murrain asked.

'He's got to be top of the list, hasn't he? He's got the motive. He's potentially got the means. He could have easily created the opportunity. Who else could have done that?'

'Do you think he also killed Vivian Turnbull?'

'What do you mean?'

'I've just been talking to Gerry Hayward, the pathologist. Turnbull was killed in the same way as Margaret Perry. An injection of diamorphine.'

Willock was clearly struggling to assimilate this new information. 'Turnbull? The one who used to be on TV?'

Murrain had mentioned Turnbull's suspicious death in passing during the briefing meeting earlier in the context of his own meeting with Romy Purslake. At that stage, he had raised it only as something for the team to bear in mind, and he'd suspected that Willock – who'd still seemed primarily to be exercised by his own perceived status within the team – hadn't really been listening. 'Yes, Colin. She was found dead. Remember?'

'You're saying she was murdered too?'

'I'm reporting what Gerry Hayward told me. The cause of death was the same as Margaret Perry's. An injection of diamorphine. And, yes, it looks most likely she was murdered.'

Bert Wallace said, 'Where did Turnbull live?'

'Out in the hills,' Murrain said. 'But only a mile or so from Perry.'

'So the two killings are linked?'

'We can't assume that,' Willock said.

Murrain nodded. 'No, we can't. And we shouldn't, at this stage. But, if they're not, it's a remarkable coincidence. I'm going to have a chat with Marty Winston but my feeling is we treat them as two enquiries but closely co-ordinated. I'll need to get the resourcing sorted out. Not the best time to be faced with this, but it never is.'

'Do we know of any links between the two victims?' Wallace asked.

'I was musing on that myself,' Murrain said. As she'd asked the question, he'd felt something again, some intensifying of the silent pulsing in his brain. His instincts were telling him there was some link, something they should be checking out, though he had no idea what it might be. 'On the face of it, it's difficult to imagine two more different people. Different backgrounds, lifestyles, circumstances.'

'Perhaps there isn't a link.' Will Sparrow had walked over to join them. 'Maybe it's just random.'

Murrain was conscious of a chill finger down his spine. It was the thought they'd all been dancing around. Random, motiveless killings, driven by nothing more than someone's unexplained desire to play God.

'You know how to cheer a man up, Will,' Murrain said. 'But it's a thought we need to bear in mind. Perhaps one of our first tasks should be to check out Margaret Perry's GP.'

CHAPTER EIGHTEEN

Murrain peered through the window before opening the door. Marie Donovan was still sitting by the bedside, one hand holding Joe's, the other idly leafing through a magazine propped on the side of the bed.

He pushed open the door. 'Marie. Do you mind if I come in?'

He was relieved to see that the smile was one of genuine welcome. 'I'll be pleased of the company, to be honest.' She gestured towards the magazine. 'I was trying to read to pass the time, but I couldn't take it in.'

'No change, I assume?'

'Nothing that's obvious to me, anyway. I thought the consultant seemed more positive when I spoke to him this afternoon, but he didn't have anything new to offer.'

'All we can do is wait.' Murrain sat down beside Marie. 'You ought to get a break. I can stay here if you want to grab yourself a coffee or something.'

'I do that periodically anyway,' she said. 'I have to get out of here occasionally just to stay sane. And they won't let me stay overnight. Probably just as well, or I'd be sleeping on the floor. To be honest, I'd rather just stay and chat to you. It's nice to have someone normal to talk to.'

'I'm not sure I've ever been described as normal before.'

'More normal than I feel at the moment, anyway. I just feel as if I'm in limbo.'

'That's inevitable, isn't it? It's so frustrating that there's nothing we can do.'

'The consultant tells me to keep talking to him. But there's no sign of anything getting through to him.'

Murrain looked at the man on the bed. As on his previous visits, he'd tried to find some way to make contact with Joe, however indeterminate and distant it might be. But there was nothing. 'We can't know what's going on inside his head. He might be hearing every word we say.'

'It doesn't feel that way. But who knows?'

Murrain could see she wanted to say something else. He remained silent, allowing her the space to formulate whatever was on her mind.

'I ran into Gill. Downstairs in the café.'

'She's been back to see him?'

'That's the thing, or one of the things. She hasn't, at least as far as I'm aware. But I kept seeing her around the hospital.'

'Perhaps she was hesitant about whether to come back up?'

'I wouldn't blame her if she was. I didn't go out of my way to welcome her last time. But that wasn't it. I saw her in the café so I thought I'd take the opportunity to apologise to her. Break the ice a bit. Her response seemed – well, odd.'

'In what way?'

'I didn't expect her to respond effusively, but I thought she'd go through the motions of being polite at least. But she was very cold, much more than I expected. Her tone felt almost threatening. As if she was warning me off.'

'From Joe?'

'I suppose so. She gave me the impression she wasn't intending to stay in Paris. She talked about moving back home.'

'To the UK?'

'Home was the word she used. I think she meant it literally.'

'That's her business, I suppose. But you say she seemed threatening?'

'Now I'm describing it to you it doesn't sound much at all. Maybe I was imagining it.'

'Maybe it's been a shock for her as well. Even though she and Joe are no longer together, this must have been unexpected. Perhaps she's going through a tricky time anyway if there are questions about her future.'

'That was one reason I approached her. I thought I'd been a bit harsh on her. I don't suppose it matters. If she turns up here, I'll do my best to be polite and make myself scarce for a bit.'

'That sounds sensible. I'm sure she doesn't mean any harm.'

'Did you know her? When she was with Joe, I mean.'

'Not really. I met her a few times at office get-togethers. Christmas and the like. She was pleasant enough but I couldn't tell you much more than that. She told me she thought she'd treated Joe badly. When she went over to Paris, I mean. She'd known they were likely to split up, and she didn't think Joe realised that.'

'She's right enough about that,' Marie said. 'It took him a long time to come to terms with the fact that she wasn't coming back. Even when he and I first began to – well, get together, I had the sense he still wasn't entirely convinced he was really a single man. But that's all water under the bridge now.'

She took another long look at Joe, still gripping his hand, and Murrain wondered whether it was time to leave the two of them alone again. 'I'd better be getting back. I just wanted to see how he was.'

'It's good of you to keep coming. How are things at work?'

'Same as ever. Looks like we might have another major enquiry, though.' He briefly told her about the Perry and Turnbull deaths. 'They may well turn out not to be related but people are getting jittery.'

'I feel bad for not being there.'

'Don't be daft. As far as I'm concerned – and I know the same goes for Marty Winston – you're signed off for as long as you need to be. Our priority's to take care of you. And of Joe. We owe it to you both.'

'Even so, it can't help having both of us absent.'

'We're drafting in more resource. We've got Colin Willock on the team at the moment.'

'Willock? I don't know how much that'll help you.'

'You've come across him then?'

'Only by reputation. I probably shouldn't talk out of

turn. I'm sure he's a good copper. But I've heard he's hard work.'

'We'll see. He seems a bit of a loose cannon. But maybe we'll benefit from someone setting a few sparks flying.'

'From what I've heard, he's certainly one to do that. Good luck with it all. And with him.'

'Thanks.' Murrain pushed himself to his feet. 'If there's anything you need, anything at all, just let me know. If you want to get away and come and stay with me and Eloise, you'd be more than welcome.'

'That's kind of you, Kenny. At the moment, I just want to keep things as normal as possible outside of this place. It feels like a kind of talisman, you know? Persuading myself this is all just temporary and one day it'll all be back to normal.'

'I'm sure it will be. It's only a matter of time.'

He said his goodbyes and made his way back out through the ward and down in the lifts to the entrance. As he passed the small café in the lobby, he glanced across at the tables. It was a relatively quiet time of day and only a few tables were occupied, but at the far side a woman was sitting with her back to him. He was too far away to be certain, but it looked like Gill.

For a moment, he considered walking over and speaking to her. But he wasn't sure it really was her, and he had no real idea what he might say if it was. In the end, he continued walking out through the main doors into the daylight.

CHAPTER NINETEEN

'So I was right?'

'It appears your suspicions were well-founded, yes,' Murrain said. He had called Romy Purslake the previous afternoon prior to his visit to the hospital to break the news to her about the cause of Vivian Turnbull's death. They had already had a similar exchange in the course of that call, but Murrain had known she would want to rehearse the same points again when they met face to face.

He had told her that, now this had become a murder enquiry, they would need to interview her again. He'd considered bringing her into the police offices, but in the end had decided he preferred to see her at home. He was likely to gain more insight from talking to her on her own territory.

He was conscious, as so often in his work, that he ought to be delegating this task to the team. He'd told himself his presence was justified by Turnbull's and Purslake's public profile – and Marty Winston would no doubt be happier he was here to smooth Purslake's ruffled feathers – but the truth was he just wanted to gain whatever insights he could from her proximity. The second question had been who should accompany him. Murrain would have preferred to have brought Bert Wallace or Will Sparrow, but he'd been conscious Colin Willock would have seen that as further evidence of his exclusion from the team. Murrain was also interested to see how Willock would behave in what might turn out to be a relatively sensitive interview.

'Vivian was murdered.' Purslake spoke the words as if selecting the inscription for her former partner's tombstone.

'We can't be sure of the precise circumstances of her death,' Murrain said cautiously. 'The cause of death appears to have been an injection of diamorphine. It may be that we'll learn more from the postmortem examination.'

Purslake snorted. 'So if not murder what else? Unless you're suggesting she injected herself.'

'At this stage, we just wish to ascertain the facts.'

'Which is why you wanted to talk to me again. Because now I'm clearly a suspect.'

'Ms Purslake—'

'You don't need to soft-soap me. I was conscious of the implications when I first raised the possibility Viv had been murdered, and no doubt so were you. If she was killed, there are only a limited number of potential suspects.'

'We're not—'

'The most obvious ones being that supposed GP who I found crouched over her body and, beyond that, me. Who else would have had an opportunity to inject the drug into her body?'

'That's what we need to discover,' Murrain said, patiently. 'At this stage we're jumping to no conclusions. Although we do have an independent witness who confirms the GP's account of events.'

'I hope you've checked her out too,' Purslake said.

Murrain had no intention of becoming involved in a debate about the detail of the investigation. 'We're following up every lead, Ms Purslake.'

Willock was sitting opposite Murrain in one of the armchairs, gazing round the room in apparent wonder at the collection of artwork and ornaments. Now, he turned his attention back to Purslake. 'Is there any reason why Ms Turnbull should have been using diamorphine?'

'What are you implying? That Viv was some kind of junkie?'

'We're interested,' Murrain said, 'in whether, for example, Ms Turnbull might have been prescribed diamorphine as a result of her accident.'

'Presumably her medical records can tell you that more reliably than I can. I've no idea what she might have been given in hospital, but as far as I'm aware the only painkillers she'd used since her discharge were paracetamol.'

'You're not aware she was in any kind of severe pain?'

'Not in recent weeks, no. She was in some discomfort when she first came home, but it had improved a lot since then. As far as I'm aware, she was using nothing stronger than standard painkillers.'

'Is it possible she was in greater pain than she told you?' Willock asked.

Purslake had been gazing fixedly at Willock since he'd asked his previous question. 'Of course it's possible. She was a proud woman, and I know she felt foolish for allowing the accident to happen in the first place. She was pushing herself too hard when she first came out of hospital, trying to prove she was as strong as ever. I had to tell her to slow down a couple of times. So if she had been in pain, she might not have wanted to admit it. But we'd lived together a long time. I think I'd have known if she wasn't telling me the truth.'

Murrain decided there was no point in pressing the issue for the moment. 'Can you tell us about Ms Turnbull's accident?'

The change in topic clearly took Purslake by surprise. 'The accident? She came off her motorcycle.' She had turned back to Murrain, and he could see she was wondering about the significance of his question. 'As I think I told you when we spoke previously, it was unexpected.'

'Ms Turnbull was a keen motorcyclist?'

'We both were. It was one of the things that initially brought us together. But she'd been riding for much longer than I had, and was much more skilled. That was why I was taken aback by what happened.'

'What were the circumstances?'

'We don't entirely know. Viv was on her way back from work in the early evening. It was autumn, so still fully light. She sometimes came a roundabout way back so she could have a spin up in the hills before getting home. It happened in a fairly remote spot, a couple of miles from here. You'll no doubt have the details on your records.' She spoke the last sentence in a tone that implied Murrain had been remiss in his research. He wondered whether she was accustomed to speaking to her students in the same manner.

'I'm sure we will,' Murrain said. 'So why did she come off her bike?'

'That's what we don't know,' Purslake said. 'And what your colleagues were ultimately unable to ascertain. They spent a considerable amount of time analysing the scene of the accident, and there were suspicions that a second vehicle had been involved. But the evidence was inconclusive, and in any case there'd have been no way of identifying the vehicle.'

Willock leaned forward. 'But surely Ms Turnbull must have remembered what had happened?'

'You might have thought so,' Purslake said. 'But she didn't. Dissociative amnesia, I understand they call it. When your memory simply shuts down after a traumatic event.'

It was a phenomenon Murrain had been introduced to during a previous investigation. 'She had no recollection of what happened?'

'Her last memory was of driving along an empty, apparently dry road in pretty much ideal conditions. The next thing she knew she was waking up in a hospital bed, festooned with tubes and wires.'

'How was she discovered?'

'Luck, partly. She'd obviously left the road, tumbled down a small embankment into a ditch and then apparently hit a tree. She hadn't travelled too far away from the carriageway and was still visible to any passers-by. She was spotted by a passing driver while it was still daylight, and he stopped and called an ambulance. It was a close-run thing. If she hadn't been spotted before dark, she'd probably have lain there till morning and by then it would have been too late. At the time, I thought we'd been unbelievably lucky. But obviously her luck didn't hold out.'

'How bad were her injuries?' Murrain asked.

'Not as bad as they might have been, but still pretty serious. She was wearing all the protective gear and that's what saved her, but she still managed to do a hell of a lot of damage. It took her months to get to anything like her former self, and we knew some of the effects would be with her for life.' She gave a hollow laugh. 'Well, we got that right. We'd envisaged a rather longer one, though.'

'What was her state of mind while she was recovering?' Willock asked.

'If you mean was she suicidal, definitely not. After the initial shock, she was quite upbeat. She felt the enforced break would give her the chance to do the things she'd been meaning to. She was playing around with ideas for books, talking to publishers. Various projects.' She had turned back to Willock. 'So if you're asking whether she took her own life, I think it's highly unlikely. I appreciate that you have to go through all this, gentlemen, but you really are wasting your time.'

There was something there, Murrain thought. Some sensation, some distant mental voice calling out to him. As always, it was too faint to hear. 'We discussed this before, but do you know of anyone who might have wanted to harm Ms Turnbull?'

'I can only give you the answer I gave previously. Perhaps someone wished to harm Viv for some reason associated with her past. She'd led a full life, and she had dealings with some unpleasant people. She was involved in exposing international scandals, potential war crimes, questionable financial dealings. Much of that was in the past but history can sometimes throw long shadows. When I suggested this before, you dismissed it as speculation. But the whole matter is now much less speculative, wouldn't you say?'

'I think we can fairly say that,' Murrain agreed. 'But if there's anything about Ms Turnbull – about her life or her past – that's likely to be relevant to our investigation, I'd urge you to tell us about it.'

'There are many things I could tell you about Viv's past, and I'm sure there are countless more things she never shared with me, but I wouldn't have an inkling of which, if any, of the countless anecdotes might be relevant.'

Murrain was increasingly sure Purslake was withholding something from them. Whether that pointed to her own guilt or to some more convoluted secret, he had no idea and, as so often, his inner sensations were steadfastly refusing to provide any clues. He could feel nothing more than a low-level white noise, his inner radio still failing to connect with any signal. 'Do you have any concerns about your own safely?'

'My own safety?'

'If someone wished to harm Ms Turnbull, they might also wish to harm you.'

'If they wanted to harm me, they've already succeeded. You might not think it, but I've found the loss of Viv genuinely unbearable.'

'I appreciate this must be a trial for you.'

'And I appreciate you have a job to do, and that you'll inevitably be treating me as a suspect at this stage. That's why I want to handle this in as pragmatic a way as possible. I can save my grief for a better time. I just want to ensure you bring Viv's killer to justice. I'll hold everything together until you've done that.'

'We'll do our utmost, Ms Purslake.' He paused, keen not to waste the moment. 'And I'm not going to insult your intelligence by pretending that we're not looking at you as a possible suspect. If nothing else, we always have to look closely at the immediate family alongside pursuing other lines of enquiry.'

'In this case I'm the only family that Viv had.'

'Is that the case?' Murrain had already had one of the team looking into Vivian Turnbull's background.

'Her mother died about ten years ago from cancer, and her father shortly afterwards from a heart attack. There's no-one else. Not even any distant cousins, as far as she was aware.'

'What about close friends? People from her past or current work?'

'All of our closest friends are joint ones. I can provide you with names and addresses if you think they're likely to be worth talking to. There are one or two former work colleagues from her TV days that she saw from time to time, but she wasn't keen to maintain much contact with most of them. She wanted to put all that behind her, to be honest. Her university colleagues tended to be just that – colleagues. She got on with them well enough but didn't socialise with them.'

'We'd be grateful for any names you can provide,' Murrain said. 'We'll be talking to her colleagues at the university. You said she wasn't keen to maintain contact with her former television contacts. Can I ask why she felt that way?'

'When we moved up here, she saw it as an opportunity to start a new life. Viv tended to be one for clean breaks.'

'Why did she leave television in the first place? Whenever I saw her on screen,' Murrain said, 'it struck me she had a real passion for what she did.'

'Television was becoming more cautious, more bureaucratic. Endless risk assessments and form filling before they'd allow her to do anything. It cramped her style. If she got wind of a story, she just wanted to chase after it, no matter where it led her. The bosses couldn't cope with that. Wanted her to sign in triplicate that whatever happened wouldn't be their responsibility. I think she just grew tired of it all. And she was becoming something of a celebrity herself. That was never what she wanted. She just wanted to be a hands-on reporter.'

'The public seemed to love her,' Murrain said. 'Wasn't she woman of the year on the Today programme once?'

'Much to her profound embarrassment, yes. She made the mistake of doing a couple of interviews for the Sunday papers, and they just wanted her to do more and more of it.

She was due to retire anyway, so she took her pension, a payoff and left it all behind. I don't think she regretted it for a moment.'

'What brought the two of you up to this part of the world?'

'Work, mainly. Mine, that is. I'd been building an academic career, and was offered a Chair up here. This was shortly after Viv had retired. At that point, she was expecting it to be a genuine retirement, giving her a chance to do the writing she'd been talking about. Then Viv was offered a visiting lectureship in journalism. She was reluctant to take it at first, but it helped keep her hand in and she enjoyed passing on her supposed wisdom to the younger generation.'

Willock had resumed his examination of the room. He had the air of an antique dealer weighing up the potential value of each item in a house clearance.

'We've probably taking up enough of your time for the moment, Ms Purslake,' Murrain said. 'We will need to speak to you again as the investigation proceeds, and we'll keep you fully informed of any developments.'

She gazed at him for a moment, and he half-expected she might demand something more. 'I hope so. I sincerely hope so.'

There was something here, Murrain thought. Something Purslake wasn't saying. Something she was holding back.

And the oddest part was that he felt that she wanted to speak, that she wanted to tell him the whole truth. The real question was what was keeping her silent.

CHAPTER TWENTY

He'd finished his final appointment and was finalising all the related administration when the knock came at the consulting room door. Before he could respond, the door opened slightly and a head peered round. 'Kyle?'

Amberson had been fearing the worst – a visit from Andrew Carnforth – and was relieved to see that the visitor was Jude Calman, one of his fellow GPs in the practice. 'Come in. I thought for a minute you were Andrew.'

'Do I look like Andrew?'

Amberson grinned. 'I'd have to be staring at you a long time before I saw the resemblance.'

'I just wanted to check you were okay, really.'

'Okay?'

'I hear you were being subjected to a police interrogation this afternoon.'

It was clear the grapevine had been very active. 'Something like that. She was very pleasant, actually.'

Calman raised an eyebrow, 'She?'

'A female detective constable. They do have them, apparently.'

'Do they? They'll be having female doctors next.'

'I don't know that Andrew would ever fully approve of that.' Amberson liked Jude Calman. She'd been the warmest and most welcoming of his fellow doctors when he'd first joined the practice, and had gone out of her way to make him feel at home. She was an attractive, athletic-looking woman, a few years older than he was, and at first he'd wondered whether there was any prospect of her friendliness leading on to a more serious relationship. But he'd quickly learned she was already very happily married, which had simply meant their friendship had flourished without the pressure for anything more.

'Are you in a rush?' she said.

'Not really. The only thing waiting for me at home is a ready-meal for one. Why?'

'Just wondered if you fancied a quick drink. It's been a long day and Charlie's playing five a side this evening, so I wouldn't mind a chat and a bit of company for an hour.' Charlie was the husband, a hospital registrar and, as far as Amberson could judge, a fully nice guy in his own right.

'Why not? Just give me time to pack up.'

Five minutes later, they were sitting in the new micropub opposite the surgery. Since its opening a few months earlier, this had become Amberson's favourite haunt for a quick post-work drink. It was a small, welcoming place with a good, constantly changing selection of craft ales and fashionable flavoured gins. They found a table in the corner, and Amberson fetched pints for both of them along with a packet of upmarket peanuts.

'So how was it?' Calman said. 'The police interrogation. Did she shine a light in your eyes, throw you down the stairs, any of that kind of stuff?'

'A disappointing lack of that, to be honest. As I said, she was very pleasant. I mean, professional but polite.'

'Disappointing. They're not seriously treating you as a suspect, are they?'

'I suppose they have to, at least up to a point. I was there. I found the body. I suppose I could potentially have the means to do it.'

'Shit.'

'On the other hand, I don't have any motive. I'd never met Vivian Turnbull. I had a pre-arranged appointment. We talked through all that, and I got the impression they were going through the motions.'

'I can see that. Makes you realise how much this kind of stuff is an occupational hazard in our work, doesn't it? So what's your theory about the death? On the assumption that you're not a serial killer.'

'It's a weird one, isn't it? I suppose her partner's the obvious candidate. I certainly thought her reaction was a bit odd. I didn't blame her for being startled at finding me in there, but she seemed oddly unemotional. As if she was more interested in dealing with me than taking care of her partner. Beyond that, I suppose anyone could have entered the room. The patio doors were open.'

'There was no sign of any struggle?'

'Nothing like that, no. She looked as if she'd died peacefully. It all seems bizarre.'

Calman was tearing open the packet of peanuts. 'She was a bit of a celebrity, wasn't she?'

'Before my time, to be honest, but I could remember the name. Some sort of war reporter.'

'Maybe she'd got on the wrong side of Al Qaeda or something.'

'Who knows? I think she'd been retired for a good few years.'

They both sat in silence for a few moments, drinking their beers. 'I hear you were called to the headmaster's study as well.'

'The headmaster's study? Oh, you mean Andrew. Yes, I was called in for a lecture.'

'Don't worry. We've all been there.'

'Have we? I mean, even you?'

'Oh God, yes. What did you think I was? Teacher's pet?'

In fact, Amberson had thought that, or at least something along those lines. He'd always had the impression Carnforth treated Jude more gently and with more deference than he did the rest of the team. But that, he reflected, was quite possibly simply because Carnforth fancied her. 'I assumed Andrew only picked on me.'

'Don't think you're special. He's picked on all of us at one time or another. It's part of his distinctive management style. And he's particularly keen on doing it to those who are new to the practice. Makes sure you're put in your place before you get too uppity.'

'Not many new partners get visited by the police in their first few months, though, I'm guessing.'

'That's true. You might have set a new record there. But, seriously, if it hadn't been that he'd have found something else. Some mistake you made. Some patient who wasn't entirely happy. Something you got wrong in the paperwork. There'd have been some reason to drag you into his office to give you the talk. It's a rite of passage.'

'What was it in your case?'

'I'm not sure I can even remember now. Something I'd cocked up. He went through the whole "more in sorrow than in anger…just want to ensure you understand the standards we work to here…I'm sure it won't happen again" spiel. Made sure I knew my place.' She took another mouthful of beer. 'Don't get me wrong. Andrew's harmless enough. He doesn't interfere much. He just wants you to understand that there's a pecking order and he's at the top of it.'

'I can live with that,' Amberson said. 'I've never been one to worry much about status.'

'There you are then. As long as you doff your metaphorical cap and tug your metaphorical forelock, Andrew'll be happy enough. And you can get on with your job.' She paused. 'The funny thing is, Andrew's got more of a skeleton in the closet than any of the rest of us.'

'Really? I'd have thought he was Dr Respectable.'

'That's how he likes to present himself. But he's been through some tricky times.' She paused, shifting slightly uncomfortably on her seat. 'I feel a bit awkward sharing this because I don't really like gossip, but it might be helpful if you were aware. Especially if Andrew does start getting on your case.'

'You don't need to tell me if you don't want to.'

'I just think it helps explain some of his behaviour. I've checked it out and I know it's not just idle gossip. It goes back to the early days of the practice. Andrew established it with a couple of colleagues who're both retired now. It all started successfully enough. It expanded rapidly, and – well, reading between the lines I think the pressure and workload got to Andrew.'

'I'm told it's not uncommon,' Amberson said.

'You do need to watch yourself. It's all too easy to become a workaholic, and that can lead to all kinds of other addictions, if you get my drift.'

'You're saying that's what happened to Andrew?'

'The details are a bit murky, but it seems to have been something like that. He was drinking too much.' She raised her glass of beer and peered at it thoughtfully. 'Which is something of an occupational hazard. But it's one thing to have a glass or two outside work. There were claims that Andrew was turning up to the surgery under the influence.'

'Really?'

'A couple of patients claimed he smelled of booze and that his behaviour seemed erratic. From what I understand, it was all dealt with very quickly and discreetly by his two partners. Apart from the professional implications, any hint of scandal would have destroyed the surgery's reputation even before it was properly established. Andrew was immediately relieved of his duties and rushed off to rehab. It never got as far as anything formal.'

'He had a lucky escape then,' Amberson said. 'I'm surprised they allowed him to return.'

'I think it took some time. Months. But, whatever else he might be, Andrew's a good doctor and they hadn't been able to find anyone suitable to replace him. In the end, he was allowed back on probation, with the partners making it very clear that if there was any repeat he'd be out of the door and charged with misconduct.'

'And there wasn't?'

'Apparently not. In fairness to Andrew, my guess is that the original issues were symptoms of some kind of mental health problem. They gave him support with that, and he pulled through it.'

'Good for him. I suppose,' Amberson said. 'And good on the partners for giving him a second chance.'

'The thing is,' Calman went on, 'I've heard rumours it wasn't just booze that was the problem, that he'd also been dabbling in stronger stuff, some of which he obtained from the surgery.'

'Ah,' Amberson said. 'Not good.'

'Not really. Especially not from the partners' point of

view. Any hint of that would have destroyed the practice. But, as you say, all credit to Andrew for rebuilding things.' She took another swallow of her beer. 'Like I say, I've told you this not as idle gossip, but because I think it helps explain some of Andrew's behaviour.'

'He did keep going on about the reputation of the practice. I thought at the time it seemed a bit overblown, but it makes more sense in this context.'

'Exactly. Andrew's not a particularly hands-on manager. He'll generally just let you get on with the job. But he wants to set a marker down right at the start. Make sure you understand how much weight he gives to the practice's image and reputation. That he wants us to be squeaky clean.'

'So you're saying I've not made the best start by having the police turn up on our doorstep?'

'Maybe not. But that might cut both ways. If Andrew thinks you handled the situation well – which in his eyes will mean suitably discreetly – you might get some kudos from that.'

'I can only hope.' Amberson gestured towards her empty glass. 'You want another?'

She looked at her watch. 'I'd better not. Charlie'll be back fairly soon. And anyway…'

'What?'

'I wouldn't want to do anything that might risk bringing the practice into disrepute.'

CHAPTER TWENTY ONE

Benny Failsworth dumped the crate slightly too heavily down on the stone doorstep and straightened to ring the doorbell. He knew this would take a while because it always did. But it was his last delivery and the end of his shift, so after this he could just head back, dump the van and go home.

This one tended to be the last delivery because it was so remote, right on the edge of their coverage. Benny would wend his way through the suburbs towards the country where the deliveries were few and further between, finally navigating the narrow road up to this place.

It was one part of the drive he actively enjoyed. Once he reached the edge of the hills and the road began to rise, the views were spectacular. Tonight, they'd been particularly good. It had been a cold clear spring day, the sun setting behind him and, as he looked to the west, the Cheshire plain was spread out under the reddening skies, offset by the darker shadows of Manchester and Stockport.

He'd arrived a few minutes early, but the old man wouldn't mind. It wasn't as if he went anywhere. He welcomed the delivery as much for the brief social interaction as for the provision of his groceries. That was fine by Benny. He was happy to chat for a few minutes after he'd helped carry the bags into the kitchen. It made the job seem more worthwhile.

He was taking his time today, though. Benny pressed the bell again, and stood staring out at the view. He couldn't imagine what had possessed the old man to want to live up here. It was a beautiful spot, but not the ideal location for someone who was now almost house-bound. The bungalow had seen better days, too, though Benny imagined it had once been a desirable residence, with its large picture windows looking out over the hillside. Now the garden was overgrown, the paintwork peeling and the windows looked as if they could do with a clean.

There was still no sign of movement from within the house. Benny rang the bell again, this time holding it down for longer. Then he banged loudly on the door.

Still nothing. Benny pulled out his mobile and checked the contact number on the order. On the previous occasions Benny had called it, the old man had always answered it very promptly. Now it just rang out, eventually cutting to what Benny knew was an old-fashioned answering machine in the hall. He gave it a moment and tried again, with the same result.

More anxious now, Benny banged loudly on the door once more, then placed his mouth to the letterbox. 'Mr Ollerenshaw! Shopping delivery!'

There was no sound from inside, and something about the quality of the silence made Benny uneasy. It was growing dark now, and no lights were showing from inside the house.

A paved path took Benny into the rear garden. The house faced west and the light was better here. The garden was mostly given over to lawn, with a paved area immediately adjacent to the house itself. Benny took another few steps and peered into the picture window, feeling uncomfortably voyeuristic.

His eyes had already grown accustomed to the gloom. He could make out a sofa, a couple of armchairs, all facing the television set in the corner. The screen was facing away from him, but Benny could see from the play of light across the room that the television was on. Facing it, in one of the armchairs, Benny could see a darker shape.

Maybe the old man had fallen asleep watching the TV and slept through the doorbell and phone. Benny tapped on the window, gently at first then, when there was no response, more loudly. The shadow remained motionless.

Benny swore quietly under his breath, then banged again on the window. There was still no response. He returned to the front door and, for lack of other ideas, tried the handle.

To his surprise, the door opened. It was unlike the old man to leave it unsecured. Usually, when Benny arrived here he had to wait patiently through a seemingly endless ritual of unlocking before the door finally opened.

He pushed open the door and peered inside. 'Mr Ollerenshaw! It's your delivery!'

There was only silence in response. Benny reached beside the door and found the light switch, flooding the hallway with light. 'Mr Ollerenshaw!'

Benny stepped inside, blinking at the sudden glare. Across the hall, the answering machine was blinking to announce his own missed call. He pushed open the door of the living room. The shape of the shadow remained motionless in the armchair. 'Mr Ollerenshaw?'

Ollerenshaw was sitting in the chair. He looked for all the world as if he was sleeping peacefully. Benny stepped forward and took Ollerenshaw's hand. It felt warm compared with own weather-chilled skin, but colder than it ought to be. As far as he could tell, there was no pulse.

Benny took out his mobile phone and made two calls. First to the emergency services to call for an ambulance. And second, back to the shop, to tell them he was likely to be some time.

CHAPTER TWENTY TWO

Murrain stifled a yawn. It had already been a long day, and he had the feeling there was more to come. He'd convened the team in the MIR for a collective update on where the two investigations stood. He and Willock had just briefed the team on their discussion with Romy Purslake.

'She's provided us with a list of names for people who were friends either of both of the women or of Turnbull alone,' Willock concluded. 'So we'll need to allocate people to interview those over the next few days. Though it's probably a waste of our time.'

Murrain and Willock had already had this conversation during their return drive from Purslake's. 'We can't leave any stone unturned, Colin.'

Willock sighed. 'Oh, I know that. Especially with a high-profile case like this one.' His tone placed ironic quotes around the words 'high profile'. 'It's just that we have an obvious suspect in the frame and we ought to focus on that.'

'You mean Purslake?' Bert Wallace asked.

'Of course Purslake. We only really have two possible contenders at present. Purslake and the GP. The GP potentially had the opportunity and may have had access to the means, so we can't ignore him. But we have a third-party witness who confirms his story, and no grounds to suspect her of collusion. In any case, what the hell would have been his motive?'

'We can come back to the GP in a minute,' Murrain said. 'Bert'll fill us in on her interview with him.'

'As far as I can see Purslake's the one who should be in our sights. She obviously had the opportunity. We've only got her word for exactly when she returned to the house. If she was already there when the GP arrived, she'd have had the chance to do the deed. Maybe that was why she was so freaked out when she walked in on the GP. It wasn't that she thought he was responsible for Turnbull's death, but that he'd realise what had happened.'

'It's worth bearing in mind,' Murrain agreed. 'What about the means? Where would Purslake acquire diamorphine?'

Willock had already given Murrain his views on this. Purslake was a left-wing, feminist academic. Why wouldn't she have access to drugs? 'She might have had contacts.'

'In which case, we'd need to identify who they are and how Purslake would have accessed them,' Murrain said. 'If we are to build a case against Purslake that side of it needs to be watertight.'

'What about a warrant to search the house?' Willock said.

'If there was any potential evidence there, it's likely to be long gone,' Murrain pointed out. 'We don't have the grounds to justify a search at this stage. But, yes, we need to have a close look at Purslake's contacts. I'm assuming we've checked she doesn't have a record?'

Will Sparrow nodded. 'There's nothing of significance, and certainly nothing to do with drugs. She was arrested during the Iraq War protests, but released with a caution.'

Willock's expression suggested Sparrow had just confirmed his worst suspicions. 'I'll get someone checking her out. Maybe some of her university colleagues can offer us an insight.'

Murrain nodded. 'Okay, Colin. But handle it sensitively, eh? Purslake strikes me as a woman who knows how to use the media. It won't help us if she stirs things up.'

'I'll be the soul of discretion,' Willock said.

'What about motive?' Murrain asked. 'What motive would Purslake have had for killing her partner?'

'Could be anything,' Willock said blithely. 'Lovers' tiff, maybe.'

'A lovers' tiff might end up with you stabbing your partner with a carving knife,' Wallace pointed out. 'It's not likely to end up with you injecting them with diamorphine.'

'You don't know my wife.' It wasn't possible to tell from his tone whether Willock was entirely joking. 'But, yes, fair point. Something more cold-blooded, then. Presumably the reason for using this approach is the killer hoped it would be accepted as natural causes.'

'Not likely these days,' Murrain said. 'Unexplained, unexpected death usually results in a postmortem. It's unlikely to be missed.'

'So why use this approach then?' Wallace asked. 'There must be easier ways of killing someone.'

'The killer might not have been aware of the protocols we follow now. And it's a relatively painless way of dying, I suppose,' Murrain said. 'If you wanted to kill someone but didn't want the victim to suffer.'

'Which again might point to Purslake,' Willock said. 'If she had a reason for wanting to rid herself of Turnbull, but wanted to do it in the most – I don't know, humane way she could.'

'What about assisted suicide?'

'It's a possibility,' Willock acknowledged. 'We raised the question of Turnbull's state of mind with Purslake. She reckoned Turnbull had been in good spirits. But if she'd helped Turnbull kill herself, that's what she would say, wouldn't she?'

'It's another avenue for us to explore,' Murrain said. 'There's nothing in Turnbull's medical records to suggest she was suffering from any illness, other than the after-effects of the accident. But I guess the trauma of the accident could have affected her mental state.'

'Maybe she hadn't managed to come to terms with leaving behind her former action-packed life,' Wallace said. 'The accident might have brought home that she wasn't the woman she once was.'

It's a long time since she retired, but I suppose these things aren't always straightforward. Speaking of the accident, we should have another look at that, too. Purslake reckoned there were potentially suspicious circumstances – suggestions of another vehicle being involved – but it went nowhere at the time. Will, can you check that out?'

Will Sparrow nodded. 'I'll see what I can find. You think it might be linked to her death somehow?'

As Sparrow asked the question, Murrain felt the familiar tremor in his brain, the sense of something kick-starting. His vision momentarily grew hazy, and he could almost see something. A road, a vehicle, woodland. The image was too brief and unclear for him to identify anything more. Paul Wanstead, on the opposite side of the table, was watching him with curiosity. 'Worth finding out what the road forensics people thought at the time. Let's move on to Dr Amberson, shall we? Bert, you went to talk to him this afternoon? What were your impressions?'

'Young – probably not much more than late 20s. Very nervous when we started but that's understandable. He calmed down once we got going and gave a clear account of what had happened. Seemed very – professional, I suppose is the word. Pretty personable. I can imagine him having a good bedside manner with his patients. He didn't leave me with any sense he was hiding anything. Seemed keen to help.' She paused. 'More than I can say for his colleague.'

'Collleague?' Murrain asked.

'Yes. Colleague. Boss. Whatever he was. The senior partner in the practice. Some guy called Carnforth. He'd obviously primed the receptionist to let him know when I arrived. So while I was sitting there waiting for Amberson, Carnforth comes out and introduces himself and asks if I can spare a few minutes. All very polite, but with a strong implication he's not going to take no for an answer.'

'So what was it all about?' Murrain asked.

'Nothing much, as it turned out. Just Carnforth bleating on about how he hoped we were going to be discreet and how he had the reputation of the practice to think of. I put up with about five minutes of this nonsense before I asked if Carnforth had anything specific to tell me. After more beating about the bush, it turned out the answer was no. The whole thing seemed to be just a shot across the bows before I saw Amberson. Marking his territory.'

'Anything else on Amberson?'

'I've checked out his background and record. Seems unblemished. No police record. Nothing to suggest he isn't just what he appears to be.'

'Too good to be true?' Willock offered.

'It's hard to see what motive he'd have had for killing Vivian Turnbull.'

'Thanks, Bert, that's very helpful,' Murrain said. 'That leads us back to Margaret Perry's death. For the moment, we're treating these as separate investigations, although it's a hell of a coincidence to have the same MO being used twice, a few miles and a few days apart. If the two killings are connected, either there must be some connection between the victims or – and this is probably even more disturbing – they're being chosen randomly.'

He pulled together his papers and leaned back in his seat. 'Okay, everyone. Thanks for your time. Any final questions or other business?' He looked around at the sea of shaking heads. 'It's early days and we've not much yet to show for our efforts, but keep on keeping on. I'll liaise with comms and do everything I can to keep the media off our backs, but that will heat up now they've got Vivian Turnbull's name. If anyone gets inappropriate approaches from journalists, let me know and I'll make sure it's dealt with. Anything you need, speak to me or Paul.'

'And we'll tell you why you can't have it,' Wanstead said. 'But no harm in trying, eh?'

Murrain smiled. In the absence of Joe and Marie, the balance of the team had shifted. The former sense of cohesion had dissipated, and they were feeling their way, not least with Colin Willock. But maybe that wasn't a bad thing. Perhaps it would do them good to be shaken up a little, and Paul Wanstead was more than capable of holding it all together with his steady good sense.

'Good luck, everyone,' Murrain said, as the group began

to disperse.

CHAPTER TWENTY THREE

Bert Wallace paused in the doorway and looked around. It was still early evening and the place was thronged with people enjoying a quick after-work drink. The hubbub of chatter swept over her, and she wondered again why she'd said yes to this. If she was going to say yes, she could have insisted on meeting later when the work crowd had begun to thin out. Better still, she could just have said no.

She hoped he wouldn't be late. There was little she hated more than standing or sitting by herself in a busy pub, fending off the attentions of half-drunk office workers who thought she might be interested in their beery conversation.

Finally she spotted Danny Fraser sitting in a corner on the far side of the bar. She made her way through the crowds towards him. He'd managed to find a table and was sitting with a pint of beer in front of him. As she approached, he half rose. 'What can I get you?'

'I'd better just have half of lager for the moment.'

'You keep the table. I won't be a sec.'

He returned a few minutes later bearing the drink. 'There you go. Hadn't expected the place to be quite so busy on a school night.'

'I've not been in here before,' she said. 'Is this a regular haunt of yours?' They were in the city centre, just round the corner from Albert Square. She rarely came into town at all in the evenings. Mostly her life was a straightforward commute from the office to home and back again.

'It's fairly convenient for the office. So we come here after work sometimes.' He looked around. 'Like everyone else, it seems. It's not normally this busy.'

'I imagine it'll quieten down soon.'

'If not we can always move on to somewhere else.'

She still wasn't sure exactly what this was. Fraser had called her earlier in the day and asked if she fancied meeting up for a drink and maybe a bite to eat after work.

He'd told her he had a couple of things he wanted to chat to her about, and had made it sound more like an informal work meeting than a date. But perhaps that had been his intention.

She'd been tempted to put him off. They were working long hours at the moment with two major enquiries under way. All she really wanted to do was get home and get a good night's sleep. On the other hand, it was a while since she'd had a night out of any kind. She'd drifted into the routine of a largely solitary life, punctuated only by the very occasional night out with friends. Mostly, she was happy with that. She enjoyed her own company, and was content to spend the evenings reading, drinking a glass or two of wine, watching TV or a film. Making her way into town for a drink like this felt like a major effort.

In the end, he'd talked her into it, and she'd decided there was no time like the present. If she'd given herself time to think, she'd probably have changed her mind. She was intending to stay for a drink or two then make her excuses.

'How's it going, then? Work, I mean.'

'Busy. We've got the Margaret Perry and Vivian Turnbull enquiries going on, and the more routine stuff doesn't go away.'

'Glad you were able to take a bit of time out, then.'

'It's good to get a break. Helps clear my head.'

'I can imagine. You're still treating the two enquiries as separate, then?'

Wallace was always wary about discussing her work with others, even those like Fraser who already had some inside knowledge. The last thing she wanted was to shoot her mouth off and find her words plastered across the front of the Evening News or the nationals. 'You said you had something you wanted to talk about?'

'Yes,' he said after a pause. 'I just don't know if I ought to be talking about it.' It sounded like a rebuke for her own reticence.

'Don't do anything that makes you feel uncomfortable.'

'I just wanted to give you another heads-up, really. I've a feeling you're about to get even busier.'

'How'd you mean?'

'Couple of things. The first is that we've had another case that resembles the Perry and Turnbull deaths.'

'Really?'

'Old bloke. Well, late seventies. Lived up in the hills a mile or so from where Turnbull lived. Bill Ollerenshaw. Getting on a bit, but no known underlying health conditions. Found dead by the supermarket delivery guy.'

'They think it looks like foul play?'

'Your guys – the uniformed officers who attended the scene, I mean – raised a couple of concerns. The main one was that the front door had been left unlocked, which the delivery guy reckoned was unusual. And there were a couple of mugs out on the table in the sitting room, as if he'd had a visitor.'

'Shades of Margaret Perry then?'

'That was what set the alarm bells ringing. That and the location. My guy was on the phone to your guys before I left. I guess it'll depend on the cause of death.'

'Why are you telling me this, Danny? If there's anything in it, I'll be hearing about it soon enough, I'm guessing.'

She was gratified to see him blush. 'It was partly just an excuse to see you again. I thought if I just asked you out you'd probably say no.'

'To be honest, you're probably right. Nothing personal. Just that the whole process of going out anywhere seems too much of an effort these days. Which just shows I've got myself into a real rut. So thanks for asking me. Next time you can do it without the added inducement of an unlawful killing.'

'I'll remember that. Anyway, I thought you might at least appreciate the warning that there might be yet more work on the way.'

'Let's hope Mr Ollerenshaw turns out to have died naturally and peacefully in his sleep. Another major investigation's the last thing we need at the moment.'

'There might be more to come,' Fraser said.

'How do you mean?'

'There's something else they're looking at.'

'Go on.'

'Some recent hospital deaths.' He mentioned the name of a major hospital trust in the area. 'Over the last month or so, there've been an unusually high number of unexpected deaths there.'

'Unexpected?'

'Unexpected in terms of timing. They seem to be different from the Perry and Turnbull cases in that the deaths aren't necessarily unexplained. They were all patients with existing serious health conditions. But they've generally occurred earlier than the prognosis indicated.'

'Presumably that isn't necessarily surprising?'

'That's the point. None of these deaths was initially treated as suspicious. In the vast majority of them, there probably wouldn't even have been a postmortem. The consultant would have signed off the death as consistent with the individual's medical condition, and nobody would have thought much about it.'

'So why are they being looked at?'

'One of the consultants raised concerns because he'd spotted two or three cases with similar characteristics. He chatted to his colleagues and they identified what they thought looked like a possible pattern among recent deaths.'

'And nobody had spotted this pattern previously?'

'Doesn't look like it, but that's not surprising. If an individual death didn't look suspicious, there was no reason to associate it with other deaths around the hospital. The statistical anomaly would have been picked up eventually, but it would have taken some time.'

'You know how to cheer a girl up, don't you, Danny? If there is anything in this, it's likely to be a messy one. Remember that case in Stockport a few years back. There were all kinds of suspicions before they finally identified the perpetrator.'

'Not the best start to an evening out. I wasn't really thinking.'

'This is why they always say you shouldn't talk shop, isn't it? It gets too depressing.'

He was looking mortified as if he'd fatally messed up what he'd presumably hoped would be their first date. The truth was she didn't mind that too much. She genuinely loved her job, and in particular she loved this kind of complex investigation. She might feel intimidated by the impending workload, but the prospect of the enquiry itself excited her. 'It's useful to know what might be coming down the line. I'll make sure I look suitably surprised when they break the good news.'

'I just thought you'd want to know. Anyway, it's probably time to change the subject. Do you fancy another drink here or shall we move on somewhere else?'

Wallace hesitated, wondering if this was the moment to cut the evening short and get herself back home. Then she looked up at Fraser and nodded. 'Why don't we go and get a bite to eat?'

CHAPTER TWENTY FOUR

'Can you spare a moment, Kenny?'

It was still early and there were few people in the office. There was no sign even of Bert Wallace, usually one of the first in here. Murrain had woken absurdly early, as he often did in the middle of a major investigation, and had decided he might as well head into the office. It wasn't as if he was short of things to do. He'd left Eloise still sleeping soundly, as she always did.

Superintendent Marty Winston was leaning against the door. He had the air of a man who'd already done a full day's work, but that was how Winston generally looked.

'Sure, Marty. Here or in your office?'

Winston looked around, as if the largely empty open-plan office might be filled with invisible listeners. 'We'd better talk in mine. Let's grab a coffee on the way.'

Five minutes later they were sitting in Winston's office bearing mugs of instant coffee. Winston had bagged himself one of the few offices with a half-decent view over the city. It was only just beginning to grow light outside, the day still heavily overcast. Winston looked as if he'd rather be falling into bed. 'Been a hell of a day already.'

'Problems?'

'Just a few. I've spent the last forty-five minutes on the phone to the Coroner's office and then Comms. First, it looks like we may have to expand our investigation. I got the heads-up at close of play last night, but I've only just got the full story.'

'Another death?'

'Worse than that. First, we might have a new domestic case. No test results yet, but the same characteristics as Perry and Turnbull.'

'If we need to extend the investigation, we'll find a way. It's not the ideal time, but we'll cope.'

'That's not the worst of it, Kenny. It looks as if we might have something even more serious coming down the road.' He slid a closely-typed page of A4 across the desk. 'Have a read.'

Murrain picked up the document and sat in silence for a few moments, skimming through the content, then he looked up at Winstone, his eyebrows raised. 'Jesus.'

'Quite. That's a summary prepared by the hospital. Again, there's no evidence as yet of foul play, but the incidence of unexpected deaths is sufficiently high that it set the alarm bells ringing.'

'If the deaths were unexpected, wouldn't any foul play have been picked up?'

'In most of these cases it could easily have slipped through the net. The deaths had been signed off by the consultant. They're going to look at the more recent ones first to determine if there's anything suspicious. If there is…'

'We're potentially opening a huge can of worms.' Murrain could feel the familiar sensations troubling his brain. 'No point in worrying till we know what we're dealing with.'

'Quite. But I do need to think about resources. We're desperately short, even with what we've got on at the moment.'

Murrain took a sip of his rapidly cooling coffee. Winston was a decent enough manager – one of the better ones Murrain had dealt with in the course of his career – but he was an inveterate worrier. 'What about this domestic case?'

'Guy called Ollerenshaw. Elderly. Lived alone. Found by the supermarket delivery driver. Similar scenario to Perry, even down to the two mugs detail.'

'We're still waiting on the postmortem?'

'But for the moment we should add it to our list. We don't want to get caught out. We can at least get the CSIs to look at his house.'

'Will do. But I won't waste too much time on it otherwise. We've more than enough on our plates as it is.'

'Not trying to hassle you. Just keeping you up to speed.

I'll see what further manpower I can draw up. How's Colin Willock fitting in?'

'Ruffling a few feathers. Don't think he and Bert exactly see eye to eye.'

'You'll lick him into shape. It's one of your gifts.'

'You reckon?'

'I reckon. What about the investigations? Making progress?'

'Not as much as I'd like.'

'What are your instincts telling you?'

Winston was well aware of Murrain's supposed gifts. Murrain wasn't sure whether Winston took them seriously, but he was at least prepared to accept that Murrain himself did. 'If you pushed me, I'd say I thought the two cases were linked. And that the link was something more than a random killer. But the two victims couldn't be more different. Margaret Perry was no-one's idea of a celebrity or an adventurer. She barely inhabited the same world as Vivian Turnbull.'

'We all inhabit the same world,' Winston said. 'And we're sometimes closer neighbours than we think.'

'Very profound, Marty. But I know what you mean.' Murrain looked at his watch. 'Due for the morning briefing soon. I take it you don't want me to mention the Ollerenshaw or hospital cases yet?'

'Not till we're sure. I'll keep you posted.'

'Thanks, Marty.' Murrain pushed himself to his feet, still clutching his half-drunk mug of coffee. 'And thanks for the coffee. The perfect start to the day.'

CHAPTER TWENTY FIVE

Bert Wallace lay with her eyes closed and a strong sense of something badly wrong. She was barely awake and her brain hadn't yet fully kicked in, so she was struggling to come to grips with the thoughts hammering at her brain, unwelcome guests she was reluctant to admit.

Finally, recognising she had no real alternative, she opened her eyes.

Shit.

It was exactly what she'd feared. Wherever she was, it wasn't at home in her own bed. She rolled over, trying not to think about the implications of her position. Several points occurred to her at once. First, that this was a double bed somewhat larger than her bed at home. Second, that she was in a room entirely unfamiliar to her. Third, and perhaps most significantly, she wasn't wearing her usual pyjamas. In fact, she wasn't wearing anything.

Shit.

She pushed herself to a sitting position, pulling the bed clothes tightly around her. Her first impressions had been correct. She was in a room she didn't recognise. An anonymous-looking bedroom, containing only the bed, a chest of drawers and wardrobe. A square, boxy room in a modern house. There were no immediate clues as to whose bedroom it might be.

The only half-reassuring sight was the pile of her clothes lying on the beige carpet by the bed, her handbag sitting on top. It occurred to her now that her head was throbbing and her mouth dry.

Through the thin curtains she could see it was still dark outside. She reached over to grab her handbag, clutching the duvet around her as if someone might be watching. It took her a moment to find her police mobile, relieved to see that, as far as she could tell, nothing was missing. The phone told her it was only a few minutes after 7am, another source of relief. She'd feared it might be much later.

She hurriedly pulled on her clothes, worried someone might enter the room. Finally dressed, she sat on the edge of the bed to think.

What the hell had happened last night?

The last thing she could clearly remember was enjoying an Italian meal with Danny Fraser. She'd been enjoying his company. He was relaxed and easy-going, with a ready supply of dark but amusing anecdotes related to his work. Her initial qualms about the evening had rapidly melted away.

After that, her memory became more blurred. She hadn't thought she was drinking excessively. They'd shared a bottle of house red in the restaurant but nothing more. After eating they'd moved on to another bar in the Northern Quarter, but she'd stuck resolutely to half pints of lager and couldn't recall drinking more than a couple.

Which would have been fine. Except that she couldn't recall anything from later in the evening. Had she carried on drinking and lost control of how much she was knocking back? It was possible, she supposed. She wasn't much of a drinker, but she'd always thought of herself as someone who could hold it pretty well when she'd needed to. Maybe she'd moved on to something stronger she wasn't accustomed to. The whole thing was disturbing. She'd never previously experienced this kind of black hole in her life.

The more immediate question was where she was and how she'd got here. There was only one way to find the answer to that. She picked up her handbag and opened the bedroom door. From the foot of the stairs in front of her she could hear the sound of a radio playing. There was a scent of coffee and toast in the air.

She made her way down. Her overcoat was thrown across the bannister, where she'd presumably left it the previous night. To the left of the stairs, there was what she took to be a living room, still in darkness. Ahead of her at the rear of the house was the kitchen where the radio was playing, the door ajar. She pushed it open.

Danny Fraser was sitting at a small kitchen table. There was a steaming cup of coffee in front of him, and he was peering at the screen of his mobile phone. He looked up as she entered. 'Oh, you're awake. I was just about to bring you some coffee.'

She gazed at him for a moment, wondering what to say. 'Thanks. I could do with a coffee.'

'Hang on.' There was a filter coffee machine on the worktop by the cooker. He pulled a mug from the cupboard and filled it from the jug. 'Milk?'

'Black's fine.' She accepted the coffee gratefully. 'I must have drunk a bit too much last night. Hope I didn't do anything embarrassing.' She couldn't bring herself to ask the direct question foremost in her mind.

'You were fine. You seemed okay till we got back here, then you just conked out. I imagine you were tired. No worries.'

'You're just saying that to make me feel better. I must have been pretty far gone.' Apart from anything else, she wouldn't have agreed to come back here if she'd been in control of her faculties. The question was what, if anything, had happened after that.

'You were a bit merry but that was all.'

So merry that her memory was a blank. 'How did we get back?'

'I got a cab.' He frowned. 'Don't you remember?'

'It's all a bit blurred, to be honest.' She was feeling more invigorated by the bitter warmth of the coffee. There was something about this whole situation that didn't feel right, but she couldn't think of a way to broach it without sounding accusatory. For all she knew, Fraser might have taken perfect care of her the previous night, judging it was safer to bring her back here than to allow her to go off on her own. 'By the way, I know this sounds a silly question, but where is here, exactly?'

'We're in Hyde. Do you really not remember coming back?'

'Not very clearly.' Wallace looked at her watch. 7.15am. 'I ought to be heading off. I need to get home and changed before I head in to work.' She was already mentally calculating whether it was feasible to do this without arriving at work unacceptably late. She didn't even know how far they were from the station.

'Did you say you lived in Chadderton?'

'Pretty much.' She couldn't recall telling him that, but there was a lot she didn't remember.

'I was thinking I might drive in today. If it helps, I can drop you at home. Would that give you time to get into work?'

'I can't ask you to do that.'

'It's not too far, and I've plenty of time.'

She expected he'd make some further reference to what had happened the previous night. But it was as if it hadn't even occurred to him. She ought to just some straight out and ask him, but somehow she couldn't bring herself to do it. 'You're sure that's okay? I really don't want to put you out.'

'Not at all.'

'Well, I'd be grateful. Thanks.'

'Just give me five minutes to get my stuff together then we can be off. How will you get into work?'

'I usually drive. I dropped the car back at home before I got the tram into town last night.' It was a good question, though. Was she in a fit state to drive? The odd thing was that, although she still had a slight headache, she didn't feel hungover. 'I'll see if I feel up to it. If not, I can get the tram.'

'If you're pushed for time, I could always wait while you get changed, then drop you off.'

'You'll end up making yourself late. The tram only takes a few minutes.'

'Well, okay,' he said. 'But let me know if you change your mind.'

She sipped at her coffee while he went to get himself ready to leave. She didn't know what to think. He was pleasant, likeable, and she had no real reason to believe he'd behaved badly towards her. In other circumstances, she'd be thinking seriously about the possibility of seeing him again. As it was, she simply felt uneasy.

She stood up to place her empty mug in the sink. As she did so, she noticed the dishwasher beside it. Glancing over her shoulder, she pulled open the dishwasher door of and peered inside. It was half full, and on the top shelf were a couple of what looked like whisky glasses. She pulled one out and sniffed at its interior. The scent of the spirit was unmistakeable. She replaced the glass and tried the second one. It also smelled strongly of whisky. It looked as if, whatever else might have happened, she'd had at least one more drink after arriving back here.

Behind her, she heard the kitchen door open. 'Are we ready to go?'

She picked up her coffee mug and placed it by the glasses in the dishwasher, as if that had been what she was doing all along. 'Ready if you are.'

CHAPTER TWENTY SIX

'You remember the case?' Will Sparrow asked.

'Oh, yes. That woman from the TV?' Steve Dawkins was fiddling with a screwdriver, twisting it between his fingers as if it was some kind of toy. At first, Sparrow had thought it was a gesture of impatience and that Dawkins resented having to waste his time on this. After a while, he'd concluded it was nothing more than a nervous tic. Sparrow had the impression Dawkins would have been much happier under the bonnet of a car.

'She was a war reporter, apparently,' Sparrow said. 'Bit before my time to be honest, but I recognised the name.'

'You're making me feel old. I remember when she was all over the TV. Reporting from the Falklands, Afghanistan, Iraq. Shouting at the screen in her flak jacket with the bombs going off behind her. Amazing to think she survived all that, and then got topped in her own home. Mind you, that was what I thought about the motorbike collision.'

Dawkins was one of a small team of Forensic Collision Investigators employed by the force. These days, they outsourced a substantial part of the investigation work to specialist consultants, but they'd retained some expertise. Dawkins was a short, solidly built man in his late 40s, who looked as if he worked out regularly, Sparrow found him a reassuring presence, with his strong Mancunian accent and slightly ponderous manner. He had the air of someone who knew what he was doing and whose judgement, within his sphere of expertise, could be relied on.

'I've had a look at the file on the case,' Sparrow said. 'I had the sense you felt there might be more to it.'

They were sitting in the small office next to the vehicle workshop where Dawkins and his colleagues carried out much of their work. 'It was one of those frustrating ones where you take it as far as you can, but you suspect you've not taken it far enough, if you see what I mean.'

'What made you suspicious?'

'Just the absence of any real explanation for the incident. We normally get to the bottom of things in here, at least to the point where we're fairly sure about what's happened even if we don't have the evidence to bring a prosecution. In this case, it felt as if something was missing. Turnbull was an experienced and skilled biker. She was driving on a straight, well-maintained road in pretty perfect conditions with clear visibility. But for some reason she lost control and left the road.'

'That must just happen sometimes?'

'Sure. Sometimes it's nothing more than a momentary lapse of concentration. The driver gets distracted by something – an animal or a bird in the road, something like that. We concluded that was the most likely explanation. We checked everything else. The bike had been in excellent condition and was well maintained. There was nothing on the road surface that could have explained the incident. Turnbull hadn't suffered from any kind of medical condition. We've sometimes had cases of drivers who've had heart attacks or some kind of fit, but there was nothing like that here.'

'You thought there might have been some other vehicle involved?' Sparrow had been assiduously taking notes as Dawkins was talking. 'There was a note to that effect in the file.'

'I just noted it as a possibility. We couldn't find any definitive evidence from the carriageway itself. It was a well-used A-road so there'd been plenty of vehicles passing. There were no signs of any skidding or similar tyre marks. We checked any available traffic cameras in the vicinity, but there were none nearby and nothing to confirm that any vehicle had passed the bike at the time of the accident. I noted it mainly just for completeness. Something we couldn't entirely discount.'

'What's your own view? I mean, just gut feel.'

'I've twenty-odd years of doing this stuff. If you want a purely personal opinion, I'd say it was likely another vehicle was involved. I never spoke to Turnbull directly, but I read the subsequent interviews with her. It was a few days before she was in a condition for your colleagues to talk to her, but she was a very articulate and well-informed witness, as you'd expect.'

'From what I remember, she couldn't recall the accident itself.'

'It's not unusual in that kind of accident.' Dawkins smiled. 'From our point of view, it's a pain in the backside. But it helps the brain cope with the trauma. The last thing she could remember was driving down the road. She had no idea what had happened after that. No recollection of any other vehicle or anything else that might have explained what happened.'

'So how does that support the idea of another vehicle being involved?'

'Only in that Turnbull clearly knew what she was talking about. I could tell from the way she spoke that she knew how to ride a bike. She described her driving in the same way advanced drivers do. The way they're taught to describe the environment around them. I wouldn't say it was impossible she might have been distracted by something in the road, but I'd say it was unlikely. But that comes from nothing beyond gut feel and a lot of experience.'

'What happened in the end?'

'It wasn't worth pursuing. Turnbull survived, and in fact was much less injured than you might have expected from the state of her bike. Which again was a testament to her skills as a biker. She avoided the worst of a very nasty collision.'

'If there was another vehicle involved, could the driver have driven her off the road unintentionally? Again, maybe the lapse in concentration thing.'

'It's obviously possible. A lorry, maybe. Goes to overtake her, gets that bit too close. Pulls in a few seconds too soon. Might have caught her without the driver even realising. It might explain why they didn't stop.'

'You don't sound very convinced.'

'I'm not. It was a straight road. Daylight. Good visibility. Turnbull was wearing high-vis gear. Road fairly wide and not particularly busy. It would take extreme carelessness not to have seen her. Not that we don't see that sometimes with truck drivers. You wouldn't believe what they get up to in their cabs while they're driving. But I think it's more likely she was driven off the road deliberately. Either as an ill-conceived joke, or because someone really wanted to hurt her.'

'Thanks, Steve,' Sparrow said. 'That's been very helpful.'

'Has it? There's no evidence. No substantive reason to think anything untoward happened. I'm not sure anyone else shared my suspicions. None of us wants to go looking for trouble.'

'Maybe not,' Sparrow said. 'But at that point Turnbull was still alive. Now she isn't. And this time we know she's been murdered.'

'Aye, you're right. It changes the picture a bit.'

'None of us wants to go looking for trouble,' Sparrow said, 'but sometimes it comes looking for us.'

CHAPTER TWENTY SEVEN

'You okay, Bert?'

They were heading back to their desks after the morning briefing session. Paul Wanstead had paused to open the office door for her, and was now looking at her with mild concern. 'You seemed a bit distracted in the meeting. Not like you.'

If it had been anyone else, Wallace might have been tempted to tell him to mind his own business. But Wanstead saw himself as a paternal figure in the office, and his concern would be genuine. He was often the first to spot if someone was unwell or going through a difficult time.

'Just a bit tired. Made the mistake of going out with a friend last night. Must have had one too many. Didn't sleep too well.' It was close enough to the truth. She could tell he'd registered the mention of a friend. He might well have a genuine concern for their collective welfare, but he was also skilled at snapping up any shred of office gossip that was floating around.

'Burning it at both ends, eh? Don't know where you youngsters get the energy from.'

'Neither do I, just at the moment. Maybe that means I'm not a youngster any more.'

'You've a good few years on me, lass. Couple of coffees and you'll be right as rain.'

She wished that were true. She felt tired, certainly, but that wasn't the main problem. The main problem was the hole in her memory that, however much she strained to recall, she'd still been unable to fill. That, and what it meant for any continued relationship with Danny Fraser. He'd seemed fine that morning, chatting amiably on the drive to her house, nothing in his demeanour to suggest anything amiss. As she'd been climbing out of the car, he'd asked if she fancied going out again. She hadn't wanted simply to say no – she wasn't sure what she wanted – but said she'd be working late for the next few days.

She'd felt relieved to be back in her own home. Showered and changed, she'd felt much more herself. She'd caught the tram into the office, arriving only a few minutes late. She'd thought no one had noticed, although she suspected now that Paul Wanstead's eagle-eye had clocked her arrival.

She booted up her computer and tried to focus on the work at hand. She was working primarily on the Margaret Perry investigation, tasked with filling out more background on Gregory Perry, for the moment still their only serious suspect.

As far as she could tell, there wasn't a great deal of background to fill out. He was only in his late-twenties. He'd completed a Master of Pharmacy degree at one of the local universities just a few years before, and joined the NHS immediately after graduation. She'd spoken confidentially to the Human Resources team at the hospital, but there was nothing unusual about Perry's career to date. He was well-regarded by his colleagues, a diligent worker with no disciplinary or performance issues. He was unmarried but was engaged to one of the nurses at the hospital, and the two of them had recently purchased a small house on a new estate just outside Wilmslow.

That seemed to be about it. An unremarkable man living a comfortable but unremarkable life. He had no criminal record and no recorded dealings with the police. There were no suggestions he had any financial problems, though that was still being checked out.

The related question, and one of the factors that potentially placed Perry in the frame, was how the killer would have obtained the diamorphine. She'd had a couple of telephone conversations with a senior pharmacist at one of the other large hospitals in the region, pitching her questions as nothing more than general background enquiries. The discussions had confirmed that it would be theoretically possible for someone in Perry's position to access the drug, but that the controls were stringent.

Another member of the team was liaising with local hospitals and pharmacists to identify any evidence of theft or unauthorised access. Beyond that, they were investigating more clandestine sources of supply.

Wallace found her concentration wavering. She closed Gregory Perry's file and went to fetch herself another coffee from the kitchenette. She hoped Paul Wanstead was right and that another couple of coffees would revive her. Otherwise, she'd be asleep before the afternoon was out.

Will Sparrow was preparing himself one of the exotic fruit teas he favoured. 'Kettle's just boiled. You okay? You look a bit tired.'

'I must look dire. You're the second person who's asked me that this morning.'

'Sorry. I didn't mean…'

'No worries. Just a bad night, that's all. How's it going?'

'Slowly. Just been talking to Steve Dawkins in Vehicle Forensics.'

'Lucky you. Been transferred to Traffic, have you?'

'Very funny. I was talking to him about Vivian Turnbull's motorbike accident. He thinks it was suspicious. That someone probably forced her off the road.'

'Really?'

'Problem is, there's no evidence. Steve was just giving me his view. There are various possible explanations for what happened but he thinks that's the most likely, once you factor in Turnbull's experience as a biker.'

'If it's true, it means someone had already tried to take Turnbull's life.'

'I've just been talking to Kenny about it. He still thinks we should focus on the partner as the prime suspect, but he's ramping up the examination of Turnbull's background in case there's something lurking there.'

'I hope they have a more exciting time than I've had. I've just been looking at Gregory Perry's background. Mr Suburban Man, as far as I can tell.'

'Aren't they always?' Sparrow said. 'Killers, I mean.'

'It could easily be. A bit too quiet to be true.'

She finished making her coffee and returned to her desk, still thinking about what Sparrow had told her. She opened up the file on Margaret Perry's burglaries. Perry had mentioned that his mother was security conscious because she'd been burgled on a couple of occasions. Wallace, with her usual thoroughness, had thought it worth checking out the burglaries. She was conscious that much of the information they had on Margaret Perry's character and personality was filtered through her son.

If anything, it seemed as if Gregory Perry had understated the burglaries. Both had happened around a year before, within a few weeks of each other. The first had been a low-key affair, while Margaret Perry had been spending a few days away with one of her female friends shortly after the death of her husband, Frank. The two women had spent Christmas together at a small hotel in north Wales, leaving Perry's house unoccupied for several days.

Intruders had gained access through a poorly-secured rear window. Little had been taken, although some jewellery and other items of largely sentimental value were missing. The intruders had created a considerable mess, but otherwise little harm had been done.

The second break-in occurred just a few weeks later. In the small hours of the morning, the intruders had entered through the front door and carried out a systematic search of the ground floor. Drawers had been emptied on to the carpets, the contents of cupboards pulled out. Even the kitchen cabinets had been ransacked.

The ground floor of the house had been left in a total mess, papers and books strewn everywhere and ornaments thrown to the ground. Almost nothing had been taken. It was as if the intruders had simply wanted to create as much mess as they could.

The most significant missing item was Margaret Perry's handbag, which had contained some bank cards but no cash or anything else of financial value. Its loss had been an annoyance – both practically and because again it was an item that Frank had bought for her – but nothing more. The only other items missing were a few ornaments and Frank's old briefcase. The latter had contained nothing more than a stack of work-related papers, Frank's old mobile phone, and a tablet computer, now a few years old, which Frank had used mainly for reading when travelling. Again, this was a sentimental loss – though she'd already been telling herself she was a silly old fool for hanging on to it – but its financial value had been small.

Margaret Perry's real concern had been that the burglary had happened while she was in the house. She had been asleep upstairs, just yards from where this devastation was taking place. Since Frank's death, she'd slept poorly, often disturbed by anxiety in the middle of the night. Her doctor had prescribed sleeping pills to help combat the worst of the insomnia. On that night, she'd woken at around 1am and, unable to sleep further, had eventually taken one of the tablets. The break-in had taken place a couple of hours later, by which time she'd been soundly asleep.

The whole experience had left her distressed and scared. She'd arranged for much tighter security at the house, replacing the front and rear doors and some of the windows.

Wallace flicked again through the selection of photographs from the burglary. The destruction looked random, but it was oddly thorough and consistent in each room. Every drawer emptied, every cupboard swept clean of its contents. It was unclear to her why any intruder would go to those lengths. Why would you risk taking the time to do that, knowing the householder was sleeping upstairs?

She reopened Margaret Perry's file and flicked through the pages. If Gregory Perry was unremarkable, his mother seemed even more so. She'd left school at sixteen and found a job as a clerical assistant with the city council. She'd married her husband, Frank, when she was in her late twenties and they'd had their first and only child,

Gregory, when she was in her mid-thirties. At that time, she was still working for the city council, having by this time been promoted to a team leader role, but she'd chosen not to return to work after her maternity leave.

Wallace wondered how Margaret Perry had filled her time once Gregory was older, but no doubt she'd had plenty to occupy herself. She clearly had a number of female friends and had been active in a number of local clubs. It was a lifestyle that left Wallace slightly baffled, but no doubt her own semi-workaholic life would have been equally incomprehensible to Margaret Perry.

Frank Perry had been some kind of civil servant, although Gregory Perry had seemed vague about what his father had actually done. Something to do with immigration, he'd thought, pen pushing of a kind that held no interest for the young Gregory. By the time Gregory might have been curious to know more, Frank had already taken early retirement on health grounds, following a serious heart attack he'd suffered in his mid-fifties.

That was all there was to know about Margaret Perry. Wallace closed the file and yawned. The coffee didn't yet seem to be having the desired effect, and she knew her attention was wandering again. Even if there was something significant in the files in front of her, she was in no shape to spot what it might be.

She still couldn't shake off her anxiety about Danny Fraser. She couldn't see him again without raising the question which, one way or another, would end any possibility of a relationship between them. If she didn't see him again, that would have the same effect but, for good or ill, would leave her anxieties unresolved.

She had no immediate answer. With her brain apparently grinding to a halt, she had no clear desire other than to make herself yet another coffee, in the hope that this time the caffeine would make a difference.

CHAPTER TWENTY EIGHT

Murrain stepped out of the lift and looked around. This area had a different feel from the rest of the hospital building. It could scarcely be classed as luxurious – even here the dominant note was one of functionality – but it had a calmer, more tranquil air than the wards and departments.

Immediately ahead was a waiting area with a hatch in the wall labelled 'Enquiries'. In the room beyond two women were working at computer terminals. One of them looked up at his knock and walked over to the window. 'Good afternoon. Can I help you?'

'I've an appointment with Alan Northcote. DCI Murrain.'

'If you take a seat for a moment, I'll let him know you're here.'

The message had reached Murrain less than an hour before, having been relayed from the upper echelons down to his lowly level. Little information had been provided, but enough to cause Murrain to pick up the phone and make this appointment.

The woman reappeared through a door to the right of the Enquiry window. 'If you'd just like to come this way…'

She led him into a short corridor and knocked gently at one of the doors before opening it. She gestured for him to enter.

There were three of them gathered round the small conference table, a man and two women, and they rose simultaneously to greet him. The man, a short, slightly overweight figure in his mid-fifties, held out a hand to be shaken. 'Good to meet you. Alan Northcote. Chief Executive.'

'Pleased to meet you, Mr Northcote.'

'Dr Emily Symonds, our Chief Pathologist, and Helen Clarke, our Director of Public Affairs.' Symonds was a slim, slightly anxious looking woman who offered

Murrain a nervous smile. Clarke looked a more robust figure, a solidly built woman with the air of someone unlikely to treat fools gladly. Both were younger than Northcote, no more than early forties.

'I'm glad you were able to get over here so quickly, Chief Inspector. As you can imagine, this is a tremendous concern to us all.'

'I've been given only very limited information. Perhaps it's best if you start at the beginning.'

Northcote nodded. 'Emily, perhaps you should start. You can describe the medical background better than we do.'

Symonds shifted slightly uncomfortably in her seat, as if she'd rather have avoided being placed in the spotlight. 'It goes back a week or so, when one of our consultants raised a concern. He was worried about a couple of deaths in his area. The two patients involved were both elderly and had been suffering from potentially life-threatening illnesses. Both were recovering from major operations, so their deaths weren't entirely unexpected.' She sounded apologetic, as if taking personal responsibility for their failings.

'What were the consultant's concerns?'

'Just that, although the fatality wasn't inexplicable, he'd been expecting a more positive prognosis. If it had been just the one case, he probably wouldn't have thought anything about it. It was the two cases in quick succession that made him feel uneasy.'

'To be honest,' Northcote said, 'when doctors raise these kinds of concerns, my first question is whether they're trying to pre-empt any accusations of negligence.'

'You don't believe that to be the case here?'

Clarke shook her head. 'He was a highly experienced doctor. He was open about the steps he'd taken, the treatment he'd recommended. The case-notes were checked and there was no sign of any errors. At this stage, no one was alleging any wrong-doing. It was simply a potential anomaly he felt we ought to check out.'

'So what happened next?' Murrain asked.

'The consultant who'd raised the original query had been talking – suitably discreetly, I should add – with various colleagues. Between them, they identified a number of similar cases in other departments. In each case, the death was not inconsistent with the patient's condition but the timing was unexpected. All within the last month or so.'

'Would any of the deceased have been subjected to a postmortem?' Murrain asked.

'In the normal course of things, probably not,' Symonds said. 'The patients in question would have been under full observation, their medical conditions well understood. Unless there was a specific reason for concern, the consultant would have signed the death certificate without a second thought.'

'Even a cluster of such cases doesn't necessarily mean much,' Clarke added. 'It may just be a run of bad luck, a statistical anomaly. Obviously, if you start to see a pattern relating to a given doctor or a given ward, you'd ask some questions. But that wasn't the case here.'

Murrain could feel something pulsing the back of his brain, a tiny cerebral spasm like a misfiring spark plug. It seemed to be telling him there was something here of wider importance, some connection that wasn't being made. 'But we're talking about more than statistical anomalies now?'

'That's the point. The number of cases was sufficient for us to carry out further investigation. Notably, a postmortem on the most recent deceased.' Northcote glanced down at the notes in front of him. 'Elizabeth Everard. Female, 65 years old. Had undergone surgery for cancer. In a fairly poorly condition, but expected to pull through. Died peacefully overnight. Apparently heart failure.'

'Exactly the kind of case that no-one would have thought much about from a medical perspective,' Symonds said. 'But given the concerns that had been raised, we conducted a postmortem.'

'And what did you find?'

'That death was due to an overdose of diamorphine.'

'Diamorphine?'

'It's a very strong opioid, used as a painkiller,' Symonds said.

'I'm aware of it,' Murrain said. Although the force had issued media statements about the deaths of Margaret Perry and Vivian Turnbull, no details had been provided about the cause of death. 'I take it that the deceased wasn't being treated with the drug?'

'She was on a relatively low dosage. Nothing like the quantity found in the body.'

'Is it possible the overdose was accidental?

'We've checked all the notes. What dosages were signed out, what were administered. Everything is consistent, and fully recorded and signed off as required. It would require an absolutely spectacular level of negligence. I just can't conceive how it would be possible.'

'So how do you believe the dose was administered?'

'That's the question, isn't it?' Northcote said. 'We're fairly sure it must have been injected, which narrows the options somewhat.'

'To one of the medical staff, presumably?'

'That seems the most likely explanation.'

'Is there a possibility someone might have deliberately injected this dose for compassionate reasons?'

'If the victim was in considerable pain, you mean?' Symonds asked. 'It's possible, of course, but it would have been an utterly wrong-headed action. There's no evidence at all that the patient's pain wasn't already being appropriately controlled. The prognosis beyond the operation was generally optimistic. There was no good reason for anyone to intervene. No-one with even a shred of medical knowledge could have seen this as a compassionate act.'

'What about the other deaths?'

'We're looking at those now,' Northcote said.

'Obviously, we didn't want to set anything in motion until we had the results back on this one. They're a mixed bunch. We've identified a number that appear questionable. Some go back several weeks, so we may already be too late to conduct a formal postmortem. We're checking on the status of the more recent ones.'

'In the meantime,' Murrain said, 'we have at least one unlawful killing on our hands, whatever the wider circumstances. This is going to be a major investigation, and we'll need a substantial resource on site. Ideally, it would be useful if we can allocate somewhere as an on-site incident room, and also have rooms available for interviews.'

Northcote exchanged another look with Clarke. 'Space tends to be at a premium here. We may have meeting rooms we could allocate but it won't be easy.'

'Anything you can do will be helpful in resolving this as quickly as possible.'

'I hope you'll be as discreet as possible in handling this,' Clarke said.

'We'll be as discreet as we can be,' Murrain said. 'But you need to recognise how disruptive this will be. The first priority must be to do everything we can to reduce the risk of further deaths. We'll need to liaise with you about your procedures and identify any steps that can be taken to improve security while the perpetrator is still at large. We don't know if this death was a one-off or whether we're potentially talking about some kind of multiple killer. We can't take any chances.'

It was clear from Northcote's expression that he was only just recognising the scale and gravity of what the hospital was facing. 'Yes, of course.'

Murrain turned to Clarke. 'I presume you've a media team. We can work with you to deal with the communications but it's going to require some careful handling.'

Clarke, like Northcote, had turned pale. 'We need to think about the hospital's reputation and public profile—

What I mean is, it's important that we can offer patients some reassurance. Something like this could cause a real panic.'

'Reassurance, yes, but we also need them to be vigilant,' Murrain said. He looked at the others sitting round the table. 'I'll head back to HQ and start getting everything organised. We'll liaise with you about what we need. We recognise you've got a hospital to run and patients to treat, and we'll do our utmost not to get in the way. But, trust us, we're used to running major investigations and we know how to make it work.'

'I'm sure you know what you're doing, Chief Inspector.' Northcote's tone implied he might still need some persuading of this, but he looked calmer than he had a few moments before. 'My primary concern is the well-being of our patients, staff and visitors.'

'The priority always has to be public safety,' Murrain said. 'I'll liaise with our senior team and Head of Communications, and ask them to contact you about issuing a public statement. I'm grateful to you all for contacting us so promptly and for being so open. In this kind of enquiry, every second counts.'

CHAPTER TWENTY NINE

Marie Donovan had been talking for fifteen minutes or more, but had no real idea what she'd been saying. It was a skill she'd developed in the days she'd been sitting here. The ability to talk incessantly, in what she presumed were coherent and meaningful sentences, but with no real clue what she was talking about. The words left her brain the moment she'd spoken them.

The key was to keep talking. The doctors had recommended it when they'd first discussed Joe's condition with her. She'd asked them what she could usefully do to help, other than simply being here. They'd suggested she talk to Joe as much as she could.

By now she was approaching it almost superstitiously. It was a ritual she had to go through whenever she was sitting here alone. If she didn't, Joe would slip further and further from her, eventually reaching the point from which he could never return. It was only her words anchoring him here.

What *had* she been talking about? Something about a holiday. Some holiday they'd take together once this was all over, once he'd come through it and was back in the land of the living. Somewhere they could just relax, sit in the sun, swim in crystal blue seas, enjoying exotic food...

The door opened slightly and a face peered in. 'Not disturbing anything, am I?'

'Not at all, Kenny. I can always welcome the company.'

'I can't stay, I'm afraid. Bit of a crisis on. But it seemed wrong to come into the hospital and not at least show my face.'

'It's always a pleasure to see it. You were visiting the hospital?'

'That's the cause of the crisis.'

Marie was looking at Joe, as Murrain told her his reasons for being at the hospital. It struck her how vulnerable Joe was, lying unconscious draped with wires and tubes. The ward was secure enough, but at night he was left lying here alone, only a handful of nurses on duty.

'I'd better get back,' Murrain said. 'I need to get this kicked off, and the Chief wants a debrief.' He glanced back at Milton. 'I take it you've seen no more of Gill?'

'Not a sighting since that odd exchange.'

'I'll pop back in as soon as I get a chance,' Murrain said. 'Though I suspect things are going to be fraught over the next day or so. Call me straightaway if there are any developments.'

'I will. And thanks, Kenny. Thanks for everything you've done.'

Murrain looked as if he wanted to say something in response, but finally just said, 'I'd better be going.'

Murrain was crossing the main foyer of the hospital when his mobile phone rang. Paul Wanstead. He'd called Paul when he'd first left the Chief Executive's office to ask him to get things moving in advance of Murrain's return.

'Paul?'

'You're on your way back?'

'Just leaving the hospital now. Thought I'd better at least show my face to Joe and Marie.'

'No news there, I take it.'

'Still the same. Nothing good or bad.'

'Poor bugger. All we can do is pray.'

'What can I do for you, Paul?'

'I thought you might want a heads-up before you got back, especially if you're seeing the Chief.'

'A heads-up on what?'

'This afternoon's Evening News headline.'

'Evening News? What's it say?'

'The headline is 'Angel of Death'. With a question mark after it, to be fair. Unconfirmed reports of a killer on the loose in the building where you're currently standing.'

'You're kidding.'

'I like a joke as much as the next man, Kenny, but there's a time and a place. No, straight up, that's what it says.'

'Christ, the bloody fools. It must have leaked from here somewhere. That's not going to make our job any easier.'

'You can say that again. Anyway, the Chief's on the warpath. Marty's already had an earful.'

'For what? This isn't anything we've done. I didn't even know about it till a couple of hours ago. If there's a leak, it can only have come from here.'

'Or from somewhere in transmission,' Wanstead pointed out. 'Which would have included the Chief's office. Maybe getting his retaliation in first.'

'That's all we need. The so-called alpha males locking horns to defend their territory. I've just been giving them a big spiel about the need for co-operation.' As he'd been speaking, he'd felt the familiar pulsing in the back of his brain, the voices growing louder. This time, there was something else, just momentary, like an object sighted in a flash of lightning. An image. Someone talking on a phone.

The image was too fleeting for him to discern more. He could tell nothing about the figure, about its appearance or even if it was male or female.

'You okay, guv?'

'I'm fine. I just had a momentary – well, you know…' He stopped, thinking. 'There's another possibility, of course.'

'Guv?'

'The story could have been leaked by our killer. If they'd got wind their handiwork had been discovered, maybe they thought this would be a useful way to keep us on the back foot.' As Murrain said it, the theory sounded far-fetched but something, perhaps the same something that whispered meanings he could never quite grasp, was telling him not to dismiss the idea. If there was any substance in what he was saying, it told them something about the person they were dealing with. Not someone to be underestimated.

'It's a thought.' Wanstead's tone suggested it wasn't one he was planning to entertain for very long. 'Anyway, you've been warned. Good luck with the Chief.'

'Thanks, Paul. Everything else okay?'

'I wouldn't go that far, but everything's under control for the moment.'

Murrain didn't doubt it. 'Okay, See you shortly.'

He glanced around the foyer, wondering whether there might already be a media presence here. There was no sign of anything out of the ordinary. But when he looked over at the small café, he saw, sitting at one of the far tables, a figure he recognised.

Gill.

CHAPTER THIRTY

So this was it then. The moment he'd known had been coming. He hadn't been able to predict the precise moment – that was beyond even his powers – but he'd felt the tension building to the point where he'd known it must be about to break.

The news had broken. He'd known that instinctively when he'd arrived at work that morning. One type of tension had dissipated, replaced by something different. It had taken him only a few minutes to check, a minor detour on his earliest round.

The young woman up there was one he'd been cultivating since his arrival here. She talked too much and was happy to talk to him. He'd caught her briefly alone that morning, and they'd chatted as they always did. A brief inconsequential exchange of pleasantries, but enough to tell him what he needed to know. She'd hardly needed to say anything at all. He could tell from her demeanour that she knew. She was excited, fearful, desperate to share news she'd been told in strictest confidence. She hadn't told him anything, or at least she'd sincerely believe she hadn't. But she'd said enough.

He completed the round on this floor and made his way to the service lift. He waited for a patient being transported into surgery, then he pushed his trolley into the lift and headed down to the basement.

It was the same routine he carried out at night. One of the routines they allocated to the less experienced porters. A repetitive task almost impossible to get wrong. It suited him perfectly. It allowed him to switch off his conscious mind to concentrate on the things that mattered. His focus was elsewhere, as he constructed in his head the sequence only he could see. Adding each piece painstakingly. Ensuring the overall edifice was growing stronger, more powerful, harder to disrupt or dismantle.

'Watch where you're going, you plank!'

He grabbed the trolley. One of the maintenance staff was in front of him, gazing at him angrily. Behind him was a metal stepladder. The man was one of the electricians, working on a unit on the wall to their left. There was an open panel, and behind it an array of incomprehensible switches and boxes.

The trolley had knocked over a metal warning notice positioned to advise passers-by of the work. He bent over to pick up the sign. 'Sorry. Miles away.'

'If I'd been on that ladder you'd have sent me bloody flying. Think on.'

'Sorry. I'll be more careful.' He wanted to get away now, fade into the background as he usually did but the electrician hadn't finished pontificating.

'You could have killed me. I'm not joking, mate. If I'd been on top of that ladder, well, there's no telling what might have happened. I've a good mind to report you, mate. Make a formal complaint.' The electrician leaned forward and peered at him. 'I've seen you down here before, haven't I? Swanning about with your trolley full of dirty laundry. Always looking as if your head's somewhere else entirely. You're a fucking menace, mate.' The electrician jabbed a figure out. 'I've seen how you waste bloody time down here. You think nobody notices you, but some of us see you. Christ knows what you get up to.'

It wasn't so much the words as the jabbing finger. There was something provocative about it. Maybe the sense of accusation. The feeling that, in his small, ill-informed way, this man was judging him. Or had already judged him and found him wanting.

'I've said I'm sorry. It won't happen again.'

'Too right it bloody won't. Because I'm going to be making a formal complaint about you. About your bloody recklessness and negligence, about your laziness. When I've finished, you'll be out of this place faster than shit off a shovel.'

In other circumstances, he'd have forced himself not to care what this man was saying. The electrician was just venting his own frustrations. He'd never get around to making the threatened complaint. He'd grumble to his workmates, and they'd agree everyone else in this place was a waste of space. It was how the world worked.

He'd long ago learned to put that pettiness behind him. He'd just tug his proverbial forelock, keep his head down and move on, knowing that in five minutes his presence would have been almost forgotten.

But, at this point, he couldn't afford any risks. He needed to be invisible. When the police started crawling over this place, he needed to be the person who could slip through the cracks, pass amongst them without being recognised.

He looked behind him down the corridor, then ahead towards the loading bay. Other than himself and the electrician, the place was empty. Even in the daytime, few people had reason to come down here.

The electrician was still talking. 'I'm telling you, mate, they'll kick your arse out of here so fast that you won't have time to think—'

'Shut up.'

'What did you say?'

'I said shut up. Now.' He reached out and seized the electrician firmly by the throat, thrusting him hard back against the wall. 'Do not move.'

By now, the electrician's expression had changed from anger to terror. He remained motionless, his body frozen as if it had lost the power to react.

It took only another minute to complete the act. The electrician was wearing a t-shirt under his overalls and his arms were bare. The syringe came from a pocket as if appearing from nowhere, and the injection was made, with some expertise, directly into a vein. The whole process took no more than seconds.

He replaced the syringe in his pocket for later disposal, and continued pushing the trolley towards the loading bay. The electrician remained motionless, as if he'd lost any control over his body.

It took only a few minutes to unload the bags of dirty linen at the loading bay. When he returned, the electrician had fallen against the metal stepladder, knocking it over. His body lay splayed over the ladder, his head hanging down on the far side.

There was an alternative route to the service lift that would avoid taking him past the electrician's body. Not that he was squeamish. It was simply he didn't want to risk being discovered in its vicinity. Now the task had been completed, he wanted to absent himself as quickly and straightforwardly as possible.

The only question was whether this unplanned death had disturbed the pattern. The answer was almost certainly yes. He wasn't doing this for his own pleasure or randomly. He was doing it because it had to be done, and it had to be done in a particular way to achieve his goal.

Any unplanned element would be outside the pattern, and would disturb its order and symmetry. The death of one insignificant individual should make little difference. But he would need to compensate for it elsewhere, restore the balance. It was something he would think carefully about.

The lift arrived and he pushed the trolley inside. He whistled softly as he did so, already considering his next steps.

CHAPTER THIRTY ONE

Murrain looked out across the assembled group. On the whole, they were an impressive bunch, pulled together in an extraordinarily short time. This was still far from the full team that would be working on the enquiry once it was fully up and running, but it was already too large a group to fit into any of the standard meeting rooms. They'd temporarily commandeered one of the spacious rooms above the staff canteen more commonly used for public events.

He was sitting at the front of the room, with Marty Winston beside him. Assistant Chief Constable Chris Rayner was currently on his feet, explaining the context and background. Murrain had mixed feelings about Rayner. He was good at the figurehead stuff, with a gravitas that came across well in sessions like this or when he was wheeled out as a spokesperson for the force. But Murrain had found him indecisive and unsupportive when faced with anything genuinely challenging. Murrain's wife, Eloise, a well-regarded senior officer who led major change projects in the force, had had similar experiences. Rayner was a political animal, who mainly had his eyes on the ultimate prize of becoming Chief Constable. Murrain had little doubt that if the enquiry wasn't a success Rayner would rapidly distance himself from it.

That was just how it was sometimes. On the other hand, Winston, for all his quirks, was a decisive figure who could be relied on to support the team, including fighting their corner with Rayner and the others on the Chief Officer team.

'...So, to conclude,' Rayner was saying, 'DCI Murrain will be the CIO for the enquiry. I'm sure most of you know Kenny, or at least know him by reputation.' It was unclear to Murrain whether Rayner intended any innuendo. Murrain's reputation tended to precede him around the force. 'For anyone who doesn't, Kenny's a highly experienced investigating officer with a tremendous track record of success in major and complex enquiries of this nature.'

Murrain was inclined to treat the complimentary words sceptically, even though they were factually true. This was Rayner already getting his defence on record in case the enquiry should turn out not to be a success.

'Kenny will be working closely with Superintendent Marty Winston,' Rayner went on. 'Again, I'm sure most of you know Marty. He'll ensure you have whatever resources you need. Well, within the usual constraints.' Rayner laughed to show he was joking, though Murrain – and the rest of the audience, judging from their po-faced response – knew full well he wasn't.

'Finally,' Rayner said, 'we all need to realise what a big deal this enquiry's going to be. We'll be working in the most sensitive of environments, and those we'll be dealing with will be understandably anxious and concerned. We need to be highly professional at all times, and our first priority must always be the safety of the public.' He paused. 'We also need to be conscious of how this will be presented by the media. There will undoubtedly be times when we will need to take advantage of the channels the media can offer us. But the media's priority will always be to obtain a juicy story. We can't entirely control that, but we can do our best to manage it. I'll be the public face of the enquiry as far as media interviews and appearances are concerned. All contact with the media on this case must be routed through the communications team and myself. If you receive any media contact, however innocuous it might seem, you must inform me or the communications team. The story's already somehow been leaked to the press. Fortunately, responsibility for the leak appears to lie elsewhere, but we can't afford any repetition.' He stopped suddenly, as if he'd finally run out of anything to say. 'I'm sure I need say no more. I suggest we take any questions you might have at the end once you've had a chance to hear the full picture. Let me hand over to Kenny Murrain to talk you through the detail of the case, the overall structure of the investigation, and your own specific roles in conducting it.' He sat down and gestured for Murrain to continue.

'Good afternoon, people.' Murrain looked around the room. 'I know most of you, and I've worked with quite a few of you previously. If you don't know me, come and have a chat at the end. As Chris said earlier, it's important we all pull together on this one. We've a lot of work ahead of us, and I want you to feel as supported as possible.' He proceeded to talk them through the proposed organisation of the team, highlighting some of the individuals around the room who would be playing key roles.

He was mostly concerned to ensure they made the best possible use of the coming days. The results of the postmortems should soon reveal whether they were dealing with a one-off murder or a multiple killer. Murrain was already working on the assumption that it could be the latter, but for the moment they were focusing on the known victim, a woman called Elizabeth Everard. One of the key questions was whether there was any significance to the victim's identity or whether she'd simply been selected at random, the result of a tragic lottery.

He urged all those present to ensure they were clear about their allocated tasks and priorities over the coming days. 'If you've any questions, come and talk to me or to DS Wanstead. Similarly, if you've any concerns or if there's anything you need. We can't promise you the earth – well, we can't promise you anything at all – but we'll genuinely do our best to help.' This time the audience did respond with at least a murmur of good-natured amusement. 'Good luck, everyone. As Chris says, this is a big one. It'll be complicated, hard work and everyone will be watching us. We're taking whatever steps we can to improve security in the meantime, but the truth is until we find who's behind this, no one in the hospital will feel safe. We need to catch this person, and quickly.'

They ended the session by taking questions from the

team. Murrain felt encouraged that the issues raised were, for the most part, pertinent and sensible. Afterwards, a few individuals, previously only known to him as names or faces, came up to introduce themselves.

'Decent bunch, as far as I can tell,' Marty Winston said, echoing Murrain's own thoughts. 'Going to be a bloody nightmare, though. We really had to scrape around to get enough resources for this. And we've still got the domestic killings ongoing.'

Murrain suspected Winston's words were aimed mainly at Rayner, who was still standing beside them. Murrain had for the moment retained the role of CIO for the Perry and Turnbull murders, with the day-to-day running delegated to Colin Willock. That was supposedly a short-term arrangement until they could arrange the transfer of a more experienced officer into the role but Murrain had no confidence this would happen quickly. And, depending on the results of the Ollerenshaw postmortem, they might soon have a third domestic murder on their hands.

Rayner nodded abstractedly. 'We're all under pressure, Marty. I'm sure you'll do your best.'

'Believe me, Chris, we're all doing our best.' Winston exchanged a glance with Murrain. 'And, believe me, I'll keep badgering you for more resources.'

'I'm sure you will, Marty.' Rayner turned to Murrain. 'How's that DI of yours doing now?'

'Joe Milton? Same as ever, I'm afraid. All we can do is hope.'

'Awful business. He was a good man.'

'He still is,' Murrain said bluntly. 'We could certainly do with him at the moment. But he's a friend as well as a colleague. I'm more concerned about his personal well-being.'

Rayner gazed at him for a moment as if baffled by Murrain's words. 'I'm sure we all feel the same. Please pass on my good wishes.' He looked at his watch. 'I'd better leave you both to it. We're going to do a round of media interviews this afternoon, so I'd better go and get myself ready.'

Winston waited until Rayner was out of earshot before turning back to Murrain. 'I suppose it goes with the rank. In fairness, he is good at the media stuff.' He shook his head. 'It's a hell of a case, this, though, Kenny.'

Murrain nodded, sensing yet again the built up of tension in the back of his brain. 'And somehow I've a feeling there's a lot more of it to come.'

CHAPTER THIRTY TWO

It took Kyle Amberson a moment to recognise her across the room. The last time he'd seen her, he'd been crouched over Vivian Turnbull's corpse, and he hadn't been in a state to take in much, including the appearance of the woman who'd been standing opposite him.

She clearly recognised him, though, and she raised a hand to wave him over. There were two pints of beer on the table in front of her.

He wasn't even sure why he'd agreed to come, or whether it had been a wise decision. The call had taken him by surprise, and he hadn't had time to think. It had come through to the consulting room toward the end of the afternoon, just as he'd finished with his final patient of the day. He'd been scheduled an early finish, having covered the evening surgeries earlier in the week.

The receptionist, ever protective of the doctors' welfare, had said, 'I've got a woman on the line asking to speak to you. Reckons it's a personal matter and very urgent, but it may just be a patient trying to jump the queue. Shall I take a message?'

'You might as well put her through. I'm just about finished in here.'

'Well, if you're sure...'

'I might as well. Just in case it really is something urgent.'

The receptionist had given a barely audible sigh before transferring the call. A crisp voice said, 'Dr Amberson?'

'Speaking. How can I help you?'

'This is Romy Purslake, Dr Amberson.'

It had taken him a moment to place the name. Vivian Turnbull's partner. The woman who had all but accused him of murder. The woman who had contacted Andrew Carnforth about him. 'What can I do for you, Ms Purslake?'

'I was wondering if you could spare a few minutes.'

'Of course.'

He'd assumed she'd meant over the phone, but she'd suggested they meet face-to-face. 'I'm happy to come over to you,' she'd said. 'I don't want to inconvenience you.' The tone was very different from the previous time they'd spoken.

'When did you have in mind?'

'I suppose it's too much to hope you might be free today?'

Amberson was free virtually every day, other than when he was working, but he had no intention of telling Purslake that. 'As it happens, I could be.'

He suggested they meet in the bar where he'd last been with Jude Calman. It was close by, likely to be quiet in the late afternoon, and a decent place to hold what he assumed might be a potentially sensitive conversation. He couldn't imagine what Purslake wanted to talk to him about, but he assumed it must be in some way connected with Vivian Turnbull's death.

'I took the liberty of buying you a beer.' She slid one of the full glasses towards him. 'An American-style IPA, apparently. The barman recommended it, which probably just means he's trying to empty the barrel.'

'Thank you. How can I help you, Ms Purslake?'

'Romy, please. And can I call you…?'

'Kyle.'

She nodded, as if consigning his name to her memory. 'First of all, Kyle, I want to apologise.'

'Apologise?'

'For the way I behaved when – well, when we met previously. I behaved appallingly.'

'It must have been a shock.'

'That's not an excuse. I've always prided myself on my ability to handle a crisis.'

'You're being rather hard on yourself. You were probably in shock. And do please accept my sincere condolences.'

'Thank you. But I should have behaved more calmly.

At least given you a chance to explain who you were.'

'I'm sure any of us would have behaved the same way.'

'Anyway, thank you for sparing the time to see me.'

'I'm only too happy to. But I'm not sure how I can help you.'

'You're aware I spoke to your colleague, Dr Carnforth?'

'He mentioned it to me, yes.'

'Again, I can only apologise. I hadn't intended to imply any criticism of your own actions. I'm afraid the way I spoke to your colleague was a little intemperate.'

'I'm sure he appreciated the way you were feeling.'

She smiled for the first time. 'Oh, he appreciated that, all right. I made sure of it.'

For the first time, Amberson felt a degree of warmth towards Purslake. If she'd made Andrew Carnforth squirm, that was fine by him. 'I imagine he's heard worse.'

'I imagine he has. He's a pompous old fool, isn't he?'

'I couldn't possibly comment.'

'But I know you were simply doing your job. In fact you did rather more than you needed to. I do appreciate that. If the circumstances had been different, your decision to come into the house might have saved Viv's life.'

'Sadly, I was too late in any case. If I'd arrived just a little earlier – well, who knows? I'm sorry.'

'Or I could have returned home from work earlier. It could all so easily have been different. There's not much point in dwelling on that.'

'So why did you call Andrew? Dr Carnforth, I mean.'

'I wanted to know more about the possible cause of Viv's death. As you'll appreciate, it was a tremendous shock for me. It was completely out of the blue. Other than the injuries she'd suffered in the accident, she was remarkably fit and healthy for a woman of her age. I never envisaged anything like this happening. So I wanted to make sure I was clear about the circumstances. I wondered if Viv had been concealing something from me. Whether there might have been some other cause of death. I wanted to eliminate all the other possibilities before I went any further.' She took a sip of her beer, which had sat untouched up to that point. 'I should have waited for the postmortem, of course. But I just wanted some certainty.'

'What did Andrew say?'

'He was as helpful as you'd expect. That is, not at all. A lot of guff about patient confidentiality and why he wasn't able to give me any information.'

'In fairness, he's right. We do have to be very careful about what we say, even to close relatives.'

'The woman was dead. I just wanted to know whether there was anything she'd not told me. Some condition or consequence of the accident she hadn't wanted to share with me.'

'Did you have any reason to suspect there might be?'

'Viv and I were as close as two people can be. But she was a very private person. And particularly so when she wanted to protect me or spare my feelings.' She picked up her beer and swallowed what appeared to be a third of the glass in a single mouthful. 'I'm looking for some help.'

'I'm not sure I—'

'Nothing unethical or inappropriate. I'm happy for you to talk in general terms rather than to say anything about Viv.'

'I still don't really see how I can help you.'

'First, before I stir anything up, I want to be fully sure of my ground. That was the reason I phoned Dr Carnforth in the first place.'

'But you know now she died from the diamorphine overdose.'

'I know that was the cause of death, yes. And I know there was no other contributory condition. Is there any possibility that the overdose was self-inflicted?'

'Self inflicted?'

'That Viv might have chosen to kill herself that way.'

Amberson took another sip of beer to buy himself time to answer the question. 'If we're talking in general terms, it's theoretically possible. You'd have to inject yourself, but some people are accustomed to doing that, obviously.'

'Diabetics and addicts,' Purslake said. 'As far as I know Viv was neither. On the other hand, she wasn't the sort to be squeamish.'

'You're thinking she might have killed herself?'

'I imagine it's a possibility the police must be considering. Personally I don't think it's remotely likely Viv committed suicide, even putting aside the practical issues. She was the most levelheaded person I've ever met. To the best of my knowledge, she'd never suffered from any mental health problems. She was incredibly resilient. She never seemed remotely affected by anything she'd witnessed in her work.'

'That in itself might have been an issue,' Amberson pointed out. 'Someone who'd seen what she'd seen could easily have been more affected than they realised. If she tried to repress that, it might have reemerged, perhaps even in a more intense form. Sometimes the ones who seem least affected are the ones to be concerned about.'

'I'm not a fool, Kyle. That thought had occurred to me. I watched her very carefully after she retired because I had the same fear. We were both prone to channelling our emotions back into our work, which isn't always the healthiest approach. But I saw no sign of any problems. And I saw no change in her behaviour before her death.'

'What about her response to the accident? That must have affected her, presumably?'

'She was frustrated by it. She wasn't happy with the loss of her independence, however temporarily. Nothing more than that.'

'For what it's worth,' Amberson said, 'it's not a method of suicide I've ever come across. Not self-administered. I'm aware of some cases of assisted suicide using this or similar drugs, usually in the context of euthanasia. But that wouldn't apply in this case.'

'Not unless I was involved.' Purslake held up her hand as before. 'Which, for the avoidance of doubt, I wasn't. There was nothing to justify euthanasia. We know that Viv was physically healthy. She was close to recovering from the effects of the accident. There was no reason for her to take her own life, and certainly no reason for anyone else to help her do so.' She paused, as if for dramatic effect. 'So we're left with murder. Which I imagine is where the police's enquiries are taking them.'

'I'd presume so. And I've assumed that, like you, I'm a potential suspect until they know better.' Amberson swallowed the last of his beer and gestured towards her now nearly-empty glass. 'Can I get you another?'

'Why not? I got a taxi over so I'm not worried about driving. And I'm rather partial to that IPA.' She smiled at him. 'Aren't you worried about being a suspect?'

'I've no motive. Why would I have any reason to harm her? I'd never even met her. Sorry, that was insensitive. But you take my point.'

'I do. I'm not trying to accuse you. Whatever I might have said in the heat of the moment, I don't see you as the killer. That's why I'm here.'

'I don't understand.'

She gestured towards the empty glasses in front of him. 'If you get the round in, I'll try to explain.'

CHAPTER THIRTY THREE

By mid-afternoon, Bert Wallace was feeling slightly more human. The effects of the hangover had worn off, and the continuous supply of coffee was keeping her alert. Murrain had spoken to her earlier and suggested that, for the moment at least, she should continue working on the Perry investigation rather than transferring to the hospital enquiry.

'I'd rather have you on the hospital case,' he'd said. 'I suspect we'd benefit from your skills, but I can't afford to deplete the other enquiries too much. We can review it in a few days once we see how things are panning out.'

She hadn't been exactly pleased by the decision, particularly as it meant continuing to work with Colin Willock. On the other hand, although Murrain would never say it, she suspected that part of the reason was to help keep Willock in check.

In the meantime, she'd continued her work on Gregory Perry's background. It was tedious work that felt as if it was leading nowhere, but necessary if they were to build any case against Perry. In practice, there seemed little noteworthy about Perry himself. She followed up her telephone discussions with his employer with a call to the university where he'd studied and tracked down Perry's former Director of Studies. The man in question, a Dr Adrian Copley, phoned back more promptly than she'd expected.

'How can I help you?'

'I'm looking for some background information on Gregory Perry. I understand he was a student of yours.' She gave him the dates of Perry's attendance at the university.

'Can I ask why you need it? Is this part of an investigation?' Copley sounded a brusque figure, not one to waste his own or anyone else's time.

'You might have seen on the local news that Perry's

mother was found dead. We believe she was the victim of an unlawful killing.'

'Dear God, was that Perry's mother? Diamorphine, from what the news report said.'

'We believe so.' She could sense Copley already adding two and two together.

'You don't think that Perry could have…?'

'We're not thinking anything at present. We're just gathering background information on the victims and their immediate family and friends.'

'I'm not sure there's much I can tell you. I remember Gregory, of course. It was only a few years ago. But he didn't make much of an impact on me. Hang on—' There was the sound of tapping on a keyboard. 'Just dug out his file. Everything's on-line these days.'

'Is there anything interesting in Perry's file?'

'It doesn't look like it, I'm afraid. Perfectly competent student. Not outstanding, but above average. Ended up with a decent upper second. No record of any performance or conduct issues. Typical student, to be honest. Comes here, gets a degree, moves on. That's about all I can tell you.' There was another pause. 'Oh, wait, there's one thing.'

'Go on.'

'To be honest, I'm not sure if I should share this.'

'I'm engaged in a murder enquiry, Dr Copley. If you have something that may be pertinent—'

'Of course,' Copley said impatiently. 'The question is whether it's pertinent.'

'If it isn't, or isn't likely to be, I'll be happy to treat it as confidential.'

'It's just that, in his last few months here, just before Finals, Perry suffered some quite severe mental health problems. There are only limited details here, so I guess you'd need to talk to his GP for a fuller picture. Some fairly full-blown form of psychosis. He was living in a shared house in his final year, and he started to demonstrate odd behaviours. Said he was hearing voices instructing him to carry out various acts.'

'What sort of acts?'

'The file doesn't go into detail. There were a couple of instances of self-harm, both relatively minor. And an incident where he was found in one of his housemate's rooms in the middle of the night holding a kitchen knife. His housemates found him sleepwalking on several occasions, and he became aggressive if they tried to return him to bed or wake him.'

'So what happened?'

'It looks as if it was all brushed under the carpet. I'm a bit shocked I wasn't made aware of it at the time, though his personal tutor must have known. He seems to have added the file note. I didn't even know it was there till now.' Copley sounded unexpectedly chastened, as if he'd failed in his duty. 'The note indicates that his condition improved rapidly once the issue was identified. He was still registered with his home GP, who suggested the problem had most likely been stress and overwork in the weeks leading up to Finals. The GP recommended that, as the condition had improved significantly, Perry should continue at university and proceed to take his finals. Looks as if it was the right decision. Certainly, Perry's performance in the exams was in line with our expectations of him, so it doesn't seem to have affected him too much.'

'That's the only mention of that kind of issue in the file?'

'As far as I can see. It looks as if it hit him out of the blue. But that's often the way with students. I've seen it happen before.'

'I don't suppose the file has the name of Perry's GP at the time?'

'I think I saw it. Wait a minute. Yes, it was a Dr Carnforth. A Dr Andrew Carnforth.'

CHAPTER THIRTY FOUR

'All under control?' Murrain dropped himself into the chair beside Paul Wanstead's desk.

'Could be a lot worse. And I'm sure it will be before it gets any better.'

'It's your cheery good nature keeps me going, Paul.'

'We're in as good a shape as we can be. We've got the first officers in the hospital already, and interviews underway. We're starting with the pharmacy and related areas, as agreed.'

'Our killer must have got his weapon of choice from somewhere,' Murrain said. 'Though it doesn't have to have been from inside the hospital. I assume this means we'll be interviewing our friend Gregory Perry?'

'I thought it best not to give him any special treatment, although obviously the officer interviewing him is aware of the background and will handle it with appropriate sensitivity.' It was impossible to tell if there was any note of irony in the way Wanstead spoke the last two words.

'He's going to make the link between this and his mother's death, but then he'll presumably have done that as soon as he saw the statement this afternoon.' A notice to all the hospital's staff had been co-ordinated with the media release, and Chris Rayner was at that moment in the middle of a round of television and radio interviews. 'The question is whether we should be looking at him as a suspect in both cases.'

'If there is a link between the hospital cases and the domestic ones, he's the only common factor we have,' Wanstead agreed.

'Assuming he's a serious contender for the hospital killing.'

'He's potentially got the means to procure the drug, just as with his mother. But he's not someone who generally visits the wards. He wouldn't easily have been able to spend time alone with a patient without arousing suspicion. Doesn't mean it wasn't possible, but it would have been risky.'

'Working in conjunction with someone else, then?'

'It's possible,' Wanstead said. 'Perry could be the source of the drug even if he's not the killer. Maybe Perry was being blackmailed if he was already involved in some dodgy procurement. Who knows?'

'For the moment, all we can do is keep a close eye on him. Bert's looking into his background, though she hadn't found much when I spoke to her earlier. Seemed to be just Mr Average.'

'Those are the ones to watch,' Wanstead said.

'Anything else I should know? I'm just about to call the CEO for an update.'

'I'm just printing off the latest iteration of the schedule of activity, so that should give you the salient facts if he starts asking tricky questions.'

'Thanks, Paul. Always one step ahead.'

'Better than being one step behind. Speaking of which, you reckon Bert's okay?'

'Okay?'

'Seemed a bit distracted this morning. Maybe even a bit the worse for wear. Like she'd had a heavy night.'

'That doesn't sound like Bert. She seemed all right when I spoke to her this afternoon. But then I don't always have your nose for such things.'

'It's probably nothing. Just might be worth keeping an eye on her, that's all.'

'Noted. Thanks, Paul.' Murrain was feeling pretty exhausted himself after several days of early starts and late finishes. He climbed wearily to his feet, retrieved the schedule from the printer and headed across to his own desk.

There were a couple of voicemail messages waiting for him. The first was from Gerry Hayward, the pathologist in charge of the Ollerenshaw postmortem. The second was from Marty Winston. He dialled Hayward's number. If Hayward had news, good or bad, it would be better if he heard it before speaking to Winston.

'Afternoon, Gerry,' he said. 'Hope you're phoning with good news.'

'Depends on your point of view, Kenny. I know you're a sucker for more work.'

'Nothing I like more. We're all just lazing around here at the moment. Break it to me slowly.'

'Our friend Ollerenshaw. Trevor Ollerenshaw, to give him his full name. It looks as if he's another one.'

'Diamorphine.'

'Almost identical to the other two in terms of dosage.'

'You've completed the postmortem?'

'Thought you'd want a heads-up before I start writing the formal report.'

'Thanks.' Murrain laughed. 'Sorry, I intended that to be more sincere than it probably sounded.'

'No worries. You've a lot on your plate. The hospital thing sounds grim. Just been talking to colleagues over there. There's a lot of anxiety. Everybody starts to suspect everyone else.'

'Tell me about it,' Murrain said. 'Thanks for adding to my burden. I'll go and break the news to my superintendent, so I can add it to his.'

He finished the call and sat for a moment. While he'd been talking to Hayward, he'd felt the familiar sensations. They'd never entirely gone away over the preceding few days, but had been little more than background noise. Now, they'd come to the fore, like voices chanting just above the threshold of his hearing.

He looked at his watch. Fifteen minutes or so before he was due to call Alan Northcote at the hospital. He made his way to Marty Winston's office. Winston was at his desk, tapping on his computer keyboard.

'You wanted a word? And I've some news. Not good news, I'm afraid.'

Winston waved him in. 'I could have done with some good news.'

'Ollerenshaw. It looks like we need to add him to our

list.'

'Bugger. I was hoping that one might just be coincidence. We deserve a break.'

'And what was your news?'

'We might have a problem.'

'Go on.'

'You know we were talking about the story being leaked to the local paper. Everyone's keen to shift the blame on to someone else. The hospital reckon no-one could have leaked it from there because only a handful of people were aware of it.'

'I'm willing to bet there were more people than they imagine.'

'No doubt. But they're never going to admit it. Next on the list is the Coroner's Office. They're getting twitchy because they don't want any stain on their reputation, so they kicked off an internal enquiry.'

'What have they found?' Murrain looked at his watch pointedly. 'I need to call Alan Northcote in a few minutes. First daily debrief.'

'They've had suspicions for a while of one of their younger employees, a guy called...' Winston checked the notepad in front of him. 'Daniel Fraser. They've had stories leaked to the media before the Coroner had completed his work, and Fraser looked to be in the frame. With a couple of exceptions, the leaked stories have been cases he was working on. They'd checked Fraser's calls and e-mails, but found nothing suspicious. But, since he was one of only a small number of people who had prior knowledge of the hospital case – he'd been preparing some of the paperwork – they interviewed him about it.'

Murrain glanced at his watch again. 'And?'

'He flatly denied any involvement in the previous leaks. But this one...' Winston paused. 'He denied having any contact with the media, but eventually conceded he'd been indiscreet. Shooting his mouth off when he shouldn't have been.'

'Shooting his mouth off?'

'Trying to impress a woman, would you believe?'

'What sort of woman would be impressed by news of a hospital killer?'

'There are probably several sorts,' Winston said, 'of varying levels of sanity. But there's one sort who might have an interest at a professional level.'

'Go on.' Murrain could already feel a knot of anxiety in his stomach.

'I'm thinking of an eager police detective,' Winston said. 'Someone like Bert Wallace.'

CHAPTER THIRTY FIVE

Bert Wallace wasn't sure what had led her to think about Margaret Perry's late husband. The thought had been partly triggered by the revelation that Andrew Carnforth had been Gregory Perry's GP, the first time they'd identified even a tenuous link between the Perry and Turnbull cases. They'd checked out the name of Margaret Perry's own GP, of course, not least to confirm whether Kyle Amberson might have been linked to both deaths. Perry had been registered with another local practice, and no one had seen any reason to check whether her son was also registered there.

In itself, the link with Carnforth was unlikely to be significant but the coincidence had led Wallace to think about Perry's family. It occurred to her that she still knew little about Margaret Perry's husband.

Her curiosity aroused, she pulled together the scanty information they had. It amounted to the fact that Frank Perry had been a civil servant working for some offshoot of the Home Office in Manchester. That information had been gleaned from Gregory Perry himself, who had seemed to know little more about his father's occupation or private life. On the face of it, the father seemed as unremarkable as his wife and son.

She began with a basic internet search on Perry in the hope of finding some relevant news stories about him. She found a couple of stories in the local paper which referenced Perry's name in connection with local Rotary Club events. She also found a brief funeral notice for him, which gave the time and place of the funeral and indicated that donations should be made to the British Heart Foundation.

Next, she tried to identify the organisations in Manchester Frank Perry might have worked for. The most likely areas were either within the Immigration Directorate or possibly the Border Agency. She picked up the phone and, selecting one of the available numbers at random, she began to dial.

After half an hour, she was on the point of abandoning her quest. She'd painstakingly explained the background to her enquiries to a succession of telephone receptionists and had been greeted generally by evident bafflement, sometimes by apparent hostility, and occasionally by a genuine willingness to help. In those cases, the receptionist had transferred her to managers who'd offered a similar range of responses. No one, though, had any knowledge of Frank Perry.

Close to giving up, she came across a helpful receptionist in the Immigration and Enforcement Directorate. 'The name does seem to ring a bell, but I don't know from where. Just wait a minute. I'll check if anyone else has any ideas...' Wallace sat for a several minutes listening to bland hold music, wondering at what point she should end the call. Finally, the receptionist spoke again. 'A couple of people here knew the name but couldn't remember anything about him. But I've just spoken to Ron Charlesworth. He's been here forever, so I thought he might be a good bet. He did know Frank Perry and he'd be happy to have a chat with you. I'll put you through.'

'Ron Charlesworth. How can I help?'

It took Wallace only a couple of minutes to pigeon-hole Charlesworth as a man rapidly winding down to retirement, happy to waste his time gossiping for as long as she was prepared to listen. The fact that she was female was probably part of that equation. Charlesworth's manner was gentlemanly, in an old school style, but with an undoubted undertone of flirtatiousness.

'Frank? Oh, yes, I knew him. Saw the awful thing about his wife in the paper, and wondered if someone would be in contact with us here. Dreadful business. Only too happy to help if I can.'

'It's really just about gathering some background. Can you tell me what Mr Perry's job involved?'

'We're basically just bureaucrats here, you understand. Processing and checking data for the compliance teams.'

Wallace was aware of the immigration compliance teams who worked with some of her colleagues on identifying and dealing with illegal immigrants in the region. 'That was the kind of work Frank Perry was involved in?'

'To be honest, we all had a bit of trouble fathoming Frank.'

'How do you mean?'

'We're a mixed bunch in here. I'm the longest serving now. Life-long civil servant for my sins. Only still here for the pension. Another year and I'll be at the maximum, then I'll be away. Most of the people I work with now are just youngsters, probably like yourself.'

'And Frank Perry?'

'He was like me. Career civil servant. But whereas I'd always worked in the department, he was drafted in a few years ago. There was always a bit of mystery about where he'd come from. It was supposedly from elsewhere in the Home Office, but no one seemed to know him. I remember asking around, just out of curiosity, but the name didn't mean anything to anyone.'

'But he worked alongside the rest of you, doing the same kind of work?'

'The short answer is no. He was notionally part of the team, but he very much did his own thing. He took his instructions from a much more senior level than the rest of us, and we had no idea what he was really doing.'

'So who did he report to?'

'No idea. Frank was supposedly on the same grade as I was. But my impression was that the work he was doing was a different level. My stuff's basically just processing. Checking information. A bit of collation. Frank's work was much more analytical. But whenever I asked him about it, he reckoned it was easier than it looked.'

'What did the rest of the team make of him?'

'He was a likeable bloke. He didn't have airs or graces or consider himself something special. In most respects he was just another member of the office. He mucked in on making tea and coffee. He joined in all the banter. I'm not sure most of them even noticed there was anything different about his role. If you've only been there a few months, you'd probably just think it was how things were. I'd been around long enough to know that it was a bit out of the ordinary.'

'So what do you think his role was?'

'Hope this phone's not tapped, lass.' The words were said as a joke, but Wallace could detect a genuine anxiety underlying them.

'Not that I'm aware of.'

'It's just that – and this will probably sound daft – I thought he was a spook.'

'A spook? You mean, a spy?'

'Well, not a spy as such. But someone from the intelligence services.'

'What made you think that?'

'A lot of what we do is just handle turning,' Charlesworth said, 'but we do work with some sensitive data at times. We have to treat it with full confidentiality, and we've all been appropriately vetted.'

It occurred to Wallace that, if Charlesworth's work involved the kind of sensitive data he was claiming, he should perhaps know better than to gossip over the phone to someone claiming to be a police officer. Even so, she had no intention of silencing him now.

'My impression was that Frank was working with the same data but examining it much more analytically. As if he was looking for patterns or even for specific individuals. Our role was just to double-check the data to ensure it was accurate before it was used to inform decisions and actions by our enforcement colleagues. It's a sensitive field, particularly if you're conducting raids on employers and the like. You don't want to get it wrong, though sometimes we still do.'

'If that's what he was doing, presumably he could have done it from anywhere, though, as long as he had access to the data? He didn't have to be sited with you.'

'I imagine it was convenient for him to be located with the rest of us. He'd quite often consult with one or other of us on some detail in the data. Because we were checking it, we were immersed in the detail, whereas I had the sense Frank was working at a higher level, reviewing the material as a whole rather than delving into each file.'

It might explain why he hadn't been keen to share much about his job with his wife or son, Wallace thought. 'What sort of man was he?'

'Like I say, pleasant enough. Not exactly outgoing – but then he wouldn't be if he was what I thought he was – but not standoffish either. He was well enough liked in the office. He'd join us for a drink or two after work, though he tended not to stay long. Described himself as a bit of a home-bird. But that's probably how the youngsters see me.'

'I understand he retired early?'

'That was a bit sad, really. He actually collapsed in the office. He was at his desk one day and just keeled over. We had the first-aider in the office doing CPR and it was clear something was seriously wrong. We didn't even know if the ambulance would get there in time.'

'A heart attack?'

'It was lucky that we called the ambulance as quickly as we did. Another few minutes and it might well have been too late. He never came back to work. I assume HR put some package together for him to take early retirement. He popped in a couple of times to say goodbye and pick up a few personal bits and pieces.'

Gregory Perry had said nothing about the cause of his father's death. 'Did he have another attack?'

'They thought that must be what had happened as there was no other obvious cause. Car accident. Went off the road somewhere out near where he lived. Car plunged down an embankment and hit a tree. The whole thing went up in flames. Not much left of the car or Frank, from the accounts I read.'

Wallace was listening more intently now. This must be in the files, she thought, unsure how she could have missed it when she'd been searching for information on Frank Perry. 'Sounds unpleasant.'

'Very much so. It was why they couldn't be sure of the cause. The car had seemed in good shape although it was difficult to be sure after the fire. Frank's body was apparently too badly damaged for them to conduct a full autopsy. Sorry. Probably too much information. It's just that, having known Frank, I followed the story in a lot of detail at the time.'

'No, that's very useful. He wasn't replaced in your team?'

'That's one of the things I found intriguing. Managers here aren't usually keen to give up a vacancy without a fight. But it never happened, which made me wonder where the original funding for the post had come from.'

'That's all been very helpful, Mr Charleswortth. I won't take up any more of your time for the present. Depending on how the investigation proceeds, we might need to talk to you again.'

'You've got my number, lass. Call if you want anything.'

It wasn't until she'd ended that call that she realised someone was hovering close to her desk. She looked up and saw Colin Willock standing in front of her, looking characteristically pleased with himself.

'Finished on the phone, then?' There was the usual underlying sneer in his voice, but something else she couldn't quite identify.

'Did you need something?'

'Not me. But Kenny would like a word.'

CHAPTER THIRTY SIX

Kyle Amberson looked at the beer in front of him and realised he was feeling slightly woozy. He'd downed two pints of the IPA already, which was as much as he was generally accustomed to drinking. But Romy Purslake has offered to buy him a third, and it had seemed rude to decline.

Purslake was also on her third pint but appeared none the worse for it. 'It's not a strong one. What do they call them? Session ales? I suppose we're on a session then. Or is it in a session?'

The other consideration, Amberson thought, was that it wasn't yet 5.00 pm. He wasn't used to drinking this early. 'Isn't it strong? It tastes strong.'

'You should try the porter.' Purslake gestured to the chalked list of available beers behind the bar. 'Nearly nine per cent. That's a real beer.' She sounded as if she might be tempted to give it a go. 'So what do you think?'

He considered pretending she was still talking about the beer, but he knew she wasn't. 'You're sure about Andrew?'

'Certain. I'm no journalist. That was Viv's talent. But I've plenty of contacts, and Viv was known and liked by a lot of influential people. I had several calls out of the blue after the cause of death was revealed. Not just the usual expressions of sympathy – though I had plenty of those – but people offering help in finding the killer. One or two of the calls were slightly unnerving, to be honest. Viv had friends and contacts in low as well as high places.'

'I'm not sure I like the sound of that,' Amberson said. 'Speaking as a potential suspect.'

'I'll make sure you're safe enough, Kyle. But that's another reason for resolving this as quickly as we can. I don't want any of these people taking the law into their own hands.'

Amberson had a sick feeling in the pit of his stomach. He felt as if he'd been dragged into a new and unfamiliar world, and he wasn't sure he wanted to be here. 'But Andrew, though. It seems incredible.'

'You said that you were already aware of some of Carnforth's history?'

'Yes, but nothing like this. All I had was gossip passed on to me by one of my fellow doctors. They told me that he'd had some kind of drink problem early in his career that had been hushed up.'

'That's part of the story. But a fairly small part according to my sources.'

'Assuming any of this is true, I don't see how he could have got himself into that position.'

'The same way people usually get into those positions. One thing leads to another. Especially if you're dealing with people like that. The only options you have are either to sacrifice yourself or just keep going. Carnforth clearly likes his current status and lifestyle too much and just kept going.'

'I still can't believe it.'

'He's not the first and he won't be the last.'

'So how long do you reckon this has been going on?'

'My guess is it started with the drinking so that must have been twenty-odd years ago. What your colleague told you was accurate enough. According to my sources, he was turning up at work stinking of booze. Patients noticed very quickly, and he was suspended by his colleagues.'

'There were also suggestions he was stealing drugs for his own use.'

'More than suggestions, according to my sources. And not just for his own use. He was also dealing them. In a very genteel middle-class way, of course. And probably not, at least at that stage, primarily for the money. More about impressing his friends.'

'I can't imagine any of Andrew Carnforth's friends being influenced by that.'

'Remember this was twenty years ago. Carnforth and his friends would have been in their early thirties. Some of them would have been only too keen to get their hands on the right middle-class drugs of choice. They'd no doubt much rather get them from someone like Carnforth than from some teenage dealer from the wrong estate.'

'So why didn't this come to a stop when Carnforth was suspended? His partners must have known what was going on.'

'No doubt they knew some of it. I'm sure your colleague was right about Carnforth going into rehab and promising to turn over a new leaf. I just don't think he meant a word of it, other than knocking back the drinking.'

'And you think he's continued the dealing ever since?'

'I have some very good sources.'

Amberson shook his head, then felt dizzy and instantly regretted it. 'But how would that even be possible? We're a group practice. He couldn't have got away with it without someone spotting something was wrong.'

'He won't be doing it through the surgery or its suppliers. Not now. That side of it must all be above board. After his original problems, he was approached by some less reputable suppliers. Maybe he was already using them, and had got his hands well and truly dirty in dealing to his golf-club friends. Or maybe he was only approached at that point. Perhaps they got wind of the stuff that had been brushed under the carpet and threatened to expose him unless he went into business with them.'

'He was blackmailed into it?'

'They were probably pushing at an open door. Carnforth was running a sideline which brought him extra money, kudos with his friends, and probably also a nice sense of risk. I think that's sometimes what drives this kind of stuff, even more than the money. The adrenaline that comes from risk-taking. I saw that in Viv. Alongside all her noble motives – the desire to uncover the truth, to get the story – she just loved the buzz. Maybe Carnforth's the same in his buttoned-up way.'

'But why would these people be interested in someone like Carnforth? Surely he'd be small-fry by their standards.'

'In the grand scheme of things, yes. But he's the premium end of the market. The people Carnforth knows would pay much bigger bucks than those your average street dealer's involved with. Think of the growth of drug-use among the supposedly respectable classes. Makes you wonder how many Carnforths are out there.' The room around them was filling up with the after work crowd and he'd lowered his voice. Purslake, for all her cut-glass intonation, had done the same. 'And of course the fact that Carnforth's a doctor, a GP, might have other uses to them.'

'How do you mean?'

'These aren't nice people. It might be useful for them to have the means of procuring a convenient death certificate.'

'I can't believe he'd do anything like that.'

'Given he's so deeply ensnared, he's not likely to refuse any request, is he?'

'And you're sure of all this?'

'The gist of it, yes. The sources are reliable and they've no reason to lie.'

'Why aren't the police aware of it?'

'We don't know they aren't. But there's no particular reason why they should be.'

'So what made you look at Carnforth?'

'I looked at your background first. Obviously.'

'Mine?'

'You'll be delighted to hear that you appear to be squeaky-clean. According to my sources.'

'That's good, I suppose.'

'Think of it as a moral credit check. I'd already decided you were genuine. But it was good to have it confirmed. Carnforth had intrigued me because I'd sensed something defensive in his manner. The way he responded to my call didn't feel right.'

'Shouldn't you be telling the police all this?'

'I've no real evidence. My sources aren't the sort of people who are going to talk to the police willingly. Look, Kyle, the reason I've told you this is because I wanted you to be forewarned. Everything I've heard suggests Carnforth is a ruthless and nasty piece of work. If he thought he was under threat, he wouldn't hesitate to throw someone else to the wolves to save his own skin. You're already on the police's radar because of Viv's death, so you could be lined up for that scapegoat role.'

'Point taken. Though I'm not sure what I can do about that. I've nothing to hide.'

'Just be vigilant. And maybe think about moving jobs.'

'I might have to do that. It strikes me this isn't going to end well for anyone.'

'So the best thing is to ensure it ends badly for Carnforth. Sooner rather than later, before Carnforth can start trying to drag anyone else into the mire. If we want to stop Carnforth doing what he's doing, we need evidence. You're in a better position to gather that evidence than anyone else.'

'I don't—'

'All I'm suggesting is you keep an eye on Carnforth and on what goes on in the practice. You're all supposed to be equal partners, right?'

'Well, yes.'

'So use your position to check the accounts, check the documentation, find anything that looks anomalous. Listen to the gossip, particularly among the receptionists and admin staff. They're the ones who'll spot something out of the ordinary.'

'But if Carnforth's operating outside the practice—'

'It'll be harder to spot. Of course. He's going to be careful. But I wouldn't be surprised if there are instances where it suits him to use the practice as a front. I've already got people looking at what else Carnforth might be up to.'

'I mean, I'll do what I can. But why are we doing this, Romy?'

'Are you happy that Carnforth's involved in this kind of stuff?'

'No, of course not. But I meant why are you so

concerned about it all? Do you think this is connected with Vivian's death?'

'I don't know. If Carnforth can do this, what else might he be capable of? Since I know I didn't kill Viv and I'm pretty sure you didn't, he's the only serious suspect we have.'

'But what motive would he have had for killing her?'

'I don't honestly know. But if it's even a possibility, it makes this even more important.'

'I can't promise anything. I imagine Andrew's pretty careful.'

'Just do what you can. You've got more chance of finding something than I have.' She smiled and Amberson was left with the uncomfortable feeling that he'd somehow been manipulated. He reassured himself with the thought that he'd made no promises or commitments.

Purslake tapped her empty glass. 'One more?'

Amberson was conscious it was his round. 'I'd better not. I'm not a big drinker. If I have any more, I won't even be able to crawl home. I can get you one if you like.'

'No worries. Let's call it an evening.' Purslake's smile widened. 'But I won't forget that you owe me one.'

CHAPTER THIRTY SEVEN

Bert Wallace had already seen that Kenny Murrain's desk was unoccupied. 'Where is he?' she asked Colin Willock.

Willock's familiar smarmy smile had transformed into something closer to a smirk. 'He asked if you could go along to Marty Winston's office.'

Wallace frowned, an uneasy feeling stirring in her stomach. This felt uncomfortably like being summoned to the head teacher. 'What about?'

'He just wanted a word.'

'Fair enough. I can find my own way, Colin.'

He nodded, still smiling, and returned to his desk. She watched him for a moment, then turned to make her way along the corridor to Winston's office. Through the glass partition Winston and Murrain were conversing earnestly. She tapped on the door and Murrain waved for her to enter.

Winston was already on his feet. 'Come in, Bert. Take a seat. Coffee?' He gestured over towards the filter machine on the side cabinet.

'I'm fine, thanks.' Winston seemed friendly enough. Despite Willock's manner, it didn't feel as if she'd been brought here for a dressing-down.

'We just wanted a quick chat,' Murrain said. 'Something's come up, and we wanted your version of it.'

'My version?' The uneasy feeling had returned to her stomach.

Winston had returned to his seat. 'It's slightly awkward, I'm afraid. Do you know a man called Daniel Fraser?'

'Fraser? You mean in the Coroner's Office?'

'That's the one. You do know him, then?'

'Sort of.' She glanced at Murrain. 'I had some dealings with him in connection with the Margaret Perry case. He did some of the initial legwork for the Coroner. I think you were aware of that,' she added to Murrain.

Murrain nodded. 'I think what Marty was really asking

was whether you know Fraser socially. Outside work.'

As far as she was aware, there was nothing to prevent her enjoying a drink with an employee of the Coroner's Office. 'He asked me out for a drink. I wasn't aware there was anything wrong with that.'

'No, of course not.' Winston looked at Murrain. 'Not in itself, obviously.'

Wallace could feel her unease giving way to a growing irritation. Neither of these men had any right to interrogate her about her private life. What the hell was this about? 'Why are you interested in him?'

Winston shifted awkwardly. Wallace sensed that he was finding this conversation almost as tough as she was, though her sympathy was limited. 'You're aware the hospital death investigation was leaked to the local paper ahead of any official announcement?'

'I'm aware it appeared there almost before we'd been informed about the death, yes.' The sense of unease had returned as she thought back to her conversation with Fraser the previous evening.

'That's the way it looked,' Winston said. 'Our assumption was that the leak had come either from the hospital itself or from the Coroner's Office.'

'That's what I assumed,' Wallace said.

'The Coroner's Office has been concerned for some time about information being leaked to the media,' Murrain said. 'They'd been observing a small number of individuals who they thought were the most likely suspects. One of those was Daniel Fraser.'

'I don't understand what this has to do with me,' Wallace said.

'Because of their suspicions,' Murrain continued, 'they've been managing the various individuals' access to different information. On this occasion, only Fraser was aware of the hospital story and had been told to keep it confidential. If the leak did come from the Coroner's Office, he was the only person, other than a couple of senior managers, who could have been responsible. He was interviewed by management this morning. He denied responsibility for the leak. But, when he was challenged, he admitted that he'd discussed the story – inappropriately, as he acknowledged – with someone outside the Coroner's Office.'

'That someone being me.'

'According to Fraser, yes. Is that true?'

She wanted just to walk out, or at least to tell them assertively that she couldn't be responsible for what someone chose to share with her. 'I suppose so.'

'I'm sorry, Bert, but we need to be clear about this. He told you about the hospital death and the findings of the postmortem?'

'It wasn't something I asked him about. I just thought he was trying to impress me by sharing some inside knowledge relevant to my job. That was all it was. Just a bit of gossip over a drink. He didn't tell me he'd been given the information in confidence. But I was smart enough to realise it wasn't something I should be sharing with others. Even if I'd had an opportunity to.'

'That's the question we wanted to ask you,' Winston said. 'Fraser gave the impression he spent the whole evening with you. Is that correct?'

'We went for a drink and a meal, then a couple more drinks, yes.'

'Fraser says that, in the course of the evening, you went outside on a couple of occasions to take a phone call. Is that true?'

'Not that I recall, no.'

'Not that you recall?'

'The truth is, I had too much to drink last night. I'm not really used to drinking and, well, it's a while since I went out with anyone socially. I ended up drinking more than I'd realised. My memory of the last part of the evening's a bit hazy, to be honest. But I wouldn't have had any reason to make a phone call.'

'You're sure about that?'

'I'm sure I'd have no reason to call anyone, yes.' A

thought struck her. 'I can show you my phone, if that would help. Any call would be logged.'

'If you're happy to do that, it would be helpful,' Winston said. 'Look, Bert, this isn't an attack on you. We just want to be clear what happened. The other parties in this will be only too pleased if they can shift the responsibility on to us.'

Wallace placed her two mobiles on the Winston's desk. 'That's my police phone, and that's my personal one. I'm happy for you to look at both. I've nothing to hide.' She picked up the police phone and unlocked it, flicking through to the call log. 'There. Nothing at all yesterday evening, inbound or outbound.' She showed the screen to Winston and then to Murrain.

She picked up her personal phone, going through the same routine. Then she stopped, staring at the screen. 'I don't understand.'

The personal phone had been in her handbag and then her pocket since the previous evening. She couldn't recall even looking at it in the last twenty-four hours. But two calls were logged from the previous evening, one outgoing and the other incoming, both showing the same mobile number and the name 'Jo'. The calls were timed roughly half an hour apart. The outbound call had lasted around five minutes. The incoming call had lasted around ten.

'There are two calls shown. But I didn't make them.' She hesitated. 'At least, I don't recall making them.'

'The contact name seems to be in your address book,' Winston pointed out. 'It must be someone you know.'

Wallace thumbed open the contacts list. The contact simply said: 'Jo' alongside the number. No other information. 'It isn't, though. I don't recognise the name at all. I don't think I even know anyone called Jo.' She switched the phone on to speaker, and then, without waiting for any comment from Winston or Murrain, she dialled the number. It rang and cut to voicemail, and a female voice said: 'Sorry, I'm tied up at the moment. Please leave a message or, if it's urgent, you can contact the news desk on—'

She ended the call and looked up at Winston. 'I didn't put that number on my phone. I didn't make those calls.'

Murrain exchanged a glance with Winston and said softly, 'Tell us what happened last night, Bert. As much as you feel able to.'

Part of her just wanted to get up and walk out of the room, save herself any further humiliation. But she knew Murrain well enough to recognise he at least would be supportive. He'd trust her as long as she gave him reason to. 'It was as I said. I went for a meal and a few drinks with Fraser. I can remember eating in the restaurant. An Italian place.'

'You made no phone calls during the meal?' Winston said.

'No. I'm certain of that. We ate quite early because we'd met up after work.'

'Tell me to mind my own business,' Murrain said, 'but you said it was Fraser who invited you for a drink?'

'Yes. He was a bit awkward about it, you know? I almost said no. Then I thought why not. I'd got myself into a rut lately, so I thought it might do me good to have a night out for a change.'

'I just want to be clear that it was Fraser who initiated the meeting,' Murrain said. 'You said you ate early. What time did you leave the restaurant?'

'It can't have been any later than 8.30. Probably earlier. Before the time of those calls, anyway.'

'What happened after that?'

'We went to a bar in the Northern Quarter that he was keen on. I just went with what he suggested. None of this is really my sort of thing. But it was fine, not too noisy. He seemed pleasant company. I hadn't thought I'd drunk very much really. I had a half of lager in the pub. We shared a bottle of wine in the restaurant, but he drank more than I did. Then I can recall having a couple more halves in the bar…'

'And after that?' Winston prompted.

'That's the thing. I can't remember anything at all after that. I mean, I'm not sure what time I remember up to. I remember him getting me a second half of lager, but I don't have much of a memory of drinking it.'

'The calls were timed quite late,' Murrain said. 'After ten. You're absolutely sure you have no recollection of them?'

'None at all,' Wallace said. 'But I've no recollection of anything then. The point is that I don't know this Jo at all. I didn't put her name into my phone.'

'You're suggesting someone else used your phone last night?' Winston was stretched back in his chair, watching her with an expression that appeared to mix sympathy and suspicion in roughly equal measures.

'That seems to be the only explanation.'

'How did you get home?' Murrain asked.

For the first time, she felt uncomfortable about continuing. 'I didn't. I must have ended up at Fraser's. I don't know how. He said we got a taxi, but I can't recall anything about it.'

She saw Murrain exchange another glance with Winston. 'And you definitely don't recall drinking anything more than you've told us about?'

'I can't swear that I didn't, but I've no recollection of it. I must have been very drunk. I don't understand it.'

'You stayed the night at Fraser's?' Winston said. 'Sorry, I'm not intending to be prurient. I just want to be clear about the facts.'

'Yes, I stayed at night at Fraser's,' she said. 'As for being prurient, your guess is as good as mine. The first thing I remember is waking up this morning. Alone, I should add. Fraser was downstairs making coffee.' She was gratified to see Winston had reddened slightly, embarrassed by her bluntness.

'What did he say about last night?' Murrain gave her a smile and she found herself feeling unexpectedly grateful. 'About your getting home, I mean. If you were as drunk as you're suggesting, you can't have been easy to handle.'

'You'd have thought not, wouldn't you? He said I hadn't seemed too drunk on the way back. It was only when we'd got back there that I suddenly seemed to collapse. As if it had hit me out of the blue.'

'But you don't recall getting back there?'

'The last I can remember is being in the bar.'

'How did you feel this morning?'

'Apart from embarrassed that I'd allowed myself to get into that position, you mean?' She hesitated. 'Actually, much better than I'd any right to be. Tired. Bit of a headache, but nothing like the hangover I'd have expected. Fraser was good enough to drop me off at home, but then I'm glad to say I got in on time.' She saw Murrain smile again. 'Well, almost.'

Winston looked at Murrain, then back at Wallace. 'Bert, you'll appreciate that leaking confidential information to the media on a case like this is a very serious matter. Even more so, if it looks as if the leak was in return for some financial inducement.'

'I'd never even consider doing something like that.'

'You're certain you didn't make those calls?'

'As certain as I can be.'

'But you don't recall the latter part of yesterday evening.'

She'd remained very calm up to this moment, but now she could begin to feel emotion welling up inside her. Part misery, part fear, part fury. She continued, trying to keep her voice steady. 'The point is that, even if I had made the calls at that point, I'd have been in no position to talk coherently, let alone to convey confidential information to a journalist in a way that sounded remotely credible. This Jo person, whoever he or she is, would have just thought I was some mad drunk. None of this makes any sense.'

'That's the problem,' Winston said. 'None of it does. At the moment, it's your word against Fraser's. He's insistent he didn't leak the information, though he admits revealing it to you. He says you spent a pleasant evening, and makes no mention of you being noticeably drunk. But he does say you went outside later in the evening first to make a call and then, a bit later, to take an incoming call. He says you told him it was some family matter you had to deal with.'

'Then he's lying. Look, you can surely check this out. You can presumably speak to this Jo person. See who they spoke to.'

'We can do that, and we will, though we'll have to handle it sensitively. I don't want to end up with this becoming a story in its own right. And any journalist is just going to refuse to reveal their source, so it may well take us no further forward.'

'There must be other ways. The taxi driver who took me and Fraser back. They'll surely be able to say what state I was in.' She was struck by the absurdity of wanting to prove that she'd been drunk and incapable the previous evening. 'Or someone in the bar we were in.'

Winston nodded. 'That'll all be looked into. I'm afraid we're going to have to hand this over to professional standards, Bert. I'm sorry, but we have to ensure we're squeaky clean. I'm going to have to suspend you from duty until this is resolved.'

She slumped back in her chair, feeling completely deflated. She hadn't expected this, even a few minutes before. She'd thought the accusations were so absurd that Winston would dismiss them out of hand. 'Yes.' Her voice barely carried. 'I can see you'd need to do that.'

Murrain leaned forward. 'I can drive you home, Bert, if that would be easier.' He looked over at Winston. She saw Winston give a barely perceptible nod. 'But there is one thing we'd like to ask. It's entirely your choice, but it might help resolve things.'

She looked up at him, baffled now. 'What is it?'

CHAPTER THIRTY EIGHT

Ninety minutes later, Murrain entered the main foyer of the hospital. He'd just dropped Bert Wallace at home. She'd appeared mildly shell-shocked, but at least now seemed reassured she was being dealt with fairly and transparently. For his own part, Murrain felt inclined to believe her version of events. He'd worked with Wallace long enough to feel she was trustworthy, and he couldn't envisage her risking her job and career for the sake of a few additional quid. But he'd seen colleagues behave stupidly over the years, and sometimes it was the people you least expected.

The worst part of this was the sense that the team was slowly falling apart. First, he'd lost Joe Milton and Marie Donovan, and now Bert Wallace was off the case. He could hope the changes were only temporary, but he couldn't shake off the sense that the stability he'd established over recent years was crumbling. That was how things were, he knew. People moved on, were transferred or promoted, took retirement. It was life, but it didn't mean he had to like it.

He paused in the foyer and looked around, wondering whether Gill might still be here. It was still only late afternoon and the place was relatively quiet, the outpatient clinics over for the day and the main round of visiting yet to start. There were a few people sitting in the café, but no one he recognised.

He'd spoken briefly to Alan Northcote earlier in the afternoon, but both had agreed that, with investigation now fully underway, it would be useful to have a face-to-face discussion on progress so far. Northcote was working long hours, and Murrain himself was expecting to be working almost around the clock until the investigation produced results, so they'd agreed to meet at the end of the normal office day.

He took the lift up to the executive floor. The

administrative staff had departed for the day, but Northcote had told Murrain to press the bell next to the internal door. He did so, and after a few moments the door buzzed open.

Northcote was standing in his office doorway, waiting for him. 'Good to see you, Kenny. You're a reassuring presence at a difficult time.'

'I'll be more reassured myself once we've identified who's behind this. But thank you.' Murrain didn't fool himself that Northcote's apparently easy-going charm would be sustained if they didn't make progress soon.

Helen Clarke was already sitting at the table, in the process of removing a covering of cling-film from a large plate of sandwiches.

'I thought we might all benefit from a bite to eat,' Northcote said. 'It's been a long day, and I didn't manage any lunch.' He began doling out plates and pouring cups of coffee from a vacuum jug.

'Appreciated,' Murrain said. 'I seem to have skipped lunch as well.'

'How's it all going?' Clarke said.

'Everything's up and running now. We've got schedules of interviews set up. We're in the process of going through all the available CCTV footage from the past four weeks. We're cross-checking all hospital staff and contractors against existing police and other records, in case we can identify anyone with a relevant history.' Murrain had taken a file from his briefcase and extracted a printout which he slid across the table to Northcote. 'That's a summary of everything we've got going on at the moment. It'll give you an idea.'

Northcote picked up the paper, his eyes running down the content. 'Looks very comprehensive. You're confident we're going to find him?'

'Or her. As confident as I can be. We're doing everything possible.'

Northcote picked up a sandwich, peering suspiciously at its contents before taking a bite. 'That doesn't sound like a yes.'

'It wasn't intended to,' Murrain said. 'I don't want to soft-soap either of you. We're doing all the right things and I'm confident that will bring a result. But there are no guarantees. The most straightforward option, from our perspective, would be if the killing was a one-off and there was some connection between killer and victim. We're looking closely at Elizabeth Everard and her family and friends to see if that provides any leads. The worst scenario is that we're dealing with a genuinely random killer. That there's no connection between killer and victim. A Peter Sutcliffe, if you like.'

'Or a Harold Shipman,' Clarke said, earning her a sharp look from Northcote.

'Exactly,' Murrain said. 'That gives us very little to work with. Our best bet in that kind of scenario is that someone witnesses the killer's suspicious behaviour or the killer makes a mistake. That's why it's so important everyone is vigilant.'

'I've sent out another communication today,' Northcote said. 'Reminding everyone of the need to be alert.'

'It's a tricky balance,' Clarke said. 'We don't want to create an atmosphere of paranoia where everyone thinks everyone else is behaving suspiciously.'

Murrain nodded. 'I appreciate that. What's the progress with the other postmortems?'

'As I said, the first couple look to be clean, if that's the right word. There's no evidence the deaths were anything other than natural causes. In particular, no sign of diamorphine. We should have the results of the next two tomorrow morning.'

'Fingers crossed, then. I'd rather be dealing with my first scenario than my second. How's the additional security working out?'

'Not bad, overall,' Northcote said. 'Obviously, it's not exactly convenient, and some of it's adding to our workload and staffing issues, particularly where we're insisting on two staff members carrying out activities normally carried out solo. But people understand the need for it and they're making it work. We've had one or two complaints, but we've also had some appreciative comments.'

'We'll give it a day or two, and see if we need anything more or different,' Murrain said. 'At this stage, I'd rather keep it low key if we can.'

'There is one other thing,' Clarke said.

'Go on.'

'We had another death today,' she said. 'A different kind of unexpected one.'

'How do you mean?'

'One of our maintenance staff,' Northcote said. 'Working on some electrical units in the basement. He didn't report back in as expected this afternoon and wasn't answering his mobile. He was found lying in the corridor. Looked as if he might have fallen off his ladder.'

'An accident?'

'We don't think that was the cause of death. We got a doctor down there as soon as it was reported, and his initial view was that the man most likely had a heart attack. Apparently the individual in question was overweight and a heavy smoker, so it wouldn't necessarily have been a surprise. It's just a pity that he wasn't spotted earlier.'

'I presume this was reported to us?' Murrain said.

'Of course. We told the senior officer on site, and he seems to have done all the right things. The area was cordoned off and I believe he had arranged for your CSI people to examine the scene. The body was moved on to one of the wards to check there was no chance to resuscitation, but other than that nothing was disturbed. I hope we did the right thing?' Northcote's tone implied that, if there was any blame to be allocated, he wasn't intending to accept any share of it.

'It sounds as if everything was handled appropriately,' Murrain said. 'Is there any evidence so far that the death looked suspicious.'

'Not in itself,' Northcote said. 'The doctor who examined the body didn't seem to think so, and there are no other suspicious factors.'

'My worry is it'll set the rumour mill going again,' Clarke said. 'It's one thing for a killer to be targeting patients – awful as that is – but it's something else again if staff think they're being targeted. A whole new level of paranoia.'

'Let's hope the postmortem confirms the doctor's diagnosis.' Murrain was conscious that the ever-present buzzing in his head had risen in intensity while he'd been talking. This time he sensed an image, a scene imprinted inside his head. Two figures, standing head to head. An argument, a disagreement. Something about one of the two figures. Something familiar but unsettling.

Then, unexpectedly, one of the figures turned to look straight at Murrain, as if staring into Murrain's head. It was a short, shocking moment, a feeling of exposure like nothing he had ever previously encountered.

'Are you okay, Kenny?'

The real world recoalesced around him, as if he'd been released back into consciousness. 'Sorry. I was just thinking about something.' He shook his head. 'Must have been what we were talking about. Just triggered some ideas. Funny how the brain works, isn't it?' He took a sandwich, saving himself from saying any more.

Northcote was watching him curiously. 'Okay, I just wanted to run through a few more admin issues. We've managed to secure more space for you on site. Small rooms but they'll be fine for interviews.'

Murrain listened as Northcote talked on, but he was taking in no more than the main points. He was still focused on what he had just experienced. That unprecedented sense of exposure. The sensation had been startling and unnerving, and he felt mentally raw from the impact of it.

'We're also limiting visiting hours as you suggested until this is resolved,' Northcote concluded. 'We don't want to ban visitors altogether, unless you think it's absolutely necessary?'

Murrain forced himself to pay Northcote full attention. 'We should keep an open mind on it. It's conceivable the killer's a visitor, though I assume it would be more difficult for a visitor to find the opportunity to administer an injection than a staff member.'

'Tricky on an open ward, but not impossible. The nurses tend to be busy and wouldn't necessarily be keeping a close eye on individual patients. But if we limit the visiting hours, it's easier for the nurses and other ward staff to be vigilant. Better than having people wandering about the wards all day.'

'We can keep it under review. I'm reluctant to disrupt the usual routines any more than we need to. Let's give it a day or so, then see what the feeling is.'

They arranged a further telephone discussion the following day. Murrain said his farewells and made his way back into the body of the hospital. They now had officers – a mix of plain clothed and uniformed - positioned around the building.

He walked around a selection of the wards, chatting to various of the officers. The general mood was one of boredom. A couple had been called to incidents which had turned out to be false alarms, but most had so far witnessed nothing out of the ordinary. 'I feel a bit of a fraud sitting around,' one said, 'while the staff here are working their socks off.'

Finally, he found himself on Joe Milton's ward. The nurses here knew him by now, but he was pleased to see they treated him with the same caution they'd been advised to apply to all visitors. Marie Donovan was still sitting by Joe's bed.

'Nothing new?'

'No change at all. It's so frustrating. He looks as if there's nothing wrong with him.'

'Let's hope there isn't, really,' Murrain said.

'I just want things to return to normal. Or to how they

were before this happened. It doesn't seem a lot to ask.'

It was nothing and it was everything, Murrain thought. In a moment, everything here could change, for good or for ill. The flickering of an eyelid that indicated a return to consciousness, or the faltering of breath that might portend the slipping away of life. He could understand her tension. She was poised in a stasis that might at any second alter her life forever.

'And now we have a killer on the wards.'

'We have a killer somewhere,' Murrain agreed. 'For the moment, we still have only the one victim, so we don't know how much danger there is to others.'

'It's unnerving, though, isn't it? I'm getting more and more paranoid. Watching each nurse or doctors who treats Joe as if they're about to commit some crime. And I can tell they're all watching each other. Everyone's afraid. What worries me is that I can't be here all the time. They've waived the new visiting hour limits for long-term patients so I'm not driven out on the dot of 8pm, but they don't want me here all night. I go home and lie awake worrying about what might be happening. It's been like that throughout, but now I've got an additional anxiety. Not just Joe's condition, but whether someone might actively try to harm him.'

'The chances of anyone targeting Joe are pretty remote. If this is someone killing at random, they're going to be opportunist. Joe's more secure in here than most patients.' Not least, he added to himself, because the officers stationed in this part of the hospital knew full well it was a colleague lying in here. Nevertheless, Murrain knew his reassuring words would cut little ice.

'I saw Gill again,' Donovan said, unexpectedly. 'She still seems to be hanging around.'

'Really?' Murrain thought back to his own glimpse of Joe's former partner in the café downstairs, 'Where did you see her?'

'I've seen her a couple of times. Once she was getting into the lift on this floor, just as I was coming out of the adjacent one. I called her name but she didn't hear me or she pretended not to. Then I saw her in the foyer going out of the main doors, again just as I was coming out of the lifts. I chased after her, but by the time I got outside she'd disappeared.'

'Has she been visiting Joe?'

'The nurses say not. To be honest, though I can't claim to be enthusiastic about the idea, I wouldn't want to prevent her. She's a right at least to visit him, but she doesn't seem to want to. She just seems to want to – I don't know, hang around.'

'Maybe she's too scared to come in,' Murrain suggested. 'Or maybe she doesn't want to offend you or hurt your feelings, but can't bring herself just to walk away.' He smiled. 'Psychology's not my strong point.'

He looked back at Marie Donovan and was struck by a sudden thought. It was something about the hospital. That was what was making him feel more than usually uneasy. It wasn't that his gifts weren't operating in here – the sensation he'd experienced in Northcote's office disproved that. But it was as if, somehow, their quality was different. He was struggling to find the words to articulate, even to himself, what he was thinking, but it was as if something was interfering with the signal.

He couldn't describe it any more clearly than that. But he realised now why the sensation he'd experienced upstairs had felt both unique and oddly familiar.

The feeling itself – that sense of utter exposure – had been like nothing he'd ever known. But something about it – the feeling of intrusion, of invasiveness – was familiar. He'd experienced something like that once before.

On the night Joe Milton had been swept into the surging river. The night all this had begun. The night Murrain had failed.

The night he'd encountered Edward Crichton.

CHAPTER THIRTY NINE

'She's what?'

Colin Willock gazed at Will Sparrow, his expression suggesting he was deciding whether the younger man was hard of hearing or simply slow on the uptake. 'She's been suspended. From duty.'

'Bert? Suspended?' Sparrow was conscious he was almost certainly confirming Willock's second diagnosis, but for the moment was too taken aback to worry about that. 'For what?'

'I'm not at liberty to divulge the full details. I believe it's connected to the hospital story appearing in the Evening News.'

'They're suggesting Bert was responsible for that?'

'I can only assume so. Or at least she's in the frame for it.'

'Frame would be the right word, then,' Sparrow said. 'Bert's the last person to do something like that.'

'Less likely than you, Will?'

Willock had a habit of twisting or misrepresenting what Sparrow said. It wasn't that Willock was smart or particularly verbally dextrous, but he had a skill for bending the truth in a way that left Sparrow unsure of his own mind. 'It's not something I'd do either. But Bert's as straight as they come. She'd never contemplate anything unethical.'

'You've probably got more faith in other people than I have.'

It occurred to Sparrow that Willock might lack faith in others because he was all too aware of his own failings. 'I've mainly got faith in Bert. It's just not the kind of thing she'd do.'

'We'll have to see how it pans out. The really bad news is that we're now even more short-handed than we were already. And it looks as if we've a third case to look at.' Willock placed a sheaf of printed out papers in front of

Sparrow. 'Kenny's just sent me the postmortem report on Trevor Ollerenshaw. It looks as if we definitely have another one. Same MO. Diamorphine. The circumstances look almost identical to Margaret Perry. Even down to the two mugs in the sink, would you believe?'

Sparrow picked up the postmortem report and skimmed through it. 'Looks like he was dead for around twenty-four hours before the delivery man found him?'

'Something like that. Lucky he was found when he was.'

'Not so lucky for him,' Sparrow said. 'But I see what you mean.'

'I've kicked off all the usual stuff with what resources we've got. He lived in a pretty isolated spot so I'm not hopeful the door-to-doors will tell us very much, but we'll talk to what neighbours there are. CSIs have already been over the house but not found much. The main fingerprints belong either to Ollerenshaw and a cleaner he had in once a week, apart from the few left by the delivery guy when he first went in there.'

'The cleaner couldn't tell us anything?'

'Nothing useful. She was contacted fairly quickly while we were trying to track down a next of kin because Ollerenshaw had her name and number pinned up in the kitchen. She'd last been there a few days before his death and said he seemed his usual self. He was only in his early sixties but seems to have been a bit of a recluse. We've not yet been able to track down any relatives, and the cleaner reckoned he'd never mentioned any close friends.'

'What was his background?'

'Some kind of doctor, apparently.' Willock had been holding a file as well as the postmortem report. He flicked through the pages. 'Neurologist. Last few years before he retired he moved into an academic and teaching role at the university medical school. Smart cookie, from the looks of things.' He dropped the file casually on Sparrow's death. 'I'd like you to look into his background. See if there's anything of interest.'

'What sort of thing?'

'If I knew that, I wouldn't be asking you to look. Anything that looks out of the ordinary. What I'm really interested in is whether there's anything that links our three victims. I'm assuming now we probably have a single killer.'

'We've not spotted any obvious links between Margaret Perry and Vivian Turnbull.'

'Not so far, no. But it's stretching credibility to believe we have three essentially identical cases, all within a few days of each other, each committed by a different killer for different reasons.' He gestured towards Bert Wallace's desk. 'Bert had already started looking at Margaret Perry's and Vivian Turnbull's backgrounds. I don't think she'd really got on to Turnbull yet, but she's made notes on the progress she'd made. You might as well take over all that, and look at the three victims.'

Sparrow gazed gloomily across at the desk. He was a conscientious and hard-working detective, but this sort of work didn't appeal to him. He lacked Wallace's analytical skills and he certainly lacked her concentration and attention to detail. Above all, he lacked her nose for something that simply didn't feel right. She had an instinct for spotting the anomalous, the detail that didn't fit the narrative. Sparrow was more of a plodder. He'd work dutifully through the material, follow up any emerging leads painstakingly and rigorously. 'What about the hospital killing? Do we think that's connected?'

'I don't think we can disregard a possible connection. Kenny's got someone looking into the background of the hospital victim. I'll check who's doing that so you can liaise with them.'

Left to himself, Sparrow examined the file more thoroughly. The first section contained documents relating to the discovery of Ollerenshaw's body. The report prepared by the uniformed officer who had been called out. The statement given by the delivery driver. The CSI report. It was comprehensive and detailed, but it told

Sparrow little he hadn't already gleaned from his conversation with Willock.

The only anomalous detail here, as in the Margaret Perry case, was the presence of the two mugs in the kitchen sink. The cleaner had confirmed this was not characteristic of Ollerenshaw. Sparrow skimmed through her statement, which focused primarily on her last visit to the house and her general impressions of Ollerenshaw. 'A very tidy man. I sometimes wondered why he bothered to employ me, because he generally kept the house spotless. He wouldn't leave crockery in the sink like that, and he certainly wouldn't have left his own unwashed mug in there. He'd either have put it straight in the dishwasher or washed it himself to reuse.'

There was little in the file about Ollerenshaw himself. The information on Ollerenshaw's previous career had initially been supplied by the cleaner, although presumably someone had double-checked the detail. Sparrow turned to his computer and searched for Ollerenshaw's name on-line. He found a few references to him, including a brief biography on the medical school website.

Sparrow skimmed through the other mentions he could find, but they added little of substance. There were a couple of local news stories about his retirement from the medical school, and a couple more about him receiving an honorary doctorate a few years before that. Bland puff pieces clearly based on press releases from the institutions concerned.

He reopened the website for the medical school and checked the names of the senior team. The only number given was the main switchboard, so he started there and eventually found himself talking to the secretary of the Dean of Faculty. Sparrow had no idea whether the Dean would have any knowledge of Ollerenshaw, but it seemed the best place to start.

'I'll see if he's available,' she said, after he'd finished explaining why he wanted to speak to the Dean.

Sparrow had fully expected to be fobbed off, either

with a vague promise of a call back or by having his call transferred to some junior employee. To his slight surprise, after a few moments a smooth sounding voice said, 'Roger Ellis speaking. How can I help you?'

'I'm really just after some background at the moment. I appreciate that you're probably not the best person to tell me about Dr Ollerenshaw, but I was hoping you might be able to direct me to someone who knew him well.'

'As it happens, I did know Trevor well. We went back quite a way. You're saying you believe that Trevor was murdered?'

'Unlawfully killed, anyway. Obviously, at the moment we don't know the full circumstances, but the cause of death was an injection of diamorphine.' This hadn't yet been announced publicly, but Sparrow understood there would be a media release later that day.

'My God. Really?'

'I'm afraid so.'

'Look, this is a bad business. I'm very happy to talk to you about Trevor. But I'd rather talk to you face to face. I presume this is urgent from your point of view?'

'The sooner we start making progress the better.'

'Just let me check,' Ellis said. There was a moment's pause while Ellis presumably checked his on-line diary. 'Look, I can free up an hour or so now if you're able to pop over.'

'No problem. Where do I come?'

Ellis furnished him with directions and some guidance on where to park nearby, and Sparrow agreed to come straight over. He ended the call and walked over to Willock's desk. 'I'm off to the medical school. Going to talk to the Dean.'

'Hobnobbing with the great and the good?'

'He knew Ollerenshaw. He might be able to offer us some insights.'

'And he wasn't prepared to offer these insights over the phone?'

'Funnily enough, he seemed a little cagey.'

'Interesting. Well, off you go, young Will. See what you can dig up.'

'I'll do my best.'

As he turned to go, Sparrow found that Ellis's words were repeating in his head.

Bad business.

What sort of bad business?

CHAPTER FORTY

It took Sparrow longer than he'd expected to navigate the university site to the building where Ellis's office was located. He eventually found his way up to the third floor. Ellis's secretary looked pointedly at her watch as he came through the door.

'Sorry. It wasn't easy to find.'

'Roger's holding off other meetings to talk to you, so I was getting slightly anxious. I'll get you both coffee.'

He was led through into Ellis's office. Ellis himself had an evident presence that presumably explained how he'd secured this job at a relatively young age. He seemed assured and in control, with an expensive-looking suit and an impressively coiffured mop of fair hair. In another life, he might have been conducting surfing lessons on an Australian beach. 'DC Sparrow. Good to meet you.' He gave Sparrow a firm handshake and gestured for him to take a seat at a table that dominated one side of the office.

Sparrow drew out his warrant card. 'I thought you might want to see this. So you can be sure I'm legitimate.'

Ellis took a seat opposite Sparrow. 'I'm sorry if I sounded a little rude on the phone. I had issues with this at this time. Calls from journalists. At least I assumed they were journalists. They tried all kind of tricks to get through to me. Sue out there was brilliant at sussing them out. That was partly why I was prepared to talk to you. If Sue thought you were genuine, you most likely are.' His smile widened. 'Well, of course, now I know you are.'

'As I told you, we're investigating the apparent unlawful killing of Dr Ollerenshaw. I'm just looking for background information.'

'You've had a number of killings like this, haven't you? And I'm aware of the death at the hospital. Do you think they're connected?'

'We're keeping an open mind. Especially on the potential links between the hospital case and the domestic ones.'

Ellis's expression suggested he didn't believe this for a moment. 'Interesting that Trevor Ollerenshaw should have been one of the victims, though.'

'Why do you say that?'

'In a way, I'm reassured you don't know,' Ellis said. 'At the time, I didn't know if we'd done the right thing. That's why I was so paranoid about being caught out by the media. I thought people would jump to the wrong conclusions.'

'I'm afraid I don't understand?'

Ellis looked surprised. 'I didn't know what the police really thought. I assumed there'd be a file on this somewhere, and that you might also feel it merited investigation.'

'I'm sorry. You've lost me, Mr Ellis. There's no police file on Dr Ollerenshaw, or at least nothing I've been able to find. He doesn't appear to be on our records anywhere. Is there any reason he should have been?'

'Not as such, no. It's just… Ah, coffee.'

He waited while the secretary brought in the coffee, and Sparrow could tell he was composing his thoughts in preparation for continuing.

'I'm sorry,' he continued when they were alone again. 'I'm explaining this badly. This goes back a couple of years, a few months before Ollerenshaw retired. As I told you, I'd known Trevor for a good few years. He'd been something of a mentor to me. I'd been unsure what direction I should go in, and at the time he gave me a lot of useful advice. Anyway, I ended up eventually moving into teaching and somehow I managed to climb the greasy pole into this role.'

'And Dr Ollerenshaw?'

'A few years ago, Trevor decided to retire from practising. I wasn't sure why at the time, but I suspect he was having some mental health problems. His wife had died unexpectedly a year or so earlier, and that had hit him hard. I'd thought he might throw himself back into work, but he seemed to do almost the opposite. He was distracted, made mistakes, was unacceptably rude to patients. The hospital management were very supportive, but he knew that he wasn't performing at the right level and he decided to call it a day. He'd planned to retire for good, and he did for a few months. But I wasn't convinced that was what he really wanted, and his departure seemed a loss to the profession. He really was an authority in his field. We were short of expertise in that area, so I offered him a part-time role as a visiting lecturer. It filled a hole for me, and I thought it would give him something constructive to do. That was probably a mistake on my part.'

'What happened?'

'The lecturing and teaching part was fine. Trevor knew his stuff. He wasn't the most inspiring teacher in the world, but he was solid. If I'm honest, he was less committed than I'd expected. He was definitely a different man from the person I'd worked with years before, but that's not surprising. He was older, more jaded, less tolerant of others. We had a few issues about him being abrupt with students, particularly if he thought they were slow on the uptake. And we had some issues with him cutting corners. Not carrying out duties or administration that were part of the job. To be honest, we'd reached the point where we were wondering whether to keep him on anyway. Sorry, I'm just reliving the frustration I felt at the time. But that wasn't really the problem.' Ellis laughed. 'The problem was he fell in with a bad crowd.'

'A bad crowd?' Sparrow was struggling to envisage Ollerenshaw as some kind of delinquent.

'Just my joke. There's a light-hearted rivalry between us real medics and some of the the other disciplines in the university. In this particular case, psychologists.'

'I'm not sure I understand.'

'We medical types are sceptical of psychologists. We see psychology as a kind of pseudoscience. Lots of statistics and unfalsifiable theories, but not much empirical evidence. Which I'm sure is unfair. But it was an area that always interested Trevor because of the overlaps with his own specialism. He was particularly intrigued by the extent to which psychological phenomena could be attributed to neurological factors or conditions. He'd done research in the area earlier in his career, and he'd been disappointed he hadn't taken it further.'

'So he was involved in some kind of psychological research?'

'He was an old friend of a chap called Gordon Fenwick—'

'Gordon Fenwick?'

Ellis looked curiously at Sparrow. 'You've heard of him?'

It had taken Sparrow a moment to recall why the name Gordon Fenwick was familiar. They'd come across Fenwick in connection with the Edward Crichton case – the case that had resulted in Joe Milton's current state. Fenwick had died a year or before, suffering from Alzheimer's Syndrome and had apparently had only peripheral links with the case, but he'd been one of the academics involved in a psychological study in which both Crichton and Kenny Murrain had participated years before. It was no doubt nothing more than a coincidence, but one that left Sparrow feeling uneasy. 'The name rang a bell. I came across a mention of him in a case I was involved in recently.'

Ellis raised an eyebrow. 'I ought to be surprised, but somehow I'm not. I only met Fenwick a few times, but there was something a bit odd about him. A bit obsessive. Mind you, it may not be fair to judge. By the time I met him, his faculties were going. I met him at a couple of university events, and it was obvious even then that he was being shielded by his wife. He was the last person Trevor should have got himself involved with.'

'I'm not sure I understand.'

'Given what Fenwick and Trevor had been up to.' Ellis paused. 'The tests.'

'Tests?'

'This was all unofficial, you understand? Fenwick apparently had history in that respect. He had a knack of securing funding from questionable sources including, as I understand it, various clandestine government bodies. There were other figures involved in the tests who were rumoured to be part of the intelligence services. All I know is they weren't part of the university and they disappeared into the woodwork after everything hit the fan.'

'What were these tests?'

'Another part of Fenwick's long-standing obsession with – well, I'm not even sure what you call it. Telepathy. Psychic powers. Second sight. That kind of mumbo-jumbo. One of the individuals involved in this study – in fact, one of the two who was rumoured to be a spook or whatever it was – supposedly had gifts in that direction. Not just telepathy, but an actual ability to influence others' thinking and behaviour. Some nonsense of that kind. I think Trevor probably approached all this in a genuinely scientific spirit. I suspect he was more unstable than any of us realised. He was still grieving for his wife, and I wonder if he was looking for some reality beyond the purely material.' Ellis shrugged. 'Who knows?'

'What was the nature of the tests?'

'They involved this individual – the one with the supposed gift or powers – trying to exercise them on a number of subjects, all undergraduate volunteers. This was followed by tests to assess the cognitive and psychological impact on the subjects. We subsequently discovered that Trevor had been making unauthorised use of medical school equipment to carry out scans on some of the subjects. Clearly, that was completely unacceptable, even putting aside what happened.' Ellis was silent for a moment. 'Two of the undergraduates involved took their own lives. Almost certainly coincidence, of course. They were both individuals already suffering from severe mental health problems. But for that reason they shouldn't have been dabbling in anything like this, and Fenwick should have taken more responsibility for their well-being.'

'Were the police informed?'

'I imagine it went through the usual formal processes,' Ellis said vaguely. 'There was no suggestion that anything unlawful had occurred. Irresponsible, possibly, but not unlawful. For the university authorities, it was the last straw as far as Fenwick was concerned. He was due to retire shortly anyway so rather than any kind of protracted disciplinary process – which I imagine might have uncovered procedural shortcomings on all sides, if you get my drift – he was allowed to leave with a supposedly unblemished record. He'd had a distinguished career, whatever his failings.'

Sparrow thought about the two students whose lives had been lost, and wondered whether he could bring himself to share Ellis's generosity. 'What about Ollerenshaw?'

'Trevor was collateral damage in the whole thing. Though unlike Fenwick he'd clearly committed an actual disciplinary offence. Again we thought it simpler just to terminate his contract with us. He'd only been on a short-term arrangement, and there didn't seem much point in going through a protracted disciplinary process if we weren't going to renew his employment anyway.' Ellis paused, as if considering what he'd just said. 'I still don't know if that was the right thing. There was part of me thought we owed it to the students who'd lost their lives to do more. Trevor must have known how irresponsible he was being. Anyway, that's the story. I thought you ought to be aware of it, and I'm not sure you'd have heard it from any other source. It was all quite effectively brushed under the carpet at the time.'

'You were keen not to tell me over the phone?'

'I wanted to be sure you weren't just some journalist who'd got the sniff of a story.' Ellis hesitated. 'And there was another reason, although it makes me sound as if I'm losing my marbles myself. When we were originally dealing with the aftermath of this, I had a couple of odd calls. Sue put them through to me because she didn't know what to make of them. Some chap who purported to be a government official. He was keen to know what we were doing about Trevor's case. Obviously, I told him that we didn't discuss our business with outsiders. There was something oddly threatening about his tone, although he didn't say anything explicitly. He even gave me his name. Hang on...' He rose and walked over to a filing cabinet in the corner of the room and, after a moment's search, pulled a file from one of the lower drawers. 'I kept a file on the whole thing just in case it did turn nasty in some way.' He slid the open file across the desk towards Sparrow. 'Here's the note I made of the call. He gave me a number to call him back if I should decide I wanted to talk to him. Needless to say, I never did.'

Sparrow skimmed through the short file note, then looked up at Ellis. 'He said his name was Frank Perry?'

'If that's what I wrote down, it must be what he told me. Does that mean something to you?'

'You may have seen that one of our victims is a Mrs Margaret Perry. Her late husband was called Frank.'

'You think this could be the same man?' Ellis gestured to the file.

'It's a strange coincidence. Do you mind if I have a look at the file?'

'Take it with you if you like.'

Sparrow pulled the file towards him and flicked through the various documents. There wasn't much. The file mainly comprised notes of the interviews conducted with Ollerenshaw at the time, along with contextual notes produced by Ellis. Ollerenshaw's main defence was that Fenwick was a reputable figure in his field, and Ollerenshaw had assumed the study had been officially sanctioned by the university. With regard to his own unauthorised use of medical school equipment, Ollerenshaw had no defence to offer other than that he hadn't realised anyone would mind.

So far, so uninteresting. But then, on the second page of the note, Sparrow found a list of those involved in

Fenwick's study. This included the names of the students who had participated, as well as the academics and others who had been part of the group. There was one name there that rang a bell in Sparrow's mind. A name he'd heard someone mention quite recently but he couldn't immediately remember who or in what context.

But it was another name that had first caught his eye. A name mentioned frequently by his colleagues in recent weeks. A name all too unnervingly familiar.

CHAPTER FORTY ONE

Murrain had received the call a couple of hours before. He'd asked for the checks to be expedited, and the police doctor had been as good as his word.

'You're sure?'

'Kenny, how long have you known me? I'm not going to cut corners on something like this.'

'Of course not. But I don't want to cause her any unnecessary distress.'

'The one positive aspect,' the doctor went on, 'is that there's no evidence of actual rape. By which I mean no evidence intercourse actually took place.'

'Can you be certain of that?'

'Not absolutely after the time delay. But my judgement would be that it didn't.'

'I suppose that's something. You'll be sharing this information with her presumably?'

'As soon as I'm off the phone to you. She was happy I should give you any information first, though. She thought you'd want to get things moving.'

'Too bloody right. And – well, sorry to ask you again, but there's no question? From an analytical perspective I mean. You couldn't have a false positive, or whatever the term is?'

'You can be confident, Kenny. Another few hours and it might have been a different matter. You were right to get it checked when you did.'

'I'm glad I got something right. You'll be sending the formal report over?'

'As soon as I've written it up, which I'll do as soon as I've spoken to her. I'll send it over by close of play.'

'Thanks. Really appreciated.'

'No worries, Kenny. Only too happy,' the doctor said. 'Little bastard.'

An hour later, Murrain was sitting in one of the interview rooms with a copy of the medical report in front of him. Colin Willock was sitting by his side, and facing him was a white-faced Daniel Fraser. Next to Fraser was Brian Thomas, a solicitor Murrain knew well from previous investigations. Murrain had finished explaining that, although Fraser had not yet been arrested or charged, the interview was being conducted under caution. 'I take it you've explained to your client what his rights are?' he asked Thomas.

Thomas nodded. Murrain's experience was that Thomas was a reasonable and realistic advocate of his clients' rights, but by no means a soft touch.

'Can you describe to us how you spent the evening before last? Wednesday, that is,' Murrain asked Fraser, once they'd completed the interview formalities.

'Wednesday?' Fraser exchanged a look with Thomas.

'Just describe the evening as fully as you can, Daniel,' the solicitor said. 'I understand you met Ms Wallace for a drink?'

'I met her after work. We went for a drink in a place in the city centre.'

'Can I ask how you knew Ms Wallace?' Murrain said.

'I'd met her professionally. Through work.'

'You work for the Coroner's Office?'

'That's right. I had some dealings with her in respect of Margaret Perry's death.'

'You must be aware of that already, Chief Inspector,' Thomas interposed.

'She was our first point of liaison with you on that. You shared various pieces of information with her in respect of the Coroner's conclusions.'

'My client was under the impression that it was a professional relationship and that he could rely on DC Wallace's discretion,' Thomas said.

'Of course,' Murrain said. 'As far as I'm aware, Ms Wallace respected that discretion.'

Thomas said, 'Perhaps continue your description of what happened on Wednesday night, Daniel.'

'As I said, I'd asked Bert – Ms Wallace – if she fancied

going for a drink sometime. She seemed keen so we'd agreed to meet that evening. Anyway, we had a couple of drinks in the pub—'

'Can I ask what Ms Wallace was drinking?' Willock said.

'Lager. Just halves.'

'You had two drinks there, or just one?'

'Perhaps it was just one.' Fraser frowned. 'I can't remember exactly. Bert said she wasn't much of a drinker.' He paused, perhaps to emphasise the significance of that statement. 'Anyway, we suggested going for a bite to eat.'

'Can you recall who suggested that?' Willock asked. 'Was it you or Ms Wallace?'

'It just sort of came up. I knew an Italian place round there. Fairly cheap and cheerful. We went there, and had a pizza.'

'You drank some more in the restaurant?'

'We had some wine. We shared a bottle of house red.'

'How did Ms Wallace seem at this point?'

'I'm not sure what—'

'Did she seem inebriated, for example?' Willock had already spoken to the manager of the restaurant. He recalled the young couple, but had noticed nothing untoward or unusual in their behaviour.

'I'm not sure my client's really in a position to offer an opinion on Ms Wallace's state of inebriation,' Thomas said.

Willock shrugged. 'I just wondered how she seemed. Whether she appeared overly boisterous or loud, for example.'

'She was in good spirits, but I wouldn't have said any more than that.'

'Did you have any other drinks in the restaurant?'

'Just a coffee. I suggested we should maybe have a brandy or a grappa or something, but in the end we decided to move on.'

'Where did you move on to?' Willock seemed in his element, now, Murrain thought, leading Fraser gently along in his narrative.

'Another bar round the corner.' Fraser gave the name of a hostelry that meant nothing to Murrain. Again, Willock had already called the place and spoken to the manager, who this time had been unable to recollect seeing Fraser or Wallace. He had however confirmed they'd had no issues with drunken customers that evening.

'You had more drinks there?'

'A couple. I can't remember exactly.'

'Did Ms Wallace continue drinking halves of lager or did she move on to something else?'

Murrain saw Fraser exchange another look with Thomas. Murrain suspected Fraser wanted to claim Wallace had moved on to something stronger, but was unsure how much information the police already had. Thomas gave an almost invisible shake of the head.

'I can't remember exactly,' Fraser said. 'I was drinking pints. I think she probably did stick to halves.'

'Can you recall how many drinks you had there?'

'Not exactly. We didn't stay late.'

Willock was silent for a moment, as if contemplating what Fraser had just said. 'When you were questioned about the apparent leakage of confidential information to the media, you said you'd shared information with Ms Wallace in the course of Wednesday evening. Is that the case?'

'I gave her some information in confidence.' Despite Willock's change in tack, Fraser had clearly been expecting the question. 'I realise now that was a mistake, but I thought I'd made it clear it shouldn't be shared any further.'

Thomas leaned forward. 'While my client regrets his action, I'm not aware that it constitutes a criminal offence.'

'I'm just trying to clarify the sequence of events across the evening,' Willock said. 'You also said that Ms Wallace went outside on two occasions to deal with phone calls?'

Murrain could almost see Fraser's mind working. 'I think so.'

'You think so?'

'We'd both had a few drinks. I can't remember it particularly clearly.' Fraser looked across at Thomas as if hoping to be helped out. 'She went off to the ladies at first, I think. She was longer than I'd expected, and she apologised and said she had to make a call. A bit later her phone rang and she went out again to take the call. She said it was noisy in the bar and she couldn't hear properly.'

'She didn't tell you what these calls were about?'

'She said it was some family issue. But looking back now—'

Thomas intervened smoothly. 'I don't think it's for my client to speculate on what Ms Wallace's calls may or may not have been about. I take it you've checked up on all this in any case.'

Willock turned back to Fraser. 'Let's talk about the rest of the evening. What time did you leave the bar?'

'About ten, maybe? I was beginning to think that Bert had probably had enough.'

'She was drunk?'

'Not drunk, exactly. She just seemed very tired. Almost falling asleep in the bar. She'd been planning to get the tram home, but I was concerned whether she'd be okay. If nothing else, I was worried she'd sleep through her stop. So I suggested we get a cab to my place.'

The police had been trying to track down the cab driver who'd picked up Fraser and Wallace, but so far without any luck. Wallace had also allowed them to examine her phone's location services, which indicated they'd left the bar earlier than Fraser had suggested.

'Ms Wallace was happy to do that?'

'She seemed to be.' Fraser held up his hands. 'I made it clear I wasn't intending to – well, try anything on with her. I just wanted to make sure she was all right.'

'What happened when you reached your house?'

'She'd fallen asleep in the cab and still seemed very woozy. I assumed she'd probably had a heavy day, and after a few drinks the exhaustion had just hit her. I got her out of the cab and into the house. I'd been planning to take her into the living room and maybe have another drink, but she could barely stand up. In the end, I helped her up the stairs and into the bedroom.'

'Your bedroom?'

'Yes. I've a spare room but it wasn't really prepared for visitors, so I thought she'd be more comfortable using mine.'

'Did you undress her?'

'I just helped her lie down on the bed. She must have undressed herself after I'd gone downstairs.'

'What did you do after that?'

'Not much. I watched a bit of the news. Then I went to bed. In the spare room.'

'Mr Fraser. You've already been informed that traces of a so-called date-rape drug were found in Ms Wallace's body the following day. Here's a copy of the report.' Willock slid a copy of the doctor's report across the desk towards Fraser, who picked it up and scanned through the contents before passing it to Thomas. 'Do you have any explanation as to how those traces came to be there?'

'I don't know. I've been thinking hard about it. I can only assume someone slipped something into her drink at the bar. It would explain why she became so sleepy.'

'Someone,' Willock said. 'But not you?'

'I— No, not me. I wouldn't do something like that.'

'Why would anyone else do it? If she was clearly with you, I mean.'

'I don't know. Perhaps they just thought it would be funny.'

'Funny,' Willock repeated. 'Isn't it more likely you doctored her drink in the hope that you'd be able to take advantage of her drugged state?'

'With respect,' Thomas said, 'my client can only tell you what he did or didn't do. He's hardly in a position to speculate on anyone else's motives in this matter.'

'Why would I have drugged her in the bar?' Fraser said. 'That would have left me with the task of getting in and out of the taxi. If I'd been going to drug her, surely if would have been better to have waited till we reached my house.'

Murrain could see Thomas momentarily close his eyes. Willock said quietly, 'Except of course, if she hadn't been drugged, she might not have agreed to come back with you in the first place.'

'I think we need to be clear,' Thomas said. 'Are you accusing my client of drugging Ms Wallace?'

'At the moment, we're conducting an investigation,' Murrain said. 'We haven't charged your client, and we're still in the process of gathering evidence. There is one other point.'

'Go on,' Thomas said.

'The location device on Ms Wallace's phone indicates that she and presumably you left the bar rather earlier than you suggested. A little before 9.30pm, in fact.'

'Like I said, I'm a bit hazy about the detail. Perhaps it was earlier than I thought.'

'The phone also indicates that two phone calls were made from her phone, one outgoing, the other incoming, in line with what you told us.'

'Well, I said so—'

'The only issue is that, from the location of the phone, it looks as if those calls were made after you'd both left the bar and were on your way to your home. In other words, the calls were made from the taxi. Do you have any recollection of Ms Wallace making or receiving calls in the taxi?'

This time the silence seemed almost interminable. 'No, I don't think so.'

'You don't think so,' Willock repeated. 'You said that she'd fallen asleep?'

'Well, yes.'

'What about you, Mr Fraser? Did you make any calls in the taxi?'

Thomas looked as if he was about to interrupt, but then seemed to think better of it. Fraser was silent for another few seconds, then said, 'I can show you my phone.'

'I was thinking,' Willock continued, 'that perhaps you

made the calls on Ms Wallace's phone.'

Fraser opened and then closed his mouth, clearly unable to concoct an explanation which made any sense. 'I don't know.'

'You don't know whether you – well, let's say borrowed Ms Wallace's phone to make a call to the Evening News newsdesk?'

'I…'

'If you know the recipient of the call, presumably you can confirm whether the caller was male or female?' Thomas said.

'At present, the recipient of the calls is refusing to confirm or deny anything about the source of their information,' Murrain said. 'Given that the leakage of the story isn't in itself a criminal matter, I think there's little we can do to change their mind.'

'So why are you seeking to accuse my client of something that isn't a criminal matter?'

'The leaking of the information isn't a criminal offence,' Murrain said. 'Though it's no doubt a disciplinary issue. But the unauthorised use of a mobile phone belonging to one of my officers with the intention of implicating her in the leak, resulting in her suspension from duty is potentially a different matter. And I think we can all agree that the administering of a controlled substance to an unwilling recipient constitutes a criminal offence.'

'Are you accusing my client of that?'

'We're asking him to provide us with a convincing explanation of how the drug came to be in Ms Wallace's body, and, alongside that, of how those calls were made on her phone while she and Mr Fraser were travelling in a taxi.'

Murrain could see Thomas weighing up the options. Murrain himself had little doubt Fraser had been lying, and he imagined Thomas thought the same. The question was whether Fraser was prepared to continue bluffing it out, or whether he might see the benefits of being more co-operative.

The usual feelings were pulsing at the back of Murrain's mind, and there was a sense of something focused on Fraser. As if there was a thread there that might be worth pulling. He could express it no more clearly than that.

Thomas was gazing thoughtfully at Fraser. Finally, he turned back to Murrain. 'I wonder if you could give me a few minutes alone with my client. There are a few issues I'd like to talk through with him.'

CHAPTER FORTY TWO

Murrain closed the door of the interview room firmly behind him before turning to Willock. 'What do you think?'

'He's lying through his teeth and guilty as hell.'

'I'd have said so. He knows his story doesn't hang together. The question's whether he's going to come clean. The main problem is that the weakest part of his story relates to the phone calls. He was clearly thrown when we told him we'd tracked the location of the phone. If the calls were made in the taxi, either he took Bert's phone and made them or he'd have heard Bert making them, which doesn't square with the rest of his story. We're on shakier ground with the date-rape drug. If he continues to deny he administered it, it's going to be hard for us to prove he's lying. It's conceivable that someone else doctored her drink in the bar for a supposed laugh. Not likely, but conceivable. We've no evidence he actually assaulted her. In fact, the evidence indicates that he most likely didn't.'

'My instinct's that he'll cave. If he's lying, he won't have the bottle or the resilience to carry it off. And Thomas is no fool. He'll persuade Fraser that, as a young man with no criminal record, he'll be better off admitting he made a terrible mistake, co-operating fully with the police, pleading guilty to any charges, and keeping his fingers crossed he's treated leniently.'

As they'd been talking, they'd gradually retreated away from the interview room towards the far end of the corridor. From here, Murrain could see through the glass partitions into the open plan office that housed the majority of the team. Will Sparrow was sitting facing them, tapping away on his computer. As he caught sight of Murrain and Willock, he hurried out of the office towards them.

'Can you spare me a minute? I think it might be important.'

'We're a bit busy at the moment,' Willock said.

Murrain offered Sparrow a smile. 'We're just in an adjournment from an interview, so we might get interrupted. But fire away. We can always finish off afterwards.'

'You asked me to dig out some background on Ollerenshaw,' Sparrow said to Willock. 'I did some phoning round and ended up talking to his former boss at the medical school. It seems Ollerenshaw left there under something of a cloud.' He briefly recounted what Ellis had told him.

'Gordon Fenwick? So he continued with his questionable studies then?' Murrain himself had been involved in one of Fenwick's early studies into supposedly paranormal abilities.

'Not just that,' Sparrow said. 'It looks as if he was working with at least one of the same subjects. Have a look.' He handed Murrain a copy of the file note prepared by Ellis.

Murrain scanned down the note then handed it to Willock. 'Edward Crichton.'

'Looks like it.'

Alongside Murrain himself, Crichton had been a participant in a psychological study conducted years before by Gordon Fenwick. The purpose of the study, in broad terms, had been to test and explore the abilities of a range of subjects who had claimed experience of paranormal insights.

In the majority of cases, the study had found no compelling evidence to support the existence of such abilities. Only a small proportion had produced statistically significant results, including Murrain himself. Murrain had had little doubt his own gifts were genuine, even if he found them unfathomable. But he had also come away from the study with a recognition – shared by Gordon Fenwick and others – that Crichton's gifts were significantly more substantial.

The study had ended in disarray when Crichton had attacked another participant, accusing him of 'spying' on

Crichton's thoughts. Even at that point it was clear that, whatever gifts he might possess, Crichton was a highly unstable figure, prone to a paranoia exacerbated by the nature of his abilities.

Fenwick's original study had not been authorised by his university, and its sources of funding had been opaque. Murrain assumed at least part of the funding had been derived from the intelligence services, who had had an interest in the subject and in Crichton in particular. It was unclear what had happened to Crichton after the study. He'd never been arrested or charged in connection with the assault, and it seemed likely that he had been subjected to further study. At some point, he had gone missing, his gifts supposedly of interest to various foreign powers. Murrain, more sceptically, had been inclined to believe the intelligence services had simply lost track of him.

To Murrain's knowledge, Crichton had reemerged only relatively recently, linked to their investigation of a series of murders. That investigation had ultimately led to the rainswept encounter in which both Crichton and Joe Milton had been dragged into the swollen river. Now, Milton was lying in a coma and Crichton's whereabouts were unknown.

Ellis's file-note implied that Crichton had reappeared earlier than the intelligence services had led the police to believe. Murrain assumed they had also funded this more recent study of Fenwick's, with the aim of trying to gain some neurological understanding of Crichton's gifts. Good luck with that, Murrain thought.

If Crichton had been back on the intelligence services' radar for some years – prior to Fenwick's retirement and increasing dementia – that raised the question of whether he had been under surveillance at the time he'd apparently committed the murders. From his limited dealings with spooks over the years, Murrain thought anything was possible. They were quite capable of allowing Crichton to continue killing if that suited their wider objectives. But it was equally possible they'd simply lost contact with

Crichton again until the killings had begun.

The combination of ruthlessness and sheer ineptitude could render Murrain coldly furious, especially if he allowed himself to think of Joe Milton as one of its victims. For the moment, though, he was more concerned about this unexpected connection – between Trevor Ollerenshaw and Edward Crichton.

'There's another familiar name on here.' Willock held out the note for Murrain. 'In the list of those involved in the study overall.'

Murrain took the note back and re-read it more carefully. Ellis had appended a list of those involved in Fenwick's study which appeared to have been cut and pasted from some another source. Most of the names meant nothing, but there was one he had heard relatively recently. It took him a moment to place it.

'You think it's the same one?'

'It's a fairly unusual name. But it might just be coincidence, I suppose.'

Sparrow was nodding. 'I thought the name sounded familiar, too. I've just been checking Bert's notes.'

'Speaking of Bert,' Murrain said. 'I think we might have a development.' He nodded over Willock's shoulder, indicating Brian Thomas striding towards them.

Sparrow took the file note and disappeared back into the office, while Murrain stepped forward to greet Thomas.

'I've had a discussion with my client,' Thomas said. 'He's ready to say a little more to you. I've explained the likely implications to him.'

Murrain and Willock followed Thomas back into the interview room. Fraser looked shrunken, as if he'd been physically beaten into submission. Thomas took a seat beside him, and Murrain went through the formalities of reconvening the interview.

Daniel,' Thomas said. 'It's probably best if you take DCI Murrain and DS Willock through exactly what happened on Wednesday evening. Take your time.'

Fraser sat for a moment as if unable to start. 'Most of what I told you was true. I met her – Bert Wallace – for a drink. She drank what I said she did, I think. A half in the first pub, some of the wine in the restaurant, though I probably drank more than half the bottle. Then a couple more halves in the second bar. Not a lot over the evening. She was quite sober.'

'Go on,Daniel.'

'Then I spiked her last drink. She went to the Ladies, and I did it while she was in there.'

Murrain was silent for a moment. 'Why did you do that?'

'I don't know, exactly.' Fraser looked genuinely bewildered, as if unable to comprehend his own actions. 'Someone had suggested it to me. I wasn't taking it very seriously. I didn't even know if it would work…'

'What did you expect to happen?'

'I don't know, exactly. But it wasn't – well, what it looked like…'

'Go on,' Murrain prompted.

'It was partly about the information leaks.' He looked miserably at Thomas. 'It's true. I had been leaking information from the Coroner's Office. I had an arrangement with a local journalist. It wasn't as if I told them anything highly confidential. Everything I told them would have ended up in the public domain, anyway. But I gave them advance tips on any interesting stories. I'd done it with the Margaret Perry death. They paid me a few quid for any good ones.'

Murrain offered no response, knowing the silence would encourage Fraser to continue his attempted self-justification.

'I asked for a bit more on the hospital story, because I knew it was going to be a big deal. But I was nervous about it for the same reason. It felt in a different league from the bits and pieces I'd fed them before. I knew there'd be a lot more interest in where the story had come from.' He looked around at the others in the room, as if hoping that one of them would offer him some kind of absolution. 'I'd phoned the journalist earlier that afternoon, before I met up with Bert. But I was getting cold feet. I realised there'd probably be some more serious investigation, and there were only a handful of people who'd had access to the information.'

'So you thought you'd put Ms Wallace in the frame?' Willock said coldly.

'I wasn't thinking very clearly, I had the drug, but I hadn't really been intending to use it. It was just one of those ideas you play around with. I suppose it gave me a sense of power.'

'Have you ever used this kind of drug before?' Murrain asked gently. 'With other women, I mean?'

'No, of course not. I mean, to be honest, I've not had many opportunities even to think about it. I hadn't really been out with anyone for – well, for quite a while.'

Willock raise an eyebrow, his expression suggesting he knew exactly what sort of man Fraser was. 'But you used it this time?'

'I just thought...' Fraser sat back as if gathering his thoughts. 'I'd told Bert about the hospital story earlier in the evening. I was trying to spread the blame a bit. Ensure more people were in on the story if there was an investigation. I hadn't thought about actually framing her.'

'But then you did.'

'The idea just came to me. I'd been told the main effect of the drug was likely to be to make the user sleepy. I thought if it affected her that way, I might have a chance to use her phone to call the journalist. It was a stupid plan, but I'd had a few drinks myself and I was getting jittery.'

'Talk us through what happened,' Murrain said. 'You added the drug to her drink while she was in the lavatory. Then what?'

'It worked more quickly than I'd expected. She started to look quite sleepy, so I thought I'd better get her out of the bar and home as quickly as I could. I called a taxi and we went outside to wait for it. The cold air revived her a bit, so it was better than it might have been. But by the time the taxi got there she was almost asleep on my shoulder. The driver obviously thought she'd just had a few too many. Once we were in the cab, she fell fully asleep again. So I did as I'd planned. I left a message for the journalist, saying I'd got a few more details I hadn't shared the first time. When they called back, I made up a few things just to make it sound as if I'd a reason for calling. Then we got back to my place. Bert woke up a bit when I got her out of the car, and I was able to help her into the house and up to the bedroom.' He looked around at them again, his expression anguished. 'After that, it happened as I said. I didn't touch her. I didn't do anything. I just laid her down on the bed, made sure she was all right, and left her. I didn't even help her undress. She must have done that herself sometime in the night.'

'Yet you had this drug with you,' Willock pointed out. 'You didn't have it just to frame someone for leaking information.'

'I can only tell you the truth. I hadn't really taken the drug seriously. It was just an idea. Knowing I could do it if I chose to.'

'And you're saying that, having used the drug, you chose to do nothing?'

Fraser stared desolately at Willock. 'That's exactly what I'm saying. I've regretted it since I did it, but I was never seriously intending...'

'So why do it? Willock pressed. 'Just to frame her for leaking the information?'

'Even that was just a spur of the moment thing. It just seemed like the perfect insurance policy if it looked like I was going to be found out. I hadn't thought it through. But I never intended anything more than that, I swear.'

Murrain leaned back in his chair and gazed at Fraser through half-closed eyes. The voices in his head had grown even louder, telling him that somehow this was important. It wasn't about Fraser and whatever he might or might not have done. It was something else.

'Funnily enough,' Murrain said, finally, 'I'm inclined to believe you. And for the moment I'm inclined to believe you didn't assault Ms Wallace.'

'I'm assuming you have no evidence to indicate otherwise?' Thomas said.

Murrain ignored the question. Thomas would know full well that if any such evidence existed, the police would have produced it by now. 'The fact remains, Daniel, that for whatever reason you administered a controlled drug to Ms Wallace without her permission. That's a serious offence.'

'My client's well aware of the seriousness of what he did,' Thomas said. 'Clearly, he deeply regrets his actions.'

'The best way to demonstrate his regret, I'd suggest, would be for your client to co-operate with us as fully as possible.'

'I'm sure my client will be happy to do anything in his power.'

'Perhaps then your client could begin by telling us how he obtained the drug?'

Fraser had clearly not been expecting the question. He turned to Thomas as if seeking advice. Thomas nodded gently.

'A friend of mine suggested it,' Fraser said. 'I don't want to get him into trouble. He's not a dealer or anything. He was just talking about various things, and I got curious. He knew where to go.'

'I can't promise we won't need your friend's name, Daniel. It may depend on how matters proceed. But that's not our primary concern. We're mainly interested just to know where you were able to procure the drug.'

'I thought it was going to be some dodgy backstreet character. It was all a bit convoluted. My friend gave me a number to call, and then I had to go through various other numbers. Then my friend had to vouch for me. It was only when I finally got to the end of it that I realised why it was so cloak and dagger.'

'Why was that?'

Fraser was talking more freely now, clearly glad to have moved on from discussing his own guilt, 'It wasn't what I expected. When I eventually spoke to him, it turned out he was a doctor. A GP. I suppose that was how he got hold of the drugs. He was quite talkative over the phone. Told me he mainly dealt in prescription drugs, but he could get pretty much anything for the right price. What I wanted was straightforward, he said, though he still charged me enough for it.'

'How did you actually go about receiving the drug?' Murrain asked. 'The practicalities of it, I mean.'

'He'd only accept cash. He had some guy who did the leg work for him, and he arranged to meet me in a pub in town. I handed over the money in an envelope, and he gave me the drug. It was as simple as that.'

'Could you give us a description of the person you met?' Willock asked.

'Probably. Youngish guy. In his late twenties, I guess. Skinny. Clean shaven. Shortish hair.'

'Nothing particularly distinctive about him?' Murrain wasn't too bothered. Most likely, the go-between was just that, some kid making a bit of money doing the doctor's dirty work. They could go through the motions of trying to identify him later, if only as a possible route to the dealer himself.

'Not really, I'm afraid.'

'What about the doctor? Did he give you any clues about himself?'

'He told me his name.'

Murrain exchanged a glance with Willock. 'Really?'

'I was surprised. I'd expected him to be very cagey given the lengths I'd had to go to contact him, but he was really relaxed. He seemed happy to talk about himself, and he was interested in my background. And, yes, he told me his name.'

'And who did he tell you he was?'

'He said his name was Anderson – no, not Anderson, Amberson. He made some reference to a film when he told me it but that meant nothing to me. That was it, though. Amberson. Kyle Amberson.'

Murrain looked over at Willock, who simply shrugged and said, 'It's a small world.'

CHAPTER FORTY THREE

Amberson looked up at the clock on the consulting room wall. Nearly eight-thirty. With one of his colleagues, he'd been covering the evening surgery, though his last appointment had ended more than half an hour ago. He'd spent the intervening period finishing off the outstanding administration from the day, as well as checking his schedule for the rest of the week.

At least that was what he told himself he was doing. It wasn't as if he had any particular reason to rush home for his usual date with a ready-meal, a can of beer and some brain-numbing television. He was happy to hang around here for as long as necessary.

Since his discussion with Romy Purslake, he'd spent his non-working hours brooding on what she'd said. At first, he'd found it hard to take it in. When he'd first joined the practice, Amberson had seen Andrew Carnforth as the model of professional respectability. Prissy and pedantic, yes, but a pillar of the practice and the local community. Everything about him was neat, tidy and precise, and he'd greeted Amberson even at their first meeting with a variant on his usual lecture on propriety, ethics and the good name of the practice.

Was it possible Romy Purslake was simply wrong? That her supposed reliable sources were misleading her? Amberson had no way of judging, but he couldn't imagine why anyone would want to badmouth Carnforth in this way unless it was true. And Purslake had seemed very certain that the revelations could be trusted. The whole account was sufficiently detailed to have the ring of truth, particularly given what Jude Calman had already told him.

These things happened, Amberson knew. The most respectable people sometimes turned out to have hidden lives, and people could be sucked into criminality even before they realised what was happening.

Amberson had been fretting and worrying about it ever

since. He had no real desire to expose Carnforth – though he supposed that if the claims were true, he would have no choice. He simply wanted to know the truth.

The main question was how he could best resolve his anxieties. Romy Purslake had sought his involvement because she wanted someone she could trust inside the practice. At the time, although he'd made some positive noises, he'd had no intention of actually doing anything. It was only later, on his own, that he'd found his thoughts returning repeatedly to Carnforth.

Amberson looked back up at the clock. 8.40pm. He rose from his seat, walked across the room, opened the door and listened. The surgery was silent. The lights were still on in the corridor, but that was to be expected. The convention was that the last person to leave turned off the remaining lights in the public areas and double-checked everything was locked up. It wasn't unusual for individual GPs to work late, even after the final appointments were concluded, catching up on administration and any other tasks they'd not managed to fit into the day.

He walked down the corridor into the main waiting area. Again, everywhere was silent and deserted. The lights behind reception were turned off, but the waiting room itself was still brightly illuminated. He stopped and listened again, his ears strained for any movement.

There was nothing. It would be unusual, but not unknown, for anyone else to be working this late, but Amberson wanted to take as few chances as he could. He was allowing himself only one opportunity to do this, and he wanted to make the most of it.

A second corridor, containing more consulting rooms, led off the far side of the waiting room. He walked down the corridor, tapped at each door then turned the handle. There was no one. Some of the rooms were locked, as he'd expected. The rest were empty and in darkness.

He returned to the end of the corridor nearest the waiting room. This was where Carnforth's consulting room was located. As befitted Carnforth's senior status, it occupied a prime position next to the reception area, with a view out over the park at the rear of the building. It was larger and better appointed than the other equivalent offices, comprising two adjoining rooms – the consulting room itself and Carnforth's personal office.

The office could be accessed only via the door of the consulting room. Amberson tapped loudly on the door and listened. There was no response. He reached down and tried the handle. To his slight surprise, the room was unlocked. Amberson stepped inside, closing the door softly behind him. He reached to turn on the lights then walked across the room and tapped on the door of the office. Again, there was no response and he turned the handle. This time, he was sure the room would be locked. This was surely the one room to which Carnforth wouldn't risk allowing unhindered access. But to his surprise the door opened.

He stepped inside, turned on the light and closed the door behind him. Amberson had been in here on only a handful of occasions, most recently when Carnforth had been delivering his admonitory lecture about the reputation of the practice. The room furnishings here were untypical of the rest of the surgery, but characteristic of Carnforth. There was an old-fashioned oak desk which looked as if it would be more in place in a long-established firm of solicitors. Beneath the window was a similarly-styled oak cabinet, which Amberson thought ought to be topped with a decanter of whisky and a selection of cut-glass tumblers but which instead held, slightly incongruously, a filter coffee machine, a kettle and a small fridge. Behind the desk, a glass-fronted bookshelf held a selection of medical books, some of which Amberson suspected had been brought largely for show.

Amberson took a breath and tried to hold his nerve. He would have one quick look around the room and then leave. Most likely, the desk and cabinets would be firmly locked, and he had no intention of trying to force them. He'd give it one shot, and make sure there was no sign he'd ever been here.

He tried the desk first. The upper drawers were unlocked, but contained nothing but Carnforth's diary, a couple of note pads provided by pharmaceutical companies, and various office items – pens, scissors, an old-fashioned calculator. The lower drawers were locked. Amberson shook them hopefully, but nothing short of brute force or lock-picking skills would open them.

The large oak cabinet looked more like a piece of domestic furniture than anything appropriate to an office or medical environment. There were three large cupboards at the bottom of the cabinet with a row of drawers above. The cupboard below the coffee machine contained mugs, packets of ground coffee and a tin of biscuits. The other two contained a selection of stationery – paper for printing, envelopes, some empty files, and various similar items.

The drawers were also unlocked, and, at least initially, the contents looked more interesting. The first two drawers contained several files filled with documents. Amberson pulled one out and flicked through it. It was nothing more than a file of bills and invoices – utilities, maintenance work, cleaning services, the various non-medical expenses incurred in running the practice. The second file contained similar material.

Amberson replaced the files and pulled open the third drawer. Again, this contained a selection of chunky-looking files. The first was more of the same, this time bills dating back several years. The second file looked more interesting. It contained a series of handwritten sheets. On each sheet was written a date, a name, what appeared to be a phone number, and some lines of typed text. The text appeared to be written largely in some form of private code. Amberson turned through some of the pages, trying to make sense of the contents, occasionally recognising the name of a controlled drug.

Was this the smoking gun he'd be looking for? Could he be looking at some kind of order book? It seemed too good to be true. Would Carnforth really have written down this kind of information? It was possible, Amberson supposed. He would need some method of recording and tracking orders, and a typed summary would probably be more secure than anything electronic.

But why would he store it here, in an unlocked drawer among an array of irrelevant and uninteresting files? Perhaps that was the answer – that this was a variant on hiding in plain sight. Even if someone did look in here, they'd probably just go through the first couple of files before concluding, as Amberson almost had, that there was nothing worth finding. Even if someone did stumble across this file by accident, they were unlikely to ascribe any significance to it. Amberson had been struck by it because it looked precisely like the material he had come to find.

He realised a moment too late that, engrossed in the pages, he had failed to register movement in the consulting room adjacent to the office. He realised someone was out there only as the door from the consulting room opened to reveal Andrew Carnforth standing in the doorway.

'What the bloody hell are you doing in here?'

CHAPTER FORTY FOUR

'So what exactly do we have?' Murrain looked round the table.

'Mainly a set of odd coincidences,' Colin Willock said. 'God knows how it makes any sense.'

They had concluded the interview with Daniel Fraser the previous day by charging him with possession of a controlled substance and with spiking Wallace's drink with intent to commit a sexual offence. He'd subsequently been released on bail including the condition that he should make no attempt to contact Wallace. Following discussions with the Coroner's Office, he had been suspended from duty pending a full investigation into the circumstances of the leak.

Murrain had phoned Bert Wallace immediately to break the news, suggesting she should take a day or two's further compassionate leave until she felt ready to return. Instead, characteristically, she'd been back at her desk the next morning, and was now sitting opposite him at the morning briefing.

Willock was on his feet behind Murrain, writing names on a white-board. He scribbled up the names of their three domestic victims. Margaret Perry. Vivian Turnbull. Trevor Ollerenshaw. On the face of it, Murrain thought, it was difficult to envisage three more disparate individuals.

'Stop me if you think I'm missing something,' Willock said, 'but as far as I can see this is what we've got so far. Ollerenshaw was involved in a psychological study of Edward Crichton.' He wrote Crichton's name on the board alongside those of the three victims. 'We believe Crichton was involved in a series of killings in recent months. Crichton himself is missing, quite possibly dead.'

'We've no evidence to support that,' Murrain pointed out. 'All we know is he was swept away in the same flood surge that took Joe. We found Joe very quickly, but we never found Crichton. My gut feeling is that if his body was there, we'd have found it.'

Willock nodded and added a question mark next to Crichton's name. 'Okay, so Crichton might still be out there. If he is, we know he's dangerous. Could he be our killer?'

'It's a possibility. But the nature of the killings is quite different from the earlier ones, which were much more straightforwardly brutal.'

'Perhaps he's just developed a taste for subtlety,' Paul Wanstead said. 'The syringe being mightier than the knife.'

'Maybe. But the original victims were all linked to Gordon Fenwick's original psychological study. The only one of our current victims with links to Fenwick is Trevor Ollerenshaw, and as far as I'm aware he wasn't involved in the original study.'

Willock drew a line between Ollerenshaw and Crichton. 'So Crichton's a possibility, but it would be a gear change if he were responsible for these new deaths.'

'Something like that.' Murrain had been listening to the rhythm of his own inner voices. Although their meaning was as indecipherable as ever, he was growing increasingly certain of one thing. Crichton was alive. That certainty had been growing ever since that terrible night. It felt almost as if Crichton was calling to him, mocking him. If he listened harder, Murrain felt he might almost be able to discern Crichton's voice among the cacophony.

'What about Frank Perry, Margaret's husband?' Wallace said. Willock immediately wrote Frank Perry's name up on the board, with a line linking him to Margaret's name.

'Tell us about Frank Perry, Bert,' Murrain said.

'A slightly mysterious figure. Boring-sounding civil servant, but his colleagues suspected him of working for the intelligence services. Working alongside immigration, but nobody quite knew what he was there for.'

'Then someone calling himself Frank Perry phoned Ellis at the medical school seeking reassurance that none of the dirty linen was being made public,' Will Sparrow added.

Willock drew lines between Frank Perry's name and those of Edward Crichton and Trevor Ollerenshaw.

'We've had suggestions that Crichton went AWOL at various points after the original study,' Wallace said. 'Weren't there suggestions he might have been nabbed by some foreign power?'

'The intelligence services seemed keen to suggest that,' Murrain agreed.

'I'm wondering if Perry's role might have been to track movements of persons of interest like Crichton? It might explain why he had an interest in the study and its aftermath. Especially if they lost track of Crichton again after the second study.'

'Anything's possible,' Murrain said. 'What about Vivian Turnbull?'

'That's where it gets murky,' Willock said. 'We've found no obvious links between her and the other victims. Nothing obvious to link her to Crichton. As a reporter, of course, she might have had dealings with all kind of people, but we've found nothing to link her to either Perry or Ollerenshaw either.'

'Except,' Murrain added, 'that, shortly after her death, she received a visit from a Dr Kyle Amberson. Who, according to allegations we've just heard, recently supplied drugs to our friend Daniel Fraser who in turn appears to have been responsible of leaking the story of the hospital killings to the press. Which again we could dismiss as yet another coincidence. Except...' He paused, waiting for his colleagues to pick up the thread.

'Except that his boss or head of practice or whatever he calls himself turns out also to be on the list of participants in the second study conducted by Gordon Fenwick and Trevor Ollerenshaw. We don't know why he was there or what his role was. But he – or at least someone called Andrew Carnforth – was definitely there.'

Dutifully, Willock wrote up Carnforth's name and draw lines from it to those of Crichton and Ollerenshaw.

'Very artistic, Colin,' Paul Wanstead said. 'But I don't

know what the bloody hell all this telling us.'

'What about the hospital victim?' Willock asked. 'Have we found any links there?'

Murrain had the file in front of him, part of a pile of documents he'd brought to the meeting. He opened the front page and skimmed through the summary, though he knew most of the detail by heart. 'Elizabeth Everard. We've found no links with any of the domestic victims. In her seventies, already seriously ill. Close family. Husband, grown-up son and daughter. Retired nurse, as it happens. Husband a retired engineer who'd worked for a manufacturing company in north Manchester. We've identified no reasons why anyone might want to harm her, and, as I say, nothing to link her to our other victims.'

'What about other hospital victims?' Wallace asked.

'We're still waiting on postmortem reports but should have confirmation today. I've a meeting with the Chief Executive later to catch up.' Murrain sighed. 'To be honest, we're making slower progress there than I'd like. I was hoping we might wrap it up fairly quickly. There was a relatively limited time frame in which Everard could have been injected with the drug and, in principle, only a limited number of individuals who could have gained access to her. She was on an open ward, but the entrance was secured so any visitors must have been given access by the ward staff. We've interviewed the ward staff and any other staff members who were known to have accessed the ward during the relevant time period. So far we've identified no leads. No one who couldn't reasonably account for their time or actions, no one who witnessed anything suspicious or out of the ordinary. We're checked out all the available CCTV on the ward and the adjacent corridor, but again spotted nobody who seems out of place.'

'That's going to be the problem, though,' Wanstead said. 'If whoever did this is one of the staff or even a visitor, if they're confident enough they'll blur into the background. Even on CCTV, unless you actually catch them in the act, they'll just look like business as usual.'

'That's exactly it,' Murrain said. 'Administering the injection would be a matter of seconds if the killer knew what they were doing. The potential time frame for the killing included one of the evening visiting hours. Everard's husband was there for a while, but the ward was busy. That might turn out to be good fortune if someone spotted something, but it means we've a lot more potential interviewees to work through.'

'What's your gut feel about the hospital killing?' Wanstead asked. 'You reckon it's connected to the domestic ones?'

Murrain hesitated for a moment before responding. 'I think it's too similar to the others for us not to consider a possible link.' Murrain knew his answer didn't address what Wanstead had really been asking, but he didn't feel ready to say more. Before Wanstead could say anything more, Murrain moved the meeting on. 'Okay, folks, that's enough idle speculation. Let's get on with the important stuff about resources and who's doing what.'

CHAPTER FORTY FIVE

He was feeling more confident now. It was all coming together.

He'd never had any doubt it would. The question had only ever been one of time. He had to make the pattern work, and he had only a limited period in which to do that. Once he fitted the first piece into place, they would soon be on his trail. He would have only a few weeks' head start on them.

In fact, it had taken them longer than he'd expected to realise something was wrong. It had allowed him enough time to identify the other pieces, and to work out how to arrange them to his desire. The fates were working with him.

He'd thought it was the others holding him captive. The others who had been part of that original circle. The others who, in their own feeble ways, shared his gifts. He'd been partly right about that. He'd felt the bonds lifting as, one by one, he'd eliminated those people. But he hadn't fully succeeded. That night by the river he hadn't been strong enough, and two of them remained. One in particular. The policeman.

He might still have to deal with the policeman. The other could safely be disregarded now. Her gift had been strong, certainly, but she'd been a woman and he felt confident now that, once the pattern had been completed, she would be powerless to hold him.

The policeman was a different matter. His gifts were less, but there was a steeliness to him, a strength of will, that was troubling. It had been there, that night by the river, and it had been enough to prevent the task being completed.

But the policeman had been weakened. That certainty of purpose had been undermined. He had lost some of his faith, some of his confidence. He had failed.

The proof of that was here. The man in a coma, the

woman sitting by his side. Both had been there that night, and both were part of the pattern. As was the other woman, the woman who haunted the hospital like the ghost of a past life.

'Have you finished?'

He'd been lost in thought, as he so often was these days. He needed to concentrate. He needed to ensure he wouldn't be caught before the work was done. Above all, he needed to be invisible, to do nothing to draw attention to himself.

He was crouching on the floor by the bed, supposedly checking one of the brakes that held the bed stationary once it was on the ward. He'd just brought it back up here after taking a patient down to theatre. The nurse was smiling at him. 'All okay?'

'Thought the brake seemed a bit stiff but it's all right.' He'd been fiddling with the bed to buy himself some extra seconds up here. This was where the final piece of the pattern would slip into place, and he wanted to be familiar with it, given his limited opportunities to visit the place. 'If that's it, I'll head back downstairs.'

'Thanks. Always good to see your smiling face up here.'

'Sounds a bit daft, but I enjoy the job. Anyway, you lot are always cheerful considering what you have to deal with.'

'It's nice to be appreciated. Rather than being interviewed by suspicious police officers.'

'You've had that, have you?' He'd have preferred to move on to another topic, but this was all everyone was talking about. 'They've not got to me yet.'

'They weren't so bad, to be honest. They've got a job to do.' She gave a mock shiver. 'I'll be glad when this is all over.'

He smiled back at her. 'Oh, believe me. So will I.'

CHAPTER FORTY SIX

'Where is he?'

'Meeting Room 4,' Wanstead said, checking his notes.

'The coincidences in this are getting too good to be true, aren't they?' Murrain was still skim reading through the short report Wanstead had printed off for him. 'What's his story?'

'He doesn't really have one. Nothing coherent, anyway.'

'The question for us,' Murrain said, 'is whether he's actually committed a criminal offence.'

'Carnforth's arguing breaking and entering, theft, intent to access controlled drugs. You name it.'

'He didn't break in,' Murrain pointed out. 'He works there.'

'Not in Carnforth's office.'

'Which Amberson says was unlocked.'

'Carnforth denies that. Says he always locks it when he leaves each evening, because the room contains confidential material. Reckons Amberson must have procured a duplicate key somehow.'

'But no key was found on Amberson's person?'

Wanstead shrugged. 'Carnforth's adamant the office door's never left unlocked.'

'The fact remains that Amberson was in his own workplace. Even if he did somehow acquire a key to Carnforth's office, it hardly constitutes a criminal offence. Disciplinary matter, maybe.'

'I'm sure you're right. I just thought you might want the opportunity to have a chat with him in the circumstances. And doing it while he's anxious about his job, his career and his future prospects as a medical practitioner might be the perfect time to put some pressure on him.'

'Did anyone ever tell you you're an utter bastard, Paul?'

'Mainly my wife.'

'She's not wrong. Anyway, well spotted.'

'I just saw his name on the morning log. The uniforms

weren't planning to do anything with it, for all the good reasons you've just mentioned. It's really something for Carnforth to deal with. But I thought we'd be wanting to talk to him anyway, given Fraser's allegations, so I called him in.'

'Always one step ahead.'

'That's me. You want to do this yourself?'

'Whites of their eyes and all that. Maybe get Will in with me, given Bert's links to Fraser. I'll pick him up on my way.'

Five minutes later, Murrain was sitting in the interview room with Will Sparrow by his side, Kyle Amberson sitting opposite. As Murrain introduced himself and Sparrow, Amberson paled. 'Detective Chief Inspector? That sounds rather elevated for an issue like this. I didn't do anything...'

'We'd like to talk to you about that and one or two other issues, Dr Amberson. This is not a formal interview at this stage, so we're not conducting it under caution. It's just an opportunity for us to gather some information. We're grateful for you agreeing to come in, and I should stress that you're free to leave at any time.'

'I'm only too happy to co-operate. I've done nothing wrong.'

'First of all, tell us what happened yesterday evening.'

'Nothing happened yesterday evening.' Amberson was silent for a moment. 'It's a long story. I was given some information that suggests Dr Carnforth might be involved in some unethical and quite probably illegal practices.'

Murrain felt a jolt in the back of his brain, almost like an electrical shock to his spine. For a moment, he saw something else – a brief flickering image of two men sitting with their heads together as if conspiring. Almost instantly it was gone, its afterimage still on his retinas, the voices still playing their interminable soundtrack. 'What kind of practices are we talking about?'

'Procuring and selling drugs illegally.'

Murrain exchanged a glance with Sparrow. 'Do you

have any evidence for this?'

'No, that's the point. It was information passed on to me. The person who gave me the information claimed it was reliable, but had no substantive evidence. They told me in the hope I might be able to find something to support their allegations.'

'That's what you were trying to do last night?'

Amberson looked mildly embarrassed. 'Pretty much.'

'Did you find anything?'

'I'm not sure. I found a folder of what looked like handwritten orders. Names, addresses, details of various drugs. But I think now I was being set up.'

'Set up?'

'I was taken aback when Carnforth reappeared like that. He's notorious in the practice for not working outside his allocated hours. I was concerned someone might catch me entering his office, but I hadn't imagined it would be Carnforth himself. I realised while he was reading the riot act that he'd set up one of those motion sensitive cameras in there. It would have alerted him I was there, and then he no doubt watched me until I found the folder he'd planted in that cabinet.'

'Why would he do that, Dr Amberson?'

'To distract attention from himself, I suppose.'

Murrain leaned back in his chair. 'What would you say, Dr Amberson, if I told you that we'd received intelligence that you were the one involved in illegal drug sales?'

'Me? That's ridiculous. What sort of intelligence? I mean, if Carnforth's your source, it just proves my point. He's trying to set me up.'

'Our source isn't Dr Carnforth. But it's also possible our source is incorrect. They purchased drugs illegally from someone who gave their name as Kyle Amberson.'

'If I was dealing in illegal drugs why would I give my name?'

'It does seem remarkably indiscreet. Tell us about Dr Carnforth.'

'One of my colleagues told me Carnforth had been

involved in a scandal in the early days of the practice. He had a drink problem and was suspended. I've also heard suggestions he was involved in the theft of drugs from the practice. He went through rehab, supposedly kicked the drink problem and returned to work. That was what my colleague told me. I haven't checked it out but I had no reason to doubt what was said.'

'This was presumably some years ago?'

'Twenty or so, I assume.'

'But you're suggesting Dr Carnforth is still involved in current unethical or illegal practices?'

'According to my source. That was why I went rooting round in Carnforth's office. I don't really know what I was expecting to find.'

'But you found a folder?'

'Looking back, that seems too convenient. It was just sitting there in an unlocked drawer, buried among a stack of apparently innocuous files. I was meant to find it, and Carnforth was watching on the camera till I did.'

'Why would he do that?'

'He accused me of planting the file. He said I was trying to plant documents in his office to incriminate him. Accused me of running a campaign to discredit him.'

'Why would he think you'd do that?'

'He implied I was trying to cover up my own ineptitude. He said he had evidence of me badmouthing him to colleagues and others outside the practice. He claimed he'd been keeping a record of errors I'd made and instances when I'd been negligent or exercised poor judgement. He even implied he still had concerns about my involvement in Vivian Turnbull's death.'

'Is there any truth in those allegations?'

'Nothing at all.'

'You've not been subject to any kind of performance or disciplinary actions at work? Dr Carnforth hasn't previous told you he's been keeping this log he mentioned?'

'All of that was completely out of the blue. The only conversation I've had with Carnforth was about Vivian

Turnbull's death, and then he was mostly concerned to ensure I'd done nothing to bring the practice into disrepute.'

'Did he think you might have done?'

'He was just covering his back. I told him what I'd done and how I'd handled it and that seemed to satisfy him.'

'And the suggestion that you'd criticised him to colleagues and outside the practice?'

'I've no idea where that came from. I might have had the odd grumble about him to some of the other doctors, but nothing malicious. I'm not aware I've spoken negatively about him to anyone outside the practice.'

'Yet someone told you about Dr Carnforth supposedly selling drugs illegally? Was that accusation unprompted or was it in response to something you'd said about Dr Carnforth?'

Amberson clearly realised he'd said more than he'd intended. 'It was unprompted. The – person in question asked to meet me. I was surprised, and had no idea what they wanted to talk about.'

Murrain nodded. 'Dr Amberson, I want you to help us. If you do, we'll help you as best we can, though I can make no promises.'

'I'm happy to co-operate. I've nothing to hide.'

'In that case,' Murrain said, 'I want you to begin by being completely honest.'

CHAPTER FORTY SEVEN

Alan Northcote stretched out in his chair and peered down his nose at Murrain. 'I have to confess we're both concerned and so far a little disappointed. The findings have been sent to the Coroner for the purposes of the inquest. But it's clear we have at least two more unlawful killings. And so far you seem to have made little progress with the first.'

Murrain knew there'd be no benefit in being defensive. 'To be frank, I'm disappointed too. We have a specific crime scene and a limited time frame in which the killing could have taken place, as well as a relatively small list of possible suspects. I'd have expected we'd have either picked up something from the CCTV or someone would have spotted something suspicious. But so far we've found nothing. Tell me about the two newly identified victims.'

'One's male. Alan Bagshaw.' Helen Clarke was reading from the notes in front of her. 'Early seventies. Suffering from prostate cancer. Had been diagnosed as terminal, probably with only weeks to live and was about to be transferred to a hospice. So, again, the death wasn't a surprise. But the cause was an unauthorised overdose of diamorphine. We've checked the treatment records and it looks unlikely the dosage was given in error. The other was a female, Nathalie Vaughan. Mid-sixties. Suffering from an aggressive form of progressive multiple sclerosis. Again seen as being in the terminal stages but was expected to live for some months longer. Cause of death the same. Again, very unlikely to have been accidental.'

Murrain noted the caveats in both cases. Clarke and Northcote were already erecting their own defences. If there was one thing the hospital management wanted less than a random killer on the loose, it was that the deaths should be in any way attributable to their or their staff's negligence. Even now there would be some cynics out there who might conclude that talk of a multiple killer was nothing more than a smokescreen.

'Presumably there are no obvious connections between the two, or between them and Elizabeth Everard?'

'Nothing obvious to us,' Northcote said. 'They were on three different wards, being treated by three different consultants. Bagshaw's ward was close to Everard's, but Vaughan's was on a different floor. There doesn't seem to have been any overlap between the various staff involved in their care as far as we've been able to ascertain.'

All of this would need to be double-checked. Murrain began to talk through the proposed process with Northcote and Clarke, keen they should understand how much effort was going into this despite the lack of progress to date. 'We're getting whatever resources we can devoted to this. We can hope for some unexpected breakthrough, but the chances are it will just be a matter of painstakingly detailed work. We will get there.'

'I wish I shared your confidence,' Northcote said. 'Every day that goes by makes this worse. People are getting increasingly paranoid. The media want to know why more isn't being done to protect patients. I'm getting more and more flak from the trustees. We need to nail this bastard before anyone else is killed.'

'What about the maintenance worker we talked about? Has his postmortem been completed yet?'

'We're hoping to have the results of that tomorrow,' Helen Clarke said. 'We've also got at least one more patient death to look at. The slightly better news is that a couple of the other deaths we'd thought looked potentially suspicious have been confirmed as natural causes.' She laughed bitterly. 'We've reached a dark point when it's good news that some of our patients haven't been murdered.'

Northcote scowled at her. 'I'm not sure this is really a laughing matter, Helen.'

Murrain could almost feel the tension in the room. Clarke's laughter had sounded brittle, and Northcote's irritation close to real anger. Murrain had trained himself to remain dispassionate about the cases he investigated, though sometimes it was far from easy. He had to remind himself how stressful this could be for those caught up in it – the friends and families of those affected or even just those, like Northcote and Clarke, who had to deal with the practical consequences.

Murrain finished talking them through the next steps. By the time they'd completed the meeting, Northcote had calmed to some degree though it was clear he was coping badly with the stress. There were no doubt countless challenges in running a hospital of this size, but this was one that Northcote could presumably never have envisaged.

Murrain needed to get back to HQ but, as before, didn't want to miss the opportunity to visit Joe. He hurried down to the ward where Joe lay, and pressed the bell for admission. Security had tightened in recent days, and he was pleased to see the nurses on the ward taking it seriously. By now, most of them knew who he was, but the nurse on reception, a young red-haired woman called Amy Kelly, still insisted on seeing his ID before allowing him to proceed. 'I know it's a bit stupid but even so…'

'You're doing exactly the right thing,' Murrain said. 'Don't let anyone get over-familiar.'

Kelly grinned at him as he showed her his warrant card. 'No-one gets familiar with me. Not unless I want them to. I'll allow you through this once, but don't go expecting special treatment next time.'

As he walked past the beds in the open ward, he could tell that a number of the patients, most of whom seemed to be relatively elderly men, were watching him uneasily. There was a growing anxiety in the place, a state of mind where every visitor was regarded with suspicion. Murrain smiled and tried his hardest to look unthreatening, though that wasn't easy with his burly policeman's frame. Like a thuggish toddler, as Eloise had once described him.

He reached Joe's room and peered through the observation window. It took him a moment to realise the woman standing with her back to him wasn't Marie Donovan. She was leaning over Joe's bed, apparently making some adjustment to the medical equipment. She wasn't wearing a uniform, so his second thought was that she was one of the doctors.

Then the woman straightened and turned slightly, and he realised his assumption had been wrong.

He pushed open the door and stepped inside. 'Gill?'

'Oh, it's Kenny, isn't it? You made me jump.'

'Sorry, I didn't mean to. I assumed you were Marie. From the back, I mean.'

'Marie?' She sounded as if the name meant nothing to her. 'I'm not sure where she is.'

'She must have gone to get a coffee or something. I imagine she won't be long. How is he?' Murrain gestured to Joe, who looked the same as ever, lying as if asleep, breathing gently into an oxygen mask.

'He's fine. It's just a matter of time.'

'Until he wakes? I hope you're right.' Murrain peered over Gill's shoulder, trying to see what she'd been doing when he'd interrupted her. There was a tangle of boxes and equipment, and he had no way of knowing if anything had been changed. 'It's good of you to keep coming to see him. When are you expecting to head back to Paris?'

'Things are a little…fluid. I'm happy to come to see Joe for as long as I need to.'

There was something odd in her tone, Murrain thought. As if she was barely engaging with what he was saying, her head somewhere else entirely.

'I can't stay long,' he said, awkwardly. 'I was just in the hospital so I thought I'd check how he was doing. It would be good to have a few minutes with him.' Pointedly, he pulled out one of the visitors' chairs and sat himself by Joe's bedside.

She gazed at him blankly for a moment, then seemed to take the hint. 'I'd better go myself. A lot of things to do.' She stood for a moment longer, then turned and left the room. It occurred to Murrain only then that, although the weather outside was still cold, Gill hadn't been carrying a coat.

Murrain walked over to the door and peered out into the ward. Gill was at the far end of the ward by the entrance, exchanging some words with Amy Kelly. After a moment, she turned and left. Murrain waited a few seconds longer, then walked up the ward. 'I'm sorry to disturb you,' he said to Kelly. 'I just wondered if you could come and check up on Joe for me.'

'Is something wrong?'

'I was a little concerned that the equipment had been disturbed in some way. It may be nothing, but I didn't want to take any risks.'

Kelly looked baffled, but rose to follow him back down the ward to Milton's room.

Milton looked unchanged, still apparently breathing rhythmically. Murrain gestured towards where he'd seen Gill leaning over. 'Has anything been changed just there?'

'I don't understand. Changed in what way?'

'I don't know. Have any of the equipment settings been altered, for example?'

Clearly humouring him, Kelly leaned over and examined the equipment. Then her body stiffened. 'The oxygen's been turned off.' She reached down and tuned on the tap. 'What's going on?'

The woman who was just in here, does she visit Joe a lot?'

'She's been in a couple of times today. I'd assumed it was okay, since she obviously knew Joe well. I'd seen her in here with you and Marie.'

'Has she been in here with Marie?'

'Only that first time with the three of you. Today, she seemed to pick moments when Marie was away from the bedside. I assumed there was some awkwardness between them.'

'You might say that,' Murrain said. 'Gill is Joe's ex.'

'Oh. I hadn't realised that.' She stopped and looked back at the equipment. 'Are you saying she—?'

'All I know is that when I came in here, she seemed to be doing something with the equipment on that side of the bed. What would have happened with the oxygen turned off?'

'Nothing immediately. We're controlling the levels of oxygen he's breathing to ensure the brain's getting what it needs. If it had remained off, it might have harmed his chances of recovery or might have affected his condition after recovery.'

'But not good news?'

'Let's just say there's a reason we're giving him the treatment.'

'Can you make sure that woman's not allowed in here again? If necessary, call on one of the patrolling police officers to prevent her. I'll see if we can track her down.'

He dug out his phone and called DS Howard Temple, the officer co-ordinating the police patrols in the hospital. He provided a brief account of what had happened and Gill's appearance and clothing. 'If any of you see her, detain her. Arrest her if necessary. Then let me know.'

'Is this our killer?' Temple asked.

'Probably not. But I want her picked up if we can.'

'We'll see what we can do.'

Murrain ended the call and turned back to Kelly. 'Where is Marie, anyway?'

'I don't know exactly. I assumed she was just going for a coffee, but she's been gone a long time. Nearly an hour. She's not normally away for that long even when she goes to get some lunch.'

Murrain could feel it then, the crescendo of voices building in his head, desperately trying to impart some information he could never quite discern. And something more. A single, recurrent note at the heart of it, a repeated tone that underpinned everything. As if his brain was an internal radio telescope picking up a pulsing signal from the heart of the universe, a rhythm too solid and steady to be anything other than an attempt to communicate.

He nodded abstractly to Amy Kelly and dialled Marie's

number on his mobile. It rang out to voicemail. He tried again with the same result, and this time he left a message asking her to call him as soon as she picked up the message.

'You think there's something wrong?' Kelly hesitated. 'There's something wrong with this whole place, if you ask me.'

'How do you mean?'

She looked up at him, and he was surprised by what he saw in her eyes. Some unexpected sense of understanding. 'You've got it, haven't you? The gift.'

Murrain's first thought was to pretend he didn't know what she was talking about, but he knew he wouldn't fool her. 'I've certainly got some kind of gift, if that's the word. How did you know?' He knew the answer even before he'd asked the question. 'You too?'

'Something like that. I can always tell.'

'Look, we should talk about what it is you've been feeling. But I need to find out what's happened to Marie. It's not like her not to respond to her phone. In the meantime don't let anyone see Joe except for authorised medical staff. We need to take every precaution. Take care of Joe, won't you?'

'It's what we do.'

'I know. And thanks.' He moved towards the door. 'Now I'd better go and do what I do.'

CHAPTER FORTY EIGHT

Wallace glanced over at Willock. 'Maybe she's out?'

'She knew we were coming.' Willock gestured to the open-fronted building to their left. 'And there are two cars and two motorbikes over there.'

'She could have gone for a walk.'

Willock looked up at the sky. It was a fine if chilly spring day but the sun was low in the sky. 'If she has she'll be back soon. We can wait if necessary. Try the bell again.'

Wallace pressed the bell a third time, this time holding it down. Finally, she withdrew her finger and listened. There was no movement from inside.

'Let's have a look around,' Willock said. 'Just in case.'

He didn't specify what they were looking around for. Wallace followed him along the side of the house into the rear garden. This was presumably the same path that the young GP had taken when he'd found Vivian Turnbull's body. The thought was sufficient to send a chill down Wallace's spine. She was already feeling more uneasy than the situation appeared to justify.

They were here because of what Amberson had finally told them. 'To be honest,' Willock had said, 'I wasn't sure what Kenny was up to. I still thought Amberson was most likely spinning us a line, and I was more inclined to believe the word of someone like Carnforth than a youngster like Amberson.'

Amberson had first admitted it was his colleague Jude Calman who had told him about Carnworth's history. 'She said I ought to know, and to know the whole story rather than some half-baked version I might hear as office gossip. I wondered afterwards whether Carnforth had put Jude up to telling me the story.'

'Why would he have done that?' Murrain had asked.

'To ensure I got the authorised version? Or perhaps to pre-empt any other rumours I might hear. It was heavy on the repentance and rehab. And it made me hesitate when I heard stuff about what he might be up to now.'

'So who was it told you about Carnforth supposedly dealing in illegal drugs?' Murrain had asked. 'We need to know if we're going to investigate Carnforth further.'

Amberson had been silent for perhaps a couple of minutes, to the point where Willock had been convinced he wouldn't respond. 'It was Romy Purslake.'

'Purslake? You've been in contact with her?'

'She contacted me out of the blue. We met for a drink after work and she told me she'd had both me and Carnforth investigated after Turnbull's death. Our characters and backgrounds.'

'Why Carnforth?'

'She thought Carnforth had seemed oddly defensive when she called him. My guess is that she had underworld sources, but she wouldn't tell me more. Anyway, they uncovered more than she'd expected. I'd apparently come out of her review squeaky clean, as she put it. She felt able to trust me, and she wanted to talk to someone about Carnforth. She felt he needed to be exposed.'

'Why was she so concerned about Carnforth?' Willock had asked. 'Whatever he might or might not be up to, it's nothing to do with Turnbull's death.'

'She seemed to think it might.'

'What motive could Dr Carnforth have for killing Vivian Turnbull?'

'Perhaps she'd threatened to expose what he was involved in. It didn't take long for Romy Purslake to find out the truth about him, so I imagine Turnbull could have done the same.'

Murrain was far from convinced but – on the assumption that Amberson was telling the truth rather than trying to deflect attention from his own actions – it was as plausible a motive as any others they'd come up with. At any rate, there would be no harm in another chat with Purslake.

Willock was looking along the rear of the house. 'No

conveniently opened windows this time,' he said as Wallace caught up with him. 'But let's take a look anyway.'

He walked across to the back door of the house and rapped sharply on the glass with his knuckles. Wallace walked past him and, knocking similarly on the patio doors, she pressed her face against the glass. 'Colin.'

'What is it?'

'You'd better come and see.' She pointed into the room.

'Shit.'

Wallace fumbled in the pocket of her coat for the pack of disposable gloves she always carried. Taking care to avoid disturbing any forensic evidence that might be present, she pressed down on the handle of the patio doors. She'd expected the doors would be locked and that they'd have to try to gain entrance through some other route. But the door opened at her touch.

The rich cloying scent of blood was unmistakeable. Romy Purslake's body was lying face up on the couch that, on a previous occasion, had held the corpse of her partner. Purslake's death had been far less peaceful than Vivian Turnbull's. Her throat was gaping open, her chest soaked with the blood from the wound. There were more knife wounds in the torso.

Wallace walked gently across the room, holding her breath and trying to disturb the scene as little as possible. She carefully took Purslake's hand, feeling for any sign of a pulse. The body still felt relatively warm, suggesting that death had occurred recently, although the blood was congealing on Purslake's body.

The killer could conceivably still be in the house or perhaps trying to leave through the front. She turned to Willock, still standing outside, who'd clearly had the same thought.

'I'll get round to the front before I call it in.'

Wallace took one last look around the room. There was no other sign of any struggle. It was difficult to imagine the killer had been left untouched by the blood that drenched Purslake's body, although there were no other signs of blood elsewhere in the room.

Wallace made her way back to the patio doors. It was only when she was back out in the open air that she finally released her breath and took a mouthful of the fresh spring air.

CHAPTER FORTY NINE

A small co-ordination room for the officers patrolling the hospital had been established on the ground floor. It provided a base where the co-ordinating officer, a sergeant called Howard Temple, could organise the rotas and maintain contact with the team. It also served as an informal rest room for the officers.

Murrain stepped inside. 'Howard. How's it going?'

Temple looked up as Murrain entered. 'It's going, I guess. I won't commit any further than that. We haven't had any luck so far with that woman you called about.'

'I shouldn't have let her leave the ward. I didn't want to start throwing accusations around, but I should have trusted my instincts.'

'We'll track her down. We've got the external doors covered. I'm not sure I'm following this, though. You're not suggesting she's our killer?'

'I don't know,' Murrain said. 'She might have a reason for wanting to harm Joe, at least in her own head. But even that sounds weirdly out of character from the person I remember. The idea that she might be responsible for the deaths of complete strangers is bizarre. And I don't see how she'd have managed it. My sense is that this is someone who's got a reason to be on the wards – a nurse, a doctor, one of the ancillary staff, something like that. Someone could pose as a visitor, but I don't know how easy it would be to get away with that in different wards.' He paused. 'The other thing is that I'm worried about Marie Donovan.'

'What about her?'

'You know she and Joe had just – well, become an item, let's say, when all this happened?'

'I'd heard that. Christ, that's awful.'

'She's on compassionate leave and has basically been spending her time by Joe's bedside. But Gill was on her own with Joe. The nurse reckoned Marie had gone to grab herself a coffee but that was an hour or so back. She's not answering her mobile.'

'Maybe she decided to get something to eat or to get some fresh air?'

'It's not like Marie not to answer her phone. She'd want to be contactable if there was any development with Joe.'

'I don't see what can have happened to her.'

'Something about this whole case makes me feel uneasy. Not just the obvious fact we have a random killer on the loose but something about the whole set-up.'

'It might be this place,' Temple said. 'It gives me the creeps.'

'The hospital?'

'Hospitals in general. I've spent too much time in them for the wrong reasons.'

Temple's wife had died from cancer just a couple of years earlier. Murrain was aware from his own experience – sitting by his young son's bed, years before, watching the boy's life ebbing inexorably away – that, however unjustly, you could still end up resenting those who'd allowed your loved one to die.

Temple seemed to read his thoughts. 'Don't get me wrong. I've nothing but admiration for everyone who works here. They do a tremendous job. But the place makes me feel uncomfortable. People being treated on an industrial scale, some living, some dying.'

'You're more imaginative than I thought, Howard.'

'I have my moments.' Temple smiled. 'But the place makes me nervous from a professional point of view, too. It's too big for us to fully control. Too many corners and crannies for someone to hide themselves. None of it quite fits together. It's just grown organically over the decades from the original Victorian core.' He gestured as if pointing to the walls around them. 'Which is this bit, basically. This block and the rooms above. Everything else has been added. Makes it a nightmare to plan the patrol rotas. I'd like to ensure we've got the whole building under some form of observation, but in practice that's impossible.'

'I'm sure you're doing a great job, Howard.'

'I wasn't fishing for compliments. We're doing the best we can. I just don't know if it's actually achieving anything.'

'You're providing reassurance. And you're making the killer's job that much harder. That could save someone's life.'

'If you say so, Kenny.'

Murrain pulled out his phone and dialled Marie Donovan's number once more. As before, the call rang out. The voices were still there in the back of his head, and the central pulse was present too, mocking in its rhythmic steadiness. He was replacing the phone in his pocket when it buzzed in his hand. For a moment, he thought it was Marie returning his call. 'Yes?'

'Kenny. Colin Willock. I thought you ought to know. We've another body. Romy Purslake.'

'Purslake?'

'Bert and I are at her house now. I've called it in, and the scene's sealed off. She was on the same couch Turnbull was found on, would you believe? Throat cut.'

The pulsing in the back of Murrain's brain was growing stronger, a signal finally being established. Something was falling into place – a pattern or plan he couldn't fathom. A destiny being worked out.

Murrain recalled that, on that rain-soaked night when Joe Milton had been swept away, a phase had entered his brain from nowhere. A quote from Shakespeare. *O God, I could be bounded in a nutshell and count myself a king of infinite space.*

That had been linked to Edward Crichton and his deranged idea that he was somehow held captive by those, like Murrain, who shared his gifts. The phrase had appeared in Murrain's consciousness again, this time with a mocking edge.

Purslake's death seemed like another message, the killer replaying her partner's death but in a different mode.

'Look, bring Amberson in. I don't think he's our killer, but we can't take any risks. If he knows more than he's told us so far, Purslake's death might loosen his tongue. Bring in Andrew Carnforth too. Given Purslake's allegations, he must be a prime suspect.'

'I was thinking the same,' Willock said. 'Are you still at the hospital?'

'There's plenty going on over here too.'

'All happens at once, eh?'

'That's what's troubling me. It can't all be coincidence. Keep me posted, and let me know when you've brought in Carnforth and Amberson.'

Murrain turned back to Temple who was watching him with undisguised curiosity.

'More trouble?'

'Maybe more of the same. I don't know.' Murrain was finding it increasingly hard to concentrate, the pulsing in his brain growing more intense with every minute. There were images too, a succession of visuals skittering through his head with the speed of a silent movie, too rapid to discern. A face, maybe. Someone watching him. Someone laughing. 'Can you get your people focused on tracking down Gill? I don't like the thought of her wandering round this place. I need to track down Marie, too. I'll head back up to the ward and see if she's returned. I'll let you know if so, but if not I want you to step up the search.'

'You really think something could have happened to her?'

'I've no idea,' Murrain said sincerely. 'I've no idea at all.'

CHAPTER FIFTY

The task had been delegated to Will Sparrow along with three uniformed officers. Sparrow had felt mildly embarrassed by the level of resourcing. It felt excessive in this leafy resolutely middle-class environment. But they had two suspects to bring in, both potential suspects in a violent murder.

They had assumed Amberson would have been suspended from duty after the previous evening's altercation, but there was no sign of him at his home address. Sparrow had made the decision to continue to the surgery to collect Carnforth and to see if anyone there had any idea of Amberson's whereabouts.

Sparrow, who lacked the performative instincts of some of his colleagues, felt acutely self-conscious as he entered the surgery reception, closely followed by the three PCs, two male, one female. The waiting area was relatively quiet, but the handful of waiting patients regarded them with a mix of astonishment and curiosity.

Sparrow showed his ID to the receptionist. 'We need to see Dr Carnforth and Dr Amberson as a matter of urgency.'

'I don't know if either's available—'

'We don't want to cause any more disruption for you and your colleagues than we can avoid. But this is part of a murder enquiry.'

The receptionist stared at Sparrow. 'Dr Amberson's with a patient at the moment. I wasn't expecting Dr Carnforth to be in this afternoon, but he just called through from his office to say he was back but wasn't to be disturbed.'

'How long do you expect Dr Amberson to be with his patient?'

'He shouldn't be long. She went in there a while ago.'

Sparrow confirmed the number of Amberson's consulting room with the receptionist, and asked two of the PCs to wait outside until the patient emerged. 'I'm afraid you'll have to cancel Dr Amberson's appointments for the rest of the afternoon,' he said to the receptionist. 'Where can we find Dr Carnforth?'

The receptionist looked about to offer some further objection, but was silenced by Sparrow's expression. 'Through the double doors on the left. First office.'

Sparrow led the third officer through to Carnforth's room. He tapped loudly on the door and then, without waiting for a response, opened it and stepped inside.

He had expected his intrusion to be greeted with anger or irritation, but the consulting room remained silent. Sparrow looked around. There was no one in the consulting room itself, but he could see a further room leading from it. 'Dr Carnforth?' Sparrow took another few steps forward and peered through the doorway.

Carnforth was slumped across the desk, his jacket was spread across the back of his chair. One of his shirt-sleeves was rolled up. An empty syringe lay on the desktop by his head.

Sparrow pressed his fingers against Carnforth's neck, searching for a pulse. At first, he thought there was nothing, but as he forced himself to concentrate he realised a very faint pulse was still discernible.

'At least we know there's a doctor in the house,' Sparrow said. 'More than one, presumably. We'll need an ambulance, but go and find someone who can give us a second opinion.'

Sparrow carefully lifted Carnforth's head, wanting to get a sense of the man's condition. It was only as he did so that he noticed the blood stains on the front of Carnforth's white shirt. They were already congealing a dirty brown, and Sparrow had little doubt that the blood was not Carnforth's own.

There was a babble of raised voices from the corridor outside, and the PC reappeared, followed by Kyle Amberson. 'I'm sorry,' the PC said, 'but they were just coming out as I arrived in reception…'

Amberson's eyes were fixed on Carnforth. 'Look, I've no idea what this is about or why you want to talk to me again, but I am a qualified doctor. If I can help here, I've a duty to do so.' He took Carnforth's head from Sparrow, leaning Carnforth back in the chair. 'He's still alive and breathing but only just. Get the receptionist to call an ambulance, and to tell them it's urgent. Let's get him into the recovery position, and I'll do what I can to keep him alive till the ambulance gets here. At least we're in the right place to help him.'

Sparrow stood back to let Amberson get to work. One of the PCs had already been dispatched to organise the ambulance, and another was sent to find another doctor or a nurse to assist Amberson. Sparrow decided he had no option but to go with the flow. He watched as Amberson knelt to listen to Carnforth's breathing.

Ten minutes later, an ambulance had been and gone, with Carnforth inside accompanied by one of the PCs. Amberson remained in Carnforth's office with Sparrow and the remaining uniformed officers. Amberson looked shocked, as if the reality of the event was only just catching up with him. 'You were about to take me in for an interview.'

'We'd appreciate another discussion with you.'

'Can I ask what this is about? Do I need legal representation?'

'It's a voluntary interview and it won't be under caution. If that changes, you'll be informed and told your rights. But at this stage we're just after information. There've been some developments.' He paused. 'To be honest, we weren't expecting to find you here. I'd assumed Carnforth would have suspended you from duty after the fuss he made last night.'

'He doesn't have the right on his own, much as he'd like to pretend he does. We're a partnership and it has to be a collective decision. The only exceptions would be if it was a criminal matter or an issue of medical malpractice. Despite what Carnforth tried to claim, he's no *prima facie* evidence of either of those. I'd heard nothing more by this morning, so I decided my best tactic was to come in and continue as normal. As it turned out, Carnforth wasn't here anyway. He'd cancelled his appointments at short notice because he had commitments elsewhere. That's all I know.'

'If you're happy to come with us to HQ, I think it would be in your own interest,' Sparrow said.

'I just want to get this cleared up.'

'That's a sentiment we can all get fully behind,' Sparrow said. 'Shall we get going?'

CHAPTER FIFTY ONE

Murrain pressed the buzzer at the ward entrance, holding his face to the window so that Amy Kelly could see him waiting. The door clicked open and he walked in brandishing his warrant card.

Kelly smiled back. 'Glad you showed me that before I had to ask you.'

'Any sign of Marie?'

'No.' Kelly's smile transformed into a frown. 'It's a bit odd, isn't it? I had the impression she was only popping out for a few minutes. It's not like her to be gone this long.'

Murrain had tried Marie again several times on his way back up here without success. 'Any more sign of Gill?'

'She's not reappeared. I'm not sorry. I wasn't looking forward to having an argument with her. Or trying to detain her.'

'We think she's still in the building but she's gone to ground somewhere. I'm assuming Joe's okay? Or at least as okay as before.'

'I told one of the consultants what had happened and she checked him over. The oxygen was only off for a short time, and it shouldn't have had any effect. Why would she *do* that? I mean, what sort of break up did they have?'

'An amicable one, or so Joe thought at the time. I don't know what's in her head, but something's not right.' He paused. 'How did you know about my – gift?'

'I can always tell. I've got it myself to some extent. But my great nan was the one. She was from one of the Scottish Isles, seventh child of a seventh child and all that. But she had the "sight", as they say.' She'd adopted a mock Scottish accent for the last sentence, although her normal voice was unmistakably Mancunian. 'There were all kind of family stories about her. How she used to go into weird trances, have visions about the future or about what other members of the family were doing. I never knew her – she died before I was born – but I had this image of her as a kind of Celtic witch.'

'We had similar stories about my supposed ancestors. Another Highland connection. Probably all nonsense.'

'But you've got the gift or something of it. My mum had it strongly. Not something she could ever use in a practical sense. Just feelings she had. Sensations. She always felt they told her something, but often she had no idea what. Must be quite useful for a detective, though?'

'You'd think so, wouldn't you? But I'm like your mum. I've usually no idea what it's telling me. What did you mean about something wrong with the place, though?'

'Just – a feeling. I've always loved working here. I've worked in one or two hospitals that were challenging. But this place has a good reputation, it's generally well run, and it's got decent facilities. Then a while ago – a few weeks ago – it was as if the atmosphere changed. I felt uncomfortable being here, especially when I was on my own.'

'This was before the first reports about the deaths?'

'A few weeks before. I felt as if there was some presence here making me uneasy. You wouldn't think so to hear me blethering on about the "gift" but I've never seen myself as the imaginative sort. But the atmosphere here was giving me the creeps. Especially in the basement.'

'The basement?'

'It's a weird place at the best of times. Thankfully not somewhere I normally have to go. It's mostly given over to storage and the usual behind the scenes stuff. But there are some public areas below the main entrance. The mortuary's down there, which might partly explain my feelings, and a couple of outpatients departments. I had to go down there two or three weeks back to pass on some documents to one of the departments. I felt it as soon as I got out of the lift. I could barely face the walk along the corridor. It was just daft. There were people in the lifts with me – patients heading to the departments, other hospital staff. The place was busy. But I felt completely shaken. It was as if there was someone – I don't know how to describe it – someone intruding in my head.' She laughed again, but the laugh was more uneasy, as if recounting the story had unleashed the same feeling. 'As if someone was trying to control me.'

He'd felt the same sense of discomfort in the hospital. He could rationalise it all he liked. But he knew in his heart – or perhaps in the deepest, most primitive parts of his brain – that Kelly was right. There was something wrong with the place. Something growing stronger by the hour.

'You must think I'm not fit to be left in charge of a ward.'

'I think you've identified something about the place that I hadn't. Your gift must be stronger than you think.'

'I've never experienced anything like this before.'

Murrain looked along the ward. He wondered how many others in this building – staff, patients, visitors – shared the sensations they were discussing. He was sure some must, to a greater or lesser degree. Most likely, they wouldn't even know what they were experiencing.

'You mentioned the basement. What sort of people go down there? On a regular basis.'

'There are a couple of departments down there, so obviously the medical and support staff for those. The mortuary staff. That's the public area at the front of the hospital.'

'What about the other areas? You say they're mostly storage?'

'It's not a part of the hospital I know well. There's a loading bay at the rear for deliveries, and there's various utilities stuff. It's mainly the porters and maintenance people who go down there.'

Still talking, they made their way along to the ward to Joe's room. Joe lay, apparently the same as ever, the machines flashing around him. The room felt oddly deserted without Marie Donovan's presence, a space left in the air. Murrain couldn't imagine what it would be like for her if, as seemed increasingly likely, Joe didn't pull through.

Murrain watched Joe for a moment longer. There was nothing else he could do here, he thought, not for the moment. It was time to find Marie.

CHAPTER FIFTY TWO

'Not bad,' Willock said. 'Surprising what you can afford on a GP's salary.'

'Isn't it?' They were in the driveway of Andrew Carnforth's house, looking up at the imposing facade of the villa. A large house for a single man, Bert Wallace thought, and in one of the most expensive villages in the area. The neighbours would be premier league footballers, captains of industry, or gangsters and major drug dealers.

Which was exactly why they were here. Carnforth might not have fitted the stereotype of the inner-city dealer, but he might be the middle-class equivalent. It had not proved difficult to secure a search warrant. Willock and Wallace were here to execute the warrant, supported by a small team of uniformed officers waiting in marked cars on the street outside. The net curtains of the neighbouring houses would be twitching frantically.

They had originally expected it would be necessary to break into the house, but a set of Carnforth's house and car keys had been found in his office at the surgery. The subsequent search would be highly rigorous and wouldn't leave much of the house untouched.

Willock and Wallace would enter the house first to check it over, and then bring in the uniformed officers to carry out the detailed search. That would allow them to note and record any immediate findings, and also ensure that, should there be any reason to treat the house as a crime scene, it could be secured and the full search postponed until the CSIs had done their work.

Willock unlocked the front door and stepped inside. They were expecting the house to be empty, but Willock was experienced enough not to take that for granted. He stepped forward and listened. The house was silent, except for the distant sound of a ticking clock.

To the left of the hallway was a large living room. This led through an archway into a dining room which looked out over the rear garden. There was nothing obviously out of the ordinary in the living room – a sofa and armchairs, a large television, a cabinet holding a cut-glass whisky decanter and an array matching glasses, bookshelves containing a mix of ornaments and paperback thrillers. The dining room contained a large oak table with matching chairs, an old-fashioned oak dresser displaying decorative plates, and a large grandfather clock. Both rooms matched Carnforth's public persona. Fussy, slightly dated, solid but unexciting.

A door led from the dining room into the kitchen. The kitchen was tidy, with only a couple of mugs in the sink revealing any sign of human presence. Two mugs. Was that some kind of message from Carnforth, a tacit admission of his guilt, or simply the remnants of a hurried morning departure?

Another door led back out into the hallway, where Bert Wallace was waiting. 'Anything?'

'Nothing obvious. He's a tidy old bugger.'

'He certainly kept his double life well tucked away if Romy Purslake's claims are true.' She gestured to a closed door on the right of the hall. 'What about this one?'

Willock pulled out a pack of disposable gloves and slipped one on before trying the door. 'Locked. Hang on.' He sorted through the set of keys until he'd identified two that appeared to match the lock. The first turned and unlocked the door. 'Must be my lucky day.'

He peered inside, then pushed the door wider for Wallace to see. The room was clearly used as an office, with an oak desk similar to the one in Carnforth's room at the surgery. There were a couple of substantial-looking filing cabinets, a large padlocked cupboard and, perhaps the most interesting item, a large lockable fridge.

'Funny place for a drinks cabinet.' Willock scanned through the remaining keys and shook his head.

'Maybe not your lucky day after all?'

'Story of my life.' He tried matching the keys to the padlock on the cabinet, but again without success.

'Definitely reverted to my typical level of good fortune. Carnforth must have another set somewhere.'

'Worth looking around for them?'

'Life's too short. Let's get the brawn in.'

The locks offered little obstacle to PC David Grodin, their designated expert in the fine art of brute force. Two minutes with a crowbar, and another couple of minutes with a pair of heavy-duty bolt-cutters, and the locks were removed. Willock opened the fridge door and gave a low whistle. 'Well, well. Dr Carnforth's private dispensary.'

Wallace peered into the fridge. 'He shouldn't have these at home.'

'Not unless he'd one hell of a headache.' Willock stepped over and opened the cabinet. 'Same here. Quite the medicine cabinet. Beats my first-aid kit.'

'I think we can take it this confirms Romy Purslake's allegations.' Like Willock, Wallace had donned disposable gloves, and she reached into the cabinet to retrieve a file that sat alongside the boxes of drugs. She flicked through the pages. It looked like the official version of the fake file Amberson had found in Carnforth's office. That one had presumably been intended to lure Amberson with something of no meaning or value, but this looked like the real thing.

The entries were typed, but occasionally annotated with what Wallace took to be Carnforth's handwriting. There were names, addresses, drug names and quantities. An order book, and Wallace recognised some of the customers' names. 'This is potential dynamite. Some of the names in here...' There were politicians, actors, sports stars – some of the biggest names in the local celebrity circuit.

'I hope you're not thinking of leaking it to the Evening News?' Willock said.

'Not funny, Colin.'

'But it suggests Carnforth had the material to turn the screws on people if he wanted to.'

'Blackmail?' Wallace said.

'It's possible, isn't it?'

'Only on the basis of mutually assured destruction, surely. If Carnforth exposed one of his clients, the first question would be who the supplier was. But I guess that's how it works. Once you're sucked into it, you can't get out without destroying your own reputation.'

'You think there's enough to convict Carnforth?'

'If he lives long enough, I'd have said so, wouldn't you? We can get his computers checked over, but my guess is he probably kept any information in hard copy. You can't hack a file and it's easy to destroy if you feel things are closing in. This file may be all there is. He wouldn't have needed much more.'

Willock glanced over at Grodin who was standing watching them. 'We can check the desk and the filing cabinets too if our friend here gets his chubby arse in gear.'

'You ever had a pair of bolt cutters forcibly inserted in your rear end, Colin?' Grodin said amiably. 'If not, I'm happy to introduce you to the experience. Okay, let me at them.'

It took Grodin a little longer to work his magic this time. Five minutes later, the cabinets were standing open and the desk drawers had been forced. 'No-one would even guess you'd been here,' Willock said to Grodin, gazing at the splintered oak. 'Efficient, though. I'll give you that.'

Inside the cabinets, they found further sets of files, these ones apparently historical, with dates stretching back several years. 'Good of him to keep the incriminating evidence,' Wallace said. 'But again I suppose that's the point. It's not just incriminating for him. It's an insurance policy in case any of his clients prove difficult.'

The contents of the desk were less interesting, though after skimming through various stacks of pedestrian documents Wallace pulled out what appeared to be an old-fashioned photo album comprising a stack of plastic wallets with photographs. She flicked through it and showed some of the photographs to Willock. He took it and turned more slowly through the sheets. 'Not old school porn, then?'

'There are some famous faces in there who'd no doubt see the photographs as deeply offensive.' The pictures showed drugs handovers to various of Carnforth's clients. The photographs had been taken from a distance using a powerful zoom., shot from behind so the identity of the supplier remained concealed.

'Definitely old school, anyway,' Willock said. 'I haven't seen a photograph album like that in a while.'

'Same argument, isn't it?' Wallace said. 'More secure, unhackable, easy to destroy if necessary. There's a lot to be said for hard copy.'

'I keep saying that when I get bollocked for not completing the on-line forms. Does anybody listen?' Willock looked around the room. 'Is that enough in here for the moment? Shall we go and check upstairs?'

'Why not?' Wallace said. 'We've already found what we were looking for. Anything else is a bonus.'

She followed him up the stairs. At the top, he paused and looked around. Then he sniffed the air like a dog. 'Can you smell that?'

'What is it?'

He took a couple of steps forward so she could join him on the landing. 'Now?'

There was no mistaking it. Rich, cloying, slightly acrid. Four doors led off the landing, three of them standing ajar. The nearest, overlooking the rear of the house, was a bathroom, clean and tidy as the rest of the house had been.

The other two half-open doors led into what looked to be spare bedrooms. They appeared not to have been used in a while and had an anonymous feel. There was nothing obviously out of the ordinary in either.

Willock opened the door of the final room, which they assumed to be the master bedroom at the rear of the house. Willock took a step forward and Wallace heard him say, 'Christ almighty.'

She stepped into the room behind him, holding her breath. The smell wasn't as bad as it would eventually become. Not yet the scent of decomposition, simply the stench of recently spilled blood.

The king-sized bed was drenched in it, the red staining beginning to congeal brown. In the centre of the gore lay a naked body, a duvet partly covering the pale skin. There were two knife wounds in the chest as well as a deep red line across the neck, although the throat had not been fully slit.

That wasn't even the worst thing, Wallace thought. It was clear the same thought had struck Willock and he beckoned her forward so she could see the victim's face more clearly.

'I'm not wrong, am I?'

He wasn't. There was no question about it, and she'd spent more time in the man's presence than Willock. Even if she hadn't remembered all of it.

The man lying on the bed was Daniel Fraser.

CHAPTER FIFTY THREE

Murrain looked around. This was the public area of the basement, just as Amy Kelly had described it. The corridor to the left led to the outpatients departments. The corridor to the right led to the mortuary and some related units. Double-doors ahead led into the areas closed to the public.

The hospital operated an electronic security system which ensured the non-public areas could not be accessed by those without appropriate authorisation. The same system prevented unauthorised entry to the patient areas, with staff allocated varying levels of access depending on their needs. In practice, as the police had discovered when analysing the access rights of the hospital's staff, the majority of staff had been given universal or near-universal access to ensure they would not be unnecessarily impeded in carrying out their duties. The analysis had not proved helpful in narrowing down their list of potential suspects.

Murrain himself, along with a limited number of the police team, had been given universal access rights. He held the security card next to the automated lock and heard the click of the doors being released. The corridor beyond was in darkness. As he walked forward, the lights came on, triggered by some unseen sensor.

He continued walking, trying to gain a sense of the topography of this subterranean area. It was a disconcerting experience. The corridor ahead remained in darkness until he entered each new section. Behind him, the lights remained on for the moment, but those areas would be plunged back into darkness as he passed. It was like walking in the beam of a moving spotlight. The thought made him feel uneasily like a target.

Most of the space here seemed devoted to storage areas. The doors had various labels – linen stores, medical equipment stores, and others where the name meant little or nothing to him. The rooms down here had physical locks rather than being secured by the electronic system, and Murrain assumed that access rights to each room would be limited.

He passed a service lift and shortly afterwards came to a crossroads where further corridors stretched off to the left, right and ahead. Each option ended in darkness.

The left hand corridor led to the loading bay. He decided to try that first, reasoning it would take him to the rear of the hospital and help him get his bearings. At what he took to be the far end of the corridor, he could see a paler patch in the darkness which he guessed indicated the outside world and daylight.

He was trying to keep his mind blank, allowing his internal voices to do whatever work they needed to. Experience had taught him there was no point in trying to force any insights. Any sensations would most likely emerge when his conscious mind was otherwise engaged. But trying to keep his mind blank was a contradictory process – consciously trying to be unconscious – and he had no idea if it would be successful here.

The internal voices were stronger and more intense down here. He could feel them like a repetitive drumbeat. The central pulsing was more powerful too. For the moment there was nothing more – no visions, no sense of any comprehensible meaning. Nothing he could firmly grasp.

Ahead of him, as another set of lights came on, he saw he was nearing the end of the corridor. The corridor opened up into a wide loading bay with retractable doors standing half open to the daylight. He expected there might be someone down here to supervise deliveries and collections, but there was no-one. An office at the right-hand side of the bay was unoccupied. Murrain walked over and peered through the door.

A ledger file lay open on the desk beside an empty coffee mug. Someone had been working in here not long before. Perhaps the storekeeper came down here only when deliveries or collections were due.

Murrain turned to look at the rest of the loading bay. There wasn't much to be seen. At the far end, there were two large hospital trolleys holding substantial-looking bags of laundry. Next to that was a pallet holding a stack of cardboard boxes. Presumably items awaiting movement elsewhere. He walked forward until he could see the interior of the two laundry trollies.

The body would have been invisible to a casual passer-by. It had been wedged between two of the well-stuffed bags, although there had been no serious attempt at concealment. It was as if the body had been tossed there for disposal.

A white male clad in blue overalls. The storekeeper who would normally have occupied the office. There was no obvious cause of death. No blood and no sign of any injury.

'It's simply part of the pattern.'

Murrain looked up, conscious he'd allowed his attention to be distracted. The man was standing at the entrance to the loading bay, just inside the corridor. He was in shadow, partly silhouetted against the light from the corridor, but Murrain had no doubt about his identity.

'What pattern?'

'The pattern I need to complete to free myself. I had it wrong before, or at least not quite right. I thought it was you and the others holding me. But now I understand it clearly. You must hear the voices too. They make everything clear.'

'They told you about the pattern?'

'They told me I had to complete it. I had to create the pattern. It was only by creating and completing the pattern that I could set myself free.'

'From the voices?'

'From the intrusions into my mind. From those who are always watching what I do and see and think.'

'The pattern means killing people like this?' Murrain gestured towards the figure in the trolley.

'They're part of the pattern. There's nothing I can do.'

'Am I part of the pattern?' Murrain asked.

'I thought you were. I thought you were a major part of it. One of the few whose gift comes close to mine. I'm not sure you matter now. You're just another of the captives, aren't you? Another one trapped with the voices and the visions and the feelings. All those experiences that surround you and incarcerate you. You're trapped with them too.'

Years before, when he'd first encountered this man – back in that fateful psychological study – Murrain had been concerned about his own mental health. It had been in his early days in the force, when he'd still been coming to grip with the demands of the job. The sensations he experienced were intensifying, and he'd feared that he was losing his reason. That had been part of the reason he'd volunteered for the study in the first place.

The man standing before him had far greater gifts. Murrain had realised, on that night by the river, that this man really had lost his reason, that he was tortured by the gift to the point where he would do anything to rid himself of it.

'So what is the pattern?' Murrain asked.

'I can't explain it in any terms you'd understand. An interlinking of action and sacrifice. Selecting the right individuals to complete the shape, the symmetry. The links are more subtle than you could ever understand.'

Murrain's instinct was to keep the man talking, hope that in the course of this incoherent discourse he would reveal information Murrain could use. 'What about Marie Donovan? Is she part of the pattern?'

'Your colleague? The woman with your friend in the coma? She's not directly part of the pattern. She's a barrier.'

Murrain felt a chill in his stomach. 'An obstacle to what?'

'To your friend in the coma. He's at the heart of the pattern.'

'What does he have to do with anything?'

'He sacrificed himself and I lived. But his sacrifice was incomplete, and so I live in torment. I have to finish the pattern.'

'What about the other patients? What about the maintenance man you killed? What about this man here? Where do they fit into your pattern?'

'It's a sequence.' The man spoke as if this was the most obvious point in the world. 'I follow the sequence until it reaches your friend.'

'What about the people you killed in their homes? Margaret Perry? Vivian Turnbull? Trevor Ollerenshaw? Were they part of the pattern too?'

'More obliquely. Those were not my victims. They died in part for other reasons. But that also makes them part of the pattern.'

'So where is Marie Donovan?'

'She's safe enough.'

Murrain had taken another step or two forward. As he did so there was a loud click and the whole area was thrown into darkness. Murrain half expected some attack which never came. For a few moments he could see nothing at all, except the line of daylight behind him. As his eyes adjusted, the pale daylight allowed him to make out the rest of the loading bay. The man had vanished.

Murrain cursed himself for coming down without a decent flashlight. He pulled out his phone and turned on the torch, shining its feeble glow into the darkness. He moved forwards, tensed for any attack. He peered ahead into the pale glow cast by the torch. Then, suddenly and with another loud click, the corridor lights returned.

The corridor was deserted. Murrain looked back behind him. The loading bay, now fully lit, was equally empty. For the moment, Murrain's priority was to track down Marie Donovan and protect Joe Milton, and he dialled Howard Temple's number. 'Howard. Kenny Murrain. Can we get some additional protection up to Joe Milton's ward?'

'I'll see what I can do. It's not the best moment because

we're just changing shifts.'

'As quick as you can, Howard. I'll be up there shortly.'

'Where are you?'

'Down in basement. Looking for Marie Donovan.'

'In the basement?'

'Long story.'

Murrain ended the call and stood listening hard, alert for any sign of movement. The pulsing in his head was still there. A signal beckoning him to follow it. He walked forward, following some unconscious urging.

Finally, he heard it, somewhere on his right, further along the corridor. He wasn't sure at first that it wasn't just his imagination, an illusion created by the sounds inside his head. He took another step forward and had no doubt.

CHAPTER FIFTY FOUR

Bert Wallace was looking up at the house, thinking about the body lying inside it. It was only now, out in the cold morning air, that she felt able to think and she had no idea how she felt. She had no attachment for Daniel Fraser himself, of course. She'd met him only a handful of times, had spent what had turned out to be a disastrous evening with him, had been set up by him in a way that could have ended her career almost before it had begun. Why would she care what happened to him?

But he was a fellow human being, and she supposed anyone's violent death was something to be mourned. She'd already seen enough not to be unduly troubled by the sight of the copiously spread blood. What had struck her more was the ordinary humanity of Fraser's face.

'Penny for them,' Willock said.

She was determined to allow no emotion to show on her face. 'CSIs are on their way. Is the place sealed off?'

'Well and truly. I've got a team of trusty PCs to ensure it stays that way.'

They'd left the house as soon as they'd discovered the body, and had it sealed off as a crime scene. Wallace had come outside to call in their discovery while Willock had overseen the uniformed officers. 'Bit of a surprise, that,' she said.

'At two levels. Fraser turning up again like a bad penny, and him turning up here of all places.'

'We know he bought the drug from Carnworth,' Wallace pointed out. 'I assume the stuff about getting it via a friend was all bollocks. Maybe he knew Carnforth directly.'

'Maybe.' Willock had the air of a magician about to extract a particularly large rabbit from an item of undersized headgear. 'Perhaps this will tell us.' He held up a transparent evidence bag.

Wallace peered at it. 'Where'd you find that?'

'In the bedroom. On the dressing table. I thought it might be sufficiently important to liberate before our CSI friends arrived.'

She took the bag from him and looked more carefully at the contents. An envelope, marked with a couple of bloody smudges. 'Should we look at what's inside?'

'I reckon so, don't you? Shouldn't do any harm as long as we handle the contents with care. Let's go and sit in the car.'

They climbed into the car, and donned new pairs of disposable gloves. Willock carefully tipped the envelope into his palm. The envelope wasn't sealed and he delicately slipped it open and eased out the contents.

There were several sheets of old-fashioned notepaper, largely covered by Carnforth's challenging copyplate handwriting. The note carried that day's date, and began without any salutation. Willock spent several minutes reading though it in silence, while Wallace grew impatient.

'Well?'

He looked up at her. 'Christ. That's some narrative.' He handed her the papers, and she read the opening paragraph.

'I don't know what's happening to me. I've lost control, which must mean I've lost my reason. I've known for a while something like this was coming, but I didn't expect it to come like this. My anxiety has been increasing, and I had become certain I would be exposed. The voices have been telling me this for many months now.'

Wallace looked up at Willock. 'Voices?'

'It gets madder.'

'I've been eliminating them one by one, as the voices told me. I did it gently and painlessly, so that they left life with no distress. My intervention was a blessing for them. Their lives were empty and meaningless, and their deaths were completing a necessary pattern. I hoped their deaths would serve as a warning to those who might betray me.'

'A warning,' Wallace said. 'Who's he talking about?' She held up the sheets by a corner. 'We're going to compromise these if we're not careful. You'd better give me the summarised version.'

He took the sheets from her and slipped them carefully back into the envelope and then into the evidence bag. 'It doesn't get much clearer. By the end it goes completely off the rails. He seems to be talking about people who would be in a position to expose his extracurricular business. He mentions several. Gregory Perry—'

'Perry? How's he involved?'

'Looks as if he was involved in Carnforth's dodgy business. I'm guessing he had the skills and knowledge to assist Carnforth. Carnforth was growing increasingly paranoid about Perry shopping him. The killing of Perry's mother seems to have been intended as some kind of warning.'

'A bit counter-productive, given that it put Perry on our radar.'

'Maybe that was the point. Make Perry aware of the seriousness of what he was involved with. Remind him he couldn't shop Carnforth without shopping himself.' Willock shrugged. 'None of it sounds like the product of a sane and thoughtful mind. I don't imagine Perry even suspected Carnforth was responsible for his mother's death – probably never connected the two. That was a revelation Carnforth was saving for when he needed to turn the screws on Perry.'

'Who else does he mention?'

'Vivian Turnbull. Romy Purslake was a user, addicted to prescription drugs. Turnbull was trying to get her clean, and threatening to expose Carnforth as the supplier. Looks as if Purslake and Turnbull were daggers drawn by the time of Turnbull's death. Purslake was mostly concerned with maintaining her own supply. I even wonder if the supposed motorbike accident had been a previous attempt on Turnbull's life. This time, they had a half-baked scheme to frame Amberson, ensuring he was there on the day. But then that was blown by the presence of a witness. Carnforth had another go with that stuff in his office, but that was never going to fly. By that stage, I reckon

Carnforth had lost it.'

'Where do Trevor Ollerenshaw and Daniel Fraser fit into this?'

'In Ollerenshaw's case, he and Roger Ellis at the medical school both procured drugs from Carnforth. That was why Carnforth was involved in that psychological study of Edward Crichton. As well as the psychological stuff, they'd been experimenting with the impact of various drugs on Crichton's supposed gifts. That study ended up with Crichton in state of dependency. He'd discovered – or at least he believed, maybe not without encouragement from Carnforth and others – that certain drugs enhanced and helped him control his powers.' Willock had clearly read Wallace's expression. 'I'm just telling you what Carnforth wrote. Nothing like as coherently as this, I should add.'

'And Fraser?'

'Ah. More personal. He was working for Carnforth. As you said, what he told us was bollocks. He was Carnforth's well-paid delivery boy. From the fact that we've just found his body in Carnforth's bed, it seems likely he was more than that.'

'Blimey.'

'Indeed. And the letter mentions other victims who aren't on our radar. We may have some exhumations ahead of us.'

'Oh, joy. What about Purslake and Fraser? Are we saying that Carnforth killed them too?'

'The letter's explicit about that. He did. The question is why he abandoned his gentle humane method of killing and resorted to what we saw upstairs.'

'And?'

'In Purslake's case, the letter suggests it was just in the heat of moment. Carnforth's paranoia had moved on to Purslake. He became convinced that, now their scheme against Amberson had failed, she'd try to extract herself by shopping Carnforth. He went over there with the intention of injecting her, but she fought back. Carnforth grabbed a kitchen knife and...'

'I get the picture.'

'After that, Carnforth seems to have lost it. He came back here, had some kind of a row with Fraser. By this stage, he suspected everyone of wanting to betray him, and Fraser had risen to the top of the list. As far as I can judge, Carnforth killed Fraser, sat down and wrote the missive you're holding in your hand, and then headed back into the surgery with the aim of topping himself.'

'Utter madness.'

'I'd say so. The odd thing is that the madness – the deep red mist or whatever it was – seems to have lifted after he'd killed Fraser. He talks about the voices going quiet. The final thing they'd told him was that his part in completing the pattern was complete and it was time for him to rest.'

'What were these voices? Some form of schizophrenia?'

'I'm a not-very-humble copper. What would I know? Carnforth seems convinced they were real. Not just real, but some form of communication. Someone controlling his actions.'

'That's convenient, when you've just committed multiple murders. I don't suppose he mentioned the name of the person controlling his actions.'

She'd asked the question as a joke, but when Willock looked back up at her, his face showed no trace of humour. 'Funnily enough, he did. One specific name. Edward Crichton.'

CHAPTER FIFTY FIVE

Murrain listened again, trying to work out where the noises were coming from. After a moment, he focused on a room on the right hand side of the corridor. He walked towards the door and pressed his ear against it.

He could hear a repetitive banging and what appeared to be a kind of muffled shriek. The noises were steady and rhythmic. Someone trying to attract attention rather than someone in immediate trouble.

Murrain banged hard on the door. 'Marie? Is that you?'

The banging became louder and more frequent. The door was firmly locked. He took a step back and examined the door. He'd broken down a few doors in his younger, uniformed days, but this solid construction was beyond his middle-aged powers. 'Hang on, Marie. I'm going to find some way in.'

He contemplated phoning back to Temple or up to Alan Northcote to track down some keys for the room, but that would be a protracted process and he was unsure how much time he could afford to waste.

A thought was nagging at the back of his mind and it took him a moment to remember what it was. Something he'd noticed, almost without registering it, back in the loading bay.

He hurried back into the bay, still trying to recall where he'd spotted the item, retracing in his head the steps he'd taken on his previous visit. In the office, he thought. On the floor. There'd been a stack of tools under the desk that the storekeeper had presumably used in the course of his work – a hammer, a couple of screwdrivers and, at the rear, a heavy duty crowbar.

Murrain wasn't sure if even this implement would be sufficient. He returned to the room and eased the sharp end of the crowbar into the gap between the door and the frame, pressing on it hard with all his weight. Murrain was a large man, but for a moment he thought that even his strength would be insufficient.

Finally, the doorframe gave way and the door sprang inwards. He kicked it open and fumbled by the door for a light-switch.

Murrain had no idea what this room was intended for, but someone had turned it into some kind of private office or refuge. There was a low table and chair, which Murrain suspected had once furnished one of the hospital waiting rooms. A whiteboard on which had been scribbled several incomprehensible diagrams. A cupboard topped with a kettle, a jar of instant coffee and a couple of mugs. The furnishings looked as if they had been cobbled together, salvaged from materials intended for disposal.

Marie Donovan was lying on the floor, gagged and with her wrists and ankles bound together by plastic ties. Murrain crouched and pulled away the gag. 'You okay?'

She gazed at him blankly for a moment as if unsure where she was. It occurred to Murrain she was probably still dazzled by the sudden light, but her confusion seemed greater than that. He wondered if she'd been drugged in some way. 'Kenny?'

'Hang on.' He helped her to her feet and sat her down in the chair while he looked for something to cut the ties. Inside the cupboard he found a selection of old stationery – yellowing pads of notepaper, a stapler and, near the back, a pair of office scissors. He uncut the ties on her ankles and then she held out her hands for him to release her wrists.

'Where are we?' she said.

'In the hospital basement.'

'But how—?'

'I was hoping you might be able to tell me that. What can you remember?'

'I'm not sure. I was sitting with Joe, and I decided to get myself a coffee. I was only intending to head down to the coffee bar, grab a takeaway coffee and go back upstairs again. But…'

'What happened?'

'I was in the lift going down to the coffee place. Then I

didn't get out at the right floor. I just carried on down. I can remember it clearly now, but for some reason I didn't even think about what I was doing. It seemed the obvious thing to do.'

'How did you get into the restricted area?'

'Restricted area?'

'The front of the basement is open to the public. But this area isn't. You have to get through a set of secured doors.'

She frowned. 'I don't know. They must have been unlocked. I can remember going through those doors, but I didn't think anything of it.' She shook her head, as if trying to clear it physically. 'It's weird. As if someone was actually controlling my movements.'

'I think someone was,' Murrain said. 'I don't know how he works the trick. Whether it's some sort of genuine psychic gift or whether it's using – I don't know – hypnosis, suggestibility, but I think it's exactly what he's doing. That's how he persuaded his previous victims to step out of their homes. That's how he stopped me intervening on that night be the river.'

'Edward Crichton.'

'He's here. In the hospital. Right now. I saw him just a few minutes ago.'

'What about Joe? Is he safe?'

'I've asked for some more back up there. He should be okay.' Murrain wished he felt as confident as he hoped he sounded. 'We can get up there as soon as you're in a state to move.'

'Just give me a second. How long have I been down here?'

'Not that long. Couple of hours, maybe.'

'Feels longer.' She stretched out her legs as if trying to regain lost feeling. 'I thought I was making enough noise to waken the dead.'

'You could barely hear it out there. He chose this place well.' Murrain looked around him. 'Made it quite cosy, hasn't he?'

'But what's he doing in here? How can he just wander round the hospital at will?'

'Mr Crichton seems to be able to do whatever he wants. Although what he wants is a mystery to me.' Murrain looked at his watch. His anxiety about Joe was growing. 'Do you feel up to moving?'

She pushed herself to her feet, looking as if she was trying out a new set of limbs. 'I think so. Let's get up there.'

She followed him out into the corridor, and they made their way back out to the public area at the front of the basement. It was late in the afternoon, the end of the outpatients clinics and the afternoon visiting session and there were fewer people around. He pressed the call button for the lift and waited impatiently. Both lifts seemed to be stalled on one of the higher floors.

Murrain had been aware, as they'd made their way along the corridor here, that the voices in his head had been reintensifying. Telling him something. The pulsing that he associated with Edward Crichton was still there, cutting through all the white noise. It was less strong than it had been when Crichton had been standing immediately in front of him, but steady as ever. 'The lifts aren't moving. They shouldn't just stay on one floor like that. Not all of them. Not for this long. Hang on.' He pulled out his phone and dialled.

'Howard. It's Kenny Murrain.'

'Where are you?'

'Still down in the basement. Trying to get upstairs. What's going on?'

'All hell breaking loose, that's what. We've got what looks like a suicide.'

'A suicide?'

'Some poor bugger threw himself off the roof. On top of that, some bastard – maybe the same poor bastard – has buggered the lift system so nothing's moving. Just at the end of visiting time. We've dozens of visitors milling around, behaving as if it's the end of the world.'

'They can use the stairs, surely?'

'You'd think so, wouldn't you? Some of them seem unfamiliar with the concept. Just gathering in the lift lobbies and milling about as if there's nothing else they can do. We're gradually getting them cleared but it's been a major distraction on top of everything else—'

'You're telling me you've not yet been able to send anyone up to Joe, aren't you?'

'What do you think, Kenny? I'll get someone there as quickly as—'

'No worries, Howard. You've enough on your plate. What about the service lifts at the back? Are they still working?'

'They're on a different circuit. But we're not using those for visitors because they're needed to move patients and the like… '

Murrain didn't bother to listen to the rest of the sentence. He turned to Marie. 'We need to get up there. Come on.' He led Marie back into the restricted corridor and then along to the service lift they'd passed earlier. The lift was controlled by the same security system as the doors, but again Murrain's pass allowed him to use it. He suspected Crichton had also used this route, having disabled the main public lifts.

It took just a few seconds for the lift to arrive. Murrain and Donovan jumped inside, and Murrain pressed his card to the security panel while stabbing the button for Floor 7. To his relief, the lift started moving.

It seemed to take them an age to reach their destination. Finally, the doors opened and Murrain hurried out, Marie following close behind. From somewhere at the end of the corridor he could hear a hubbub of voices – real physical voices for once. Presumably the crowds Howard Temple was trying to disperse.

When they reached the ward he didn't wait for the nurses but pressed his card to the security panel and heard the door click open. He stepped inside and looked around.

The ward was eerily quiet. There was no sign of any

nursing staff, and most of the patients in the open ward were sleeping. At the far end of the room, an elderly man was sitting in the chair by his bed reading a paperback. Murrain paused by the man's bed. 'Excuse me. Do you know if any of the nurses are around?'

The man looked up, surprised. 'Sorry?'

'The nurses. Do you know where any of them are?'

'I'm not sure. They were here not long ago. There was some kind of kerfuffle out in the corridor earlier so they might have gone to deal with that.' He pointedly flicked over a page in his book, his demeanour confirming he had no desire to continue the discussion.

The voices in Murrain's head were as loud as ever, urging him on in some way he could barely explain. He'd expected that if Crichton had been close by, the pulsing would have intensified. So far, though, that hadn't happened. The sensation was still there, still strong, a radio beacon pounding through his brain. But it was no stronger here. He hoped that meant Crichton was elsewhere in the building. Unless, he added silently to himself, Crichton had already been here and done what he believed he needed to do.

He peered through the door into Joe's room. There was no sign of Crichton in the room. But what he saw made Murrain catch his breath.

Gill was sitting by Joe Milton's bed, stroking his hand and talking gently to him. At first glance, the scene looked innocent enough. But Murrain had already registered what was in Gill's other hand.

A syringe. Filled and ready to use.

Marie Donovan had pressed her face against the window and turned to Murrain in horror. Murrain's fear was that, in her desire to protect Joe, she might startle Gill into taking some precipitate action. 'Gently,' he whispered.

He opened the door as quietly as he could. 'Gill. What are you doing?'

Gill shifted the syringe into her other hand, making no effort to conceal it. 'I'm looking after Joe.'

'What's in the syringe, Gill?' Murrain could feel Marie standing close behind him.

'Something to make Joe sleep.' Gill's face was expressionless. Her eyes seemed to have no depth to them, as if they were disconnected from her brain.

'He's already sleeping, Gill.'

Gill looked at the man lying on the bed here as if to confirm what Murrain had said. 'He has nothing now. I have nothing now. We can be together, though.'

Murrain felt rather than heard Marie move behind him. Before he could prevent her, she'd moved towards Gill. Murrain expected Gill to try to defend herself, but instead she calmly took the syringe and placed it on Joe's bare arm, the needle pressed against his flesh. 'You can't stop us now.'

Marie had stopped as she watched Gill start to press down on the syringe. Then she threw herself forward, reaching for Gill's hand, dragging it up and away from Joe's arm. Gill twisted round, still holding the needle. She held it out, jabbing it towards Marie's face. 'Don't come any closer.'

Murrain had circled round, positioning himself so that he could intervene without risking Gill using the syringe on either him or Marie. But before he could move, Gill's hand was grasped from behind, the syringe slipping from her grip to the floor below.

Murrain pulled Gill away from the bed, dragging her to the floor. He'd expected Marie to assist him, but he looked up to see she was still standing by the bed. Holding Gill down beneath his weight, he said, 'What is it?'

It was only then that Murrain finally registered who had grabbed Gill's hand from behind. He was there, on the bed, his eyes open, looking around bewilderedly.

'What the hell's going on?' Joe said, and then, almost as an afterthought, 'And where the hell is this?'

CHAPTER FIFTY SIX

Murrain climbed to the first landing and paused, partly to regain his breath and partly to allow himself a moment to think.

He'd left Marie and Joe in the room downstairs. The doctors were checking Joe over, and for the moment Murrain's presence had felt superfluous.

Moments after they'd dragged Gill away from Joe, two uniformed officers had entered the room, presumably ordered there by Howard Temple, along with an anxious-looking nurse. The police officers had taken care of Gill, who was being driven back to police HQ for questioning. She looked shell-shocked, as bewildered as Joe had been, with the air of someone released from a trance. The contents of the syringe had been collected as far as possible and would be tested. Murrain guessed they were unlikely to be harmless.

As for Joe, he seemed to have fully regained consciousness. One of the doctors had said to Murrain, 'It's unusual for a coma patient to wake suddenly like that, but not unknown. Maybe the trauma of the struggle in some way replicated the trauma of the night he entered the coma. So much of the brain remains a mystery to us.' He'd continued talking but Murrain's own brain had already moved on to other things, notably the absence of Edward Crichton.

He could still feel the pulsing, too, drawing him as if he were being pulled by a magnet. Drawing him upwards. 'The suicide,' he asked one of the uniformed officers. 'Did I understand he'd thrown himself off the roof of the hospital?'

'Looks like it. Hell of a mess.'

'Has he been identified?'

'Not yet,' the officer had said, laconically. 'There's not a lot of identify.'

It was possible the suicide victim was Crichton himself,

but it seemed unlikely. The pulsing in his brain was as strong as ever, and, rightly or wrongly, Murrain was associating that with Crichton.

He left Marie watching as the medical staff fussed around Joe, and made his way on to the corridors and round to the landing by the lifts. The lifts were working again now, and the area had largely been cleared although there were still people standing around chatting. Murrain assumed that Crichton had been behind the lift failure, presumably as a distraction from whatever he was up to.

That was the question. What was he up to? How did all this fit together? Murrain did not believe Gill had been the hospital killer, but it was surely no coincidence that she'd apparently tried to use the same murder weapon with Joe. And was Gill really a killer? She had seemed as bewildered as Joe as the police had led her away.

Murrain continued his upwards trek. As far as he'd been able to ascertain, this was the only way up on to the roof of the building. The entrance to the upper staircase had been secured as a potential crime scene following the suicide, pending the arrival of the CSIs. Murrain had showed his ID to the two uniformed officers guarding the stairs and been allowed through. 'I just want to have a quick look,' he'd said. 'I'll be careful not to disturb anything.' He wondered how Crichton had been able to gain entrance, but it was possible he'd been concealed up there all along.

Murrain reached the top of the stairs. Secured double-doors led out on to the roof-space, accessible for maintenance purposes. Murrain pressed his security card to the security panel and pushed his way into the cold late afternoon air.

From here, it was possible to look out to the city to the west, the familiar landmarks of the Beetham and CIS towers visible in the distance. The sun was setting behind him, the first lights coming on. The sky was clear, translucent with the approach of evening; the roof was buffeted by a strong wind.

Edward Crichton was at the far end of the roof-space,

leaning casually against the barrier surrounding the perimeter. Murrain walked towards him, alert for any movement.

'You're too late,' Crichton said. 'By now the pattern must be complete.'

'Then what happens?'

'Then I'm free.'

'Which means what?'

'You must have a better idea than most, though you can only get a glimpse of what I see. Once I'm free, I can exercise my powers.'

'Which means what?'

'You've already seen the first examples,' Crichton said. 'Those people who acted at my bidding. Those I enticed out of their homes to become my first sacrifices. The way I used Andrew Carnforth to complete the sacrificial pattern outside. The way I used Gregory Perry and others to assist in my work. The way I used the woman downstairs to complete the pattern with your colleague.'

'You're claiming you made them do that? Against their will?'

'Not against their will. That's the point. I help them achieve what they want.'

Murrain was silent, absorbing what Crichton had said. It made an absurd kind of sense. Carnforth wanting to exercise power and influence, and then no doubt wanting to escape from the mess he'd created. People like Gregory Perry and Daniel Fraser wanting to make a quick buck, without too many scruples as to how they did it. Gill, her career unexpectedly stalled, wanting to take Joe away from Marie. As if Crichton had taken individual desires, and exaggerated and perverted them to achieve his own ends.

That didn't necessarily imply paranormal gifts. It might be a question of psychology, of suggestibility. The ability to isolate a small germ of corruption and magnify it into something destructive.

'You believe your powers are increasing?' Murrain asked.

'Now I'm free, I'll be able to exercise them at will. No-one will be able to prevent me.'

Murrain wanted to dismiss this as insanity, but he could already feel – as he had on that night by the river – an inertia creeping over him. That same reluctance to intervene.

Perhaps this was nothing more than the phenomenon Crichton had just described. Tapping into his own fears, his own weaknesses, and exaggerating them. Murrain had spent years agonising about his inability – his failure – to prevent the death of his own son. He'd been too slow to help the boy just as he'd been too slow to prevent Joe Milton being swept into the river. As if Crichton was drawing on Murrain's fears and mirroring them back to him in intensified form.

The realisation was unexpectedly liberating. Murrain took another couple of steps forward, approaching Crichton. 'Your plan didn't work. The pattern's not complete. Your keystone is missing. Joe Milton isn't dead. He's awake.'

'That's not true.'

'It is true. This is just your fantasy. This nonsense about patterns and control and gifts. You've some gifts, no doubt, just as I have. But this web you've woven around yourself, it's all nonsense.'

He'd expected some sharp retort from Crichton, but nothing came. Crichton was staring past him, as if seeing something Murrain couldn't imagine. He looked back at Murrain, his eyes hollow. 'You're serious? He's awake?'

'Awake and apparently in good health.'

'But that's— He sacrificed himself. That was how…' He trailed off, gazing blankly at something Murrain would never see. He took a step backwards, as if in retreat, and stumbled into the low barrier behind him.

Before Murrain could move, Crichton had tipped over, his own body weight pulling him backwards. He scrabbled vainly in the air for a moment as Murrain reached for him, but it was already too late.

A few moments later, the pulsing in Murrain's brain finally ceased.

CHAPTER FIFTY SEVEN

'You're sure you're okay?'

'I'm fine,' Murrain said. 'Never better.'

Marty Winston gazed at him for a moment. 'You know, Kenny, I almost believe you. You look better than you've looked in weeks.'

'Joe's okay.'

'More than okay,' Winston says. 'He reckons he's ready to return to work. I've told him to take a couple more weeks off. And Marie. Get away somewhere. I assume you're happy with that.'

'Couldn't be happier. I've got Colin Willock filling the gap in his own inimitable way.'

'How's that working out?'

'He's an acquired taste, but we're all slowly acquiring it. Even Bert.'

'He's been a square peg wherever we've put him. Trust you to knock the corners off.'

'We'll see. But he'll do until we're fully back up to strength.'

Winston was silent for a moment. 'There'll be an enquiry, you know, Kenny. Especially about what happened on the rooftop.'

'I've nothing to hide.'

'I hope not, Kenny. For your sake. You've one blot on your copybook.'

'That was years ago.'

'It was you trying to take revenge on the person you thought was responsible for killing your son.'

'In the heat of the moment. I was wrong. I paid the price at the time. You don't seriously think…'

'I don't think anything, Kenny. You told me what happened and I believe you. And frankly I don't much care what happened to Crichton. We've no doubt now that he was responsible for the hospital killings. He was working there as a porter so he had easy access to all the wards. We know he was associating with Andrew Carnforth and Gregory Perry, and had access to the necessary drugs. I don't pretend to understand what was going on between him and Carnforth, but Carnforth was responsible for the parallel deaths in the community. There's a whole mess there we'll never entirely untangle.' He was silent for a moment. 'In the end, weirdly, it's as if all the loose ends were messily tied up.'

'With Gregory Perry throwing himself off the roof just before Crichton did?'

'I don't imagine we'll ever know the full story.'

'I don't imagine so.'

'So nobody's likely to be shedding tears for Edward Crichton. And, to be honest, I don't imagine anybody's going to want to open this particular can of worms too far. Especially as we know our friends in the intelligence services were involved at various points. If this becomes too public, it could be embarrassing for everyone. So I'm hoping any enquiry will be little more than going through the motions. I'm just warning you, Kenny, that if they do end up looking for a scapegoat, you'll inevitably be in the frame.'

'Very reassuring. What about Gill?'

'That's an odd one. She claims to have no recollection of what she tried to do to Joe. The syringe contained diamorphine, just as in the other deaths. There's no evidence she was an accomplice of Crichton's – in fact, she wasn't even in the country when the first hospital murders occurred – but she can offer no explanation as to how she came by the syringe. She was in a mess. Her contract in France had been abruptly terminated as a result of funding cuts. She hadn't been able to find other employment out there and had decided to return to the UK. It looks as if she'd been hoping to resume her relationship with Joe, but then she discovered what had happened and that he and Marie were an item. Maybe that tipped her over the edge.'

'What'll happen to her?'

'It was attempted murder. She's been charged and she's on remand. It's a sorry business.'

Murrain had heard much of this from Marie and Joe already, but, following the events at the hospital, Eloise had insisted he take a few days leave himself. He hadn't objected, knowing he needed to get his head straight again after that last confrontation with Crichton.

He wondered now about that confrontation. In his memory, Crichton had been staring at something and had toppled back and fallen to his death, Murrain reaching out to try to save him. Was that really what had happened? Surely it wasn't possible that, in that frantic moment, Murrain had finally taken the action he'd failed to take that night by the river?

He'd never be certain. And there was another aspect that troubled him.

Crichton's gift, whatever its nature, latched on to the dark longings that individuals denied even to themselves. He seemed somehow to bring those desires into the open, take them to fruition.

Was it possible that in those final moments, his plans in disarray, he'd driven Murrain to act on his own buried desire? To take the action that would atone for his previous failings.

There was no way of knowing. An enquiry would reveal nothing either way, regardless of its formal outcomes. The secret, if there was a secret, would remain buried in Murrain's own mind.

'Too right,' he said to Winston. 'It's a bloody sorry business.'

Printed in Great Britain
by Amazon